The Digger's Daughter

By

Rosemary Noble

This is a work of fiction. Names, characters, businesses, places, events and incidents are either the products of the author's imagination or used in a fictitious manner. Any resemblance to actual persons, living or dead, or actual events is purely coincidental.

With thanks to:

Colette McAlpine, my mentor at the Female Convicts Research Centre in Tasmania;

Werribee Historical Society for sharing Jim Dugmore's story with me

Fern and Jan Hames, who donated their copy of Jim Dugmore's story to the historical society

Julie Moten for reading the drafts

Richard Noble, my husband, for his patience as I bury myself in research and writing

Arun Creative Writing Group (Arun Scribes) for their guidance and suggestions

Karen Wells at Verité CM, Worthing for the cover design

And last but not least, the Dugmore and Timms families who experienced these times and provided such a rich source of material. I apologise for any liberties taken in the name of fiction.

Chapter 1

Melbourne 1932

Jane lay in bed, her restless bones complaining as she tried shifting them to a more comfortable position. She patted the sheet underneath her with gnarled fingers hoping to find a cooler spot, but it felt damp and sticky in the early morning heat. I'll most likely never leave this bed again, she thought, without any sign of dismay. What life remained was ebbing away and she was relieved. When the moment came, she would cast it off without regret. Her body had always been strong and ramrod straight, and she no longer recognised this thin shell she inhabited, the puny muscles in her arms and legs flaccid against the white cotton of her nightgown.

A cup of tea cooled on the cupboard beside the bed, but she did not have the energy to reach it. How long had it been since Sophie brought it? She had no recollection. The minutes, the hours, even the days, no longer had shape in her mind and she wondered what day it was. Was it even still February? She dozed some more. She did not hear the heavy footsteps of Sophie re-entering the room with a tray where a fine porcelain cup decorated with swags of peonies lay beside a similar plate of egg sandwiches.

Sophie sighed as she saw her mother still asleep. She picked up the untouched tea, replacing it with a fresh cup and put the spare saucer over the sandwiches to stop them from drying out too much. The sun rose higher, burning through the bricks of the bungalow. As Sophie left the room, she switched on the ceiling fan which started in slow revolutions to stir the lazy morning air. The gentle swoosh did not disturb Jane, but a slight waft of cooler air found her wrinkled cheeks and her mouth slackened in pleasure. She began to dream.

Her older brothers and sisters were playing a game of tag on the rough patch of ground near the washing line. No sheets or clothes blew on the line or Mother would have had a fit to think of the dust undoing her hard work. Jane wanted to play too, but Jacob told her she was too little and could not run fast enough. She toddled off towards Hannah, pleading with her oldest sister and when she said no, Jane broke into great gulping sobs, fat hot tears sliding down her cheeks and onto her pinafore. She wiped her runny nose against her rough woollen sleeve, still bawling until Mother came out of the cabin, drying her hands on her apron to pick her up, snuggling Jane against her thin neck.

'There, there my sweet,' she said, her voice soft as butter. Her nose rubbed against Jane's gently. 'Come with me. I've baked bread and you my little dumpling, shall have some with apple jelly.'

She carried Jane into the kitchen and set her on the flattened earth floor where her toes soaked up the warmth from the fire. Taking the new loaf Mother carved off the crust, laying it steaming on the wooden table, before taking a spoonful of jelly and spreading it thinly. As she sat down on her stool, Jane crawled towards her to be picked up again. She felt Mother's arms snake around her and her lips nuzzling Jane's cheek as she bit into the crust. The sweetness of the jelly calmed her; her mother's tenderness soothed her. Mother licked Jane's tiny fingers of their stickiness, and she wiped her face with the edge of her apron, spitting on it first to moisten it.

'Remember this,' she said. 'You have to work for what you want. If they will not play with you now, grow a little, run faster and soon they will be happy to play with you. There's no point in tears. They will never get you what you want, Jane.' Mother set her back down on the floor, walked to the rough-hewn door and clapped her hands. Jane's brothers and sisters ceased their running and their laughter.

'Chores.' was all Mother said and they stopped their brief game and set back to work; Hannah and Jacob to fetch water from the carrier whose cart was already lumbering along Bourke Street; James and Sarah to weed the vegetable plot. Jane stood watching until her mother turned around and saw her.

'Jane, you can help James and Sarah weed. They will show you what to do. Be careful not to pull up anything we can eat.'

'Mother, Mother, are you awake?'

Jane stirred. She opened her eyes and took a moment to adjust her vision, her eyes watery and sticky from sleep. Sophie handed her a handkerchief to wipe them allowing Jane to see her youngest surviving daughter since poor Florence died of diphtheria. Was it twenty years or more? She sighed.

'Let me help you sit up, Mother. See if you can sip this tea.'

Sophie plumped up another pillow, then hoisting her mother up to a sitting position, placed it behind her to support her back.

'Oh, that feels nice and cool,' whispered Jane.

Sophie was concerned at how light she was becoming. Her mother had taken to her bed a few days before, and she had certainly lost weight since. She still managed to slide herself out of bed to visit the bathroom with the aid of sticks, but for how much longer?

'Nellie will visit later this morning, Mother. We'll get you out of bed. Jean can change your sheets while Nellie and I wash you. But for now, please drink a little tea and try one of these sandwiches I made.'

Sophie helped Jane to sip the tea which was cool now, but Jane did not mind. She managed to nibble half an egg sandwich before pushing it away. Her appetite was gone.

'Sophie, I dreamt I was a tiny child, here in Melbourne. It was so real that I smelt the wood smoke. Mother gave me bread and jelly, and it tasted wonderful. It must have been our first spring here, and still cool as the cold nipped at my bare feet.'

Sophie pulled up a chair and sat next to her mother. She picked up one of her hands, the blue veins standing proud under the thinning skin and she stroked it with tenderness. She remembered her mother's hands as strong and hard, matching her demeanour. No, you could not say she had been a gentle or affectionate mother, but now her toughness was disappearing and her frailty distressing for her daughters to witness. Perhaps in her final illness she might allow herself to be loved.

'I'm dying Sophie. I'm tired, and I want to go.'

Sophie did not know how to answer her mother. She was always so direct and plain speaking. There was never any attempt to gloss over a subject. What was it she used to say? 'Speak the truth and shame the devil.' Yes, that was it. Her mother interrupted her thoughts.

'Hire a nurse, Sophie. Lifting me with your rheumatics will only hurt you. There's enough money, and you can't spend much more time away from your lodgers and your son. You need that money.'

It's not as if I have grandchildren to care for, Sophie thought with sadness. With her sole surviving son nearing thirty-five, both an invalid and a bachelor, it was unlikely she would ever be called Granny, and she so longed to be a grandma. Could she not have a little happiness in her life?

'I need a nurse Sophie.' Her mother's tone changed to one of pleading. 'I don't know how much longer I can get out of bed. I don't want you to ...' She tailed off. Sophie was inwardly shocked and saddened by her mother's sudden vulnerability. For the first time in her life, her mother was showing signs of weakness.

'Don't worry Mother, I will do as you ask. The doctor will recommend someone suitable, I'm sure. I'll telephone right away if that's what you want.' She lumbered to her feet and left the room, and a few moments later Jane heard her speaking on the telephone.

How much has changed over my life? Jane thought. Whoever dreamt of telephones or electricity or even aeroplanes? Her youngest son, Charlie, on one of his few visits, told her of his flight to Broken Hill and then onwards to Alice Springs. The railways, which Joseph her second son built, were a miracle at the time but flying, it did not seem natural. Thank God Joseph passed away before the worst of the financial crash. It would have broken his heart to live in Australia now. God's own country he used to call it.

Stories on the radio of poverty, hunger and proud working men losing their jobs upset her beyond measure. The spineless politicians in Canberra were in thrall to London bankers demanding their pound of flesh, but it was always the working men and their families who

8

suffered. She had seen it time and time again throughout her life. Will things ever change? If they did, she would not live to see it.

Why was she chosen to live so long? Ninety-four was a ridiculous age, who on earth lived that long? No one she ever knew. She assumed her brothers and sisters had short, troubled lives. She did not know what had happened to them after the trouble they each got themselves into. Remembering her dream and seeing them so clearly after all this time made her catch her breath in hope. Was it a message? Were they waiting for her? Would she be forgiven? The dream felt so real, although she had no memory of time for play, or of her mother's softness. Perhaps this is what happens, she pondered. They say a drowning man sees his life flash in front of him before he dies. But her life, might it appear in dreams before she went? Or was it an aberration, the only one that would really mean something she could understand?

As she drifted back to sleep she pictured the first house she remembered. It was not the kind of house people think of today, but a log cabin with no windows, just holes on either side with canvas flaps pinned back during the day. Sacking divided the cabin into areas for sleeping and eating, disguising neither the sounds nor smells of life. For how many years of her life did she live in huts like that? And yet, it was a palace compared to the tents on the goldfields. Her great-grandchildren had no idea of living conditions as they were then. Whenever she checked them for vanity or squandering water and food, they became petulant and impatient with her. But this was what she had worked for, that her children and their children would know a better life.

Sleep came, and this time no dreams disturbed her slumbers.

Chapter 2

There was a rap on the door. It wasn't a loud rap, more of a signal, just one tap and a second later, two more brief taps. Sophie rose with difficulty from the comfortable chair in which she sat reading the newspaper. Mother was right; she felt old herself these days. After opening the front door, she found a tall, well-built woman aged around forty beaming at her. She wore a thin blue jacket over a grey uniform, which spoke for itself.

'I'm here about the position of nurse. The doctor said you needed someone to care for a lady who's dying. My name is Mary O'Hara.'

'Do come in Mrs O'Hara. It is Mrs I assume.'

'Yes, though I lost my hubby in the Great War. It was a long time ago, and I've got used to it.' Her tone made it plain she was not looking for sympathy, and she found none.

The plump woman of around sixty years of age, standing in front of Mary, had her own share of worry lines, and she appeared on edge. Mary wondered who the woman was because she had not introduced herself. No doubt she would get around to it, but for now, she smiled vaguely at Mary in welcome and ushered her into the sitting room.

Sophie asked Mrs O'Hara to sit while she made a cup of tea for them both. Disappearing into the kitchen, she left Mary to glance around the room. It was a square shaped room with double doors opening onto a large dining room. She guessed it was an old person's place by the heavy old furniture and the number of photographs on every surface and every wall. She walked over to take a closer look. On the piano were the usual photos of men in the uniform of the Great War, and wedding portraits with groups of people sitting stiff and unsmiling in their best clothes. But there were also expensive hand-tinted society photos of women in evening gowns and photos of racehorses and, if she was not mistaken, even a winner of the Melbourne Cup. This surprised Mary for the bungalow did not appear to be that of a wealthy woman but more one comfortably placed. She picked up one photograph of a pretty young woman sporting a broad-brimmed hat worn at a jaunty angle and a sumptuous fur coat, maybe even a mink. She had a small dog nestling in her arms, and Mary was studying it when Sophie returned with the tea.

'Lovely lot of photographs here Mrs..?'

'Oh, sorry I should have introduced myself. My name is Mrs Eliot, and it is my mother, Mrs Timmins, who needs nursing. Yes, the photos are of my brother's family and his horses. He lived here for a while before he died three years ago.

As Mary sat drinking her tea, Sophie explained that her mother was in her ninety-fifth year and until recently managed with a daily help coming in to clean and do the heavy work. Doctor Goodison was now of the opinion that her mother's heart was failing, and that she had only a few weeks to live.

'This morning my mother asked for a nurse because she is finding it difficult to get out of bed. It's come so quickly, although we should have expected it. We always thought her indestructible.' Sophie wiped a tear from her eyes.

'Quite understandable Mrs Eliot,' Mary reassured her. 'That's why I am here. Look I carry several recommendations with me because you wouldn't want a stranger in your mother's home unless you're sure she is trustworthy.' She opened her handbag and dug out a sheaf of letters.

'So many,' said Sophie taking them and briefly scanning them.

'I am not blessed with children to care for, so I have spent the last few years doing this kind of work. I think you will find them very satisfactory.'

'No doubt. They're excellent I am sure.' She paused and smiled at Mary and found herself relaxing. Her anxiety about her mother's care disappeared. This woman in front of her looked competent and capable. So long as Mother did not take a dislike to her, perhaps she could hand over the worry which had been building inside of her for the last few weeks. The rest would do her aching bones good.

'When you have finished your tea, I will take you in to meet Mother, and if she's happy, then I hope you can move in to look after her. There is a pleasant bedroom here for your own use and Jean, the help I told you about, will cook and clean for you. The pay will not be a problem; we are happy to pay your usual rate. Um, I must warn you that mother can be difficult. Her mind is as sharp as a tack. It's just that she can be quite fierce.'

'Don't you worry yourself about that. I have met all sorts, and there's none got the better of me yet.' Mary stood up straight and waited to be taken in to meet her new patient.

'Well, let's see if Mother is awake.'

Chapter 3

'I used to have a sister called Mary.'

'Did you now? Well, it's a common enough name for sure.' Mary straightened the sheets on Jane's bed having helped her use the new commode, one of the first things she organised. The poor woman had been struggling to the bathroom. It's a wonder she never fell and injured herself.

'It was my job to rock her cradle and try and get her to sleep.'

Jane had not thought of Mary in years. Mother always gave one of her daughters the job of rocking the cradle and shushing asleep the newest addition to the family. Hannah rocked Jane, and Sarah rocked Ellen, and now it fell to Jane to rock Mary. Her pride knew no bounds. Jane loved to stroke Mary's soft pale cheek and one day was rewarded with a broad gummy smile. She called for Mam to look, and when the baby smiled again on cue, Mam patted Jane on the back and said, 'Well done Jane. Now you are her special sister; always watch out for her,' and Jane promised she would.

It was her hair she remembered most; it was like fine spun gold, curling over her tiny head. Jane never owned a doll, but her granddaughters had plenty, and some might have been fashioned on Mary, rosy cheeks, big, blue eyes and a pink bud for a mouth. She recalled her mother saying that Mary would grow up to be a beauty. Jane winced as she remembered her mother's screams the morning she found Mary stiff and cold in the cradle.

Children dying happened often enough in those days. But Mary's death was the first she experienced. An icy stone lodged in Jane's heart that day, one of many over the years, and it never completely disappeared. Had she ever dared to love a baby again quite as much as she adored Mary? It was a question she could not truthfully answer. She may well have held something of herself back from her children? If so, she regretted it now, when it was far too late.

She remembered promising Mam to watch out for Mary, and then worrying herself into a state of terror that she had rocked the cradle too hard. Maybe Mary dying was her fault, but she dared say none of this to her mother.

One of her sisters, probably Hannah, asked Mother why the baby had died, and Jane felt sick thinking Mam might blame her, but Mam replied, 'Mary was so perfect and so beautiful that God wanted her for his own.'

The relief washed over her, and she thanked God that neither she nor her other sisters were pretty. They had each inherited their father's muddy brown hair and their mother's sharp features. The elder boys fared better, at least they had chestnut hair, a fact much bemoaned by their twin sisters.

She could picture her mother washing and wrapping Mary's tiny body with great tenderness and then placing her gently in a small box which Father made. After that, she sat silent, grieving, her face a mask of stone, while Jane's father and the boys carried the box away to bury under a tree. Over the following months, Jane left offerings on the grave, praying that angels would look after Mary, a brightly coloured parrot feather, an unusual coloured pebble, anything that she found and liked. She smiled at the memory.

'So, what was she like, your sister Mary?'

'She died Mrs O'Hara, she was about six months old.'

'Oh, I am sorry. No mother should have to go through that pain.'

Jane studied her nurse. For a moment, she was sure she saw a flicker of anguish in her warm brown eyes, but her face quickly resumed its cheerful expression. Doctor Goodison had done well to send her this nurse. She had shown strength enough to help her in and out of bed, but she was also gentle and motherly. Jane realised, with a sudden pang, that what she wanted most was her mother. Then she felt the usual guilt that she was not there for her own mother's death.

Life was a circle. You are helpless at the beginning and at the end, Jane realised with sadness. Why had she never thought it before? She recalled one of her grandsons telling her of injured men in no-man's land crying out for their mothers, Germans as well as the British and Empire troops. At the end, let's face it, we just want the love and comfort that only a mother provides. Would her children feel like that when their time came? Would they somehow remember how she had caressed them as babies with love and devotion, or only remember her as she was now, a cantankerous old woman? She shook her head. It did no good to ponder over these things. She turned her attention to the nurse.

'Was your husband Irish Mrs O'Hara?'

'Do call me Mary, Mrs Timmins. Of Irish stock, that he was.' Changing the subject, Mary asked, 'How long have you lived in Melbourne?'

'Eighteen thirty-nine we arrived. We were pioneers.' Jane answered her with not a little pride. 'The town was only two years old, the same age as me. I would wager they are starting to plan for the centenary, but I will be long dead by that time. Melbourne will continue to grow stronger as I moulder in my grave. No, don't shake your head at me. I know I have only a few weeks, maybe days left.'

'My, my! I can't imagine that. You actually remember the city from the 1840s. I have never met anyone who was here then.' Mary looked astonished. She sat down on the chair beside the bed. 'Can you remember what it was like?'

'Smoke and mud. Mud and smoke.'

'Surely you remember more than that. Go on, describe it for me. Your daughter complimented you on your sharp mind.'

'Well, she'd no business discussing me with you.' Jane turned her face towards the window. Was this nurse going to be another of those tiresome gossips? She hoped not, for she wanted to die in peace and not worry she would say something which should remain private. Who knows what you might blurt out when you are about to meet your maker.

'I shouldn't have said that Mrs Timmins. I am sorry, forgive me. I phrased it badly. It's just that we are going to be spending a few weeks together, and it really helps to talk. I am interested in my patients.

They often have such wonderful stories to tell, but what they say never goes any further. I'll leave you to rest for now.'

This old lady was no apple-cheeked, cuddly granny, that was for sure. Mary placed a cloth over the commode pan, lifted it up and left the room to dispose of the contents. There was calculation in Jane's pale blue eyes which almost unnerved her. She shook her head at the thought that a lady of her age could upset her. Wasn't she used to cranky and crotchety old folk?

Jane turned to watch her go. Wonderful stories indeed! Jane's stories were of mud and fire, hardship and violence and life sometimes so near the edge that starvation and death waited around the next corner. Life was a battle to be fought, and all her life she had fought hard and won. She had been relentless, dragging her family out of the slime and into respectability and society. What hardships had this nurse known, a widow yes, but did she have any understanding of what it takes to survive when the odds are against you?

She closed her eyes, but sleep eluded her. She found herself thinking of her parents and her childhood again. It was so long ago, but the memories were flooding back, and she lost her anger. Perhaps I have spent too much time being tough and secretive. How much harm could it do to talk about her life, as long as she never mentioned the the 'C' word? How else was she going spend the time? Her hands were too arthritic for sewing and knitting. She never felt comfortable reading and was barely able to sign her name. To think only a month ago, she managed to walk out to the shops and take the tram to visit her children. This sudden decline came too rapidly, the slightest exertion making her so breathless she could scarcely put one foot in front of the other without gasping for air. Now even getting out of bed was a struggle. Dying is so undignified

Mary came back into the bedroom with the clean dish; her tread soft on the thick carpet trying not to disturb her patient. But Jane called her name, asking for help to sit up. Once comfortable, she indicated to Mary to sit in the chair beside the bed.

16

'Smoke and mud. That is the memory I have of early Melbourne. Smoke from the kitchens, behind the cabins where we slept; a few hundred log houses, each on its half-acre plot. Ours was on Bourke Street, near where Spencer Street Station is now. The streets were laid out and named as they are now, a city waiting to happen. My father came from Birmingham, England and he told me that towns and cities grew there over hundreds of years, street by narrow winding street, with no real plan. Whereas our streets are broad and straight, wide enough for two laden bullock carts to pass and turn around with ease and then some.'

'What about the alleys and lanes?' asked Mary.

'Oh, they came a few years later. The price of land rose so high that plots sizes were reduced, and it was difficult to reach the backs of houses, so they built the alleys. We had moved out by then. But the mud, oh the mud, none of the streets were paved you see. The trees had been cut down when the city was laid out leaving stumps, but when it rained it all turned into a quagmire, the water running downhill towards the Yarra River. Elizabeth Street was the worst. It was built over a gully, a natural waterway. My father said a horse and cart went down into the mud there never to be seen again, and a mother lost her baby there, swept right out of her arms. I used not to believe it until I saw that kind of thing for myself on the goldfields; horses up to their knees in mud, their stomachs impaled on the horns of the drowned bullocks below. Mother never let us stray too far when the mud was at its worst.'

'I saw mud like that in Flanders,' Mary sighed. Her eyes looked far away.

Jane stopped talking. It was her turn to be astonished. She stared hard at her nurse, appraising her. Beyond the open cheerful face, was that a flicker of sadness she noticed again in her eyes?

'You nursed in the war?'

'Yes, first in Egypt and then on the Western Front.'

Jane clutched at Mary's hand. 'Then you will understand.'

'Understand what?'

17

'What you must do to survive.'

'How I survive is to nurse people like yourself, those who have lived a good long life.' Her voice took on an edge that Jane recognised. It was one she used herself when she did not want to discuss things which made her uncomfortable.

'I never wanted to see another young man torn apart by shrapnel or maimed and disfigured or gassed. All those beautiful young men who never made it back home to ...' Mary choked back her tears.

'Your husband was one of them?'

'Yes, him too, God rest his soul.' Mary crossed herself.

Jane remembered her grandson Bruce telling her of the selfless devotion and hard work of the nurses in the dressing stations and hospitals. He told her how they worked until they dropped through exhaustion and then got up and carried on again. 'If it weren't for those nurses, neither I nor Stanley would have made it home,' he'd said. Bruce died eight years ago from the effects of gas poisoning, but at least he had made it home. He married a girl he met soon after arriving home and fathered three children. Jane always believed he knew his years were numbered, and he just best get on with it.

But there was something more to Mary's story. Married women did not nurse, not even now. She must have her own secrets. There was an affinity between them. She felt it in her gut. Mary's expression may be cheerful, her widely spaced eyes may look open and frank, but there were a few too many worry lines on her forehead. Jane appraised her some more before making her mind up. She had spent a lifetime refusing to talk about her life, refusing to acknowledge certain aspects and once, just once before she left this shell of her body it might be a relief to talk to a stranger who would not blab. Priests and doctors were bound by oaths of confidentiality. She imagined a nurse must be the same.

'I like you, Mary O'Hara. You must have guts to go to war. I'll tell you my stories, but first I need to sleep.'

Chapter 4

'Look in that drawer Mary, the one on the left-hand side.' Jane pointed to her mahogany dressing table the following morning.

Mary wandered over to it. Glass and china ornaments littered the top. She picked up a double pewter shell to admire.

'This is gorgeous; I love the way they have cast the whorls.'

'The grandchildren keep buying me ornaments for Christmas. I wish they wouldn't; they just collect dust. In the drawer, you should find a wooden crucifix.'

Mary opened the drawer and lying above a pile of fine cotton handkerchiefs was an elegantly carved cross made from huon pine, the distinctive scent permeating the contents of the drawer.

'Oh, how exquisite,' said Mary, picking it up. She lifted it to her nose and breathed deeply; the scent was heady, slightly medicinal but pleasant for all that. Peering closer, she admired the polished golden colour of the cross and its finely carved image of Jesus in his final agony. It begged to be stroked.

'My dear father carved it from wood he brought with him from Tasmania. The tree never grew around Launceston, and I don't have the slightest idea how he came by it. He made the first crucifix for my mother, a fervent, Irish Catholic, although he was Church of England. Then he made one for each of us children for our confirmation. Mother made us go to short-mass every day while we lived in Melbourne.'

'Did you go to St Francis' Church? That was built before St Patrick's Cathedral, wasn't it?'

'We watched it being built. Mother was so in awe of it. She thought it magnificent, and I suppose that rubbed off on us. They did not finish it by the time we left Melbourne, but I have vague memories of services there before its completion.'

Mary closed the drawer and went to sit beside Jane, handing her the cross.

'This is my most prized possession. The only thing that remains of my father. I want you to swear on it that anything I tell you will not be repeated. Can I trust you Mary? There are things my children don't know, and I mean to leave it that way.' Jane's expression was fierce, and Mary saw how she must have been as a younger woman, tough, uncompromising and determined.

Mary nodded and took the cross back, bent her lips to it and promised Jane she would not divulge anything. She sat beside the bed silent for a moment. Jane glimpsed sadness again in Mary's eyes.

'When I am at my lowest and find myself thinking of the war, I turn my mind turn to the stories my patients told me over the years. It gives me renewed hope. So many of them struggled, arriving here as penniless refugees from different countries and finding some peace in this new country of ours. There are struggles here I know, but when I nursed in Flanders, I couldn't wait to get back home to the sun, to a blue cloudless sky, and a land where the endless thump and roar of guns wasn't the accompaniment to everyday life. Those stories are the few precious nuggets of gold left in my life now.'

'Struggles, I fear my parents' lives were one long struggle.' Jane sighed. 'That crucifix you are holding, I'm lucky to have it. It's the only one left. Shall I tell you about the day I saved it?'

Chapter 5

Geelong February 1851

Jane woke at first light to a fine, fresh morning. Her mother was already up and about and chivvying the youngest children to stir themselves. Bread and tin plates lay on the table. Jane nudged Sarah, who lay beside her.

'Come on sleepyhead; it's time to get up.'

Sarah opened an eye, grimaced and sighed, before stretching her arms and legs. Not for the first time Sarah wished she had a mattress to herself.

Jane rose first and went to the privy hut. Next, she washed her hands and face in a bowl of tepid creek water from the bucket that Sarah's twin, James, had fetched the evening before. After slipping on a black skirt over her petticoat, she put on a blue cotton blouse, both hand-me-downs from her eldest sister, Hannah. Tying on her white apron, she set to her chores before breakfast. Jane's first was to collect rainwater for making tea. She looked in the barrel, noticing again how little was left. Six weeks had passed since they had seen more than a light shower, and in a day or two they would have to use creek water for drinking, and if that failed? She did not want to think of the possibility, although it was a perennial problem. She would make sure to say a special prayer for rain this evening.

Next, she stoked the fire in the kitchen before putting a heavy pan of water on to boil. Sarah's chores were to hunt for eggs in the chicken coop, and then pop them into the boiling water for a few minutes, removing them before Jane put in the tea leaves. They worked in unison, chatting, or singing as the mood took them. When everything was ready, they carried the jug of tea and the eggs across the yard to the hut.

The family sat expectantly on benches either side of a table of rough planks. Father was telling James what he wanted him to do that day, before asking Mother if she needed anything from town when he made a delivery of wood there later. She thought a moment before asking Thomas to bring back some mutton and candles, and he nodded as Mother cut the bread and passed the eggs and salt. Jane told her parents that the rainwater was low, watching their frowns, always another problem, their expressions said.

Breakfast fare rarely changed, unless the hens were not laying, and it was a meal that Jane always enjoyed. She felt relaxed after a good sleep, another summer's day lay ahead and who knew what it might bring? By nature, she was an optimist. In contrast, by supper time she was tired from the long uphill walk home after a day of hot and dirty manual labour, looking forward only to her bed.

With breakfast over, Father got up and kissed his wife on the cheek, signalling James to follow him out to the saw-mill. Mother inspected the tidiness of the two youngest children, the first in the family to go to school, before sending them off on their journey. They were accompanied by Sarah and Jane, who were bound for their jobs as chambermaids in the Lord Nelson hotel.

It was a four-mile walk to Geelong along the Settlement Road. Their hut was to the southwest, and that morning a pleasant breeze from the Southern Ocean cooled Jane's back as they set off along the dirt track towards the road. No more than five minutes into the journey there was a sudden shift in the wind and temperature. Ellen and Joseph were running ahead when Jane watched them stop and turn around, their hands spread out in front of their faces. A moment later Sarah and Jane felt the same blast of hot air mixed up with dust that sandblasted into their eyes, nose and mouth. With smarting eyes, they tried turning to walk backwards into the dust but could hardly catch a breath. Beckoning to Ellen and Joseph, Jane and Sarah ran back towards the hut. Their anxious mother met them all a few yards from home with gritty wet rags for their faces, then ushered them inside where they ran to seal any openings with those same rags and some spare sacking. Mother went over to the kitchen to fetch a lit taper to light her few remaining candle stubs. As the candles flickered into life, Jane noticed that the dust was already covering the table and remains of their breakfast. A minute or two later her father and James ran into the house after stabling the bullocks.

'Phew, I've known some dust storms, but this is as bad as any we've had, or worse,' grumbled Father. 'We'll have to stay put for as long as it lasts, although I'll be late with that wood delivery to Mr. Chepstow, and I'm counting on that money Mother.' He put his arm around her shoulders, pecking her cheek.

Was there ever another day when all the family sat cooped up together in the small hut? Jane wondered. She picked up some knitting. Her sisters did likewise, and Mother turned to darning a pile of socks while Father settled down to whittle. He was carving a horse's head on a walking stick he had begun working on weeks before. He rarely had a moment to spend on it, but when completed he knew there was a market for it. A shopkeeper in Geelong took everything he made and always wanted more.

Thomas doubted that the dust storm would last the whole day. He prayed silently for enough time to take the wood into Geelong, and be back before dusk. As the minutes and hours passed, he grew increasingly irritated about losing valuable working time. Time is money, and he needed that money, for theirs was a hand to mouth existence. He tried to remember how much was left in the bank, no more than five pounds, he thought, and this after a lifetime of labour. His sixty years hung heavy on him and he worried about his young family should anything happen to him. After he had risen from his stool and wandered over to the canvas flap to peep out, for what seemed like the tenth time, Mother lost her patience.

'Thomas, will you stop your pottering and sit. You're as bad as Joseph. Every time you lift that flap, more of the dust pours in. Joseph, you get back to your slate and practise your writing.'

The heat and dry atmosphere inside made them all fractious, and the worst of it was that there was nothing to drink. As it got to dinner time, Mother wondered what she could prepare for their meal as the food was stored in the kitchen across the yard. Putting down her darning she dusted off the bread, and in vain hope rather than expectation opened cupboards until she found a near-empty jar of pickled onions which she sliced into fine slices. They sat again at the table to eat the small repast but were thirsty more than hungry. They sucked at the vinegary onions, dredging up every bit of moisture from the thin slivers and were desperate for more.

The dust crept into their mouths and eyes, but the bucket of water was also in the kitchen. They struggled with their thirst until James cursed that he could stand it no more, and with a rag over his mouth and nose, opened the door a fraction enough to slip his slim frame through. While running across to the kitchen, he caught sight of something that made him stop dead. Peering through the dust, he was chilled by what he saw, despite the temperature being over a hundred degrees. He spun around and ran back into the hut, bursting in through the door crying the most dreaded of words, 'Bushfire!'

Father shot up from the bench and ran outside. Mixed up with the swirling dust, he glimpsed an orange pall of smoke to the southwest. Cape Otway was burning, and the fire was travelling in their direction.

'Grab everything you can,' he shouted to Mother. 'I'll get the cart.' He and the boys ran outside towards the stables while the girls fell over each other grabbing up mattresses, clothes and plates. Mother ran to the kitchen to collect pans. The dust was still flying everywhere but now was not the time to hide from it. They could smell the acrid smoke drifting towards them. Jane wondered how far away the fire was and fear made her mouth as dry as dust itself. They each knew the risks of a bushfire but had never experienced one so close.

Minutes later, Father brought round the cart, and they threw on what they could. The bullocks were snorting and stamping the ground in fear. Patch, the black and white mongrel dog, barked madly, his ears flat against his head. They began to hear the trees exploding into flame in the distance. Sarah clutched at Jane in fear, while James helped the younger children climb up onto the cart. Wasting no time, Father whipped the bullocks to force them to move, their terror making them reluctant. He thrashed them harder, and suddenly they set off at a gallop, panicking so much that Jane worried they might never stop.

The children were thrown jolting around the cart with Jane hanging on tight to Ellen, while Sarah grabbed hold of Joseph. Patch ran after them as they careered towards Geelong.

They could hear crackling as the fire spread amongst the tree canopy. In silence, each offered prayers that the flying embers would not jump over them and set more fires further along the potholed track in front. If that happened, they were done for. The wind was no longer blowing from the north bringing the dust, but had turned southeasterly, and they were directly in the path of the fire, maybe a mile or two behind them.

Kangaroos and wallabies careered out of the forest ahead, trying to escape the flames, it was a miracle they missed them and that the cart stayed upright. Mother cried out as she remembered they had left behind the hens, but this was no time to go back. It felt like the longest ten minutes of Jane's life, but at last they were out of the bush and into open farmland. They watched in passing as other families went through the same panic to pack possessions and flee their wooden farmhouses. One farmer hustled animals out of their barns and into the open fields, where at least they stood a chance of not perishing in the flames.

Everyone sighed with relief as they crossed the Barwon River and entered the outskirts of Geelong. Father brought the bullocks to a walk for fear their hearts may burst. Their coats steamed as they walked through the deserted and eerie streets; shops and public houses stood shuttered fast against the dust. Father drew the cart up outside his son-in-law's butcher's shop in Chilwell and James hopped down to hammer on the door. After a few moments, Isaac opened the door an inch or two but seeing his wife's family, called out to Hannah and went to help his mother-in-law from the cart. Hannah ran towards them from the kitchen, hugging them each in turn, relieved to see them safe, before running back to put water on the fire to boil for tea. Father and James took the cart and bullocks around to the sheds at the back.

'Will the fire reach us here?' Joseph asked Isaac, his frightened eyes searching for reassurance from his solid, jovial brother-in-law.

'I hope not. There's a good break between the forest and the town, with the river in between. If it does, we need to head to the waterfront. We'll be alright, I'm sure.' Isaac patted Joseph's head. The five-year-old relaxed and turned to play with Patch, who had managed to worm his way into the house in all the confusion. Isaac was a Welshman, not a Catholic, but a good-humoured, steadfast man with a thriving butchery business. Hannah's parents thought it a good match at the time, their opinion only confirmed over the last three years.

Jane and Sarah went through to the kitchen to help Hannah, chatting with relief at their escape, praising James for raising the alarm. Their mother sat there on a stool wringing her hands in despair. Jane bent to kiss her, but she would not be comforted. Jane noticed that her mother still wore her battered old spectacles.

'Thank goodness we're all safe Mother, and you saved your precious eyeglasses,' said Jane trying to cheer her up. Her mother put up her hand to her eyes in reaction to Jane's comment, but she gave no glimmer of a smile, nor even any recognition of the comment. She appeared frozen in misery.

'Jacob,' she whispered, when Thomas entered the house.

'Don't worry Helen. He's able to take care of himself.'

'Yes Mother,' said Hannah. 'I'm sure he will be fine.'

The girls bustled around her preparing food and drink for the extended family, thankful that there were more than enough mutton chops to go around. The shop had closed early because of the dust and a lack of customers, but the meat had to be cooked before the heat made it inedible. Isaac believed it was still over one hundred degrees although it was nearing four o'clock. He walked into the kitchen, patting his wife on her bottom in affection.

'Let's hope this heat disappears before it bankrupts us,' he said. He joked but with an undercurrent of truth, and Hannah turned towards him with concern showing in her eyes. Chucking her under the chin, he bent to kiss the concern away.

Just before supper, a loud knocking was heard at the door. Isaac opened it to see Jacob standing there, his face and clothes covered in soot and his hands blistered and raw.

'Thank God,' said Mother, rushing to embrace her son. He held his hands out above her head. Realising that they were burnt, she immediately called for mutton fat and cold water.

'Tell us what happened,' Father said, as Mother tended to his wounds.

'I was reaping a few miles south of here, and we started to run as soon as we saw the fire coming towards us. Anyhow I came upon a woman carrying a baby. She was done in from running. Her bark hut had caught alight, and she only just escaped. I flung her over my shoulder, heading for a waterhole. I told her to stay there, while I took the baby to safety, for it was hardly breathing with the smoke. I got across the river, handed the baby to someone then ran back for her. By that time the grass was burning, but in the distance, I saw her staggering around, calling for her child, her outer clothes steaming. I had to push her back into the water and jumped in myself, holding her under the water as flames flew over us. The fire sucked up the air from all around, so it took time to catch our breath. We stayed in the water until it was safe, then I carried her to the river where people looked after her, until her baby was found.'

Mother looked at him with pride and adoration. 'You could have been killed, my brave boy. That woman will thank you for the rest of her days.'

His sisters clucked around him, kissing his face. Father draped a hand across his shoulders. 'Well done son.' He said no more, for fear that emotion would overcome him.

After supper, the boys brought in the mattresses and laid them out in the sitting room; the girls would sleep in a bedroom upstairs. They had no idea how long they might stay there. It was fortunate that Isaac had a brick two-storey house ready for the family that so far had eluded them.

As they were readying the rooms, Jane heard her mother whispering to her father. 'How many times do we have to start again, Thomas? I'm so tired of it.'

'Helen there's a chance the fire never got to the hut. Let's wait to see what the damage is.'

'You know it will be bad; you can't fool yourself. You remember how you never wanted to work for another man. You worked so hard to achieve that. Oh, the thought of having to start again at our age. The Lord knows there's no spare money this time.'

'We've still got the cart and the bullocks.'

Jane heard no more because her mother clammed up when she saw Jane listening.

Four days later her father felt it was safe enough to travel back to their home. He took his wife and Jacob, leaving the younger children to go to school or their work in Geelong. When Jane returned from her work that evening, she knew by the despair in her mother's eyes that all was lost. She appeared to have aged in the last few days, there were strands of grey in her chestnut hair, and her face looked haggard and pale with worry. Jacob told Jane and Sarah that nothing was salvageable. They had lost the contents of the hut, kitchen and stables, including the flat-bed wagon used for hauling timber.

'It was awful to watch their hope turn to despair,' he told them. 'They walked around the camp with little remaining of their labours other than black soot, twisted metal and the smell of cooked meat. Everything was burnt to a cinder. You couldn't tell a koala from a possum. On the road, we came upon some injured koalas which had escaped the fire. They were sitting underneath blackened trees screaming, their paws blistered by the heat. It was awful to hear. The first one Father shot to put out of its misery, but there were so many.' Jacob had tears in his eyes remembering the sound.

'Even the flies seem to have deserted the forest. You can hardly call it the Bush now with all the undergrowth gone. It's just blackened twisted tree branches, no leaves, none of the sounds we remember, no birdsong, nothing. It was eerie, and I hope I never see anything like it again. The newspapers are calling it Black Thursday because so much of Victoria has burnt.'

Jane sat down at the Evans's table after the younger children were asleep that evening. The sun had disappeared, and the room was as gloomy as the expressions on their faces. She watched her father's grizzled face with a mixture of love and concern. His hazel eyes looked tired, but while her mother sat tight-lipped and despondent, his face showed the resolve she had always admired. Father placed his thick powerful hands on the table, fingers spread out and before opening his mouth to speak, he stared at them for a moment.

'We can recover from this,' he began, looking directly at his wife. 'Many folks have lost as much as us, if not more. There's going to be a meeting at Mack's hotel on Wednesday to start a relief fund. If we can get but a few pounds to tide us over, we'll be alright. I need to apply for a new licence to cut wood, but that means finding a few acres of forest which haven't burnt. I'll take Jacob to scout around the bush for a suitable site. James, I want you to find paid work so that we can buy wheels for the new timber wagon I'll need to build. Sarah and Jane, I will ask the landlord at the Lord Nelson if you can live in for a while, although he'll want to reduce your wages, but needs must. Isaac, can you take in my wife and Ellen and Joseph until we get ourselves a new hut?'

'What if we can't get money from this fund?' asked Jacob

'I will find a domestic position,' said his mother, 'and ask for an advance.'

'Then the whole family will be split up!' Jane whispered in distress.

'Needs must,' said her mother turning her face towards Thomas who nodded his thanks and smiled at her.

That night Jane held her crucifix in her hands. It was the one thing of her own she had rescued before fleeing the hut. She dared not ask if her mother had hers, she feared not. She prayed for her family, not knowing it was the last night they would ever sleep together under the same roof.

Chapter 6

Melbourne February 1932

'Good heavens! How frightened you must have been,' said Mary, patting Jane's hand.

As the story drew to its end, she sensed Jane's distress and wondered if she had done the right thing asking her to share her reminiscences. Some patients itched to tell their tales while others refused for whatever reason. Maybe Jane would become one of those and, in that case, she should respect her wishes. There were other ways to kill time such as playing cards or reading aloud to patients. She aimed to play it by ear, so she asked a question to gauge Jane's reaction.

'But what happened next? Did you get any money from the relief fund?'

'Ten shillings is all they gave us.' Jane spat it out. 'Ten shillings, although they raised over eleven hundred pounds on the night of the meeting, they said other people had lost more. It was enough to feed us for a week. We weren't of the right class, that was the truth of it, not farmers or squatters but sawyers, labourers.' Jane took the crucifix back from Mary and held it near her face to look once more at the carving. Her expression softened and became wistful.

'I wonder if any of my grandchildren will take good care of this?' said Jane, fingering the crucifix. 'None of them are Catholics. Mother lost hers in the fire, and she only saved those old glasses because she was sewing when Jacob shouted the alarm. I often wondered why they were so precious to her, but she would never tell.'

'How did you manage after the fire?'

'Father and Jacob found a block of untouched trees ten miles northwest of Geelong and used the last of his money to pay for a licence to cut them. It was too far for us to walk in daily, so they stayed there under canvas for six days a week returning to Geelong on Sundays. Mother got a live-in position as housekeeper to a widower and James worked with Isaac butchering sheep. Father managed to buy a second-hand dray to move the wood, rather than build another one and we got by somehow. None of us was happy to be apart, but on Sundays, we met up at church, and afterwards ate a good dinner together at Hannah's.'

'Your brother Jacob was a hero for saving that woman.'

'Jacob was the light of our lives. He was so full of fun and adventure. We never knew what he would do next. I'll tell you about him tomorrow.'

Mary made her comfortable, picked up the crucifix, kissed it gently and put it back in the drawer. She could understand why Jane treasured it. How she wished she had something left to her from her own father, other than a few happy childhood memories.

Jane dreamt again that night. It was a warm day in Melbourne, and her mother and siblings were walking to St Francis's. Mother carried a baby, while Jane held Ellen's hand. Her older brothers and sisters followed behind. It was a joyful occasion, but faces were solemn as they joined a throng of people waiting to enter the finished nave. They were wearing clean but patched clothes. Mother must have insisted they were washed the day before. They were all agog to see the church.

As they waited, a stranger tapped Mother on her shoulder. Her face looked as though it had once been beautiful, but now was sad with fine lines around her eyes, and deep ones across her forehead, underneath the fading red of her hair. Where Jane's mother wore her only Sunday dress of sober brown cotton, this woman wore a silk dress the colour of emeralds and in the latest style. Her green soulful eyes lit up on seeing Jane's mother and a brief smile made her appear younger than at first glance. Mother turned towards the lady and almost dropped the baby in shock, before whispering the name Nora. Jane stared at her mother's face registering pleasure and disbelief.

'I had to come today,' the woman said, 'although George prefers me not to hold to the Catholic faith. I am so glad I came. Look at you with your tribe. What a lovely family.'

'And you?' Mother asked the woman.

'No, I am not blessed with children. Sometimes I wonder if it is God's way of punishing me for my sins and leaving the true Church. I must go Helen. Pray for me.' The woman moved to disappear back into the throng, not before Jane glimpsed a tear rolling down her cheek as she looked briefly back. Jane's mother looked wistful and sad.

'Who was that, Mother?' asked Hannah.

'Someone I knew a long time ago in England.' Mother stared after the woman, trying to catch another sight of her. Turning back to her children, her face hardened. 'Mark what she said, that turning away from the Catholic Church has brought her nothing but sorrow.'

Jane woke from her dream. Once again it felt real, but was it? She tried to dredge up her memories of St Francis's as it was then. Hadn't there been a ceremony when the nave was consecrated and hadn't Mother insisted they make the trip in from the bush? What age would she have been, five, maybe six? She remembered the large space, the crowds of people and her mother. Was it sadness or awe that overwhelmed her? Jane remembered the tears streaming down her mother's face, and Ellen burst into tears too, not liking to see her mother cry. 'Don't worry' Mother had said. 'These are tears of happiness.' The scene grew clearer in Jane's mind the more she thought about it.

Over the last few years and unbeknownst to her children, she often slipped into the old church for a rest, after shopping in the city. Sitting in the pews, she enjoyed staring at the walls and roof, admiring the wooden tiles. Had her father sawn wood for the church? In all probability, yes, and it gave her great pride to think so. It may not be large or grand but St Francis's church, in all its elegant simplicity, brought her a measure of peace. She never left without lighting a candle for her mother.

With a pang, Jane remembered Hannah's arguments with their mother about not bringing their children up as Catholics. Her mother was horrified and doubly so when Jane followed suit, making her feelings very clear in the letters Isaac wrote to her husband after her marriage. In one letter, she told Jane that sorrow would mark her family. When Jane's firstborn died, her mother had intimated that his death might not have happened, had he been christened in the Catholic Church. But what did God have to do with dysentery? It took Catholics and Protestants alike.

But then her mind flitted back to her mother. Poor Mother, why were her children so much a trial to her? A single tear moistened Jane's eye. Too late for that, she thought and shrugged away the sadness she was feeling to get back to sleep.

Chapter 7

Victoria 1842

It was after the bushranger incident that Jacob decided he wanted to leave home and discover the world. He was thirteen and man enough for adventure; he told Pa. Hadn't his voice already broken, and hairs started to sprout on his sunburnt face? Pa did not disagree, but Mam did. She pursed her lips into the permanent frown they all knew well and feared; but spoke no words. Her body said it all, from her cold glittering eyes to the way she moved around Jacob; she emanated disapproval. But nothing could sway him, not even Pa's recent dice with death. Jacob had fallen in love with the idea of excitement.

It was not that he wanted a bushranger's life. He was too honest for that, and he wanted to live a long and productive life, unlike the outlaws. Now that the men had been caught, no one doubted that a hangman's noose awaited them. Even Jacob could see sense in avoiding that fate. But it was the idea of shaping his destiny, learning new things, and exploring the land that got him so fired up.

It had been the end of an ordinary February day when the bushrangers appeared at their hut. The family was sitting on a log around the campfire, companionable in the warmth of the ebbing day and their satisfied bellies. At the time, there was nothing to suggest danger. The three men were armed, but who did not own a rifle when travelling in the bush? The oldest called himself Yankee Jim, and when Jacob picked up his rifle to admire it, as Jim took tea with his parents, he did not tell Jacob off but told of his adventures on the high seas, holding the children rapt. The youngest of the three men was scarcely more than a youth himself, callow-looking, with scarce a hair on his chin. The third one, Mick, sounded Irish when he chose to speak, which was not often and unusual in an Irishman.

As darkness fell, the men wore their welcome out, for Mam had to get the younger children ready for bed, so they bid farewell. In the early hours, as the family slept, came a knock at the door, and receiving no immediate acknowledgment, the latch lifted. Pa, still half-asleep felt around for a weapon to defend the family, but before he could find one, Mick, the Irishman, crept in, a rifle at his shoulder. The children did not stir, dead to the world; only Pa moved to intercept the intruder.

'I don't mean you any harm,' the man whispered. 'Only go to your neighbours at the station beyond the hill in a couple of hours. They will need your help.' He disappeared through the door as silent as a wraith.

Pa dare not go before dawn, but when he did, he found his neighbours, the Lawrence brothers, tied up, one to a post and the other to a cask, their mouths gagged with rags. After setting them free, one of the brothers asked Pa if he had seen any strangers. With his heart thumping in his chest Pa said no, knowing that if he were suspected of consorting with thieves, his life would have been worth nothing. No further questions would be asked. Justice was instant in the lawless Bush. He prayed that no one had seen the men at his hut.

'It's just that I heard horses riding from this direction in the middle of the night. Well, I said to myself, that's unusual. I'd better check on my neighbours, and I'm glad I did.' He said this slowly, knowing the brother who was deaf and dumb could lip read. Suspicion faded from their eyes. The handicapped brother clapped him on the back and smiled, while the other vowed to fetch neighbours to chase the men. They had been rampaging over the area around Plenty the last few weeks, and it was time they were caught and dealt with.

This story would become one of the family legends, told time and again around the campfire, as the younger children asked Pa to tell them about the day Yankee Jim, Fogarty and Brown, the notorious outlaws, came a calling. Jacob contributed his own legends as his years of adventure found their way back to the family.

On the day he left, his younger sisters clung to their mother's skirts, eyes wet with tears. Hannah hugged her twin before dissolving into tears herself, which melted his mother's heart. She pressed food on him for the journey, insisting that he at least visit within the year. Six inches taller than his mother already, he scooped her up and kissed the top of her head and vowed he would do as she asked. He shook his father's hand and turned to go before he changed his mind. Carrying nothing but a swag and a few pounds in his pocket, he set off, first for Melbourne and then who knew where.

From Melbourne, Jacob caught the paddle steamer, Diamond, to the opposite side of the bay. The rough crossing made his stomach heave but did not daunt his spirit. Twelve hours later he was in unfamiliar territory, the burgeoning settlement of Geelong. Its main street lying under water, reminding him of Melbourne, when in the wet season, a boat was necessary to travel from Flinders Street to Bourke Street

He was tempted to buy some bullocks to haul wood down to the wharf for the paddle steamers. This was a job he understood, and no one could doubt the amount of forest around, ripe for sawing. He mulled the idea around in his head and eventually decided that it would not do. What would it gain him but more of the same life he knew? There was a whole world out there waiting. He picked up his swag and headed west on a trail through the She Oaks that grew so abundant around the town, encountering numerous kangaroos and blacks on his journey. The land was being taken up by squatters. As he trekked, bullock carts passed by carrying families intending to settle on the land. Escorted ladies also, who were travelling to join husbands, once they were convinced it was safe. Past Colac he walked, past Terang, finding himself at Glenormistan, he got a job sheep washing where there were only two white men and all the rest were blacks. They were good workers, and he had no argument with them. One day he overheard that a Corroboree was to be held half a mile away on the flat. He and his mate thought they would take a look out of curiosity.

The two youths walked until they came upon a camp of women and children and knowing no better, they sat down on the ground and tried talking with them. They were yabbering away with sign language and pidgin trying to make themselves understood, when a slight movement made the lads turn around. Flying towards them were firesticks and spears from hundreds of naked and painted black men. They had no time to react as the women threw opossum skins over them and the spears fell close around them, but miraculously not through them. All they could hear was the hiss of the spears flying towards them and the thuds as they hit the ground. As he lay in the thick darkness of the skins, Jacob thought his time was come, cursing his foolishness. The blacks and their gins yabbered some more until the chief came and throwing his stick into the ground close to Jacob's foot; it was made plain that they needed to scarper fast. Pulling the rugs off them, the chief's daughter gestured 'run quick now,' and the boys needed no further encouragement before fleeing for their lives. It was only the following morning, seeing the huge grins of the black fellahs, that Jacob realised that anyone of those spears could have hit their mark, but they only intended to frighten them. A couple of the blacks threw blankets over their heads, quivering with pretended fear, and then burst into laughter. Jim joined in. He did not mind the joke, now that the danger was over.

Moving on, Jacob learnt how to shear sheep, after some trial and error, when he cut his first ram so badly, he had to be taught to sew up the wounds with string. But shearing was a skill he could carry with him, travelling around more stations, moving ever northwards through wild country, savouring the life of an itinerant shearer.

One day, he arrived at a station owned by a man called Mr Francis, a genial man who gave Jim the job of driving bullock carts of timber from Mount Cole, until the shearing started. One of the men on the station was a morose cranky fellow called Moloney. Jacob stayed well clear of him as did most of the other men. Moloney's job was to grind wheat. Everyone was happy when he stuck to that and kept out of the way. One morning, for no reason, he emptied a jar of corrosive sublimate over the cobbles of the yard. The boss was outraged and threw a stick at him, cutting his head slightly.

Something in Moloney was twisted because, far from admitting it was his own fault, he harboured the resentment overnight, letting it fester in the further reaches of his soul. The following morning, he took a rifle, and attempted to shoot Mr Francis, but was thwarted by the shearers wrestling him to the ground. He was instantly dismissed, and Jacob was relieved to see him leave, cursing and muttering to himself.

It was not the end of the matter. Maloney was determined to get even. He returned to the station early the next morning, as the shearers were finishing their breakfast. Jacob watched as Mr Francis grabbed hold of Maloney, pushing him backwards the way he had come. It appeared to be working, until the master stopped for a breather. No one saw the knife until it was too late. Maloney stabbed Mr Francis in the stomach. Jacob saw the shock on his boss's face as first he stumbled and then tried to run back towards the shearers, before collapsing on the ground. Maloney tried to escape but one of the men untied the dogs, and they were away chasing him until he was caught in the shallow river. No one bothered to call them off as the men ran towards the boss.

He lay on the ground, blood and bowels spilling from his body. One of the older men tried to push the bowels back into his body as Jacob ran to fetch twine. This was no ram nicked by the shears and as hopeless as they knew it was, they prayed for a miracle. Jacob watched him being sewn up, the blood oozing red from the wound, with flies gathering above ready for a feast. He stroked his boss's face with a damp cloth that someone pressed into his hand, the skin clammy and growing paler by the second. As one man rode off for help, Jacob helped the others carry him into the farmhouse to hold vigil for their kind boss.

The nearest doctor was over a hundred miles away. It was a long day and a half as they waited for the doctor, but he was too late. They buried Mr Francis under a tree, and Jacob stuck the boss's shearing blades into the tree to mark his grave. This was the first murder which Jacob witnessed. It would not be the last.

These were the tales he told his sisters.

Chapter 8

Mary was shocked by the tale of murder and the matter of fact way that Jane told it. 'Do you know what happened to Maloney?'

'He was tied up until the police came and I should think he was hung. It was pretty lawless back then. The nearest police were in Geelong, and there were lots of bad characters roaming the bush. That only got worse over the next few years.' She paused looking speculatively at Mary. 'You will know why. You must have learnt about it in school. Teachers don't just teach the history of English Kings and Queens now, do they?' Jane said it with distaste, feeling nothing but scorn for the history lessons her own children had to endure.

Mary thought for a few seconds and as realisation dawned she asked: 'Gold, was it gold?'

'Yes, gold. It changed all our lives,' Jane sighed. 'Jacob came and went over the years that followed, always with more tales. He convinced my father to move over to Geelong, and we saw more of him as he travelled around the land between there and Camperdown. He did anything that was going on the stations including cattle-droving but he never stayed anywhere for long. There was always a new adventure to be had. He and James were cut from the same cloth, although it took gold to bring that out in James.' Jane paused and sighed. 'I am feeling tired now, but I will start to tell you about the gold tomorrow. It became my life for the next thirty years.'

Mary itched to ask more questions. She had always thought Victoria a law-abiding, civilised kind of place, a safe-haven for the immigrants who piled in from Europe. It was difficult to reconcile this view with the things Jane spoke about. Everyone knew of Ned Kelly, he was thought of as some kind of hero, especially to those of Irish descent, but Mary knew nothing of other bushrangers. As for the aboriginals, she was ashamed to say she knew very little, rarely encountering one, being a city girl through and through.

Jane tried to sleep, but so many images of her brothers played in her mind. She had not thought of them for years, and had never told any of the stories to her children. For one thing, there was never any time. What was it about a campfire that encouraged stories? Once the move was made to live indoors, storytelling appeared to fade as a source of entertainment.

She pictured James now in yellow trousers and a plaid shirt returning from the diggings, his eyes alight with excitement and his pockets full of gold. The image changed to her son, Joseph. He looked nothing like his uncles, apart from his height, but for the first time, she realised he had inherited their adventurous spirit, tempered by his father's Presbyterian belief in hard work and sobriety. While Jacob and James lived without worrying where the next penny was coming from, Joseph had a plan and enough ambition to conquer whatever he set his mind to, but he too loved spending his money, just like the uncles he never met and knew nothing of. As she drifted into sleep, she wondered if her brothers were waiting for her on the other side. She hoped so. They had always brought a smile to her eyes and a chuckle to her lips.

Mary brought Jane tea in the morning and thought that she looked refreshed. A good sleep had brought some colour back into her cheeks.

'Before you tell me about the gold,' Mary said, as she was washing her, 'tell me something about the aboriginals.'

Jane frowned. 'That's not something I care to talk about. Back in those days, it was hard, always conflict between the settlers and the blacks. They each did their share of murders, and for each white man killed, whole tribes were massacred in return. We didn't treat them as people, still don't, more like vermin. I don't know the right of it, but somehow, we need to learn to live with what was done to them. I won't say any more.'

Chapter 9

Geelong, September 1851

The news spread around the town like the wildfire they had escaped. People were congregating everywhere, in shops, in hotels, on street corners, their faces lit with excitement. Some carried the latest edition of the Geelong Advertiser, reading it aloud to any who would listen. Some had it on good authority, that an acquaintance of theirs found sixteen ounces of gold in a week. With the price of gold at three pounds ten shillings an ounce, that's a year's wages for a labourer earned in one week. Jane and Sarah could not escape the news, and they too were caught up in the speculation, wondering what it might mean for them, and the town.

Father arrived back in town early on Friday that week, describing how the day before, while sawing wood, he had seen a dozen or so travellers on the road heading north, where a week before there had been none. He stopped to ask a party of men carrying an assortment of tools where they were going, and they told him to Buninyong, to pick up gold.

'As though it's lying there, just waiting to be gathered like pebbles on a beach.' He laughed at the thought. 'One or two of them were as old as me and looked as though a breath of wind might knock them over. They're clogging up the road north, and already it's churned up with mud as deep as a shovel. Soon enough it will be impassable.'

'What are you going to do Thomas? Why are you back here today?' Asked Mother. She had taken an hour off from work after Hannah ran to tell her that Father was back in town.

'If this gold find is true I will load up the dray with food and provisions and head off to Ballarat. I am going to make and sell cradles. There'll be lots of demand for good tools, and I will be there to make the best.'

'You're not going to dig are you, Thomas?' asked Mother, anxiety clouding her pale blue eyes.

'We'll see. If there's gold in plentiful amounts, I'd be a fool not to. Helen, this could be the answer to our prayers. If we could just make enough money to build a house where we can live again as a family, with enough money to provide a nest-egg, then I can take a rest. I may only have a few years of good health left.'

'Pa let me go with you,' said James, his eyes burning with anticipation. Butchering lambs had much less appeal than mining for gold.

'No James,' his mother's tone abrupt and adamant.

'Why not, Helen? I think he should come with me and Jacob. He's a strong boy and a good shot. I bet the only cheap meat up there will be 'roos so he'll be useful.

'What about the timber licence? Are you going to abandon it?' Mother sounded shrill.

'For the moment. We can always go back to it if the gold doesn't work out.' He stroked her hand to calm her.

Mother saw from his expression that he was determined, and she could not change his mind. More than just a bit of her hoped that he might be lucky and come back with a fortune. The thought was too tempting. She pushed it to the back of her mind. When had they ever been lucky?

Father spent that night in the bar of the Victory Inn, talking to anyone who had information on the diggings at Ballarat. Someone read him the news, and he returned to Hannah and Isaac's house even more convinced that he should go. He stayed up talking with James and Isaac into the early hours. There had been good advice in the Advertiser describing a cradle which he knew he could manufacture. He drew it on scrap paper, telling James that they would spend the next day making one up and then find out how much it might sell for.

The cradle was ready before the close of business on Saturday. Father and James carried it to an ironmonger for evaluation. It measured three feet long by two feet wide and a foot in depth. A smaller square hopper stood proud of the cradle, with a fine mesh to allow the earth to pass through, before being rocked in the water. Father explained how gold particles would sink through a smaller sieve to the bottom tray, where they would glitter on the blue felt covering. It was not a pretty piece of equipment, showing none of the skills of an expert wood carver, but as James and his father carried the cradle into the shop, men surrounded them asking how it worked. He did not need evaluation because the cradle sold in an instant for a whole pound sterling.

Mother said after mass on Sunday that there was scarcely any need to go to the diggings if they could make money that easily. But Father replied there was no way of knowing how long the gold fever might last. It might be a flash in the pan, and he needed to be there to judge for himself.

As they sat around Isaac's table to eat dinner, Jane listened to the conversation, comparing it with the one back in February. This had such a different tone. Gone was the gloom and despair of that evening. Now everyone was talking about a rosy future and spirits were high, fuelled by a generous portion of ale.

Father said he intended to make three more cradles during the week to pay for the provisions he needed to take. On Thursday, he and James planned to pick up Jacob, collecting the tent and his tools and be in Ballarat by next Sunday.

'When do you think you'll come back?' asked Jane.

'By Christmas, I wouldn't miss Christmas with my family for all the gold in the world.'

Jane and Sarah left for their tiny box room in the hotel, having kissed their father and James and wished them luck.

'Don't you think it sounds a huge adventure? I wish I could go,' said Jane.

'I just hope he makes enough money for a house in Geelong,' replied Sarah. She hated being apart from her family.

On Sunday, the remaining family gathered for their dinner, and afterwards, Isaac read the news of the diggings from the Advertiser.

They heard how the peaceful wilderness now had three hundred diggers camped there. How allotments were marked out, and holes dug; how men cocooned themselves in their blankets at night under canvas or a stringy bark hut thrown up in a moment. How shaving was dispensed with; how language was changing and how campfires lit up the night sky and the smell of frying steaks wafted over the land. The dawn was heralded by laughing jackasses and magpies and the night's peace disturbed by serenading frogs, the possum's snarl and the bullfrog's bassoon. The journalist made it sound so romantic, but Mother poured cold water on the description with a snort of derision.

Jane wondered whether her father and the boys had arrived there by now. She tried to picture the scene. It did sound great fun.

The following Sunday, Isaac read of a new cradle from Geelong which was spoken very highly of, and the family at the table cheered. It had to be father's, didn't it? The article also stated that a digger had to be Jack of all Trades, able to fell a tree, strip bark, dig sods, make an embankment, mend clothes, fry a steak, make roadways and so forth. The list went on and on, Mother nodding her head in agreement. This was much more to her taste.

'My boys can do all of that and still not draw breath,' she said, looking at her daughters with pride.

They smiled and said, 'of course they can Mother.'

Next Isaac read how one nugget weighing twenty-one ounces had been found, and their mouths opened in amazement. But their spirits were dampened by the description of cold wet weather, with a heavy fall of sleet on the goldfields turning the roads to mud.

Later that week, Jane heard angry murmurings on the streets. She was sent on an errand to the ironmongers, to buy a new laundry pail at the behest of her mistress, and the gossip in the long queue was that the government had begun to charge monthly licences for the digging of gold, to be paid up-front.

'It is outrageous. They're taking the money and not doing anything for it. Licences are a tax on the working man my husband says.' A middle-aged woman was pointing to the latest article in the paper.

46

Two days later Isaac read the whole piece to them. The writer was incensed by the tax and the way the government was doing nothing in return, offering no protection to the miners nor building any roads or bridges to the diggings. Worst still, miners might not earn a penny if their bit of ground yielded no gold. His article ended with 'Government is the greatest Gold Digger after all, and the most lucky -- for where they dig they find it in the pockets of miners and are saved the expense of outfit or licence -- work when they please, and sink a shaft in every man's purse -- and, perhaps his heart too.'

'Goodness,' said Mother. 'He sounds like a trouble maker to me. But I don't think it is fair to charge men before they find gold, surely it would be better to charge on what they find. I wish we had news from Thomas about how he's faring.' Her wistful tone ended the discussion.

Geelong was changing. Each day more men left the town to take their chance on the diggings. Women were left to take over jobs which had been the preserve of men, such as delivering the post, working as clerks, even taking over their husband's businesses as shopkeepers or hotel owners. Isaac joked that he wished he could take on little Joseph to help him slaughter sheep, now that James had gone. Labour was in such demand that wages rose, and there were still no takers, while hundreds and then thousands of men passed through Geelong on their way to the goldfields. Some of the men looked rough, already full bearded, wearing mostly cabbage tree hats, blue shirts, and canvas trousers. They stopped at the shops in Geelong for provisions, leaving with a pick, a swag and little else.

'Damned convicts,' Jane heard repeatedly, as women watched. 'We'd best lock our doors at night with that scum around.'

But mixed up with the ruffians were lawyers, doctors, bank managers, even soldiers and sailors deserting their posts. The hotels in Geelong were full to bursting with gentlemen, who cast up everything to go to the diggings, but wanted a good bed for the night before leaving Geelong with their carriages piled high.

47

Jane and Sarah were run off their feet at the hotel. Each room was let to more than one man at a time; every space crammed including the breakfast room, and men willingly paid the high prices demanded. The box room where Jane and Sarah slept was wanted back. Mr Greenwood, the owner, knew he could let that tiny space, and be paid a fortune for it. So, the girls packed up their meagre belongings and decamped back to Hannah's house.

'I'm glad to be out of that box room, but he hasn't talked about putting our wages back up, and he's raking in the money,' complained Sarah at dinner on Sunday.

'Wages are going up all around the town,' said Isaac. 'What men I have left are coming to me and demanding a wage rise or they will go to the diggings. I am putting up the price of meat almost daily to pay for it. The papers say there are now thousands at the diggings and every day hundreds more turn up.'

'Where are they coming from?' Asked Mother.

'From all over Victoria and New South Wales. People are even travelling across the Murray from South Australia,' Isaac replied.

'There's some from Van Diemen's Land too,' said Jane.

'Aye,' said her mother shuddering. 'They'll be the worst. I'm glad the boys have Father with them. But it's not right that your wages haven't been restored. Sarah, Jane, I want you both to ask for a pay rise. If he doesn't give it, you can look for new jobs.'

Hand in hand the sisters approached the owner, Charles Greenwood, the next day. Sarah, being older, spoke for them both.

'Now we are back living with our brother-in-law our wages should go back up,' she began.

Mr Greenwood looked up briefly before going back to his accounts. The girls saw the mound of coins and paper money on the table in front of them.

'In fact,' Sarah began again, 'we should get a pay-rise for the extra work.'

The master laughed but without mirth. 'Have you seen my bills? Your brother-in-law has put up the price of meat. All my costs are rising. I will agree to your wages going back to what they were before, but I can't pay you more.' He waved them back to work.

'That's not right,' said Jane. 'We have more than double the sheets to wash and iron.'

The landlord stood up, he was a large man, and he meant to intimidate the sisters. Never in all his days had girls demanded more money. Fifteen pounds a year for a chambermaid was a good wage. He glared at the girls, expecting them to be sufficiently cowed to make themselves scarce and get back to work.

Jane stared back at him. Her sister shuffled her feet and was prepared to retreat if Jane had not grasped her hand. 'Eighteen pounds a year or we give a week's notice,' she declared.

The master roared in displeasure, his black bushy eyebrows appearing to meet in the middle of his forehead in a scowl of anger. Jane gripped Sarah's hand tighter and repeated her demand, refusing to be frightened by him.

'I'll not be blackmailed. You can go at the end of the week.' He dismissed them, thinking they would now beg to stay, but Jane turned on her heel and pulled Sarah out of the room.

'What are we going to do? Surely, we should try to get a new job before giving our notice. Mother will be furious with us.' Sarah's troubled face had tears in her eyes.

'I can get us new jobs,' said Jane.

'Where?'

'I have an idea. Come with me at dinner time.'

At midday, the girls got thirty minutes off to eat dinner. Usually, they ate in the hotel's kitchen, but on this day, Jane asked the cook if they might have a hunk of bread each with a slab of cheese.

'We can eat this when we get back,' said Jane putting the bread and cheese on a plate in the laundry room.

Jane led Sarah down Corio Street to the ironmongers. The girls could scarcely get through the door. Men of all ages milled around waiting to be served. Some wore work clothes, others looked far too well dressed to be queuing in a shop selling the necessities of labour.

There were two counters, one at the far end of the shop where the owner was engrossed in serving a man whose bulk almost hid him from view. The other counter on the right was unmanned. Around the sides of the shop were shelves packed with goods, underneath sat large wicker baskets holding more tools, each with a white card. bold black writing stating the price. Tin buckets and canvas tents lay piled up next to the counters. The dark wooden floorboards were littered with clumps of mud from the boots of impatient customers.

'Watch this,' said Jane.

Jane marched up to the empty counter to the right and beckoned to customers. The first to arrive was a man dressed in obvious new working clothes, for they were far too neat and unsullied. He was clean-shaven, apart from a fair moustache which barely shaded his upper lip. His air of uncertainty gave Jane courage.

'Sir,' said Jane. 'How may I help you today?'

The man looked at Jane and smiled in relief, his long wait over.

'I am going to the diggings,' he said in a cultured English accent. 'I need tools, but I am not sure which would be best.'

'Well Sir, there I can help you for I understand exactly what you need. First, you need an axe, and an American axe is the one we recommend. It will cut through wood far better than any British axe.'

'Oh!' said the man grateful but perplexed. 'Why do I need an axe?'

'For firewood Sir.' Jane saw his bewilderment.

His face showed dawning realisation that he must do his own cooking.

'Then you will need a good spade and a pick, and do you have a tent?' Jane gathered the goods he would need from the shelves and baskets around, until a pile stood on her counter. She totted up the prices in her head. Mentally she thanked the owner for labelling all his tools although she knew the value of them.

The owner still had not noticed Jane. She asked her customer for twelve pounds seventeen shillings and sixpence, and he handed her thirteen pounds. With her heart in her mouth, she went over to the far counter and tapped the owner on the shoulder, before asking him for change.

Mr Richardson was utterly confused, but when Jane's customer pushed his way over to the far counter and complimented Jane on her most helpful advice, he smiled and handed him his money. In the meantime, Sarah began to serve another customer, and between them they served four satisfied men within their dinner break, taking a total of fifty-three pounds.

'We have to go now,' Jane told the owner. 'You know our family, and we know our tools. We have been brought up with them and can add up quick as anyone. If you want to hire us, it will cost you twenty pounds a year each.'

Mr Richardson's previous assistants, who had both left for the diggings cost twenty-five pounds a year. But girls, he never employed girls. He thought for a moment and then said 'Deal.' He had tried to get men to work for him over the last two weeks. The only one who started demanded thirty pounds a year and only lasted a week, before he threw over his job for goldfields.

'We'll start tomorrow,' said Jane.

The girls made their way to the door as men clamoured for service before they left. 'I'm in a hurry Miss,' said one, and Jane was sorely tempted to stay. But they needed to pick up their belongings, and she so wanted to look at the expression on the landlord's face as she told him they had new and better-paid jobs than his.

The girls skipped back to the hotel laughing. 'How on earth did you come up with that idea?' Said Sarah in amazement.

'I stood in such a queue last week and guessed he needed help. We may not be able to read but we know our numbers, and I thought why not try for a job there. It beats making up beds and boiling dirty sheets. But did you ever meet such greenhorns? That first customer of mine has no idea what's ahead of him. I wonder how long he'll last as a digger.'

Chapter 10

Melbourne 1932

'What did you say to the hotel keeper?' Asked Mary, laughing.

'Oh, I knew he would bluster and call us names, which he did. But what could he do about it? I remember his face to this day. It was puce with fury, but I didn't care. My mother and father were tough bargainers, and they didn't back down, not if they knew they were right. They taught me a valuable lesson. Never give in, unless your back's against the wall.'

'You must have had guts to bluff your way in and start serving in the ironmongers.'

'Not as much as you think, because what I didn't tell Sarah was that I had been in the shop the week before, and Mr. Richardson asked if any of my brothers were at home and would like a job. I told him only my six-year-old brother, and he was maybe a mite too young, but it got me thinking.'

'You crafty thing! I can see I need to watch out.' Mary teased but then paused, becoming more serious. 'But your mother must have been thrilled with your pay rise.'

'Yes, because within the month the old man she kept house for died. I persuaded her to take on the lease with our extra money. None of his children wanted the furniture, so she bought it at a fair price to be paid over twelve months. We moved in and let out the two spare rooms. We filled them over and over again.

The town was growing fast. When the gold-rush began, only eight thousand people lived in Geelong. Inside of a year, it grew by twelve thousand or more. Imagine it, ships arriving in the harbour and when the sailors learnt of the gold, they abandoned the ship, and the Masters did too. It was complete bedlam. In the ironmongers, we sold out of our stock of axes, tents and pannikins regularly. We could not get enough, and prices soared.'

'And did your father come home for Christmas.'

'That's another story.' Jane sighed, and her expression changed in an instant. Her girlish gleefulness disappeared, and she appeared more thoughtful and strained. Mary was sorry she asked, sensing sadness in her expression.

'Yes, you need to have a rest before your daughter arrives. She rang to say she would visit this afternoon.'

'Which one?'

'Mrs Eliot, the one who was here when I first knocked on your door.'

'Ah, Sophie. She travels here all the way from Prahran. She's very good to me, but I wish her life was easier.' She did not expand upon the comment. It was Sophie's business, but Jane worried about her. Two husbands she'd had, and both deserted her. Now to make ends meet she let out rooms, as Jane had done and her mother before her.

Some might say it was strange how some people attracted bad luck and others sailed through life without a care in the world. Jane knew better. People made their own luck. If Sophie made bad marriages, it was because she did not listen to her mother's advice. She was too swayed by looks and charm, often signs of weakness in Jane's book. She thought about it for a while, concluding that perhaps her older children were tougher than the younger ones. Being born in a tent or a hut must have hardened them up.

Later that afternoon Sophie closed the bedroom door gently, and came into the sitting room, leaving her mother asleep.

'Mrs O' Hara I can't thank you enough, Mother seems very happy in your care. She was telling me how you have been helping her to remember her early days in Melbourne and Geelong. She appears quite animated by it. When her grandchildren ask her to tell them stories about her life she clams up tight.'

'I find that getting my older patients to talk about their life helps ease their passing. They come to realise that their lives have been worth living, even those who tell me at first that they're very ordinary, and have done little with their lives. Your mother's stories, and I have only heard a couple so far, are fascinating. I hope you don't mind her telling them. She has asked me not to repeat them and I wouldn't.'

'That sounds like her. Sometimes I wish she had been more open and warm. She is hardly likely to change at this late stage, is she? Well if it helps her, I'll I not complain.'

'Mrs Eliot, we need to arrange for a priest to visit when the time comes. Who is her priest?'

'Priest!' Sophie was aghast. 'Do you mean a Catholic priest? Why would she need one? She's not a Catholic.'

Mary cast her eyes down, feeling that she had fallen at the first hurdle of confidentiality. Recovering she smiled and said, 'So sorry, my mistake. She told me about watching the building of St Francis, and I assumed she was Catholic.'

'No, no. Father was a Scottish Presbyterian. He had no truck with Catholics. Oh, sorry Mrs O' Hara, I did not mean to be rude. My youngest sister, Florence, married a Catholic, but that was long after my father died. He would never have approved, even though her bridegroom was filthy rich.' Sophie laughed to take away her momentary confusion. With a name like O' Hara the nurse was bound to be Catholic, thank goodness she hadn't mentioned her father despising the Irish as well.

The next morning dawned cool to Jane's relief. As Mary washed Jane, she remarked at how much better her legs looked.

'They're not nearly so swollen this morning. Let's hope we have seen the last of this heat wave. It's March now, and we have the cooler weather to look forward to. Yesterday you were going to tell me about your father and if he made it back for Christmas.'

'Yes, he did, but on his own. My brothers stayed to guard their claim. He rode into Geelong on Christmas Eve. How thrilled we all were to see him.' Jane's shrunken face relaxed and smiled at the memory. She did not talk for a while, but the smile remained as her mind swept back eighty years to that Christmas.

'He rode first to Isaac's shop, and they told him where we were living. He was so pleased that we now had our own house, and picked

54

me up in a bear hug and swung me around when he heard the story of how we got our new jobs. 'That's my Jane' he said laughing. I felt so proud when he said that. It was a lovely Christmas, even without my older brothers. Father told us what it was like on the goldfields, but he did not make it sound as romantic as the stories in the paper. He told us as much as he thought we should hear, but I know there was much he left out. He said it was no place for a woman and he was adamant about that.'

'Did he bring any gold back?' Asked Mary.

'Yes, he did and gave it to my mother. It was in a small knotted bag, which she took with something approaching devotion. She untied the string and peered inside, gasping at the colour of it. Of course, we all wanted to have a look. The bag was passed around to each of us, but none of us dared stick a finger into the fine golden grains. I remember it weighing much heavier than I expected. Father told us it weighed about fifteen ounces and was worth fifty pounds of any man's money. He grumbled that there was not more gold, blaming the cost of licences and the price of food.

We asked him if he had made any more cradles. At first he told us, but all the trees were being chopped down, and he did not want to waste time searching for wood, when it was more important to dig out their claim. I came to understand that later, when I lived on the goldfield. He was angry that some poor fellows dig and dig but find nothing, but still have to pay for the licences.

Mother could tell my father was tired. He had aged in those few months, so she begged him to stay longer than a week, but he told her no. The boys needed him. It was hard graft, harder than anything he had ever done, and he had spent all his life labouring. Maybe a few more months, he promised her. 'if I can just find enough gold to buy this house for you Helen.' I watched mother shush him and plant a kiss upon his lips. She was worried about him, and he worried about her, so much younger than him, he fretted about leaving her a penniless widow. He often mentioned that in our hearing, and we all told him not to worry, that Mother would always be taken care of.

Before he left, I reassured him that I would make sure Mother was alright. 'Will you promise Jane?' He asked me. I crossed myself and promised with my hand on Mother's hand. He smiled at me and planted a kiss on the top of my head. 'Lucky will be the husband who gets you,' he said, before mounting his horse. I nearly died with pleasure. But I tried to keep my promise to him, as much as I could.'

Jane turned her eyes away but not before Mary saw a single tear in each eye. Jane paused after a surreptitious wipe of her eyes with her handkerchief and then turned back.

'That was such a happy Christmas. But Mother said it was her last happy one, though she lived for another thirty years. Gold ruined our family Mary, not financially you understand. It was gold-fever that ruined it, and Mother came to curse the day someone found the yellow dust. It didn't just destroy us though. Countless men and families came from around the globe to join the thousands already here, using any means to get to Ballarat. I'll tell you tomorrow about one of them.'

Chapter 11

Victoria 1852

By mid-February the first ships began to arrive from Europe and America, bringing hordes of men chasing after the riches of Ballarat. Only now it wasn't just Ballarat; it was Bendigo and Mount Alexander too. Gold finds were reported all over the north of the State of Victoria and in some parts of New South Wales.

The Americans came from the goldfields of California and knew what they were about, but the Europeans were dubbed 'New Chums' because many had no inkling of what was ahead of them. Jane thought the term too kind, but later realised it was a form of gentle mockery.

One morning in late March, she served a man who looked so out of place that Jane immediately guessed he was one of those 'New Chums.' He wore a white shirt beneath a deep lapelled waistcoat. His legs sported chequered trousers finished off with shiny leather shoes. Over his arm, he carried a long woollen coat and outside the temperature must have been ninety. His dark curling hair and sideburns were damp and stuck to his head, dripping pearls of sweat onto his broiled face and narrow shoulders. Jane was politeness itself, but inside she veered between amusement and feeling sorry for him. Before she served him with the usual paraphernalia required by a new digger, he asked her if she knew of somewhere where he and his family could stay. She told him her mother had vacancies, and directed him to her house, thinking little more about it over the course of the day.

Arriving home that evening, Jane found her mother sitting down with a well-dressed young woman in the small breakfast room, a pot of tea beside them.

'This is Mrs Adams, Jane. She's the wife of the gentleman you sent to us today. They have a real bonnie boy, who's fast asleep in bed.'

Jane went over to the woman and greeted her, noticing her tiny waist held in by a boned corset no doubt. She looked uncomfortable and vulnerable, but Jane could not help but admire her dress. She wore a skirt made of silk, in a plaid pattern of green, blue and magenta, the top mirrored the dark blue of the skirt, matching her deep, blue eyes. There was no doubt in Jane's mind that such an exotic creature had never before set foot in their house.

'Go and fetch your supper to eat in here Jane. Mrs Adams is going to tell us about their journey. Mr Adams has gone over to the Lord Nelson to collect their luggage and talk to some men he met earlier today.'

Jane did as she was told but felt a little resentful that after a busy day at work, she had to listen to the woman, when all she wanted was to kick off her boots, eat and flop on her mattress. Sarah was lucky to have escaped to Hannah's this evening.

All the rooms, bar the kitchen, in the single-storey brick house were in use as guest rooms. The parlour was used as a bedroom by single men. There was a small dining room where Mother served breakfast and supper. Beyond that were two small bedrooms. Neither of which were used by the family now, paying guests being too numerous and a good earner. They knew this state of affairs would not continue more than a few months, a year at best, so Ellen and Joseph lodged with Hannah while Mother, Sarah and Jane slept on mattresses in the scullery.

Jane returned to the breakfast room carrying a plate of shepherd's pie, as Mrs Adams said, 'I am so thankful that the waitress at the Lord Nelson mentioned you Miss Jane. There were no rooms to be had at any hotel, and I so wanted to sleep in a bed again. You have no idea what it has been like these last two weeks.' She had a slight lisp to her voice which sounded thin and reedy in her cultured English accent.

Jane inclined her head in acknowledgment, thinking it must have been Milly who directed them. She was a friendly soul, always happy to stop work for a gossip. She was the only thing she missed about the hotel.

'Do tell us how you came to leave England,' said Jane's mother, her voice acquiring a vague accent in a misguided attempt to appear more refined than she was. Jane chuckled to herself. She had never heard her mother put on airs and graces before, and had thought her incapable of it.

'Well it was the talk of the city, London I mean. When the newspapers reported the gold finds in Victoria, it was all anyone could gossip about. Mr Adams, my husband, is a lawyer. He had a good job, but he was impatient for his talents to be recognised in London, where so many lawyers depend upon patrons. He resents the way that others advanced through patronage rather than talent.'

Jane became fascinated by the woman's hands. They fluttered as she talked rather than lying still in her lap. They were like the wings of a dove caught in a net, struggling to escape. She longed to capture one and see if it was really as soft as it appeared.

'We had a pleasant home in Clapham, near the common, but Mr Adams came home one evening and said that he was determined to come here to seek his fortune. I have to say Mrs Dugmore, I was shocked, but he explained it to me, and it made sense at the time.' She sighed. 'He is something of a romantic, you understand.'

Jane looked at her mother. Neither showed any expression knowing what each other was thinking. What is romantic about being a digger? Those newspaper reporters had much to answer for.

'He wants to start a business in Australia when he has found enough gold.'

'What kind of business?' Mother asked.

'Oh, he doesn't know yet, but something will occur by and by.' Jane caught her mother's eye. The woman was childlike in her innocence and ought not to be blamed for the decisions of her husband. He, on the other hand, sounded reckless in the extreme.

'He sold everything we had and bought what he thought we would need, and we set sail, or rather steamed on over.' She laughed a little girl's laugh, but Jane had an inkling that it masked something else, possibly fear.

'At the end of the voyage, we sailed into Hobson's Bay with such trepidation in our hearts. Were the tales of gold true? Would we find it all a terrible hoax? When the pilot arrived onboard, he brought newspapers from Melbourne with him, and the men fell on them. At first, there were cheers of joy when they read the news of the gold finds and the prices gold was fetching. I remember jumping up and down with glee to see my husband's smile. It was true. Everything was going to be alright.' She paused to take a sip of tea and then put her hand over her mouth, choking off her words.

'You could feel the silence descend on the ship. It was as though a hundred of the brightest candles had been blown out in a second. What's wrong, I cried. My husband showed me the advertisements further down the column. Can you believe that horses selling in London for fifteen shillings are selling in Melbourne for seventy pounds! Freight to Melbourne from the ship is three pounds per ton, as much as it cost from our home in London to Hobson's Bay. We stood at the side of the ship looking on to the shore, and we realised how little our money would buy. At that point, I wished more than anything we had never started on this venture and nothing since has made me change my mind.

We had to pay three shillings each to be landed on the beach without our luggage, and another charge of the same to be taken into Melbourne. That was just the start of our problems.' She dabbed a handkerchief to her eyes.

'Mrs Dugmore, I am so worried about what will become of us. My husband scoured Melbourne for accommodation for us, but there was none. Even the stables were full, not of horses, but of people, and they wanted five pounds for the privilege of sleeping on straw. I sat and waited for him in a rough hotel with my little boy and our nursemaid, and I felt so homesick. I thought Melbourne would be a civilised city, but it's not, is it?'

'It's a long time since I visited,' said Mother, somewhat put out.

60

'It's mostly wooden hovels as far as I could tell from where I sat waiting. There's no paving and so much mud. I imagined a city with fine buildings and parks.'

'It hasn't changed that much then,' said Mother, even she was surprised.

'We had to travel south of the river to a tent city. They are hiring tents out at five shillings a night. My maid took one look and gave notice there, and then and I can't say I blamed her. We stayed there a week, and I don't know how we stood the heat and the flies. I am a wreck just thinking about it. To be able to have a good wash in warm water is so wonderful. I can't tell you how grateful I am that you took us in. That was a filthy experience and one I never wish to repeat. My husband even had to walk to a cart with our night soil. I felt so ashamed.'

'Then you don't intend to go up to the goldfields Mrs Adams?' Mother asked innocently.

'Well yes, of course I do Mrs Dugmore.'

'You do realise that you will have to live in a tent there.'

The shock showed plainly on her face. Jane guessed she was around twenty but acted more like a child.

'Will there not be houses to rent?' she asked in a whisper.

'No, a slab hut at most and only if your husband can build one.' Jane hid her smile as her mother spoke. 'You will need to know about the snakes and the insects. We've got some horrors here.' Mother's voice returned to normal, and so had her patience. The woman paled, her English complexion took on a pasty hue.

'Excuse me, Mrs Dugmore, I must see to my son. I think I heard a cry.' She fled from the room.

'Why ever did you send them to me? I'm sure they are going to be more trouble than they're worth.' Mother looked at Jane, her eyes accusing.

'You were all over her a few moments ago,' retorted Jane.

'Was I? Well, I suppose I have never entertained someone who thinks herself a lady before. I should know better at my age. If she has

61

any sense, she'll talk him out of digging and into getting a job as a lawyer.' Jane agreed with her mother.

'I'll ask Mr Richardson if he'll take back the purchases he made. I don't know why she wasn't told about the tent I sold her husband today. Perhaps he's keeping it from her.'

Mr Adams returned an hour or so later. Soon after they heard the couple arguing followed by a sustained period of weeping.

'It sounds like she hasn't convinced him,' Jane whispered to her mother. 'He'll never make it as a digger. I doubt he's cut a sod of earth in his life. If she doesn't go, then she can rent a room in Geelong, no doubt, maybe even stay here.

Jane thought little of it the next day beyond getting Mr Richardson's agreement to take back the goods at a small loss to Mr Adams. If possible, the day was even busier than usual. She felt worn out by the time seven o'clock came and time to return home to eat. Sarah threw off her boots as soon as she got in, rushing to the scullery to find her supper.

'I am so hungry I could eat a horse,' she said, giving her mother a quick peck on the cheek.

Jane noticed that her mother was troubled because of the furrows in her brow.

'What am I going to do Jane? Am I to throw a woman and small child out on the street?'

Jane sighed. 'Just let me get my supper, and I'll join you.' Why did she feel her mother wanted to blame her for whatever had gone amiss?

'So, what's happened?' she asked as she laid her plate on the small kitchen table.

'He's gone to the diggings with two men he met at the Victory and abandoned her here to fend for herself.'

Jane chewed at her mutton chop, wondering what the problem was. Sarah joined them, but Jane did not feel like explaining all that had gone on the night before. Her mother was going to tell her anyway, was itching to tell her.

'What she didn't tell us last night was that they have almost run out of money.'

'Who has?' Asked Sarah. Jane shook her head at her as much to say, 'don't ask.'

'Mrs Adams, the lady who Jane kindly directed here.' It was not worth saying that Jane had not set eyes on the woman until last night, and that her mother had been fawning over her to begin with.

'When he left this morning, he gave me two weeks rent for his wife and child, and his father's precious pocket watch in case I needed more money. He expects me not to sell but pawn it, so that he can retrieve it upon his return. We'll see about that. I don't mean to be out of pocket. Mrs Adams has been weeping in her room since he left, and has not even come for her supper. So, Jane tell me, what am I to do?'

'About what?' Jane asked in confusion.

'Do I turn the woman and her child out on the street when the money's gone?'

Jane paled as she noticed the woman in question standing in the doorway. Her elfin hands flew to her mouth, all the horror of her situation written in her eyes.

'My husband does not mean to abandon me,' she cried. Jane's mother softened a little as she saw the sorry creature.

'Come and sit down, Mrs Adams. Sarah, fetch the lady some tea and supper.' She pushed her daughter towards the scullery as Sarah only had eyes for the lady's dress, the same colourful plaid she wore the day before. Sarah wanted it, desperately.

'Well here's a-to-do. I am sure we can work something out,' said Mother.

'How I wish we had never set off, never heard of the gold.' The woman sobbed. 'He told me it would be fine. Even when we slept in that awful tent with goodness knows what insects in the mattress, biting me and poor little Freddie to bits, he told me it would work out. I believed him, and I still want to. He is my husband, after all. When we had to pay a fortune to bring our luggage ashore, he reassured me everything would sort itself out. There were people worse off than us who were trying to sell what they had brought from England. It was all wrong you see; none of it of any use in this climate. At least we didn't do that. But I can't live in a tent again. I told him, no, and now he's gone!'

'You poor thing,' said Mother, but her words did not match the expression in her eyes.

'He'll be back within two weeks,' said Jane. He'll get to Ballarat, realise he hasn't got what it takes to be a miner, then return. It's happened before, at the shop. We have had half a dozen men trying to sell back their tents and frying pans after they gave up on digging within a day or two.'

Mrs Adams looked cheered by this and sipped at the tea which Sarah set in front of her.

'That dress, Mrs Adams, it's beautiful. Is that what they are wearing in London?' asked Sarah. 'I wager you could sell it here. Have you more like that?' There was avarice in Sarah's voice which upset Mrs Adams anew. Was she even to lose the clothes off her back?

'Perhaps I could get some employment,' she said, hopefully.

'What experience do you have?' Asked Mother. 'Can you cook?' Mrs Adams shook her head. 'Sew?'

'Embroider. I can embroider.'

'Not much call for that,' sniffed Mother. 'How about being a nursemaid?' She smiled, of course, that was the answer. What satisfaction it would give her to have this English lady reduced to a nursemaid. Not even bothering to wait for a reply, she said. 'I will start to ask around tomorrow if anyone needs a nursemaid.'

Mrs Adams looked forlorn. How had it got to this? She did not want a job as a nursemaid. Jane saw the stricken look on her face. She reached over the table and took one of Mrs Adam's hands in her own, marvelling at the softness of it.

'It will not come to that. He'll be back in a fortnight,' Jane reassured her.

Jane was wrong it only took ten days to find him back knocking on their door, before they turned in for the night. Mother grumbled when she heard the rapping.

'All of my guests know they must be back before nine o'clock.'

'Perhaps it is Father and the boys,' said Jane, running towards the door, in anticipation.

When Jane opened it, she scarcely recognised Mr Adams. A sorrier sight was hard to imagine. The darkness could not hide the fact that he was not the same man who had set off with such optimism and excitement a few days before. He looked as though he had lost some weight. Not only was he shoeless and hatless, but his clothes were ripped and torn and coated in mud and filth. Lit by candlelight, his face showed several days worth of beard, but through the beard were raw blisters where the sun had burned him. Above his eyes was an ugly gash where dried blood had gathered, and his eyes were red and streaming with puss, infected by insect bites by the look of it.

'Please don't tell my wife I am back until I have cleaned myself up.' He whimpered in embarrassment. Jane thought it would take more than a wash to make him look presentable. She led him stumbling into the breakfast room, sitting him down on a wooden chair, and told him she would get some warm water and a cloth. Her mother was hovering near the kitchen door in her night clothes.

'Who is it? Who's ever knocking at this time of night?' She complained.

'It's Mr Adams, and he is in a bad way. I need to boil up some water, and he probably needs a doctor, but I doubt he has money for one.'

Mother donned a large shawl, wrapping it firmly around her shoulders and went to investigate for herself. When she saw him, she was shocked into action. She ordered Sarah to bring cold tea and vinegar.

'I'll find an old sheet for cloths and a blanket for you, Mr Adams. Please take off your clothes down to your drawers.' This he found hard to do because his hands were a mass of blisters. He fumbled with his buttons but made little progress, before Mother returned carrying a clean but threadbare sheet. Tutting, she helped him out of his outer clothes. They felt unusually heavy and stiff with caked mud, and she dropped them in a pile on the floor, thinking It would take a deal of scrubbing to get the filth out, but they might be salvageable. Jane brought in a bucket of clean, warm water.

'I'll need more water than that Jane. Find two bowls and put in enough hot soapy water to cover his hands,' Mother said. She held one of his hands up to examine the damage. 'Right I will start on your face, it's not going to be pleasant, but I need to clean it and then see what to do.'

She tore the sheet into strips and dipped one into the water and began to clean his face and eyes. He flinched several times and cried out in pain more than once. Next, she took some vinegar and poured a little onto a clean cloth and dabbed at his sunburn. Around his red and weeping eyes, she worked with a cloth dipped in cold tea. When Jane came back with the two bowls of water Mother put a finger in to test the heat. She placed his hands in them and held them there, even though he complained it was too hot.

'It needs to be as hot as you can stand,' she said. 'Sarah please mix oatmeal into a paste with water. Jane, we need more hot water for his feet.'

Mother worked on cleaning him up and tending to his wounds, before binding his hands and feet in rags, coated with the oatmeal mixture. As she worked, she asked him what had happened.

'Thank you for your help Mrs Dugmore. You have been more than patient with me and my family. I have been a fool. This whole journey was foolhardy, wasn't it? I can tell, you knew I would be no use up there at the diggings, and you were so right.

'Tell us what happened for you to be in such a state as this Mr Adams.'

The men waited for him outside the Lord Nelson not long after sun-up. They helped him stow his belongings in the cart, covering them up with canvas. He scrambled up and sat on his tent while his two new companions sat up front, with their backs towards him. He had never travelled in such a clumsy looking vehicle before. Being a city man born and bred, it reminded him of the big carts used to deliver coal or beer around the streets of London. The man called Harry flicked the reins, and the powerful looking horse set off pulling the wagon. It jolted forward. He grabbed hold of the side, to stop himself from tipping out.

This felt like the start of a real adventure into the wilds of a continent, he had never dreamed of visiting six months ago. Slowly they passed through the streets of Geelong and up a steep hill onto the road north. The sun already shone bright in the cloudless sky, and he was glad of the wide-brimmed hat he had bought in Melbourne. It cast a good shadow over his eyes letting him see the land. The broad-leafed trees he was used to, the London plane, the oak and the horse chestnut were nothing like these trees. Many of them appeared to have scorched trunks, and their bluish, elongated leaves originated much higher in the canopy. A flock of large birds flew up screeching raucously as the wagon lumbered past. He was expecting seagulls being so near the coast, but although they were white they sported bright yellow crests, and the beaks weren't long and pointed but stumpy, pointing down and inwards, no use for catching fish.

His companions could not be described as conversationalists, and when he asked what the trees and birds were called - 'gums, 'toos mate' was the response, which did not help much. He settled himself down for a long, tedious and uncomfortable journey.

They had been travelling for a couple of hours before they made their first stop at a grog tent. It was too early in the day for a drink he thought, but not according to his chums, who told him it was never too early. He declined their offer to imbibe and sat under a tree waiting for them, twiddling his thumbs, and becoming impatient, but what could he say? It was hot, and flies gathered around his face, buzzing greedily. He took off his hat to swat them away, but it did little good, so he had no choice but to join the men in the tent where they happily cajoled him to buy them another drink. Other wagons rumbled past as he stood waiting. He had half a mind to ask the drivers for a lift, but it seemed ungracious.

At last, after relieving themselves in the bush, the men told him it was time to go on, because they wanted to get to a certain campsite they favoured by the end of the day. The day wore on. They made another stop for a drink and a bite to eat at midday and this time the men put their heads down in a shady spot, and had a snooze, while he kicked his feet in annoyance. Were they deliberately trying to provoke him?

'We're making good time,' they told him, when he enquired how long it would take. 'The track is dry after the summer, no need to rush Mate.'

He thought better of them when they reached the place where they wanted to camp. There was a creek where the water ran clear, and they could fill up their billycans; the Bush too was close enough for them to gather a supply of wood for the campfire. He found it difficult to tell the men apart, but he had already established that they were not brothers. They both wore rather shapeless wide-brimmed hats, their features hidden by a thick mass of unkempt facial hair. One he guessed was older than the other as his face was more wrinkled, and it was this one who showed him how to make a campfire. He made it look so easy. Take an axe to chop wood; dig out the fire pit; surround it by a ring of stones; place the dry kindling in the centre; build a pyramid of sticks before striking a piece of steel against a flint to set fire to a singed scrap of cloth; lay it against the kindling and blow gently to make the flames grow. So few words were exchanged, and yet the lawyer felt an elemental thrill going back to his boyhood. He had been raised on the novels of Sir Walter Scott and Daniel Defoe, unlocking in him a spirit of adventure, which his father tried to quash but without success.

'You can have a go tomorrow Mate,' said the man, who called himself Harry. 'Time now to put up your tent.' He stamped on the cloth, once the fire had taken and stored it away to reuse.

Once again with few words, Harry showed him how. What a magical evening it was, everything he had longed for as a boy. Sitting around a campfire in companionable silence after a meal of fried chops and potatoes cooked in the fire, with a flagon of beer to share. The darkening sky lay above him where a bright moon and the first stars were appearing. And yet it was balmy; the temperature akin to the warmest summer eve in England. Something caught his eye in the growing dusk; large shapes were moving towards the grass by the creek.

'Roos there Mate.' Animals he had seen only in books appeared before his eyes, kangaroos and wallabies if he were not mistaken. He caught his breath admiring them. The kangaroos were so much bigger and more powerful than he expected. He swore later that he felt the bullet whistling past his ear, before he heard the shot which felled one of the larger beasts.

Turning, he saw Harry with a rifle. 'What have you done?' He cried. The man looked at him puzzled.

'Tomorrow's dinner Mate. I'll show you how to skin it.'

The moment was spoiled. Building a fire and skinning and gutting a kangaroo were two different things altogether; the first made him feel noble; the second made him want to throw up. He felt that first moment of doubt since beginning the journey.

Their second day on the road followed the pattern of the first; unnecessary stops for grog, which he reluctantly paid for, conscious of his dwindling supply of cash. He had long hours to think, once the scenery had lost its novelty. He tried to recall the heroes of Scott and Defoe, but his mind played tricks on him as it kept returning to John Bunyon.

He heard his father, in his grave three years past, saying 'When will you learn, that life is not one of those accursed novels of yours but a journey, full of pitfalls? Throw away those books and learn your lessons from Pilgrim's Progress. It will stand you in better stead.' He had not listened, and he tried not to listen now.

His attempt to build a fire at the end of the day put him back in a good frame of mind. He found the wood harder to chop than he had imagined, but all the other things he accomplished after a fashion. Harry may be a man of few words, but he was a good teacher. His tent was up, so they settled around the campfire to eat kangaroo steaks which were surprisingly good, somewhere between beef and venison.

'We'll be in Ballarat tomorrow. Time to pay us what you owe Mate.' Harry's words stunned him.

'What do you mean?' He asked. 'I paid you three pounds before we set off.'

'Two pounds should cover it.'

'I never agreed to pay you more.'

'We have expenses.'

'What expenses?'

'Lamb chops, bullets, horse feed.'

'I bought you grog, and I don't have two pounds spare.'

'Course you do. You can't dig without the licence money.'

'I'll give you one pound. It's all I can manage.' Reluctantly he fished out a note from his pocket, alarmed at how little was left and stomped off towards his tent. He could not bear to sit with those scoundrels a moment longer.

It took some time for him to sleep but once he got off, he slept soundly. When he woke, the sun shone through the canvas of his tent, and he concluded it must be way past dawn. Poking his head out of the flap, he expected to see the men taking down their tent in preparation for leaving camp, but he was alone with no horse or wagon in sight. He did not believe his eyes or his ears, how had they managed not to wake him? He stood looking around him in a state of shock, before realising that the men had left with his tools. His axe and a spade, which he used the evening before, were all that he had left. His pick, spare clothes, frying pan, all gone, together with his pistol.

He grasped his head in despair. If only he had given them the extra pound, he could have avoided this. What was he to do? Last night they told him it was seven miles from here to Ballarat. Should he make for there or turn back and give up? After five minutes of mulling over the arguments in his mind, he realised he must decide, and the first thing was to take down his tent and gather any possessions which remained. He began to strike camp, when he heard the familiar rumble of a horse-drawn wagon and prayed they had come back for him. He rushed to the track looking north but saw nothing. The sound grew louder behind him. A wagon came into view around a bend in the track from the south. He waved frantically, and the driver drew his horses to a stop a few yards from him. He said nothing and looked wary, a rifle slung across his knees with the barrel pointing towards the stranger standing by the track. His wife and child sitting beside him stared at him with alarm in their eyes.

'Please, can you give me a lift?' Richard cried out. 'The men I travelled with have stolen my goods and abandoned me here.'

His cultivated English accent reassured the family, and the man gave a curt nod of agreement while the woman fussed over him, offering him some bread and cold tea which he gratefully accepted. So began the final leg of his journey.

Those good people dropped him off outside the gold commissioner's tent. After thanking them profusely for rescuing him, he entered. Men stood grumbling and impatient in a queue which stretched towards the entrance. He joined the back of the line to wait his turn. There appeared to be only one man selling licences and dealing with other matters. Minutes passed and then an hour before it was his turn. The official beckoned to him, and he went into a long explanation until he saw the glazed expression in the man's eyes.

'Can you describe them?' He asked.

'They were brown haired with long beards, wore blue shirts, brown boots and dark trousers and floppy hats,' he told him.

At this point the official roared with laughter. 'Just look out there,' he said, gesticulating out of the open-sided tent.

He looked and understood his point. The description fitted every man he could see.

'Do you have their names?' The official asked.

'One was called Tom and the other Harry,'

'And are you called Dick?' He questioned, chuckling.

'Richard, I don't like Dick, how do you know that?' Once again, the commissioner roared with laughter, until Richard's face flushed with embarrassment.

Realising he had been conned, he apologised, shamefaced for wasting the official's time and was about to go, when the commissioner asked him for money for the licence saying, 'You do intend to dig, I assume.'

The erstwhile lawyer said he had not decided. He had four pounds sewn into his clothes and only two pounds in his pocket. At that point, he was almost ready to give up.

'If you want to dig, you need to mark out a claim and come back here for the licence,' the official told him as he left the tent.

He wandered around the diggings for the rest of the day in something of a daze. How does one mark out a claim he thought? What should he look out for? Which land is best? He watched men sifting the dirt and attempted to ask questions, but they mostly told him to scarper and stop wasting their time. He wished he had Harry to advise him. Then a man tapped him on the shoulder and said: 'If any of us knew which land to make a claim on, do you think we would tell you Mate?'

After meandering around the diggings for a while more, and unable to take in the vastness of it all, he found a spare patch of land, thinking t he would at least pitch his tent for the night. He hadn't had anything to eat since the bread and cold tea of the morning, but was so dispirited he could do no more than crawl into his blankets and go to sleep.

He awoke to the sound of guns being fired off all around. It was dark, but he could see the glowing embers of fires, and there was the tantalising smell of fried meat wafting towards him. He poked his head out of the tent, but all looked peaceful, so he crawled back to his makeshift bed and tried to sleep again. But the experiences of the last two days kept him awake, together with a growing hunger and thirst. Why at least had he not thought to fill up his billycan with water?

At first light, he sniffed the smoke of campfires, and his stomach groaned its emptiness. He hastened to find food to fill it. Leaving the tent, he stretched his weary muscles while observing the scene around him. There must be thousands of men, he thought, all engaged in cooking up breakfast, surely there will be one willing to share some food. He set off to find such a man, and he did not have to travel far before he found him.

The man was cooking up thick rashers of bacon, making Richard's mouth drool with anticipation. Richard tried asking for food, but the man indicated he did not understand. He pointed to himself and said 'Richard' and then pointing to the man he elicited the reply 'Friedrich,' who patted the space beside him. Richard fell to the ground looking longingly at the bacon. Friedrich offered him a mug of black tea, and he took it with a grateful smile. His new friend pointed to the bacon and held up three fingers, and Richard nodded in enthusiasm. Three shillings was a fortune to pay for some bacon and bread, but he did not care. Rarely had he savoured food so much, the grease ran down his chin, and he wiped his face with his hand then sucked his fingers clean.

After breakfast, he wandered back to his tent. Invigorated by food in his stomach, he decided to mark out his claim and dig the patch of unused ground next to his tent. Not having a pick was a problem, so he tried using the spade. The ground was rock hard, and he could hardly get the blade through the caked earth, but battled on until his hands became raw, and his back couldn't take any more. Straightening up, with his hand massaging his weary knotted muscles in the small of his back, he looked at his efforts. He had managed to shift four feet across, to a depth of ten inches. It was hardly a good start.

Feeling dispirited, he studied his hands, which he had always looked after; taking pride in the fact they had held nothing more than a quill or a pencil during his normal working day. His manicured nails were broken, and his palms encrusted with dirt and blisters. He compared them mentally to the broad calloused hands of Harry, if that was his name and his mood darkened again.

His head began to thump, and he felt sick with dehydration, cursing himself for not having found water to fill his billycan before digging. As tired as he was, he recognised the urgent need to go in search of water, rather than crawl into his tent and sleep, which his aching body demanded. Why did he not think this through before? He walked off in search of a creek. An hour later he returned with a billycan full of fresh water, but not from a creek. He had paid for water after wandering around looking for the stream which had long since been spoiled or diverted by diggers.

Richard returned to Friedrich who cooked up a mutton chop with some potatoes and more tea for five shillings. He sat there thinking hard. If he paid for a license he would have no money left by the end of the week. What he was doing was madness. His hands were burning, and he understood that he would not even be able to touch the spade tomorrow, let alone dig.

Back in his tent that night he knew he had to give up, and the weight shifted from his shoulders. This has all been a silly pipe dream. He thought of his wife and child and loneliness and guilt overwhelmed him. What was I thinking of bringing them all this way in the pursuit of gold? What if I don't make it back to Geelong in one piece and leave them without the means to support themselves? He sank into his bed, chastising himself, and cried himself to sleep. He slept through the nine o'clock gunfire and the rain that began to beat down on his tent, first in fat drops, and then in a steady drumming noise.

He was woken in the early hours by water seeping up from the ground. He listened to the rain for a second or two before shaking himself from his wet blankets. He sloshed his way to the tent flap. Outside he couldn't see anything; it was pitch black. There was nothing for it but to sit on a pile of his damp blankets, becoming increasingly miserable as he got colder and wetter throughout the night. Even when the rain stopped somewhere close to dawn, he dared not move.

At first light, he put on his boots, climbed out of the tent. He registered immediately the mistake he had made in pitching his tent in a hollow, which is why no one else had bothered. The hole dug the previous day was overflowing with mud, washed back from the heaped spoil. Men were stirring. He could not bear to see their laughter, could not face their pity or his humiliation, so he started to walk, leaving everything behind him.

He walked in a daze back the way he had come, ignoring anyone who passed. As the light began to fade, awareness dawned that his stupidity was even worse than he first imagined. He carried no tent, had not so much as a blanket. Luckily the sun had dried his clothes, so he tried to find some shelter under a tree. He had eaten nothing all day but slaked his thirst from puddles or waterholes he passed. He dared not stop at any grog tents, for fear of the questions he would be asked. He passed an inn a couple of hours back. Why had he not thought to stop for the night? The shillings left in his pocket would have meant a bed and food. Cursing his lack of forethought, he settled down a few feet away from the path, shivering as the sun sank, and fearful of the noises of wildlife around him. He faced a second sleepless night trying to fend off the insects without success.

On the second day, he was walking down the track having seen no one for a while, when two rough men on horses trotted by. As they passed he noticed them staring at him, then a while later he saw they had stopped just before a bend in the track. There were trees to one side of the track and a gully to the other side, with a thin stream of water flowing through. He knew they meant him ill. His heart started to race, and his head pounded with fear. He tried shouting for help, but no sound came from his throat.

He stood still as they rode towards him. 'I've got nothing of value,' he managed to say. 'I'm not a digger.'

'Everyone has something of value. If you were a woman in a birthday suit, you'd still have a value,' one of them sniggered. At that, he turned and ran, which was utterly pointless but was the only thing he could do. Stumbling over a tree root, he was felled by a sharp blow to his head and knew little more.

How long was it before he woke up or even knew what had happened? The sun was high in the sky, burning his face and the top of his head. He was lying in the gully with his feet in the water. They had taken his boots and hat. Something trickled down his face and flies buzzed around his forehead. He put a finger to his face, and it came away red and sticky with blood. His head throbbed, and he touched it with his other hand and winced. He had been pistol-whipped.

Richard felt in his pockets for the few coins and notes he had left, but they were gone, of course, even the ones sewn into his clothes. He lay for a long time, darting in and out of consciousness, thinking he might as well stay in the gully and be done with life. How could he return to his wife in this state? He rolled himself over as his lips were so dry and swollen, a drop of water, just a drop of water he promised himself. Was it possible to drown in this stream? That might be a quicker end than burning in the unforgiving sun. As his mouth descended to the cool water, he glimpsed something bright like sunshine glinting on the surface. He drank a mouthful and wanting more, gulped it down, but every time he lifted his mouth from the stream he saw it gleaming. It did not shimmer as sunlight does on water, but shone through the water, steady and solid. His fingers worked their way over and rested on the smoothness of it. A stone, he thought, just a stone. His hands closed around the object, and he pulled it out of the river bed, slowly towards his face. As the stone came closer, his eyes filled up with the honeyed colour of gold. He could not believe his luck. Surely not! He grasped his fingers around its smoothness, hiding it from view. His eyes scoured the stream for another golden rock, his blistered hands scoured the pebbles on the riverbed, turning the water reddish-brown, but he saw nothing else of value. The rain two nights ago, must have washed it downstream. But what if the men come back to finish me off he fretted. They must not find this gold. Start walking. Get away from here a voice in his head commanded.

Somehow, he got himself up and hobbled out of the gully. He stumbled onwards, praying he would find an inn or somewhere he might shelter, forgetting that his money was gone. Eventually, it got too dark to see the track, and he knew better than to continue. He saw a campfire in the distance, but his mind was in turmoil. What if they set upon me and steal this gold? How can I survive another night out here with blood oozing from both head and feet? His stomach was also in rebellion. It demanded food.

He stopped and thought about it until he had the idea of hiding his stone somewhere where thieves would not find it. Finding a tree about fifty yards from the fire he wrapped the stone in some grass, then inched it into a hollow by the tree, covering it up with more grass, wishing he had a knife to make a mark. Instead, he counted each tree between it and the campfire. Nine trees, remember nine trees in the morning, he said to himself. By that time, he felt sick with fear and hunger, and his head was pounding with pain. Please God, he prayed. Let these men not be brigands and murderers. I swear I will live the life my father wanted. Let me only get back to my dear wife and child, and I will be a changed man. No more dreams of adventure for me.

He attempted whistling through his swollen lips as he approached the campfire, trying not to alarm them. Coming closer, he said in as loud a voice as he could muster, 'Can you help a poor man who's been set upon by thieves?' He hardly dared hope for a friendly voice in return. When it came, he willed himself to trust it. Slowly he stumbled into the light of the fire and collapsed onto the ground.

His second piece of luck that day, was to find two of the friendliest men he had ever met since landing on those infernal shores. They sat him down, brought food and drink and gave him some water to wash his bleeding feet.

'I fear I wept, Mrs Dugmore, wept with relief. True Samaritans they were. They let me ride most of the way back with them, leaving me on the outskirts of Geelong. They would have brought me directly here, but I did not want my wife to see me like this. I hid until it was dark and then I hobbled back here.'

'Praise be to God Mr Adams, for your deliverance. I fear you have had a dreadful time, but there are good folk here in Australia. It's the gold. It attracts too many villains.'

'Did you recover your stone Mr Adams? Jane cut in, impatient to see it.

'I did Miss Dugmore. Shall I show it to you?' Jane and Sarah nodded. He lifted his trousers from the heap and felt in his pocket, then drew out a pebble covered in mud and grass, before dropping it into the bucket of water. The grass floated on the surface, but the pebble sank with a clank as it hit the bottom of the enamel pail. Jane dug around in the dirty water and lifted out a lump of gold shining a honey colour in the flickering candlelight. It was solid. She felt the weight of it in the palm of her hand.

'How heavy do you think this is?' She asked.

Her mother took the gold from her weighing it in her hand. 'More than a pound I would say, maybe twenty ounces, about seventy pounds sterling.'

'Enough to resettle us somewhere else,' breathed Mr Adams in relief. 'Mrs Dugmore, I let you hear this story, but I will never tell another soul, especially not my wife. I had to tell someone, but tomorrow we'll be gone from Victoria and never return. I want you to warn any of my countrymen from making the same mistakes, as I did. Will you do that for me Mrs Dugmore?'

Mother nodded, her expression impassive.

'I would leave Australia altogether, but my wife could not face another long voyage so soon. Where should we go do you think, Mrs Dugmore?'

'Adelaide or Sydney. They say Adelaide has lost so many people to the goldfields that there are empty properties and jobs galore for anyone who wants one.'

'Adelaide, it is. Thank you so much for your help. Is there anywhere I can sleep now? I am so weary, but I don't want to disturb my wife at this hour.'

'There's a spare mattress in the parlour.'

With a blanket wrapped around him and his right hand clutching his gold, he followed Mother to the parlour. She indicated a pallet behind the door. The other men in the room were already snoring and did not stir as Mother closed the door. She came back into the breakfast room where her daughters were clearing up the mess.

'Poor man,' she sniffed 'but I suppose there will be plenty more like him over the coming months. I hope they're not all as gullible and foolhardy. Just don't send any of them my way, do you hear girls? Send me the sensible ones, those that won't cause me sleepless nights. Just think what would have happened if he had been murdered, I don't know what his wife would have done. She and little Freddy would be out on the street. She didn't seem that eager to be a nursemaid, but it's a better option than being a woman on the town.' She glared at her daughters, an implicit warning in her expression.

Mary chuckled throughout the story. She could picture the scene, and it brought back memories of some of the English officers she encountered during her time in France. New boys, scarcely men, fresh out of Public School. They too had a rude awakening, but unlike the hapless digger they had no choice but to stick it out or die, and die they often did, and quickly too. Jane's digger was more fortunate.

'What happened to the watch?' She asked.

'Mother sold it of course. She used the remaining money to buy him boots, a hat, and passage to Adelaide. He stayed skulking in the parlour the next morning, until his wife took the child out to see the ships in the harbour. Then mother lent him an old pair of boots of my father's, stuffing paper in the toes before he set off for the boot makers to be fitted out with new ones. After that, she pointed him in the direction of the shipping office where he secured tickets for a ship leaving on the evening tide for Adelaide.

How his wife fussed over him when she got back to the house, and he gave her some rigmarole of what happened to him, all nonsense and nothing about how stupid he'd been. He made light of his injuries but when he showed her the gold pebble she called him her hero. 'How brave you are,' she cried. Mother said she felt fit to wet herself and daren't look at him, for fear she would collapse on the floor in fits of laughter. The family had left by the time we got back from work but how we roared that evening, as Mam told us what happened, and the tale he spun to make himself appear brave.'

Jean walked into Jane's bedroom with a tray of lunch and Mary saw the surprise on her face as she caught them laughing. Jean had already told Mary that Jane was a difficult mistress. She would have left already, had jobs been not hard to come by in this depression.

'I've a husband, been out of work twelve months and more, and two boys who have joined the army to escape this hardship. I need her money but I cannae like her.'

As soon as the door had closed again, Jane said 'I took her on because of her Scottish accent. It reminded me of my husband. But she's slapdash. I always had to pick her up for her cleaning. I don't suppose it matters now. She'll be out of work soon enough.' Mary winced at her comment. Had she no sympathy for the woman, who was a decent soul at heart?

Chapter 12

1852 Geelong

The year started off well. Hannah announced she was with child. Jane's mother was so overjoyed that every spare minute, she knitted and sewed baby clothes, enough for a trio of babies.

'They will come in,' she said, smiling when Jane quizzed her on the amount she was making. 'It will be the first of many, I'm sure.'

It was difficult to tell who was most happy, because Isaac stood fit to burst with pride. Hannah sat grinning contentedly with a protective hand across the slight mound of her belly. Talk of a baby was a welcome change from the talk of gold, despite the extra business it brought.

The family still met for dinner in Isaac's house after mass on Sundays. One Sunday in March, Jane was helping Hannah to wash dishes after a good meal of roast beef. Hannah suddenly grabbed the bowl, in which the pans were soaking, and moaned. Jane rushed to her sister's side, taking her hand to lead her to a chair.

'Is it the baby, are you in pain? '

'No, it's not the baby Jane. I felt a sudden chill and something strange. The hairs stood on the back of my neck, but I don't know what's wrong, but something is. I'm sure of it.' Hannah looked up at Jane; her face was white and drawn instead of a healthy pink.

'Come and lie down. I'll finish the pots. Perhaps you should have a little brandy.' Jane took Hannah through the house and led her upstairs to her bed, then went to find Isaac who rushed up to his wife.

'Mother I think we should go home after I finish clearing up. Hannah needs a rest.' Jane explained to her mother what had happened. Her mother's eyes became troubled, and her brow furrowed in puzzlement.

'And you say it was nothing to do with the baby? No twinge, nor discomfort in her belly?'

'No, just a chill, and a strange feeling. I am sure it's nothing to worry about.'

'Oh it is Jane. It sounds like a premonition; something has maybe walked over her grave. My mother felt that way sometimes, and nothing good ever came of it.'

As the months wore on Jane forgot what happened that day. Hannah bloomed and had no problems until one day in May, Isaac turned up at the house at breakfast time.

'You'd better come. It is Hannah's time.' He gasped, out of breath from running.

Mother ran out of the door with Isaac in tow, leaving Sarah and Jane to clear up the dishes. Luckily the gentlemen lodgers had eaten their breakfast and were downing their mugs of tea.

The two girls arrived a little late for their work, but their boss forgave them with good grace. They were reliable, honest workers, and knew how to help these greenhorns spend money, but without fleecing them. It didn't harm him that his new assistants were young ladies of an age to attract the male clientele. Sarah was the prettier of the two, Jane's features might be described as too sharp, but she had the better brain, a business brain at that. Were he a widower, and younger he might try for her himself. But his wife, after hearing of his new assistants, made sure she came into the shop at odd intervals throughout the day to keep her eye on him.

After work that day, Sarah and Jane rushed over to Isaac's shop, wondering if their nephew or niece had made an arrival into the world. They were delighted to find Hannah sitting up in bed, with her arms wrapped around a small bundle.

'Come and meet little Isaac,' she said in a soft voice tinged with weariness. 'Look he has his father's nose and his grandmother's hair.' The girls could see fine chestnut coloured fuzz on his tiny head. A wide squashed nose adorned his face, making them giggle with delight. His eyes flickered open at the sound, and he seemed to regard them severely before closing again. He gave a great yawn showing toothless pink gums.

'Oh, he is so adorable!' cried Sarah. 'I can't wait until I have one of my own.'

'Well you better wait,' said her mother, entering the bedroom. 'First find yourself a respectable young man like Isaac, preferably one with good prospects, and a Catholic.'

'Oh Mother,' said Sarah. She wondered how many times her mother had told her that.

Jane glanced at Hannah who looked happier than she had seen her in quite a few weeks, since that strange Sunday in March. The baby gave a loud cry, making Jane jump.

'Time young master has his first feed. Girls go downstairs and make Father Isaac something to eat, while I show Hannah how to feed this hungry chap.' Mother pushed the girls from the room.

Mother spent most days at Hannah's but was always back to put Joseph to bed, and to get some sleep herself. The lodgers had disappeared on their road to the diggings. Mother did not want any more until Hannah was settled with the baby.

About four days after Isaac's birth, their mother walked through the door earlier than expected. Her eyes were red-rimmed and her mouth set in a grim line.

'Whatever's the matter?' Asked Sarah.

'Your sister and her husband are refusing to have little Isaac baptised as a Catholic. When they married in a Presbyterian Church, it was on the understanding that their children be raised as Catholics. Hannah promised me. I would never have agreed to her marrying so young otherwise.'

What could they say to pacify her? There was nothing as important to their mother as her faith. Sometimes she seemed to put it before them. If they stayed true to the church, then everything would work out, and if they didn't, well woe betide she used to say.

'I wish your father was here. He knows how much this means to me.' Mother put her head in her hands and sobbed in her chair. 'He let me bring you all up as Catholic, though he is Church of England. Why can't Isaac do the same?'

Sarah hurried out to the kitchen to make a brew, leaving Jane with the younger children, who were back living in the house since the baby arrived. Jane was at a loss to know how to comfort her mother.

The atmosphere in the house was icy and fraught for a few days. Mother stayed away from Hannah's. It was left to Isaac to come and try to mend the relationship between mother and daughter. He came over on Saturday evening to invite them for dinner the next day.

'How could you do this to me, Isaac? Hannah promised your children would be brought up as Catholic.' Mother turned her reproachful eyes towards Isaac.

'Now Mother Dugmore,' he said. 'We pray to the same God. Some of us just like to do it in a simpler way.'

Best of luck with that argument, thought Jane. She worried that Hannah might have blown it for all of them. Her mother would be on guard after this, and out searching for Catholic husbands and wives for her older sons and daughters.

Whatever arguments Isaac tried they were each cast aside in contempt. But Mother could not bear to lose her grandson, and when she thought that Isaac had grovelled enough, she consented to dine with them the following day. An uneasy peace prevailed for a few weeks.

The winter months began with tremendous rainstorms and flooding. Bridges were swept away, and the newspapers were full of the difficulties of getting to and from the diggings. Roads were impassable, and little news came from Ballarat. By July Mother was anxious for news. Whenever she saw men returning from the diggings, she asked if they had met the Dugmores. But no one had heard of them.

Some laughed and said 'Do you have any idea what it's like there Missus? It's a madhouse. I wouldn't find my own brother if he were there.'

It was late September, with the weather turning a little warmer, when a party of weary miners, escorted by armed troopers rode into town. The fear of bushrangers and horse thieves deterred lone travellers with gold in their belongings. All the men were coated in mud, the men, the horses, the bullocks, and whatever carts or drays they pulled, so much mud it was difficult to tell the troopers from the miners.

The sight was still novel enough to bring everyone from their houses. Being a Sunday and most citizens at leisure after church, the sight attracted a large crowd. By the time Jane and Sarah arrived at the scene, a journalist was already moving down the line, noting down names and the amount of gold they brought to town. Mother came running after the girls calling Thomas by name, and the three women were overwhelmed with joy, when they received an answering reply. Two men, one sprightly and one with more difficulty got down from one of the carts and waited while the women threw themselves at them, oblivious to the mud and filth.

'Where's Jacob?' Mother's tone fled from joy to cold suspicion in an instant.

'Let's get the horses stabled, and us washed before you pound us with your questions wife.' Father sounded old and dispirited. His muddied face did not disguise the new furrows in his brow and his battered dirty clothes hung loose on his frame.

'Where's Jacob?' Mother repeated, ice forming around her heart.

'We don't know, and that's the truth of it,' Father said, looking down at the ground, shocking Jane by choking back a sob.

'Mother, we need to get Father home. Sarah, will you run to Isaac, so we can get these poor horses stabled? I'll stay with them until he comes. Jane, you help mother and father home.'

James was in charge. Jane looked at him in surprise. He'd grown into a man in the twelve months since she'd seen him. But it should be Jacob standing there; he was the eldest. Where was he? The happiest moment since Isaac's birth turned to dread in the space of a second. No, she said to herself, don't worry, Jacob's fine. He always goes wandering off, and he's well able to take care of himself, harbouring these thoughts to keep up her spirits until she was told different.

Once more they sat around the dinner table to listen to what father said, but this time he spoke no words of comfort or resolve. Pain and sorrow ravaged his face. Their family's rock lay crumbling before them as he recounted what had happened over the last nine months.

He told them how he returned to Ballarat in January, only to find Jacob gone to see what the Mount Alexander diggings were like. At each new find, rumours flew around the diggings that this was the best yet. Impatient men upped tents in an instant, and off they went in the hope of easier gold, not ceaseless, hard graft.

Father told the family how he waited for Jacob to return as weeks went by, cursing him for his thoughtlessness, but neither Jacob nor any message came back. He and James discussed what to do, but because they were still finding gold in their claim they did not want to abandon it. One of James' friends arrived at Ballarat in mid-April, and he agreed to work the shaft with James, while Father travelled to Mount Alexander in search of Jacob. He promised to be back by the start of June. They agreed that whatever happened, they would return to Geelong together, as soon as the roads were passable after the winter rains.

Mount Alexander lay a further fifty miles to the north-east of Ballarat, and the terrain was terrible. There were no roads, just tracks scored by the thousands of miners who had made the journey over the previous few months. A few years later a man and a horse might travel the distance in less than a day, but the mud and the traffic and the lack of bridges meant that he arrived at the beginning of May, enough time to find Jacob and return to Ballarat by early June, he thought.

The diggings were spread out over a wide area. The gold was indeed much nearer the surface than in Ballarat, a fact enjoyed by the thousands of diggers camped there. Father realised he needed to divide the Goldfield into sections, visiting each claim and then double check each evening by going around the campfires and grog tents.

Miners were generally a friendly bunch of men, always willing to share a meal and a tale. Father took care to put in his share if he had it, so his hunt took a while. On the first day, he had no luck but learned that there had been a fatal outbreak of dysentery in March. His heart had sunk. He had confidence that Jacob was well able to look after himself, but dysentery was a killer for someone on their own. He searched those diggings meticulously over the next two weeks, not finding anyone who recognised his son's name, but he discovered a whole bunch of graves with simple wooden crosses bearing the inscription, 'A Miner, died 1852.'

'I wanted to dig up each and every grave, in case Jacob was buried there.' He sobbed.

Mother looked stricken. Her hands flew to her mouth, and she groaned like an injured animal. Father clutched her arm and laid his head on her chest, willing her to hold him tight. She did not; she looked wretched but offered her husband no comfort, having none to give.

Hannah sat in silence while he told his tale, her face a mask of misery. At last she spoke, her voice choking with tears for her twin.

'Jacob is dead, and I know when he died. You remember Jane, you were with me when I had that sudden sense of despair. It felt as though I had lost part of myself. I suspected my brother was in trouble, but I dare not speak the words out loud. It has lain so heavy with me. Sometimes I dream of him calling to me, asking for absolution. Mother, we must pray for him.'

Isaac turned to hug and console his wife, while Mother and Father looked at her in abject horror.

'I have been praying that he would suddenly turn up somewhere on the diggings,' Father cried, 'but there's no hope is there? He's one of those poor dead miners, with no name on his grave.' His face looked ashen beneath his sunburn, and his shoulders shook again with sobs.

Mother stared at him, her face a mask of stone. 'For twenty-eight ounces of gold, I have lost my Jacob. Was it worth it?'

Jane had never heard such bitterness in her voice. They were all in despair, but it was not right to blame Father. She remembered the scene at Christmas when they passed the bag around admiring the gold. Mother was for it then.

Jane put her arms around her father's neck and lay her head against his and kissed it. He patted her hand, but his body shook with sorrow.

Chapter 13

Melbourne 1932

Jane stopped telling her story as tears blurred her vision, and ran down her nose. Mary handed her a handkerchief; she too was close to blubbing with Jane.

'So long ago Mary, but I still feel and hear their pain. How we missed Jacob, a light had gone from our lives. For years, I asked strangers on the goldfields if they knew of Jacob Dugmore. We clutch at straws don't we, when there is no body to bury?' Jane sighed.

'Father was delighted with his new grandson, of course, and that helped. He held him and stroked him, but you could see his thoughts were still far away on Mount Alexander. But that was not the end of the bad news that week. James and his friend, John, did what all young men do when let off the leash. They got blind drunk and were picked up by the police and fined five pounds each for their trouble.

Mother, who had scarcely spoken since hearing about Jacob, took her anger and pain out on James. She screamed and swore at him saying wasn't it bad enough that Jacob had died for a few ounces of gold, and now there was even less of it, because James was squandering it on drink.

Father tried to calm her down. He told her James had done everything he could and more to help his father. She should be proud of him. James was beside himself with shame at her words. I don't know what Father and he talked about, but the following week James returned to Ballarat to dig gold. Mother came around to it in time. She was distraught at first, thinking she had driven him away, but he returned around December with a bag full of gold and his own escapades to regale us with.

I often wonder how he survived to tell the tale. There were so many bad characters on the goldfields in those days. One of them, Black Douglas he was called, held James up in his tent with some of his cronies, but James had buried his gold, and they didn't find it, even though they threatened to shoot him. Another time, Captain Melville, he called himself, held James up on the road south, but somehow, he escaped on horseback. He knew the Bush so well thank God, and he was an expert horseman. Anyway, Melville was captured near Geelong in December. His real name was Frank McKullen, and he was sent to Melbourne in chains on the paddle steamer, and as luck would have it, James also took that paddle steamer. He had a fancy to visit Melbourne for a while. He told us the prisoners were down below singing, and the diggers flung money down to them. I can never get over how much money James and all the other young men threw away. In those early days, it was all squandered on drink and women. Father despaired of him. Once he even offered a reward for news of James who kept returning to the goldfields. It turned out he was in Geelong, drinking, gambling and worse no doubt, until his money ran out.'

'Did your father go back to the diggings?'

'Oh no! He never wanted to see them again. It wasn't just that his heart was broken by losing Jacob, he told us how the land was being ripped apart by mining, and that saddened him too. No, he went back to sawing, because he said he could choose which trees to cut and leave the younger ones to take their place. He wanted to leave a land of plenty, not the hell which the goldfields became. I know what he meant.'

'But he couldn't chop down a tree on his own, and you said James had left.' Mary looked puzzled.

'My half-brother David went with him,' Jane let slip. Then realising what she had said, cursed underneath her breath. 'I am tired and too upset Mary, to say anymore. I am not sure all this talking is good for me.'

As Mary opened her mouth to speak, Jane turned her head to face the window and closed her eyes, her heart throbbing. Mary grew concerned and felt for her pulse, and found it racing.

'No more exertion today, you are right. Rest now, and I will bring you a cup of cocoa in a couple of hours.' She drew the curtains to help Jane sleep and left the room.

Mary sat knitting in the sitting room surrounded by Jane's photos and mementos. She recalled Jane's reaction to letting slip a name. It had upset her far more than was good for her, and Mary thought she might know the reason. She did not want Jane to clam up, as Sophie said she did with her grandchildren. A peaceful death was what she hoped for Jane, but she sensed there were things buried deep in her mind. She needed to let go of them before making her peace with God.

Mary knew that Jane had spent her life building a hard shell around her, so that she could cope with all that life threw at her. It was time the shell cracked and let in the affection her children had for her. Mary had met death countless times, and when it came down to it, love was all that mattered. She wanted Jane to feel loved and to love in return. She made two cups of sweet cocoa and found some Lamingtons, which Jean had baked that morning. Putting them on the bedside table, she went to draw the curtains back to let in the late afternoon sun.

'Let's have a treat this afternoon,' Mary said, before taking her patient's pulse again and was relieved to find it slower, she shifted Jane to a sitting position.

'Are you cold? Let me find a warm bed jacket to put over your shoulders.' When Jane was comfortable and sipping her cocoa, Mary said, 'It's time for me to tell you a story. It's one my grandmother told me before she died. I am incredibly proud of her, and while Australians might not want to hear these stories from their past, just yet, I think one day they will, and learn to be proud too.' Mary noticed Jane frown.

Chapter 14

Melbourne 1907

Mary stood in front of the mirror, a child of twelve dressed in her confirmation dress of yellow poplin. She preened and spun slowly around, admiring her dress.

Her watching mother had worked extra hours as a housemaid to buy the fabric. She was proud of the way Mary looked. She would pass muster amongst any of the girls being confirmed that day. A tear or two escaped from her eyes, saddened that her husband, Mick, was not alive to watch his daughter's confirmation. He would have been fit to burst

'Don't you look lovely, my pet. Go and show Nana Kathleen, she'll be over the moon to see you dressed for your confirmation but mind her tea. I don't want it spilling on that lovely dress.'

Mary ran through to the old lady's bedroom, where she lay propped up on her pillows drinking tea. When she saw her, she beamed that lop-sided smile which Mary loved so much. There was a special bond between them that no stroke could break. Kathleen had brought her up while her mother and father were at work. After Mary's father died, they grieved together; Kathleen for her only son and Mary for her beloved father, although now she scarcely remembered him.

Mary used to love helping her grandmother bake, and while they baked Kathleen told Mary fairy stories, the ones her mother had told her. Mary often asked her to talk about her father and Kathleen's childhood in Ireland. Sometimes she would, but there were times she looked too sad. Mary to cheer her up, sang songs, songs taught by Kathleen. After Mary started school, she brought her friends around to visit Nana. Soon the old lady was an auntie and provider of home-made biscuits to half a dozen other children.

It was Mary who found her on the floor one day after returning from school. She ran to get help from neighbours, who picked her up and put her in bed. Mary, only twelve years old, cleaned her up and made her some tea, spooning it into her mouth. No doctor was called. Kathleen might live or die, but a doctor would only advise nursing, and that is what Mary and her mother did. Each day they saw a little improvement until Kathleen began to talk again. Between Mary and her mother, they kept her clean and somehow avoided bed sores, by getting her to sit in an old armchair during the day. Neighbours popped in and out of the unlocked back door at odd times. They all loved her.

Kathleen, hearing her granddaughter run into the room, looked up from her cup of tea. It was a sight which made her poor old heart soar. Her hand shook as she put the cup back on the table beside her bed. She waved Mary to come closer.

'Darling girl, did I ever see a better sight? How I wish I could come to the church with you.' Her voice was slurred and halting, but Mary had no trouble understanding. She lived the past two years rejoicing in every small improvement her grandmother made, and now it was as though she never lost her voice, but it just turned into a different sound. Most surprisingly she lost her broad Irish accent and spoke with an Aussie twang. They giggled together over that.

'You're all grown up now, and I want to tell you a story, but first you have to enjoy your confirmation. It's a true blessing to be received into the Holy Church. Take my prayers with you sweetheart.'

'I will Nana. Thank you.' Mary kissed her cheek, twirled around in her dress once more and then ran back to her mother, ready for the most important day of her life since her first communion at seven. Only her wedding would surpass it.

How Kathleen loved that child, just as she had loved the son born to her weeks after her new husband, like so many men, abandoned her to run off to the goldfields. She remembered with sadness how many of her shipmates, also became deserted wives, they and their children sinking quickly to the bottom of the heap in Hobart. Their lives were almost as bad as they had ever been in Ireland before transportation. The demon drink often becoming the women's only release from misery. That led to a worse fate, fallen women and children abandoned to beg on the street.

She shuddered to think how it might have been her, but how could she have faced her father or mother at Judgement day if she sank to that level? No, she kept herself clean, and she raised her son with all the love she had to give, and in return, he loved her until the day he died in a factory accident.

Back from church, Mary took off her veil, changed out of her dress and helped her mother prepare dinner. Nana wanted to hear all about her day, so Mary took in a tray with two soup bowls and sat beside her on the bed. After she had finished telling her about the service and describing the procession of children, girls all dressed up in their smartest dresses and boys in their suits; she reminded Nana that she wanted to tell her a story.

'I hadn't forgotten child, but I want you to remember how happy and joyful it was for you today. The story I am going to tell is a difficult one. I thought long and hard whether to tell you, but I feel I owe it to my parents to bear witness to their pain. The message I have for you is that when times are so difficult, you think it might be easier to give up, don't. Instead, remember this sad tale and let it guide you. Do whatever you must to survive. Sometimes a prayer to God for help is not enough, and you must act for yourself. I truly hope that you never have to use this message, but who knows what lies ahead.' Nana sighed, and Mary took her hand.

'Does Mother know what you are going to tell me?'

'No, because I never told your father. I would have done, but then he died. It has lain heavy in my heart for years. But I can't go to my grave without telling you, because who else will remember my Mam and Dada. I want you to pray for their souls Mary. It happened such a long, long time ago, but I remember as if it were yesterday.

You know I was born in Ireland. Times were hard for us all throughout my childhood, but we were happy. Dada was a cottier; we

94

had our patch of land and grew potatoes, as did our neighbours. We used to eat our potatoes with buttermilk, never bread, nor meat. If we had any money, maybe we would eat fish because we lived in a village near the coast. In 1845 I must have been fourteen, the oldest of six. That was the year it started.' Nana paused for a few moments. She had not talked this much since her stroke, and it was already tiring her.

'What started?' Asked Mary.

'The blight, the potato blight. It came from Europe to England and then to Ireland. The trouble for us was that potatoes were all that we had to eat, and suddenly we had no food and no prospect of any for that year or the next. We didn't know then it would be for two years after that as well. Four years of famine were what God sent us!' Nana crossed herself.

'Do you blame God?' Asked Mary. She was a little frightened, for she thought of him as a merciful God, only bringing retribution for those who had sinned profoundly. What sin could merit bringing famine to a whole country?

'No, I don't blame God. None of us did, and the priests worked tirelessly to get us relief. I don't want to scare you with the sights I saw, that isn't necessary.' She paused, worrying that even the few details she had to give might disturb the child, maybe give her nightmares. No, she would not tell her how it was to watch your family starve, or how hunger gnaws away at you until the pain consumes you. The pain of seeing your brothers and sisters lay down to die; skin and bones blending with the earth of their cabin, so little substance remained.

'My family died of hunger, all of them. I need you to continue to pray for their salvation.' She watched her granddaughter's tears wash the brown of her beautiful eyes. 'It was a long time ago my sweet, do not weep.'

If she cries at that, then Kathleen could not tell her of watching her mother die of a broken heart and typhus in the workhouse. Nor could she tell her how her cousins were sent from the country by their parents with the hope of new life in America, only to hear later that they died of fever on the ship.

'My father, bless his soul, dragged himself to work on building roads that were never meant to be finished, all to get a handful of corn to feed those of us who were left, but in the end, he too died.'

She paused again. Telling the tale was using all her energy. She had an image of herself being thrown out of the workhouse because there were those in more need clamouring to get in. Another image flashed through her mind of searching her village to find Dada. In every stinking hovel, the living lay with the dead, and she knew every one of them, but found it difficult to recognise any. No one had the energy to bury their loved ones. Twenty houses in the village, all affected, all her friends and relations dying or dead. She found him, at last, lying on some floor in rags and no more than a bundle of bones, the skin stretched taut over his skull. His toothless mouth opening and closing, saying those words, the words that would save her.

'Before Dada died, he told me to leave Ireland, and he told me how to do it, and this is what I want you to remember. After he died, I walked or crawled back to the town a few miles away. When you have so little energy, it can take days to cover a short distance. As soon as I got there, I flung a rock I'd picked up on the road, through a shop window. It did not matter which window, any would do. The magistrate only gave me fourteen days in prison for that, but at least I was fed. When I got out, I stole clothing to replace my rags, but I only got three months. That time in prison, there were some women waiting to be transported. I asked them what they had done. Don't look so scared child. You're thinking your old Nana must have been bad to do this, aren't you?'

Mary nodded, unable to speak, wondering what was coming next. Her dear Nana, so kind and gentle how could any of this have happened to her?

'Perhaps I'm wrong to tell you all this, but I'll finish what I set out to do. Two of the women said they stole a sheep from a farmer and slaughtered it. I thought you could get hung for that, I told them. Even the magistrates are not hard enough to hang a starving woman for trying to stay alive, they said. So, when I got out, I stole a sheep and killed it like I had seen the butcher do. I slit its neck with a knife I stole, poor thing. I sat there with its blood on my hands waiting to be caught. I did not care if they hung me for I had nothing left to lose. But that did the trick. I was sentenced to transportation to Australia. There were lots of women on the ship like me. Some were joining brothers or fathers who had been sent out before them. We were the lucky ones, the ones who found a way out of the horror of that time. Every day I thank God for sending me here, and my Dada for telling me what to do.' She sighed, but gripped Mary's hand as tight as she was able.

'I have told you enough now Mary, and I am tired. Just remember sometimes it's necessary to break the rules if you must; if it's a matter of life or death. May the Virgin Mary protect you, as she did me.'

Chapter 15

Melbourne 1932

'Long after my grandmother died, I read a book about the Irish Famine and what they went through was horrific. It made me angry too. Did you know the poor souls were blamed for being apathetic and feckless by the English government?' Mary brimmed with indignation.

Jane listened to the story, knowing how it would end. So Mary had convict grandparents, but why did that make Jane feel sad? It was never discussed or even acknowledged these days. Australia is a fine country; forget how it began, forget the thousands transported to its inclement shores, was an unspoken rule. And then the famine; she had a vague memory of collections in church for the poor and starving children of Ireland when she was a child. The recollection stayed with her because of her mother's tears, something she had scarcely seen before, not even when Mary died.

'When I nursed on the Western Front, I remembered what my Nana told me, and I took strength from her courage. It helped me knowing her story.' Mary continued, before looking at Jane and seeing that her eyes were closing.

'You're looking tired, and I am sorry it's my fault. You need a good night's sleep.'

Mary left Jane to doze, and she fell at once into a deep sleep and dreamt; a dream she had had many times before. Her father was being dragged away from a woman and baby. He cried out for help. Jane became the woman, and she cried to Thomas not to leave her. Then she saw him again, this time bound by chains at the ankle hauling great logs along a roadway. Someone she couldn't see, whipped his back until it became a mass of scarlet blood and strips of skin. He cried again to Jane saying, 'You promised to help me,' but her father's face then became her mother's, and she cried out, 'For the love of God Jane, don't leave me here.' Jane moaned in her dream. She wanted to help them, wanted to comfort them, but someone held her back, laughing at her until at last, she woke with a start.

Her brow felt moist with sweat, but her mouth was dry with terror and pain, and that awful sense of guilt. She knew the origin of the dream, and she thought back to the scene etched deep in her soul.

She was trying to slip out of the house in Geelong, when David caught sight of her. 'Where are you going to all dressed up in your finery?' He sneered.

'I'm getting married,' she said, in defiance because an argument was inevitable.

'You're not old enough to marry without Mam's permission.'

'Well she's away in Melbourne, so she's not here to give it.'

'You'll break her heart. Don't you think she's had enough trouble?'

'No, she'll be pleased when she meets John. He's a good catch.'

'You're just another of his children to bring her sorrow; Hannah, Jacob, James, Sarah and now you. You're all the same.' Disgust coated his voice with contempt.

'That's not true.' She was angry. 'You're just a loser and always will be, but I'm going to make something of myself, so that I can look after Mother.'

'Make something of yourself! A convict's daughter with such airs and graces, well you can leave Mother to me. I'll be the one looking after her.'

'Convict, what do you mean? Father wasn't a convict?'

'Where do you think he got those stripes on his back?'

'The Navy, Mother said he'd been in the navy, and they flog sailors, don't they?'

'A chain gang, that's where he got the lash, hundreds by the look of his scars. Mother too, she came to Australia as a convict. Do you think your fancy man would marry you if he knew he was marrying a currency girl, the daughter of convicts?' David was scornful.

'How do you know they were convicts?' Jane cried, on the verge of tears. 'They never mentioned it.'

'I lived in the bloody convict orphanage for four years, didn't I? Do you think I can forget that misery? But don't worry I'll not stop you from marrying this fellow. I suppose you've already lied to him about your age and religion because you wouldn't be rushing to marry him if he were Catholic, or are you in the family way? No, I'll not stop you because I don't care what you do.'

He stormed out of the house, banging the door behind him, while Jane shook with rage and horror. If it were true, it explained much, but if John found out would he call off the wedding? Jane stood in the hallway of the house wondering what to do, before deciding to act as if nothing had happened.

John understood she was not twenty-one, and yet he had been happy to apply for the licence. She felt in her gut that this marriage was right for her. She would make it work, even if it meant sweeping some things into a dark corner and leaving them there. Her support for John needed to be unquestioning as any wife would be. She was never going to give him cause to doubt her. Jane went to find water to rid her face of tears. Then fixing her expression into one of determined happiness, she opened the front door and strode towards the church to attend to the business of marrying.

Jane recalled the day down to its last detail. Hannah was her maid of honour and witness, yet she had not breathed a word of what David said to her. To this day, she did not know if Hannah went to her grave in ignorance of her parents' past. Oh, she missed her sisters. She wondered what happened to them but guessed they died years ago. Poor mother, all her children apart from Jane, had died or disappeared before her.

She felt around for the bell which Mary put by her bed and rang it in distress. The trouble was that she remembered that awful scene as if it was yesterday, and she remembered the feelings of guilt, all through her wedding day. She despised David while growing up. He was apathetic and feckless and later, he was a drunkard and a gambler. He said he loved Mother. She always protected her firstborn and sometimes, God forgive her, Jane was jealous of what they had between them. Then there came a time where his love turned into something else, and Jane could never forgive him for that.

If she had waited for Mother to return from Melbourne, a week or two later before marrying, would she have been able to persuade her that John was good husband material, even though another Presbyterian? The thought gnawed at her. She would never know the answer.

Mary slipped through the door in her dressing gown and padded towards the bed looking bleary-eyed.

'Mary I'm sorry to wake you, my mouth is terribly dry. Can you fetch me a glass of water please?' When Mary came back with the water, she plumped up the pillows and helped Jane into a sitting position.

'I had a bad dream. I haven't told you this before. My mother had a son before she met my father. David and I didn't get on. I always thought him spoilt. She said it was because he needed to be looked after while he was young, and she was working.'

'Was he in the orphanage in Hobart?'

Jane looked harshly at Mary, astonished she could see the truth so easily, but not willing to admit it. 'I never said that he was in any orphanage.'

'Oh, I just remembered something my Nana told me. When my father was born, she had to work to keep them after her husband left. She went to visit the orphanage and told me how awful it was; damp, stinking mattresses all over the floor, blank-eyed children, ragged and half-starved, and convict helpers who didn't care less. She walked out and vowed never to place him there. Nana found an elderly widow who wanted the money, and took him there every day so at least she made sure he was fed and loved.'

Could Mary see into Jane's soul, and if so how? She told Mary she wanted to sleep, and tried hard after Mary switched off the light and left the room, but Mary's description of the orphanage upset her. Why is it only now I ever gave a thought to why David was so insufferable, and why Mother put up with his behaviour? Jane tried imagining leaving one of her children somewhere so dreadful and couldn't. She would have fought like a tiger to protect any of her children. But perhaps Mother did not have a choice.

No one could describe the goldfields as comfortable, but there was food and affection for all her children, and they had each other, just as she had her siblings, but not David. He never fitted in. Jane pictured him now standing there, an outsider watching them from a distance, moody, resentful, and belligerent. She realised they never tried to include him. By the time they moved to Melbourne, he was fifteen and working as a reluctant sawyer with her father. Once Jacob and James began to work with father, David escaped to Geelong to do any job which came his way during the day. He drank his earnings away at night. When her father returned from the goldfields, David was forced back to sawing. Father never even considered taking David with him to Ballarat, but he needed someone to continue working with him as a sawyer. How David must have resented that.

She almost felt sorry for him except, that his behaviour worsened until even her mother grew tired of it. He became cruel, selfish and manipulative. God knows if he were somehow to appear in front of her now, she would want to kill him with her bare hands for what he did to Mother.

She turned her thoughts to Mary's story. What was she trying to tell her? Mary appeared to have guessed that Jane's parents were convicts, but how? Was it written on Jane's face? No. more likely that Mary knew that Irish Catholics were sent in their droves as convicts both before and after the famine.

And what was the point of the message from Mary's dear old granny? Had Mary broken the rules? Was that why she sometimes looked so sad? Jane was intrigued. Although she knew herself to be growing physically weaker by the day, her spirit felt alive as her memories flooded back.

102

Chapter 16

Geelong 1853

Who in the Dugmore family might have guessed that 1853 would follow on so badly after the anguish of losing Jacob? The family went to holy mass at Christmas. They prayed for Jacob and that the coming year would see their fortunes improve. Jane was painfully aware of the tension which still lay between her parents, which even Christmas could not heal.

The first two months were hot and dry. David and Father sawed their way through the blistering heat. In Geelong, Sarah and Jane served the ever-increasing numbers of men who thought a fortune was a day's horse ride away. The lucky men, who found their fortune, rode into town determined to lose it as fast as they could on booze and women.

The pubs were full and raucous each night, attracting fast women and fist fights in equal measure. Men with their pockets full to bursting arrived from the goldfields throwing sovereigns on the bar, and the champagne flowed freely. Even the barmaids got rich on their leavings. Fights broke out with regularity, and the diggers paid up for the damage caused. No one cared, as long as the gold kept on coming.

Geelong had lost its best policemen to the goldfields. The police who replaced them were either too lazy to hunt for gold or hardened Van Demonians, who were more than happy to concoct a tale which brought honest citizens in front of the magistrate. Father fell prey to one of them in early March.

Mother listened in outrage as he told the story of having a quiet drink in the Victory, after another gruelling week sawing timber. A woman he vaguely knew burst in through the door and looked around. Making a beeline for an off-duty policeman drinking at the bar next to Father, she slapped him hard across the cheek and clawed at his face with her nails.

'You, filthy scoundrel! You've no right to treat me like a whore,' she cried.

Father looked at the woman's face. It was bruised and cut about the mouth, but before he had time to react, the policeman grabbed the woman's hand, twisting her little finger with the other hand until she screamed.

'No,' said Father. 'Stop that; you're hurting her.'

'What's it to you?' Growled the policemen. 'She assaulted me; you witnessed her slapping me.'

'Nothing to what you deserve,' cried the woman. 'You thought you could have me for free, but I'm not a harlot, I'm a respectable woman.'

'Let her go Mate,' said Father.

'Keep out of this. She's coming with me to the lock-up.'

Father stood up and pried the constable's hands away from the woman's fingers, because he saw the pain on her face. As soon as she was loose, she scrambled for the door, sobbing, and ran back out into the night.

'That's it; you're nicked, aiding and abetting the escape of a prisoner.' The policeman got out his handcuffs and slapped them on Father's wrists. He spent the night in the lock-up and went before the Magistrate next morning to be fined five pounds.

'Oh Thomas,' Mother cried. 'That's a lot of money to be fined for helping that poor woman.' She did not blame her husband, finally casting off the anger she had held inside since Jacob's disappearance.

'This place is getting to be like Van Diemen's Land. I thought we'd escaped that life; corrupt policemen, grasping government; debauchery on every corner. We should go to Adelaide, but I'm too old to move again.' His shoulders drooped, and his hands covered his eyes and rubbed his forehead. Mother had never seen him look so defeated, but then he had never got over losing Jacob and blaming himself for it. She tried to soothe him, forgetting the harsh words she'd said when he came home without Jacob. But there was no disguising that his body was getting old and worn out, as were his spirits which appeared to sink further every time he returned home from sawing.

A little respite came with the birth of a granddaughter, Emma, just a year after her older brother was born. Hannah had a difficult time with the birth and Emma was premature. Mother worried about them both, but while Hannah recovered, Emma was slow to gain weight and had a yellow tone to her skin. She dared not tell Thomas, who was overjoyed with his darling little granddaughter.

'This is what it's all about,' he said, to Mother, 'new life.' Holding his little princess, as he called her. 'I wonder if my Sarah has children, maybe even grandchildren? She'll be thirty-seven now.'

'Hush,' said Mother.

'What did he mean about our Sarah, she's only seventeen?' asked Jane later.

Mother looked flustered for a moment, then said that Father had a younger sister called Sarah and he named his second daughter after her. Jane did the calculation in her head. Father was sixty-five which meant that he was twenty-eight years older than this other Sarah. It did not seem likely unless his father had married again. She was about to ask her mother another question. but was forestalled by her rapid exit from the room.

In July Isaac was involved in a court case of his own, regarding a disputed contract of employment. An employee on a three-month contract claimed that he had not been paid each week and was claiming over twenty-five pounds in wages. Isaac told his father-in-law that he needed to call both Hannah and her sister Ellen as witnesses.

'I'm sure it will be straightforward,' he exclaimed. 'My account book will show he was paid.'

'I don't like it,' said Father. 'Courts are nothing but trouble, and I don't trust the magistrates. Not after what happened earlier this year. That policeman was lying about what he did to that woman. He had no business hurting her, but the magistrates always take the side of the police.'

'But there's no police involved. It's a civil case.'

'I still don't like it, and Ellen is far too young to stand up and give evidence.'

'My lawyer assures me there's nothing to worry about. Please let her do it Thomas.'

Father came back to Geelong the evening before the court case, determined to support his daughters. Jane could tell he was on edge as he picked at the food Mother had prepared for him. Minutes later he made an excuse to go out for a walk in the dark, returning in less than half an hour, then sat silently smoking his pipe, his fingers drumming on his knee. He escorted Ellen to the court the following morning and found a seat in the public gallery to observe the case.

Cob Leigh, the complainant was a runty looking man with a bulbous nose and bloodshot eyes. He's a drinker, Father realised, wondering why Isaac had ever employed him. Isaac looked uncomfortable, but confident until Leigh produced in evidence a copy of his employment agreement, showing an altered starting date.

Father watched his son-in-law's face go pale in shock as Leigh's lawyer produced the paper. He told the magistrates that if Mr Evans was duplicitous enough to alter a contract, then any evidence he gave could not be believed.

A reporter for the local paper sat busy scribbling as the magistrate said, that in his opinion, the two documents were written by the same hand and in the same black lead pencil.

This was not what Father wanted to hear. He felt the blood drain from his body. His hands became clammy as he realised that the case may already be going against Isaac, even before his daughters gave their evidence.

Isaac was called to the stand. He disputed the existence of the duplicate contract and told the magistrate he had never seen it before. Father stared at the magistrates and saw an expression of disbelief which made his heart sink further.

Ellen was called next. Father observed his youngest daughter walk to the stand, looking tiny and nervous, wishing he could take her place. Ellen's evidence centered around the date she had witnessed the contract being signed. She told the magistrates she remembered the day because it was her birthday. But the lawyer questioned her about it being a Sunday, and would she not have been at church? Ellen began to get flustered and rambled on about the length of a Sunday mass rather than the short ones she went to on weekdays. She ended by saying she was sure that the contract was signed on her birthday. This should have been enough.

Father had watched her becoming confused by the questions. She looked at him for help, but all he could do was smile and nod his head in encouragement, trying to disguise the sickness he felt in his stomach. His hands gripped the rail in front so hard. that his knuckles showed white through the brown liver-spotted skin of his work-hardened hands.

The magistrates also looked at Ellen, weighing up her credibility, and Father again saw disbelief written on their faces. If possible, he would have snatched Ellen off the stand and taken her back home to her mother, but Hannah was up next.

Hannah backed up her husband's and Ellen's evidence. She disputed the second agreement and told the magistrate how the complainant always ran out of money before the end of the week, and she advanced him money until the next payday on several occasions. The final witness was Isaac's other employee who gave his evidence concurring with Isaac and Hannah's. Mr Evans always paid wages promptly and was a good employer, he confirmed.

One of the magistrates asked if he still worked for Mr Evans and when told that he did, dismissed his evidence as bought by his master.

Father sat fixed to his seat, knowing that his gut feeling about this case had been right. Justice was as much a joke in this country as it was in England. When the chief magistrate gave his verdict, it was worse than he could have imagined. He found against Isaac because of the writing on the second disputed contract, but worst of all he stated that he and his brother magistrates agreed that the witness, Ellen Dugmore, had been most shamefully coached to perjure herself.

Isaac's lawyer stood up to protest that his reputation as an honest lawyer was at stake. Father worried about the reputation of his daughters and family; nobody was protesting about that. Ellen ran to him crying in distress. He tried to comfort her; his old tired body determined to protect her. She lay in his arms, sobbing in humiliation at the magistrate's words. He too was angry and sickened to think that the case would appear in the newspaper for everyone to read and judge his family.

Father struggled to his feet, assisted by Hannah. Isaac was grim-faced and angry at the prospect of paying that rogue another twenty-five pounds. He could not understand why, if the dispute had been over two weeks work, he should pay a full three- months wages. No one had proved the man was not paid. Surely the magistrate did not believe any man would work for twelve weeks without wages before bringing charges.

Mr Ellis, his lawyer, approached them saying how sorry he was, and that the magistrates' remarks were despicable. He promised to write to the newspaper protesting on Ellen's behalf, in the strongest of terms. He received a wan smile from Isaac and Thomas.

As they left the courtroom and walked back to Isaac's shop, none of them felt like talking. They were shocked by the outcome, locked in their own thoughts, not noticing Thomas's ashen face and his brow beaded with sweat, until he stumbled and cried out. Pain gripped his heart, as Hannah and Isaac caught him before he fell. He clutched at his chest, his face the colour of paper. Hannah screamed 'Father.' That was the last word he heard before his eyes dimmed, sound withered to nothing, and he dropped to the ground dead in front of the two daughters he had failed to protect.

The journalist's report appeared in the newspaper that evening but not the death of Thomas Dugmore. He lay in his house on the table, waiting for a coffin. But the man who made the family coffins was himself lying there. The remaining family gathered around Thomas, weeping in disbelief until Mother shooed her children away.

'This is my job. The last thing I will do for him.'

She waited until they left the room, and then she undressed him slowly, folding each item in a neat pile. Thomas would not be buried in his best clothes; they were worth saving for the living. At last, she began the ritual washing, beginning with his feet. She wanted to save his face for last, such a dear face. She remembered well the first time she saw it, twenty-five years before. He promised to take care of her and raise a family with her if she consented to be his wife. He had fulfilled his promise and so much more, for he had given her love and affection too. Helen picked up his strong hands, washing each finger carefully, scrubbing the nails until the grime from the forest and the sawpit were erased. How hard he worked for his family. They may have been poor, but she could never remember a day when they had gone without food. As she washed him, she traced each scar on his hands and arms, remembering the little accidents and cuts which she had dressed with astringent oils, distilled from native plants. Working up his chest through the thick greying hair, she remembered the nights he had lain close comforting her when worries or sadness threatened to overcome her. She struggled to turn him, so she could reach his back but refused to call for help. With her cloth of soapy water, she traced the ridges of his scars and felt anew his pain as the cat of nine tails had ripped through his flesh, seeing the seeping blood through her tears.

Finally, she lay him back down on the table to wash his face. Taking a razor, she neatened his beard, and with great gentleness stroked the water around his eyes, into his ears and finally his lips. She bent to kiss them, tasting the soap but feeling the coldness as the heat left his blood. After drying his body with a towel, she found a clean nightshirt to use as a shroud, and lifted it over his head, struggling to lift his arms before smoothing it over his stocky frame. She should have had help with this, but did not want to share this last moment, it was too precious. Never again would she know a man's body so intimately. He was hers and she was his. That would always be the case, although he might lie under the ground.

When she finished, she sat holding his hand until the light began to fade from the sky, talking about the conversations they would never have. Sarah was ready for marriage; she was his second daughter called Sarah. The other one, far away in England, had never known her father. It did not stop him from thinking about her, she knew that, but he often told his wife he never regretted his marriage to her and the birth of their children. She too had never regretted finding him. This she told him now, and of her dreams for the grandchildren, he would never meet. Her voice was low and inaudible through the door, but none of her children dared to open it as the minutes and hours passed.

Jane could not believe that her strong, loving father would not be there for them anymore. In the room, next door, where his body lay growing cold, she still expected him to rise from his slumbers and bid them all good day and laugh about what a good joke it had been. It was not real to her until her mother opened the door, and she saw her father laid out, cleaner than she could ever remember, dressed in a ghostly white shirt. His absolute stillness convinced her he had gone, and the pain in her heart was unbearable.

Isaac sent a messenger to ride for David, but there was no time to contact James in Melbourne. On the day that Mr Ellis's letter was published in the Advertiser, denouncing the magistrate's accusations, a lonely party of mourners stood around Thomas's grave in the pauper's area of Geelong's Eastern Cemetery. Mother insisted upon attending, supported by David and Isaac. Hannah stayed at home with Ellen and Joseph. Jane and Sarah also insisted on going and were the only other mourners. They clung to each other, their eyes red with tears. The winter weather was cool and damp, more like English weather their mother said, in a vain attempt to be positive.

'He would have liked this weather; he was never too fond of the heat.'

Jane was the last of them to cast a handful of soil on the coffin. She repeated her promise to look after Mother if David would let her. She thought of him with anger. It was he who insisted they did not spend

110

much-needed money on the funeral. Isaac wanted to pay for it saying he felt responsible for Thomas's death, but with having to pay out twenty-five pounds to Leigh Cobb, he was a bit strapped right now.

'But Father, in a pauper's grave.' Jane sobbed at the thought of it. 'Not even a church service, just a few stark words uttered by the graveside. He deserved better.' The chilly wind made her shiver in despair.

Mother looked to David as the eldest male in the family. 'We can't afford any other way,' said David, standing behind Mother, mocking Jane with his eyes.

'It's all well for you to say that, because he's not your father,' Jane replied in bitterness.

'Jane, how could you? Thomas treated David as one of his own and David loved him. Apologise to David right now.' Mother was angry too.

Jane mumbled an apology to keep the peace but did not mean it. She saw through her half-brother. Something in his manner and expression told her he was pleased that Thomas had gone. It left him in charge with no Jacob or James to interfere. Until that moment she was indifferent to David, but the seeds of hatred were planted in her heart that day. When he announced that he intended giving up the sawyer's license and was selling off her father's tools and his horses, she was beside herself with rage. He said he was moving back to Geelong to look after Mother.

Jane held her tongue with difficulty. How he was going to earn a living was another question. He did not seem in a hurry to find a job. Jane tackled her mother a fortnight after David moved back into the house.

'David has been looking for a suitable position,' her mother claimed.

'Well, shopkeepers are crying out for help. We're still rushed off our feet in the ironmongers. It shouldn't be too hard. Maybe Isaac knows someone who needs somebody?'

Perhaps Mother gave David a shove, because a day or two later he landed a job in a hotel as a barman. Jane was underwhelmed, knowing he would drink away his wages, but didn't dare say anything. Inside she seethed with fury.

'Father would not have let him do that.' Jane said to Sarah on their way to work. Sarah just shrugged and told Jane she was too hard on David.

Sarah, at seventeen, was enjoying the attentions that men were paying her in the shop. While Father was alive, it rarely went further than a chaste escort home after work, with Jane as an unwilling chaperone. Her mother thanked the gentleman for his kindness followed by an invitation to stay for a cup of tea to slake his thirst. Faced with an eagle-eyed mother and mention of a powerfully built father, these men often took the hint and looked elsewhere, much to Sarah's chagrin.

But with Father gone and Mother grieving, Sarah stayed out later. Jane did not mind covering for her. Sarah was old enough to marry, and she thought the carter, Sarah was currently involved with, an honest man with a decent business of his own. When an escort arrived in Geelong with miners in a rush to spend their gold, however. Sarah threw off her latest beau for a man who waved around bundles of notes and promised her much.

Jane took an instant dislike to him, and tried to talk Sarah out of seeing him, but her sister refused to listen. The man, an Englishman, purported to be a gentleman, the younger brother of a squire in Devon. He turned Sarah's head with tales of parties and hunting. Jane thought him most likely the bastard son of a squire or a servant dismissed for dishonesty. He had an oily, swaggering personality and the luck of the devil in finding a large nugget with only minimal effort. Not wanting to bother Mother, Jane confided her worries to Hannah, who got Isaac involved. Unbeknownst to Sarah he found the man in a pub and warned him off.

'A nasty piece of work,' said Isaac 'and a coward too! He scarpered off to Melbourne as quick as he could after I went looking for him.'

Sarah accosted Jane when the man didn't turn up to meet her the following day. 'You've done something, haven't you? He promised to marry me and take me to England. I can't believe you've spoiled my chance to get away from here.'

'Sarah, you must be mad if you think he intended to marry you. Trust me you have had a lucky escape. If he was a so-called gentleman, he would never marry the daughter of a sawyer and a boarding housekeeper. English gentlemen don't do that. No, he was a cad and a bounder.'

'But a very rich one, with that kind of money I would never have to worry about being poor again.'

'Trust me, Sarah, he will lose the lot. He's not a grafter. It'll get spent on grog, gambling and women and then he'd send you out to work to keep him in booze.'

'I don't believe you.' Sarah turned away from her sister and walked on alone. Later that night as Jane got into bed Sarah again turned away from her. The two sisters had shared a mattress for as long as Jane could remember, but now Sarah froze Jane out. The easy sisterly relationship never recovered. Sarah became secretive. She still went out with men, but never in   Jane in her chatter and confidences. Mother knew someth   but could get neither girl to talk, with Jane blaming   Mother's troubles.

Chapter 17

'What happened to Sarah?' Asked Mary.

'We never knew. One night early in the New Year she disappeared. We don't know if she found another man to run off with, or the one Isaac warned off came back for her. But she did not contact anyone in the family again. I always wondered if I had told Mother what happened, she might have been able to stop it. A few months later James sent Mother a note to say he thought he had seen her, and arranged for Mother to visit Melbourne. I was told they traipsed the streets for weeks; Mother during the day and James at night, but they didn't find her.

It was a dreadful time. Hannah lost baby Emma who never really thrived. After Father died, Joseph mixed with some wild boys, getting into trouble for stealing bottles. David laughed and said if he were to go around stealing bottles, they might as well be full. But Isaac had to promise to thrash Joseph to stop the police from arresting him.

Ellen left school and found a post in the nursery of a good Catholic family, but they decided to move to Adelaide, and she left with them. Times were getting difficult in Geelong. There was not the business there had been. Too many stores opened, and prices dropped. I was concerned about my job, and my boss did not replace Sarah. Isaac was suffering too with all the other butchers starting up.

But then I met my husband, and my life changed. John walked into the ironmongers, and I served him. I knew at once that he was no greenhorn. His hands were workmen's hands; he was not tall but a strong man nevertheless. It took a while for me to understand his Scottish accent because it was quite broad. He wore mining clothes; they were clean but well worn. So many of the miners who struck lucky, geared themselves up in the latest fashion when they came back to Geelong. It seemed as though they couldn't bear to waste a minute before chucking their new wealth around. John came in the shop three days on the trot before he plucked up the courage to ask me out. I think if he had not done it by the third time I would have asked him myself.'

'Love at first sight was it?' Mary asked with a chuckle.

'No, not love. I would call it a recognition that we would fit together, that we were both cut from the same cloth, as they say. Love would come later. Mother had left for Melbourne to search for Sarah and John told me he wanted to be back on the goldfields in three weeks. He only came back to Geelong for supplies.

He was honest about the hardships of living on the goldfields, but I knew that anyway. If we were to marry we would live together whatever the conditions, I told him straight, and he said that is what he wanted too. My biggest worry was leaving Geelong before Mother returned to give us her blessing. After Sarah's disappearance, it would be a terrible blow to her.

I asked Isaac to write a letter for me, intending him to give it to her on her return. Both Hannah and Isaac liked John and supported my decision. John arranged for a special licence and we married in the Presbyterian Church with Hannah as a witness.'

'How did your mother react when she found out?'

'Badly, especially with David feeding her poison.' Jane sighed at the memory.' Poor Hannah tried her best to talk her round, receiving short shrift for her trouble. In the end, she accepted it, because when Mother met John, she discovered he was a good man. She told me he reminded her of my father, the highest praise in my eyes. And I never regretted marrying John. We had a good life together, working hard, bringing up our family, despite the hardships, and of those there were many, but I was used to that.'

Jane yawned. Mary knew that she needed to rest. She helped her back into bed and left the room, after closing the curtains on another bright sunny afternoon. No visitors were expected.

Before Jane drifted off to sleep, she tried to picture her husband when she first met him. She had no photograph to remind her, not even one taken as a middle-aged man.

Why did he stand out from any of the hundreds of other diggers who came into the shop? They looked so similar in their blue shirts and cabbage tree hats, all long-bearded and tanned, leathery faces. They were only distinguishable by height and colouring. John was of middling height, not unduly stocky, and his beard was mid-brown with glints of red. His hair was dark brown and his eyes, pale watery blue, almost matched hers.

John would never stand out in a crowd, but it wasn't his looks which attracted Jane. His interest in her at first piqued Jane's curiosity; she felt his presence minutes before she served him. How could she not be interested? He only had eyes for Jane, who was unused to that level of attention. Many of the diggers tried to flirt with her, and some asked her out, but she brushed them off. John did not flirt. It felt like he was looking into her soul, weighing her up.

Chapter 18

Geelong 1854

John strode into the ironmongers in search, not of a wife, but of replacement tools and a tent. The weather that winter had wrought havoc on the canvas; the wind and driving rain combining to slash it to ribbons.

He stopped to talk to the owner who was marking up a new consignment of picks, when John's eyes were drawn to Jane. Mr Richardson saw him looking at his assistant and said, 'You'd be a lucky man if you were to court our Jane. She has a fine head on her, unlike her sister, a flighty wench she was, before she ran off with God knows who.'

'Your daughter, is she?'

'No, just a currency lass, father dead a year now, but a hard worker and her mother too. Mrs Dugmore keeps a boarding house here in Geelong. A clean, God-fearing woman, so I'm told by men who've stayed there. She's away in Melbourne at the moment. Otherwise, I would recommend that you try for a room there.'

John was not a man to decide in an instant, remembering his mother's homily about deciding in haste and repenting at leisure, but it was in his character to be wary. He considered himself a good judge of horseflesh but took his time, studying a horse's behaviour, touching it to check for nervousness, or worse, fear. After observing it and talking to it, if he felt the horse responded to him, he expected to saddle it up and ride it for a few minutes to judge whether the partnership would work. If horses were in short supply, he refused to be hustled or cajoled by snappy salesmen but stood firm, keeping his counsel until he made up his mind. He knew less about women, so he would do well to be cautious.

When Jane finished with her customer, she turned to him, and he bought just one item he needed, noting her knowledge of the stock, her directness, and quick, precise movements. There was nothing fancy about her, not her looks, which were ordinary, not her clothes which were neat and plain, nor her manner, which was business-like. He liked all of those things. Even so, he would be hard-pressed to describe what drew him to her, but there was undoubtedly something.

For a while, he had been thinking of getting a wife. This trip to Geelong was not only to deposit the gold he and his partners had mined, but a chance to find a likely woman. If he should happen to meet one who would consent to live on a goldfield, with its attendant deprivations, he would not be averse.

A wife should bring order and comfort to his life; children to carry on his name, and, he had been considering this for a while, an additional income. Digging was becoming more unpredictable. The more men who turned up at the diggings, the less revenue, it went without saying. The easy gold was running out, and this meant deeper pits and no certainty of success. But a wife could be useful running her own business alongside mining, selling stores or drink to thirsty diggers.

When he returned to the shop the next day, he had already found out that Jane's brother-in-law was a well-regarded butcher, and bringing up his son as a Presbyterian, despite his Irish Catholic wife. That Jane had Irish blood in her was not a problem to him, she and her family were grafters, and that meant more. What he refused to tolerate was her remaining a Catholic. Scots were canny, educated and able, unlike the Irish, he thought. In general, he despised the Irish, not only for their religion but their fecklessness. He did not hold with their excuse that the English landlords were to blame for their ills. Yes, he held no truck with absentee landlords, but it was no excuse for apathy. That and slovenliness, he despised most in life, but so far, he had seen no sign of these two evils in Jane.

Jane served him again on the second morning, this time with a slight smile which lightened her face. Her pale blue eyes regarded him shrewdly. An observer, such as Jane's boss, might say they were a couple of birds at the start of a mating dance. Slow movements and steps, no preening as yet, aware of each other's interest but not yet ready to dance.

The fact that her mother was away made it easier for John. A Catholic mother, who may get the priest involved, would be fatal to his plans. What John did not know was that Jane also thought along the same lines.

On the third day John arrived in the shop just before dinner time, and when he asked Jane if she cared to step out with him after work, she answered with an invitation to supper with her sister's family that evening. This without so much as a pause for consideration, a woman who knew her mind, and not one to spend time shilly-shallying or being coy. He liked her more and more.

With the dice cast, play normally follows, but in this instance, each player capitulated and within two days, marriage was the prize.

Chapter 19

Ballarat August 1854

Two days after their marriage Jane and John set off on the journey northwest towards Ballarat. At first the roads were dry, and their horses made good progress. Jane had ridden before but never with a saddle, let alone a side-saddle. She scorned the idea of a side-saddle preferring to hitch up her skirts and display inches of black, woollen-stockings. Around a third of the way along the track, winter rains had churned up the bullock driver's path, and thick mud made the going much slower. John cursed the government for the lack of a metalled road, let alone a railway.

'The goldfields were opened up three years ago,' he told Jane, 'but still there's no decent road. One's been marked out, you'll see it later on, but if we tried to use it, the mud would trap the drays and carts within yards.'

John told her how he arrived in Victoria around the time the gold rush started. His father was a fitter working on the railways in Scotland and John thought there must be opportunities in a country as big as Australia for railroads. He was shocked and disheartened on arrival to find no realistic plans underfoot, turning instead to the goldfields. He was one of the first diggers at the Creswick Creek goldfield and had made a decent living so far with his partners, both Scotsmen he teamed up with on the ship. None of their claims had been shicers so far, but then none of them led to a life-changing nugget either.

'What's a shicer?' She asked.

'A bad claim, one that takes your gold but gives nae in return.'

John did not want to rush the journey. With good weather, it should take a couple of days, but it was also their honeymoon and a chance for him to get to know his new wife before the reality of a digger's life set in. He decided to camp early on the first night, choosing a spot by a creek where a few more tents were already erected. There was always safety in numbers. They hobbled the horses in a patch of good grass and unloaded the packs. While they were pitching the tent, John told Jane the problems that bushrangers caused the miners.

'It's not just the gold they're after; it's horses too. I'll sell these as soon as we get to Creswick or we'll lose them soon enough. The police spend so much time checking licences, but they're no' keen to go after horse thieves, mostly Irish and Vandemonian scum.'

Jane felt a little sick when he said that, following David's revelation, but she knew her parents were different. They escaped the slur of being from Van Diemen's Land. Her father was right to insist on the move to Melbourne.

While John went off to find firewood and water, she prepared the steaks they brought from Isaac's shop. It was hard parting from Hannah that morning. She wondered when she might see her sister again. The past three years had brought them very close together as they dealt with one tragedy after another. John could read and write and Isaac too, so Jane hoped that letters between the two couples would stop her from being homesick. This journey was the start of a great adventure. Maybe not as great as her parents' voyages from England. That had been made in far worse circumstances than she had ever imagined.

After a meal of steak and fried potatoes with a billycan of tea, the evening grew cold, and Jane was happy to wrap up in warm blankets and drink a drop of grog, before settling down for the night under canvas.

They woke to a cool, wet morning. There was no chance of a fire, so they made do with bread and the remaining milk they brought with them, which would grow sour by the end of another day. Rain fell hard during the night. Packing to strike camp was unpleasant, as each drop of water seemed to find a way of sneaking under their waterproof capes of gutta-percha.

The day before they passed carts pulled by bullocks with ease but now the mud made the going difficult, and several times John stopped to help the drovers pull out their wagons. Jane didn't mind the delays, once the worst of the rain stopped. The countryside was beautiful. Flocks of fat sheep grazed the fertile land, and the grass appeared greener than the yellow grass she was used to. Valleys and gentle, rounded hills formed a wonderful changing landscape where weak sunlight played with long winter shadows. The drovers' road took a wide sweep around the hills sticking to a level path. Further on, cultivated fields with early spring crops, hayricks, poultry and cattle added to the rural idyll, 'Like a Scottish lowland farm,' John said.

'One day, when they change the land ownership rules, I will buy land. The government must unlock land soon, or diggers will be in revolt against this government. I'll no stay here if they don't. It will be America or Canada for us, maybe even New Zealand. I've heard that's a right bonny country, a lot like Scotland.'

Jane chose not to dwell on the thought they might not get land. She saw herself with John and a bunch of children riding over this country, claiming it for their own. A sparkling river fringed by deep grass amongst red river gums, tea trees and myrtle overwhelmed her senses. This was what she wanted, no craved. Land like this, Australian land. Jane had no wish to leave. Her parents never mentioned any thought of returning to England, never spoke of it with regret, quite the opposite. Their lives were the better for leaving they told their children.

John interrupted her thoughts. 'Wait till we get to the goldfields and see the difference Jane. The earth has been torn apart, and it's nae more beautiful than a charnel house, with men as the beasts and mud instead of blood. But one day we'll be out of it. We just need enough money to buy a decent parcel of land.'

Jane's spirits dropped as they left the Moorabool River and arrived at Muddy Water Holes, a new township. It was in an area of good, flat land but destitute of water except for those ominously named waterholes, while a few miles further back there was a charming river and even better land.

'I'd not like to live here,' she said.

'It'll not survive, this poor wee town. More fool the people who buy plots. There's nae work and nae land being offered for cultivation. How are the people supposed to make a living?'

Pubs flourished along the length of the drovers' road, attesting to the capacity of miners and bullock drivers for drinking beer and grog. Outside each was a mound of broken glass bottles, and Jane calculated the profits of a hundred drovers a day plus all the other folk, who appeared to stop at every opportunity to slake their thirst. A good business to be in, she reckoned, as long as you did not drink the profits.

Three days after leaving Geelong they arrived in Buninyong. At first sight, it looked a thriving township, having been there since 1837. Shingles outside wooden buildings advertised stores, wheelwrights, doctors and all the professions you would need, but then Jane noticed that many of the buildings were empty. Only the inns and a post office appeared to be occupied.

'What happened?' She asked John.

'The only work is in Ballarat seven miles north, and until they release more land, people can't survive in a town with no industry. The squatters around here don't want to give up any of their thousands of acres or stock. What is so stupid is that with all this good land around, none of it is being used to grow food for the diggers and their families. In fact, the squatters are forbidden from growing vegetables for sale by the government. What utter madness! Jane, you will despair when you see the price of a lowly cabbage or cauliflower in Creswick. I hope that you can cultivate a little plot for food around our tent.'

She nodded her agreement. Wasn't it what she was brought up to do? Her mother grew vegetables and fruit in any plot of land available to her, and her children had helped as soon as they learnt to walk. She had paper packets of her mother's saved seeds ready for planting. It was the perfect time because spring approached.

Jane was saddle-sore and weary, so they treated themselves to a night in an inn, and a good wash before the short ride to Ballarat, where John said they would spend the weekend seeing the sights. She told John how her father and brothers were diggers in the early months of the gold rush.

'They would nae recognise it now,' he said, frowning.

As they rode to the outskirts of Ballarat, they came upon a road to Geelong, all marked out with trees removed, and boulders moved to the side. Not a dray travelled on it because of the thick glutinous mud. Jane wondered when it would be passable, 'not until it's metalled,' John told her.

'If only they built a railway, goods could travel up in a day, and there'd be no need for all those bullock carts and pubs. Prices would drop to a reasonable level, and we'd be better served with fresh food.'

Jane heard the racket before she saw Ballarat. The barking of a thousand dogs filled the air, drowning out the noise of the diggers themselves. As they rode over the brow of a hill, John stopped for Jane to view the scene. Gone were the trees and grass and sparkling water, replaced by thousands of tents, with dogs tied up outside as guards. The men dug and puddled their way through the mud. Flags of all sizes and different colours flapped amidst the tents, many were of Union Jacks but others she did not know. Jane saw tiny children scampering and toddling around some of the tents, while mothers worked and watched them. Beyond in the distance, wooded hills were a cruel reminder of what this land had been like three years before.

Their horses picked their way through clay mounds, sludge holes, pits and tree trunks. John told her how foolhardy it would be to arrive after dark and she could well believe it. The diggings appeared to go on mile after mile, with groups of men scattered randomly cradling the soil and pebbles, to catch the tiny grains of gold. Alongside muddy pools, white canvas awnings stood to protect the miners from the weather. Everywhere was a scene of noisy and confused activity amongst the wholesale desecration of the land. It most reminded her of the priest's description of hell and damnation, except for the lack of heat on the cool winter's day. She shivered, aware of the hardships to come, far worse than she ever imagined. Had her father been right when he told her a goldfield was no place for a woman? Possibly, and yet here were women and children getting on with life amidst the mud. Some of the women greeted her as they passed. They looked cheerful enough, and if they were happy to live like this, so could she. Most likely, she was better equipped, knowing the land as she did.

As they passed through the diggings, Jane saw an enormous wooden building way over to the right. 'What's that she asked?' But John did not know.

'It's over by the Eureka diggings. Let's find out.' So, they turned east to pick their way towards it. As they got close, John stopped to speak to a digger asking him about the building.

'It's the Eureka Hotel, but I wouldn't stay there myself mate. The landlord, Bentley, is as great a villain as you'd find anywhere, mind that doesn't stop the troops and the Joes from drinking there. He was a convict, not so long back, so how did he get the money for it, we ask ourselves? I bet it cost a fortune. He's never been a digger, that's for sure, but he's happy enough to fleece us of our hard-earned cash.' He spat in the mud before raising his hat to Jane and apologising.

'What did he mean by Joes?' asked Jane.

'Oh, that's just a name we have for all the government men. There's rarely a good Joe up here; you'll find out why they're not liked soon enough.'

Jane stared at the weather boarded hotel. She had never seen one as big, or as grand, it must have fifty rooms or more. A gorgeous lamp hung over the door, and Jane admired the sash windows and tiled roof. She ached to see inside.

'Can't we stay here?' Jane pleaded.

'No. The Eureka Hotel is not for us. Trust me, Jane. You're a digger's wife now, and we diggers stick together. I'll have nae truck with any friend of a Joe.' His expression brooked no further argument, and Jane gave in with good grace.

They continued to ride towards the government camp, over to the left, where some streets were laid out for the burgeoning town.

Several two-storey wooden buildings were already erected. John stopped outside a smaller hotel and helped Jane to dismount.

'Do you see that Jane?' He pointed across the street to a tented theatre. 'It's the Theatre Royal and recently reopened. Would ye like to go this evening? There'll be music and dancing and a play if we're lucky. I am nae normally minded for that kind of entertainment, but ye might like it.'

Jane immediately forgot her disappointment over the Eureka Hotel, grinning at him in excitement. Whoever would have thought it? The goldfields had a theatre! There were theatres in Geelong, but they were rowdy places, full of diggers throwing nuggets of gold to the actresses on the stage James told the family. Her mother would not dream of allowing her daughters to visit a theatre. Jane did not know what to expect from a play. She asked John if he had seen one before. Smiling, he answered 'no,' so it would be a first for both of them.

She unpacked her so recently worn wedding dress. The soft grey cotton offered a welcome change from the full mourning black she wore for her father over the last year. When she made the dress, she had no idea she would be married in it. The style was simple and serviceable, because she had been expecting to wear it for several years. But if babies came, she doubted that the tiny waist would allow her to wear it for long. The skirt was full and the sleeves long, ending in a tight cuff. There was no ornamentation, no lace, no frills and yet it was the most beautiful dress she had ever worn, because it was hers. No hand me down or reworked dress of Sarah's or Hannah's.

When she was ready, John bade her sit. In his hands was a parcel, carefully wrapped in brown paper.

'This is a present for you from my mother. She told me to give it to my bride, with her love and wishes for a long and happy life.'

With trembling fingers, Jane unwrapped the stiff paper, to find a fringed paisley shawl in dazzling shades of blue and mauve. She was overcome by the exquisite colours. She stammered her thanks.

'She may never meet you, but she wanted her daughter-in-law to know that she is loved, and she will pray for many children to bless our marriage.' John kissed her and wrapped the soft shawl around her shoulders, before leading her to a mirror, so that she could admire herself in it.

Jane looked at herself and John, standing behind, a wistful expression on his face. The shawl was so beautiful, too beautiful for her, and yet it was perfect. A lump came in her throat. She could not ever remember being so happy. She felt for his hand, turned and kissed him, almost wishing to forget the theatre and stay there in his arms. But he wanted to show off his wife to the world, so they made the short journey over the muddy street to the theatre.

Alas, the play did not live up to their expectations. The programme told them that the play, The Hunchback, had been brought to Ballarat after successful seasons in London and New York. As Jane looked around at the people waiting for the show to start, John read out snippets extolling the play and the actors. At last the candle lights were extinguished. A heavy curtain was drawn back showing a wooden stage, and Jane settled down, her hand in John's, shivering in anticipation.

But the story was all so alien and beyond her understanding, that disappointment made her stomach ache to think of the money wasted. The story hinged around men who gained fortunes and lost them as relatives died and then somehow were found alive. A girl was betrothed to one of the men, then not, then betrothed to the other man and then decided she wanted the first man she spurned.

Jane tried to understand the flowery language but gave up, what had any of this to do with her? She thought the story nonsense. The audience appeared to enjoy it, or did they enjoy anything with a couple of pretty women prancing about in silken costumes? They oohed and aahed, booed and hissed and clapped in delight, and when the play finished, as a man, the diggers stood to salute the company, cheering and stamping their feet and throwing money at the stage. Jane turned towards John, thinking there was something she had missed, but saw his mouth turned down.

'Well maybe not that play again, eh Jane? The programme says there's music now, The Royal Irish Quadrille, I hope is more to your taste.' Jane prayed that it was.

The lively stirring music instantly captivated her. This was another first, but one she did want to repeat. Her head rang with the tunes long after the music stopped, and she found herself humming the music over the next day or two.

Jane and John left the theatre and wandered the streets for a while watching the wealthier diggers and their womenfolk parading in the latest of fashions. She immediately thought of Sarah and peered at each of the women she passed in their peacock colours and feathered bonnets.

Jane felt suddenly dowdy even in her best frock, but how silly to waste such money on fripperies when it could be saved for a rainy day. She had no intention of letting the money John earned to be frittered away as James had done. It had always slipped through his fingers like water through a sieve, and so little of it came her mother's way. She watched John looking disapprovingly at some of the more fanciful women, and was thankful she had picked a canny Scot who minded his earnings.

Chapter 20

Melbourne March 1932

'I still have the shawl. Would you like to see it? Fetch it from the second drawer down in the tallboy?'

Mary walked over and opened the drawer hunting through until she found it wrapped carefully in flimsy tissue paper. She took it out from the paper and then unfolded it. The shawl had seen many years of use, and the silk was worn through in places, but the colours remained bright. She took it over to Jane and wrapped the material around her shoulders.

'Now don't you look a picture!' She said, as Jane stroked the shawl.

'I never met his mother, and she died not long after we married, but I always wished to thank her for her blessing and this shawl. I had never owned anything as beautiful before, and it still is, isn't it?'

Mary nodded and smiled, 'Did you ever see Lola Montez?' She asked mentioning one of the famous music hall names of the time.

'Oh, that hussy, no I didn't. But after that night I could never get enough of music and singing. My son was a friend and neighbour of Nelly Melba's father. One of the best evenings I spent was listening to her give a private performance at his home at Yering. I never heard a voice so pure and true. She sang Home Sweet Home. It brought tears to my eyes and my grandson, Stanley, well he was entranced. I always wondered if that was why he bought an opera company after the war.'

'He bought an opera company, what a strange thing to do!'

'Disastrous more like. He arrived back from the war with a pretty English wife, another Jane like me. He told us he met her when she sang for the troops and her voice enslaved him. She had a sweet voice; it's true, but not on a par with Dame Nellie. Anyway, this opera company arrived in Melbourne, and the two of them went to a performance of La Bohème, and within a few nights, it suddenly closed, bankrupt. What must Stanley do but rescue it? He paid off their debts, and it reopened at the Princess Theatre. Stanley attended every performance for a month, becoming quite the impresario until the Spanish flu arrived. The audience disappeared, the theatres closed, and he lost all the money he invested.'

'Poor man!'

'A fool and his money are soon parted they say. What did he know about opera? He should have stuck to farming or contracting. His head wound addled his brains.' Seeing Mary's disapproving look, she added more softly. 'You think I'm hard on my family, don't you? I am proud of my children and grandchildren, but I cannot show it, I don't know how to.'

Mary stroked Jane's thin grey hair. 'You just have to say those four words, no make it five, 'I am really proud of you.' It will mean so much to them.' She kissed Jane's forehead and said, 'I have had an idea, why don't I bring in the gramophone from the sitting room, Jean can help me carry it, and then you can listen to some music.'

'I'd like that.' Jane smiled at Mary, 'You are good to me.'

'See you can say something nice. That wasn't difficult, just practise on me.' Mary laughed.

As Mary lay in bed later that night, she thought about Jane's latest story. She could picture the scene, masses of tents, diggings rather than trenches, campfires, men filthy from their toil in the mud, not that much different from a field hospital. At least they wouldn't have whizz-bangs and gas to contend with. But Mary knew there was a battle of a different kind coming; one that resonated with every Australian and which had made it the country it was. Was there anyone else still alive today but Jane, who had seen the Eureka Hotel in its very short life she wondered?

Chapter 21

Ballarat August/September 1854

Sunday on the goldfields was a day of rest. A time for the many thousands of single men to do a bit of washing and attend one of the canvas-roofed churches and chapels. For the first-time Jane attended a non-conformist Sunday service with John, feeling just a smidgeon of guilt when she thought of her mother, but in truth, she was enjoying herself too much. Gossip amongst the congregation was that the new governor had arrived in Ballarat late on Saturday afternoon. He would be inspecting the diggings on Monday. After the service, John bumped into a man he knew, Tom Kennedy, who invited them to a meeting in the afternoon.

'What kind of meeting is it John?' Jane asked over an excellent dinner of roast beef and potatoes.

'The diggers have many grievances, and this new Governor of Victoria needs to listen to our complaints and begin sensible reforms. I suspect Tom wants to organise a petition.'

'And the licences? Father raged about them when he was up here.'

'Yes, that and the land issue. The squatters have huge tracts of land, the best land too, paying next to nothing for it. When the government sells off small plots, it's often of the poorest land and yet it goes for ridiculous prices. Things need to change. Let's hope this Hotham fellow is the man to do it because La Trobe was nae friend of the diggers.'

'How do you know Mr Kennedy?'

'Oh, he's an old tub-thumping Chartist. I went to one or two meetings in Glasgow, but they got nowhere in Britain, and I'd be surprised if they succeeded here. After all, it's the same jumped up men in charge. You'll see them in their fancy uniforms braided in gold, strutting around like the peacocks they are.'

The meeting was held at the Adelphi Theatre on Bakery Hill, and like the Theatre Royal, it was a large tent with benches and a stage at the far end. The owner, Mrs Hanmer, greeted Jane warmly and as Jane and John took their seats, he told her that the owner and her daughter had arrived from America, but were English born, and as far as he knew no husband was on the scene. Jane thought that quite daring.

The tent filled up with men and a few women. She heard all sorts of languages and accents around her, recognising some from the shop, but what struck her most was that everyone was young. No one around was a day over thirty-five.

A man stood up and clambered onto the rough stage; it was Tom Kennedy who had invited them to the meeting. After a second or two, the voices ceased, and Kennedy started to speak in a growling, Glaswegian accent. He was a short, heavy man, bald but with a bewhiskered, lined face, a striking man none the less. He talked of rights and liberty and the need for representation for the heavy taxation paid by the miners, of the need to unlock the land so that miners could settle down, build a house, grow food, but most of all he wanted the licence fees abolished.

'How many of you,' he cried 'have no money to pay your licence when you've found no gold for weeks on end?' Jane watched as about a quarter of the hands went up.

'How many of you struggle to feed your bairns? And yet the Joes demand you pay your monthly licence?' Again, more hands went up.

'How many of you have seen your taxes being used to pay for better roads and bridges to the diggings?' No hands were raised.

'How many of you would like to own land in this fair country and raise a family, and say a permanent farewell to the despotism of old Europe? 'Most hands rose, and a cheer sounded from every side.

'What are we going to ask of this new governor tomorrow?'

'Abolish the licence fees and sell us land.' A voice from the audience shouted, followed by another cheer.

As they left the theatre, the men were asked to sign a petition to give to the new governor. The men queued to sign their names or make their mark. While they were waiting in line, a man tapped John on the shoulder. He turned to see a young, smiling, bearded Scotsman, who cried 'It's John Timmins, isn't it? Do you remember me, James Scobie? My brother George and I sailed on the ship here with you.'

John clasped his hand and shook it. 'Of course I remember you. This is my wife, Jane.' James shook her hand in a hearty grip.

'Look would you care to share a drop o' whisky with me after signing this petition? I have a bottle of best malt in my pocket. Come back to my tent the both of you,' he said smiling at Jane.

'Why not use our room at the hotel, it will be more comfortable, and it's only across the road,' said John pointing. James nodded his agreement,

'A pure malt. However did you manage that?' Asked John, as they made their way over to the hotel.

'My brother and I run a carting business between here and Geelong, and he got lucky last week. He had a game of poker with a new chum from Scotland who put it up as a wager. George said the man was pig sick to have lost it. He brought it all the way with him from Inverness to toast his first gold find. Now we reckon that it will bring us luck instead. I have a new claim up at Eureka, and I feel it in my waters, this is going to be our big strike.'

John asked the barman for three glasses, and they took them up to their room. Jane sat on the only chair while James took out a half-empty bottle of golden Glen Livet. After carefully removing the cork. he poured three small measures into their glasses.

'I promised George, I would leave some to celebrate our find. As you can see, it had better come soon because I doubt I can wait to finish this amber nectar.'

Jane sniffed the whisky before taking a sip. It was nothing like anything else she had smelt. It was heady but sweet like honey, and she looked forward to tasting it. At first, she was lulled by the silky smoothness as it glided over her tongue. Then the fieriness hit the back of her throat making her gasp with pleasure as the warmth filled her. 'Oh,' she said, in complete surprise, and both James and John laughed and slapped their knees.

'There now, ye are now a true Scots woman with a liking for the only water of life a Scotsman understands,' said John.

The remains of the afternoon they spent in happy conversation. James and John caught up on the news from home, and about people they knew. Jane was content to listen until James took his leave, before the light disappeared. His way back to his tent was fraught with danger from deep pits, waiting for any unsuspecting victim.

'You take care of this guid man, Jane you hear. And John, you are a lucky man finding such a bonny lass.' Jane blushed. What a kind man, no one had ever called her bonny.

Chapter 22

Melbourne March 1932

'James Scobie, the name rings a bell. Oh, my gosh, the man murdered by Bentley!' Mary exclaimed, recalling her history lessons.

'Yes, poor James. I only knew him that one afternoon, but he was a generous, likeable man and very popular on the diggings.

That whole spring the temperature rose, and it was nothing to do with the weather. The atmosphere grew feverish. Even though I was new to the diggings, I felt the anger growing. You could almost touch it. There was another murder at Creswick in October too, some silly digger got shot for peering into a tent that didn't belong to him, but everyone was on edge.

More and more men arrived when gold was found at Bald Hills, just to the west of us. The price of food kept on rising, and everyone complained bitterly of the licence hunts. They even reported in October that the diggers at Creswick burned down the government camp, and troops were being sent to quell the rebellion. All nonsense of course!

I always wondered if we hadn't helped James Scobie drink his whisky that afternoon, maybe he would have lived to enjoy his lucky gold strike. I know it's silly because anyone could tell he liked his grog, so, if not that night, perhaps the next.

The diggings were a cauldron about to boil over at any time. The miners had had enough of the licences and the commissioners. It needed something to spark it off. We just wished poor James Scobie had not been the touch-paper.'

'Did your husband get involved in what happened?'

'Tom Kennedy tried his best to get the Creswick diggers mixed up in it, but for the weather, it may have happened. But that's another story. Tomorrow I'll tell you what it was like to live on the goldfields.'

Jane felt exhausted. Was it good for her to keep dredging up all these memories for Mary's benefit? Did it matter if it was good for her or not? The truth was that she was enjoying the telling. Her grandchildren and great-grandchildren did not care about the past. She could see their eyes glaze over if she told them they did not know how hard life used to be. But then she had never tried starting off a story by saying 'Oh I remember Eureka, or I remember Ned Kelly.' Their ears might prick up at that. Perhaps she should try and then it might not be such a chore to visit their old granny. Too late now!

Chapter 23

Ballarat and Creswick Creek September 1854

As Jane and John prepared to leave for Creswick Creek on the Monday a party, including the governor and his wife, rode out from the government camp heading for the diggings.

'He's heading for Canadian Gully,' said a voice from the crowd. John led Jane on horseback to a vantage point on Soldier's Hill where they could watch the governor's procession.

'He'll think us all as rich as Croesus,' said John. 'They're finding nuggets of gold down there, not just grains and the Commissioner knows it. He should show him the diggings where men find nothing and go broke, leaving their families to starve.'

They listened to the rousing cheers for Sir Charles and Lady Hotham as they made their rounds. It seemed to Jane that the miners appeared bucked up by his visit. The applause sounded genuine. As the procession moved to a shaft behind the Ballarat Dining Rooms, the governor paused to take the petition prepared the day before. Whatever he told the miners, caused them to give an hurrah.

John turned his horse, saying he'd seen enough and they must make a start on the last leg of the journey. Jane asked him if he thought the governor would act to reduce the licences fee.

'We'll have to wait and see,' he said, in his dour voice. 'If he doesnae I can see trouble brewing. There are thousands of young miners here, and some are hot-headed and not all bound to Britain. They'll be all too ready to stand up for their rights when the time comes, make no mistake.'

'And you John, what will you do?'

He did not answer. He was not a political man but was keenly aware of the situation and the injustice. He would do well to bide his time and see what was afoot.

They arrived in Creswick an hour before sundown. Jane was horrified to find the dirt track littered with yawning chasms waiting to swallow up the unwary traveller.

'Ye need to be careful here Jane. I hate to think how many men and beasts have fallen to death in pits such as these on the goldfields. Claims are not supposed to overrun the road, but who monitors it? You would think the gold commissioners, wouldn't you? But sense and officials have nae in common it seems.' Jane began to see the scale of the problems facing the diggers. The lawlessness and disorder were as bad as ever it was, if not worse.

John led the horses to where his mates were camped around a fire, warming their bone wearied bodies. There were two men, a woman and a child. When the men recognised John, they clapped him on the back and greeted Jane with great good humour. John introduced her to Will Geddes, Jack Monroe and his wife Maggie, who had accompanied her husband from Scotland. Will rushed into his tent to fetch some grog to toast the happy couple. Jane began to lose her shyness, under the onslaught of the welcome and regard these people had for her husband.

Maggie promised to take Jane under her wing and show her the ropes of being a digger's wife. Jane smiled her thanks. Drawing her close, Maggie asked for her help in preparing a meal for the men. They chatted ten to the dozen, while the men erected their tent and stowed away their belongings. Jane realised within minutes that Maggie would become a friend, as she basked in the warmth of her open, sunny smile. Her toddler son clung to her skirts, and there was another bairn on the way by the look of it.

There were a few years between them, maybe six or seven, but Maggie had a prettiness which had matured into a striking beauty. Jane was intrigued by her colouring; she looked like no Scot that Jane had ever seen. Her skin was olive in tone and unmarked by freckles, her hair dark and sleek and her eyes almost black. High cheekbones added to her beauty and Jane longed to ask her about her origins, but politeness held her back. There was no doubting her accent, for that was Scottish, beyond doubt.

They spent a happy evening around the campfire, with John telling his friends of the news garnered from his travels, and the sights seen at Ballarat. In return, they told him about the progress of their claim. John breathed a sigh of relief as they described the amount of gold retrieved over the last few weeks.

The first chore after breakfast the following morning was to buy his licence.

'Another thirty shillings to the government and for what?' He grumbled to Jane as they walked towards the licence tent. 'And if you set up a store in our tent that's a further thirty shillings a month.'

Jane had arranged with her boss in Geelong to send tools up for her to sell. On the way to buy John's licence, she noticed several other tent stores and made a mental note to visit them that day to see what they were selling, and how much they were charging.

John pointed out where he and his mates were digging, in the area where Spring Creek met Creswick Creek. Jane looked beyond the diggings towards the hills which were overgrown with peppermint gums and wondered what lay beyond.

'The number of diggers grows and falls as tales come of new finds elsewhere. But I reckon there's about five thousand men here at the moment.' John took her arm as she stumbled on a heap of pinkish coloured spoil.

She told John about her brother Jacob going off to Mount Alexander on such a tale and never being seen again. 'I looked around for him in Ballarat, you know, him and Sarah. I don't suppose I'll ever stop looking, hoping that one day I will find them and ..' Her voice trailed off and John, seeing tears at the corner of her eyes, stopped and held her close for a moment, no longer than a second or two, both conscious of being watched and becoming the butt of diggers' humour.

The licence tent was at the government camp, a brooding presence set on a hill, as it was at Ballarat. John seethed at the waste of time queuing. The commissioner was not in any hurry to begin his day's work, and it was eleven o'clock before the licence was in John's pocket. They made their way back to their tent where John changed into his work clothes and set off for his claim. Jack and Will had already been hard at work for several hours.

Jane organised their few belongings in their tent. John told her it was not worth owning more than you needed for everyday use, as thieves were ten a penny. Each of them had two changes of clothes, and apart from that, they made do with a pail for laundry, tin plates and cups, a mattress with blankets, crates to sit on with another acting as a table, a few tins for food storage and pans for the fire. All were replaceable for pennies or shillings. For now, with just a tent to keep tidy, a tiny patch of land around it to cultivate and meals to prepare, until babies came along, she worried that time would hang heavy. She was not used to being idle.

Her immediate need was food for their dinner, so grabbing a basket she set off to see what was available and to learn about prices. She had two pounds in her pocket, more than enough for a week's worth of food. She strode towards the burgeoning town, no more than a single street, where a new hotel and a few stores stood, along with the recently opened post office, nought but a simple slab hut with a calico roof.

'Four shillings for a loaf of bread!' Jane exclaimed in horror at the first store she came to. 'You mean four pence, surely.'

'You'll not find it anywhere cheaper,' said the storekeeper, eyeing her up and down. 'New to the diggings, are you?' Jane did not answer, turning away in disgust to try another store. But it seemed the storekeeper was right; she could not find bread any cheaper. The most outrageous prices were for fresh vegetables, cabbages at three and sixpence each, potatoes at one shilling and sixpence a pound. She would need a pound to feed them each day until she got her garden growing.

The prices for tools were high too, and Jane felt confident she could make a profit on what she had arranged to be sent up to her, but there were many stores selling tools. She wondered if the competition would lower prices. She listened in while a digger attempted to bargain with a storekeeper for a new pick, but the storekeeper was having none of it.

'The price is the price,' he said, and the digger swearing under his breath paid up. Without a pick, he could earn no money, and the storekeeper knew it.

Returning to her tent, she saw Maggie outside pegging up clothes on a line. 'Let me peg these last few things. I have a billycan boiling. Would you like some tea?'

Jane accepted and as soon as she had stowed away her few purchases, she joined Maggie outside her tent, where Jane told her about her little excursion to the stores.

'I knew the prices would be high, but not that high. How can people afford them?'

Maggie agreed that the prices were ridiculous and getting more expensive all the time. She made extra money by baking pies and selling them, and her prices were high because of the cost of ingredients.

'The wives have a really important role here to supplement income, especially when the gold disappears from a claim, as it often does. The men can be digging out several ounces a day and then, without warning it stops or turns and goes into a neighbour's claim. They have to stand around watching their gold being brought up by someone else. Meanwhile, their children have their bellies hanging out from hunger. There's nothing can be done unless their wives are selling a little something on the side.' She blushed. 'Oh, that sounds rude. I didn't mean...' Maggie did not finish her sentence, but Jane knew what she meant.

Jane told Maggie that she wanted to open a store and was expecting a consignment of tools within a week or so.

'Another tool store?' Maggie looked uncertain.

'Don't you think it will work? Jane asked.

'Yes, I am sure it will. It's just that we have so many, but there isn't anywhere to buy things you need for a baby, like bottles with teats or material for baby clothes.'

'Joe, Joe, Joe.' Jane heard the call as she was kneeling in the dirt by her tent planting seeds. John joked that she should puddle any soil she dug up to make sure she was not throwing away gold. She looked up as a wall of voices continued the refrain.

'Joe, Joe, Joe.' She caught sight of men diving towards their pits. Maggie next door hurried to remove the sign outside her tent listing her homemade pies. Jane stood brushing the mud from her skirt, and the chant continued.

A pair of horsemen worked their way around the diggings. As they got nearer, Jane saw that one of the horsemen was a trooper and the other she assumed was a gold commissioner, dressed in a fancy uniform, with of all things, gold lace at his cuffs and throat. The men above ground were each asked to show their licences, which they did with bad grace. Jane caught sight of several men disappearing underground, in the certain knowledge that a commissioner would not dirty his fine garb by following down the hole.

'You were only inspecting them last week. Is a week now as long as a month?' She heard a digger say.

'New orders,' said the commissioner. 'All licences to be inspected twice a week from now on.'

'Whose orders?'

'The Governor, Sir Charles Hotham himself.'

'So much for the new governor and his promises,' said John later, as he washed the worst of the mud off his hands and face, before sitting down with Jane to eat the meal she had prepared. 'Does he want a riot? He's going about it the best way to get one. The diggers won't stand for much more. What did he say only a month ago, 'all power proceeds from the people'? He might as well have said that all power proceeds from those who squat on the land, and it's the diggers who will pay for it.'

Jane had never heard John say so much and in so forthright a manner, for he was normally a taciturn man. In the few days she had been on the goldfield, Jane and John had turned in after a companionable dinner and maybe a drink of grog. But this evening, men gathered in groups around fires. Grog passed freely amongst them, and raised voices vented their anger at the new rules.

The temper of the Goldfield ebbed and flowed as license hunts vied with new finds, but the commissioner's license hunt soon merited additional troopers as the diggers grew surly. There were always miners who chanced their luck. As soon as the cry 'Joe' came, they would run to get themselves below, or had taken the precaution of swapping licenses with other men working their claim. On the other hand, Creswick Creek was doing well. Gold in the existing diggings continued to be found in good quantities, and new claims also proved fruitful. Word, as it does, passed around, and the numbers of diggers swelled throughout October.

Jane was particularly pleased as she sold her tools at a good profit to some of the new diggers, just by a having a hand-written notice outside the tent. She did not bother with a licence and copied Maggie by removing the sign as soon as she heard the warning, 'Joe.'

In early October, Jane received a letter from Isaac. She worried all day about her mother's reaction to her marriage, and was on tenterhooks as John opened the letter. She looked at his face as he began to read, seeing him frown and then grimace.

'Well John what does it say? Is there news of Sarah? Did they find her?'

'No, I'm sorry love, they didnae find her.'

Jane had hoped and prayed for better news. Would they ever find out what happened to her? She longed to console her mother, regretting she could not be with her to hold her and wipe away her tears. For the first time since her wedding day, she truly understood her thoughtlessness in marrying while her mother was away from home.

'And my mother, is she angry with me?'

'Isaac writes that she will need time to recover from the news.'

'Is that it?'

'He says that Hannah and little Isaac are doing well and your sister, Ellen, has written that she is happy in Adelaide.'

Jane thought there was more in the letter, but John screwed it up into a ball and aimed for the fire. The letter did not quite find its target, and in the darkness, Jane stuck out her boot and nudged it underneath her dress, stamping gently on it in case any embers caught. Next day she took the smoothed-out pages around to Maggie, and asked her to read it to her.

'Are you sure?' Asked Maggie, after she read it through quickly, but Jane nodded. 'I think John was wise in trying to save your feelings. These words are harsh.'

'Read the letter please. I need to know. Otherwise, I will not rest.'

Dear Jane

Your mother insists that I write this down word for word as she speaks. She says she will ask someone to read it through before sending, to check my truthfulness. By this, you will understand her anger and despair. Dearest Jane, I am so sorry to write these words. Take comfort from knowing that Hannah and little Isaac are well and that Ellen is happy in Adelaide. Of Sarah, there is no news.

Your loving brother

Isaac

Jane your father, God rest his soul, had no favourites, but he always saw something special in you. He trusted you to be a good daughter. How do you think he would feel now to know that you have abandoned your mother and your faith? He wanted you to be named Jane Elizabeth after his sisters. For me, those two names spoke of treachery, for reasons I have never shared, but I gave in as he was a good man. Whoever would have thought God would seek to punish me with a daughter as hard and treacherous as you. I pray that none of your children gives you so much heartache. Have I not had as much sorrow as any mother could bear, to lose my husband and two beloved children so recently? Now I have lost three; for you are gone from me also.

Mother

144

Jane gasped and cried out. She should have known how her mother would react. Religion and loyalty were her touchstones.

Maggie took her in her arms. 'I should not have read it to you,' she whispered in her ear, as Jane sobbed on her shoulder. 'John was right to protect you.'

'She cannot mean it. She will forgive me, won't she? I left her a letter explaining why I needed to marry in a rush and begged her to understand. She is always so unforgiving.'

'Your mother loves you, but is hurting from her other misfortunes. Give her time.'

'Yes, she came around to baby Isaac being baptised into the Presbyterian Church. Why would she not accept me marrying a Presbyterian, as my sister did before me?'

John could tell that Jane had something on her mind that evening. All through supper she was quieter than usual, frowning rather than smiling.

They had been married barely a month, but he had grown very fond of the wee lass. Jane did not have the vivacity of Maggie for which John was thankful. He sometimes found Maggie too unsettling. His wife Jane, and he felt proud when he breathed those words, was more down to earth and steady than Maggie. He hated to see Jane upset or troubled and was pleased he had destroyed Isaac's letter. The message from her mother was written in the heat of the moment, and when she had time to reflect, she would calm down. If she did not, John intended to give her a piece of his mind. He did not doubt that he was more than a match for her.

With supper ended and the washing up finished, John drew his wife to him and asked her what was wrong. Jane did not dare tell him about the rescued letter. But there were other things she had not told him. She was now worried they were bound to come out some time in the future.

'I was not completely truthful with you before we married,' she ventured studying his face to gauge his reaction. But seeing none, she continued. 'I did not tell you my right age. I am seventeen, not twenty.' John chuckled slightly and emboldened she carried on in a rush to get the words out. 'I was brought up in the Catholic Church, but my father was a Protestant.' John remained silent for a few seconds, and his face became grave. Jane clenched her fists tight in anxiety and then watched in disbelief as he began to laugh, something she had never seen him do. She did not think he was a laughing kind of man.

'Oh hinny! My Jane, ye are an innocent. Did you think I didnae know? Before I ever asked you out your boss told me all about you and your family, and he was full of praise for you.' He watched as Jane's face flushed with embarrassment. 'Don't be upset. Ye and me, we'll make a good team, and we'll bring your mother round to accept more Presbyterian grandchildren. I'll bet ye, she's eating out of my hand when ye have lots of little ones to call her Granny.' He took her face in his hands saying: 'Let's try to make that happen sooner rather than later hey?' He kissed her mouth and led her into the tent, closing the flap firmly behind them.

Chapter 24

Creswick Creek Autumn 1854

The Goldfield was a vast, undulating expanse of stricken land. Three years ago, virgin bush surrounded a sparkling creek. It was now a wasteland. All trees and bushes, the tall red river gums, the acacia, even the stringy bark had been cut back for firewood, or to provide shuttering and ladders for the deep shafts, pock-marking the surface of the land. The creek long ago diverted and dug, out was now a muddy, polluted gash, trickling through the reddish earth.

Most of the wildlife had beaten a retreat. The sleepy koalas had fallen with their trees, still clinging to the branches. New chums may have been tempted to club the shocked animals for food, but soon learnt their meat was poor stuff in comparison to a kangaroo or possum. But the skin and fur were useful for lining sleeping bags and so few escaped. And those that did escape were picked off by the wild dingoes or the black men whose hunting grounds were desecrated without apology. Even the birds no longer found a home in this sterile wilderness. Gone the high-pitched whistle of the magpie larks or the raucous cry of cockatoos; instead came the cries of barking dogs and the sound of thousands of men at work, or the jingling harness of the troopers.

The behaviour of the white men baffled the blacks. Could yellow dust feed you? Could it give you shade in the summer months or fire in winter? Why use precious water for washing the muddy earth and not save it for drinking? All of nature's bounty, their ancient Dreamtime lands destroyed for a golden pebble, and for what?

But nature abhors a vacuum, and so the mice, rats, ants, scorpions, and flies infested the goldfields and became the bane of every digger and his wife. Jane was used to flies. Her father complained that there were no flies like Australian flies, they were bigger, greedier, and altogether more insistent than any British insect. Even the lice of his childhood could not compare with an Australian fly for voracity. Wearing a veil attached to a hat was the only way to deal with them for if you did not, they would get in your eyes, nose or mouth and bite any available piece of skin. It was a wonder how they found their way between clothes, but the evidence of their appetite appeared in itchy red blotches, which Jane treated with the oil she distilled from tea tree leaves. Mosquitoes also did not like the smell of tea tree oil, and she applied it to her and John's hands and face religiously whenever the sun sank on the horizon.

In the early days of her life on the goldfield, Jane pestered John to show her the mine. She wanted to see what he did every day for a living. He was reluctant. It was dangerous, no place for a woman, maybe even bad luck, but he soon found that no excuse would dissuade her. One Sunday, as the spring sunshine warmed the land, Jane dressed in a pair of John's old breeches. She tied them up around her neat waist with thick twine and tucked the legs into her boots. Wearing an old, patched shirt with the cuffs folded back, she fastened her hair, hiding it in a slouch hat. To other diggers, she looked like a young, fresh-faced boy.

Their claim was one hundred yards from the tent. With three men to operate it they had twenty-four square feet marked out. Single men were allowed eight-foot square, the size of just two wagons placed side by side. Jack was waiting for them. He had volunteered to turn the handle of the windlass for them. He chuckled at the sight of Jane.

'You'd make a mighty fine digger there Mrs Timmins. Are you sure you don't want a job? I cannae see my Maggie going down this pit. She hates the dark at the best of times.'

Jane stood at the top of the shaft peering into the inky darkness.

'Are you sure you want to do this?' John asked.

She swallowed hard. It did not seem like such a good idea now, but her man, her husband, faced this descent every day. Looking at him she gave him a single nod, her throat too dry for words.

'It's an eighty-foot descent in the bucket. You need to stand up. I will go first and meet ye there.'

Jane was grateful there was a windlass rather than a ladder. She tried to imagine what it would feel like to climb below, rung by rung with scarce enough room for the toe of a boot between the ladder and the sides of the shaft. But some men did, for not everyone had a windlass, and those that did often had them perched perilously on unstable piles of earth. She could tell that John knew his business, because his windlass looked sturdier than many on the goldfield, neatly straddling the shaft on firm ground. The bucket, attached to a thick chain wrapped around the spindle, looked hardly big enough for a child, let alone a grown man.

John gave her a peck on the cheek and then hopped into the bucket, showing the assurance which comes with familiarity. The bucket swayed as Jack began to turn the handle. John held the chain firmly above his head and disappeared into the gloom. Jane could just see the tiny flame of a lighted taper which he held in his hand. Then not even that. The clank of the turning chain showed that he was still descending. When Jane heard his voice far below, Jack began to turn the handle in the opposite direction. Slowly the bucket reappeared, and it was Jane's turn.

With her heart in her mouth, she grabbed hold of the spindle. Jack held the bucket as she lifted first one foot and then the other. She climbed into the bucket, hardly daring let go of the spindle, until Jack told her to grab the chain and she felt the bucket begin to move. Bit by bit she descended, the square of blue sky above her head grew smaller. Jane smelled the boarding of the gum tree lined shaft, rather than seeing it. In Jane's mind, the descent took ages, but better this bucket than a ladder. She would not have had the strength for that. Her arms and legs would have been trembling uncontrollably before she ever reached the bottom. John's reassuring voice was close by. Almost there, she thanked God. Looking up, the sky appeared as a distant speck of blue. A slight bump and John's arms around her told her she was at the bottom. Jane climbed out of the bucket with relief. John gave her his lit candle, and while he lit another from his taper, Jane crossed herself and muttered a quick Hail Mary in thanks, hoping John didn't notice.

Telling Jane to follow him he turned into a narrow passageway. The ground was uneven. Jane stumbled once or twice before John turned into a yet narrower, descending passage. As short as she was, she had to duck to miss being struck on the head. The air was damp and cooler than at the surface, and in the faint candlelight, she saw water droplets seeping through the earthen walls. Pit props held up the roof, but she suddenly became aware of the weight of the earth above her head.

'Does the earth ever fall on the diggers?' She asked, heart in mouth.

'Aye, it does.' John could be very taciturn at times, a feature which she regretted at this moment but after a pause, he continued. 'Ye need to know what you're doing, and take account of the wet, but accidents happen a' the time.'

Jane sensed they were still walking downhill, wondering how far beneath the earth they were. The low rock ceiling felt as if it was closing in on her; she prayed the mine would not end up being her tomb. John stopped suddenly causing her to bump into him.

'There is it Jane. That's why we're all here.' He held his candle to a vein in the rock. She caught sight of fine specks of gold below the darker rock face. 'What we want is for that gold layer to continue in this direction for a while longer. See where we have dug out the vein so far. But there's a danger the vein will turn and follow another way into a neighbouring claim. If it does, we're done for here.'

He told Jane to move away and took up a pick that was lying at his feet, before swinging it to free a chunk of the rock. It showered down as fine gravel, which he swept into a bark-lined basket, pointing out some fragments of the yellow gold glinting in the candlelight. 'Much of this is just dust and chips. When we wash it at the surface, we'll be lucky to find a few ounces every week. Fourteen ounces was our best week, and we are fortunate that it has never gone below six. I doubt we could all live on just six with the price of everything so high.'

'How did you know where to find it at all?' Jane asked in wonder.

'Ye have to understand the structure of rock and gravel. The gold in the creek-bed has all been dug out, that's the shallow lead, so now we must go deeper. Imagine a stream diving underground and the gold captured in the sandy gravel of this underground creek. The water disappears, but the river bed is still there, most likely under harder rock such as the lava flow from a volcano. If we were digging at Bendigo, we'd be searching for gold in quartz and pipe clay, but here it's in gravel. I suspect far beneath us here, lies quartz, but to get that gold out requires much better machinery and a lot of investment. In a few years, all the lone diggers will leave, and mining companies will reap the big rewards. Mark my words.'

At that moment one of the candles guttered and blew out. It felt like an omen of hard times, and Jane shivered. John managed to light it again before leading her back to the shaft and up to the glorious sunshine and fresh air. She would hate working in the mine; was even more in awe of the thousands of men who were doing just that, every day, and with no certainty of reward.

Chapter 25

Creswick Creek Spring 1854

The news came in dribs and drabs; rumours spread like Chinese whispers percolating the diggings. There was no telling what the truth was. A man murdered at Ballarat, maybe two men or even more. It was an Irishman, no it was a Scotsman killed by an Irishman. The diggers were rioting because of injustice. It was all anyone talked about. The newspapers arrived, and John read the report in the Argus with mounting anger. Jane watched his expression changing from interest to shock, his mouth and eyes narrowing in disbelief. He threw the paper to the ground and cursed.

'What's happened?' Asked Jane

'They've killed puir James Scobie.'

'Who has?'

'That scoundrel, James Bentley, the one that owns the Eureka Hotel. What's mair they have let him off, no case to answer. It's all fixed of course. The magistrates are in cahoots with the man. But the diggers wouldnae stand for it. They only tore down the hotel and set fire to it. Guid on them I say. But thes gonnae leid tae trooble.' John's accent became thick with anger.

'What, the Eureka Hotel, the one we passed. It's gone?' Jane was astounded. It was unbelievable to think of it burnt down.

'Aye.'

'But poor James, how did he die?'

John picked up the paper, smoothing it out and read the whole article to Jane. He told how James, celebrating his long-awaited gold find, drank until the early hours and wanting more grog went with a friend to the Eureka Hotel. But it was closed, and in drunken frustration, James swore and broke a window. Making his way back to his tent, he and his friend were set upon and James beaten to death. Witnesses swore that they recognised the voice of Bentley before the attack, but the magistrate gave no credence to that evidence and let Bentley off.

'There's magistrates for you! My father had no faith in magistrates. Our family got no justice from them. But something must have happened next. How did the hotel come to be burnt?'

He looked back at the article and continued to read. 'The diggers held a public meeting, calling for the case to be referred to more competent authorities. They decided to petition the governor. But as the men then left for their tents, the commissioners and troopers rode towards the Eureka Hotel, angering the men even more. They started to shout 'Joe'. Gravel was thrown at the windows of the hotel. It started as a gesture, but then the men got carried away, and over the space of an hour or two the whole place was burned down.'

'And the troopers stood by and watched? I can hardly believe that!'

'Aye It seems so, but I cannae think that will be an end tae it. James was well liked on the diggings, and his brother George will be beside hissel. He promised his mother he would tak' guid care o' him'

'No, it won't be the end John, but we should pray for the family and ourselves I reckon.'

Throughout that spring the diggings seethed, and men began to flex their muscles, no longer willing to succumb to the indignities which those in authority heaped upon them. Diggers were prepared for the hardships and dangers of their work. They accepted the mud, the heat, and the flies, but they expected something in return for their licence fees. They wanted fairness and justice, but instead, they got intimidation, corruption, and brutality. Around the campfires of an evening, the Creswick diggers discussed their discontent, and the news which came from Ballarat. It was not just the Melbourne Argus; now they had the Ballarat Times and the Digger's Advocate to stir them up.

Jane, as a childless woman, sat with John around whichever campfire they happened to be invited to, listening to the men's conversation. Hard upon the news of James Scobie's death came details of an earlier outrage which angered Jane. The crippled servant of a Catholic priest was badly and wrongfully abused by a trooper on a licence hunt. The man did not need to have a licence, but that had not stopped the trooper from detaining him nor trampling him with his horse. Worse still the priest's servant was then accused of assaulting the trooper. The Ballarat Times called the trooper savage and cowardly and a monster too. How much more would the diggers put up with?

And still the licence hunts continued, with the troopers always more demanding and with a brutality that came from fear. They knew the mood on the diggings; tension and disgust with authority were everywhere.

'This is outrageous,' Jane heard one digger say, as he dug out his licence for the third or fourth time that week. 'We are living in the British Empire. This is not Russia. And we are lawful citizens. If this were England the people wouldn't stand for it.'

'Good on you, mate,' a few voices called, but the trooper took no notice other than to threaten the digger with his rifle.

Later that evening as they sat around the campfire a friend of John's told them a story that was going the rounds to cheer them up.

'A prosperous looking man was travelling on 'orseback just east of the diggings when he was accosted by troopers demanding to see 'is licence. Anyways 'e 'as a bit of a barney with 'em because he's not a digger but a storekeeper. And although he 'ad a licence for that, he refused to show it to the Joes.'

'I know this story,' said John, 'but go on. Jane will love it.'

'So, these troopers demanded 'e ride back with 'em to the commissioner. On the way some diggers catch sight of 'em and call out to ask why he's in custody. When the man told 'em what had happened, they gathered round and one said, 'Do you need a licence now to be riding an 'orse?' Another called out 'this is a Christian country mate. You can't arrest some poor cove for going for a ride.' Jane laughed at that.

'Oh, it gets better,' the storyteller said. 'The troopers start to get flustered, and one says to the man 'Have you got a receipt for that horse? It looks too good for the likes of you.' 'You can go to the devil,' says he, amidst hoots of laughter from the diggers. 'Bravo', says one of 'em. 'Take the man to his 'orse's old mare and ask her for a line to say she gev birth to it, why don't you?' Jane burst out laughing. 'Well, the jest spread far and wide, so that all you could hear was laughter and mockery. The troopers were so shamefaced that they set the man free.'

Jane caught the faces of the men lit by the glow of the dying fire. All young, heavily bearded men with tired eyes, but which sparkled in that instant of laughter when the story ended with the loss of face of the hated Joes. She felt the warmth of their companionship as they sat on the dusty ground, their stomachs full and with enough grog drunk to blot out the disappointments of that day, or the homesickness they suffered. I wouldn't be anywhere else she thought. She caught the eye of John who smiled at her with good humour.

One bit of good news lightened the general mood on the diggings that Spring, the arrest of Bentley and his wife, Catherine, for the murder of James Scobie. At last a change of heart and someone is listening to the diggers' complaints, they thought. But they were quickly disillusioned as they heard that a couple of men had been scape-goated for the destruction of the Eureka Hotel. One of them, McIntyre, had been trying to restrain the men, and Gold Commissioner Rede, was a witness to that, but what did the authorities care about truth and justice? The miners grew sickened by this latest arbitrary show of strength, and they were not prepared to put up with it. Over nine thousand miners gathered towards the end of October in Ballarat to decide what to do. They determined to set up a defence fund for their arrested mates.

The diggers at Creswick only got to know about this by word of mouth and newsprint. As yet, they did not want to get involved in the Ballarat miners' fight with authority, but they were forever watched by spies and troopers from the government camp. They also knew that the trouble brewing at Ballarat could spill over into Creswick. Tension mounted throughout the diggings.

In early November Jane received another letter from Isaac. This one John read to her all the way through. It contained a plea from her mother to return to Geelong because she was frightened for Jane's safety. Isaac wrote how the newspaper reports were getting increasingly concerned about the dangerous situation on the goldfields.

The talk was all about hundreds of troopers being sent up to Ballarat to contain a possible riot. This at least, had caused Jane's mother to soften her heart.

'Do you want to go back to Geelong?' asked John as he finished reading.

'Never, my place is here with you. Anyway, I think they are being overly concerned, don't you?'

'Yes. The situation is nae guid, but Victoria needs the income from gold, and eventually, someone will see sense. If there is any real danger at Creswick, I will get ye out, but I think if the situation blows up it will be at Ballarat, nae here. It is guid that your mother has come round. I thought she would. All it takes is time.'

Jane hugged the letter to her and smiled to herself in relief. She never wanted to fall out with her mother, and here was evidence of a slight thaw in her temper. She wagered that the thaw would continue. Jane was old enough to know what was best for her, and her mother needed to understand that.

'I hope that when we do go back to see them in Geelong, we will have a son or daughter with us,' she replied.

'Are you saying ye are with child?' John caught her up in his arms.

'It may be too early to say, but my courses are late this month,' she smiled shyly at him.

'Dear Lord that the best news. Perhaps I should take ye down to Geelong.'

'No. When we agreed to marry, we promised we would stay together on the diggings. This is my home,' she said, pointing to the tent. 'This is where I will stay. Let that be an end to it.' She stood by the canvas flap of their tiny abode, her arms crossed, her mouth a thin line and eyes daring him to speak further of her leaving. He looked at her petite, determined form and knew he had chosen right. She was not yet eighteen but had inherited the soul and toughness of the mother he had yet to meet. He looked forward to the encounter and, pray God, there would be a healthy bairn with them.

Chapter 26

Jane's eyes closed in exhaustion. No visitors had called to interrupt the story, and Jane, far from being reluctant to discuss her past, now relished the telling. A dam had burst in her mind with words pouring from it. For a woman of near ninety-five to have such clear recollection was unusual. In Mary's experience, a mind of that age often became cloudy, indistinct, and what was remembered, repeated again and again, enough to drive the listener to distraction.

Jane's memories had been screwed down tight in an ancient bottle. One she stored away and forgot. Now that the bottle had been found and opened, the preserves inside were as fresh as the day they were made.

In the morning, Jane's face welcomed Mary with a smile. This in itself was unusual, her normal expression, one of patient resolution or worse, sour disapproval, but that was seen less and less over the last week. Her appetite was better too, with a whole boiled egg and slice of buttered toast eaten for breakfast. Mary put on a gramophone record while they both drank a cup of tea. The mid-March air felt cooler, but the day outside looked bright and promising.

'Do you know Mary, what I would love above anything, is to take a drive into the bush once more before I die.'

'Well we have two problems there, neither you nor I own a car, and we would have to drive a fair way to see the bush from here.'

'That's true, ah well...'

'But why don't we go into the backyard this morning? You own a bit of garden, and there are chairs on the veranda. I'll get you your warm dressing gown, and a blanket for your knees. Maybe Jean could bring us some lemonade.'

'Oh, a picnic, I should like that. But I'm not strong enough to walk to the yard.'

'I know. Just wait here a few minutes. I have an idea.'

'I'm not about to go anywhere without you.' Mary grinned at that and departed purposefully.

Returning after ten minutes, she pushed open the door with her ample behind. She appeared to be pulling something through the door, which Jane could not see from the bed. But soon enough Mary brought it close enough for her to realise what it was.

'Why it's Joseph's old wheelchair. I'd forgotten all about that. Where did you find it?'

'In that old shed, you have out back. I helped Jean to look for something yesterday and came across this. Jean's given it a good wipe over. It was covered in dust and cobwebs.'

The chair was a simple design. Two large wheels in front, two smaller ones at the back, and a woven rattan chairback and seat, with leather armrests. It had not been new when one of Joseph's sons brought it for him, and Joseph only used it once, his decline and death being so rapid. Because of that Jane had forgotten she ever had such a thing. But it was ideal for what Jane needed.

Mary helped her put on her dressing gown. With some shifting backward and forwards, she managed to get Jane into the chair. She placed her slippered feet on the footrests and they set off. Jane weighed so little that she was easy to push. Soon enough they headed for the back door, passing Jean who stood at the kitchen table with her hands covered in flour. Jane grinned at her and Jean almost dropped the egg she was about to crack. She could not ever remember her dour employer grinning in that way.

As soon as the door opened Jane's spirits soared. The sun was warm but not too hot, and it played through the delicate leaves of the jacaranda tree, the beautiful blue flowers long gone. Jane regretted that she would not live to see them return next spring. She remembered the first one she planted so many years ago, just before her husband died, but that one she never saw flower before she moved elsewhere. This tree had given her years of quiet pleasure although it was getting too big for the garden. No doubt the next owner would cut it down. The thought saddened her.

The roses were still in flower. Their scent drifted towards her as she wrinkled her nose to sniff more of their perfume. An occasional agapanthus still flowered in the borders, but others had died off, their leaves grown straggly. The small vegetable garden was a mess. It was a year or two since she had touched it and the weeds grew wild. Whenever she had the opportunity, she grew her own vegetables. Poverty and hunger always a mere step away in her mind if not in reality. But now in 1932, poverty was back, and there would be many glad of a garden such as hers, small though it might be.

Mary pushed her to the best spot on the veranda and put on the brake. 'Well isn't this nice? I sometimes sit here when you are taking a nap, but until today I never thought of bringing you outside.'

'I always loved gardening, so did my mother. She taught us all to care for plants from an early age. I taught my daughters too, did your mother teach you?'

'No, because we never had a garden. I remember a British nurse who asked her mother to send her packets of seeds to France, and she planted a garden outside her tent. We told her she was mad, but she said it brought her calm after the sights we saw.'

'I can understand that. When your mind's in turmoil, and you don't know what to do for the best, then doing some weeding or pruning or anything in the garden brings a peace it is hard to describe. I remember when John marched off towards Ballarat and the Eureka Stockade, I waited, my heart thumping painfully in my chest until I could see him no more. Then I turned and grabbed a trowel and dug until not a weed stood in my little plot. Even then, I just dug and dug until my hands bled, but by and by, I grew calmer.'

The back door opened. Mary thought that Jean was bringing the lemonade, but a woman in her seventies, followed by a younger woman, stepped through the screen door. The older one was plump with tightly permed, white hair, the younger one wiry, with mid-brown hair, under a jaunty straw hat. As they drew closer, Mary saw the same sharp chin and thin lips, but they were smiling, and their pale blue eyes had laughter lines around them. They were younger versions of Jane. The resemblance was uncanny.

'We never thought to find you out here Mother. Sophie told us how ill you were, so we borrowed a car to drive over from Sale. We're here for two nights but will stay at Nellie's, so we're not putting you out.' Both women stooped to place a light kiss on Jane's cheek. It was more of a peck than a kiss.

'This is my eldest daughter Hannah and Flo, her daughter. And this is Mary, my nurse.' Jane gestured towards Mary. 'And this contraption was Joseph's. Mary found it in the shed and so I am outside for the first time in a month. I feel better for it,' she said, with some defiance in her voice. She saw a quick look pass between them, a raising of the eyebrows as if to say, well she hasn't changed, even now when she's dying.

'Jane was just going to tell me about the Eureka Stockade and your grandfather's part in it, Flo, may I call you that?'

'What! Oh, by all means, call me Flo, but what on earth do you mean? Grandpa had no part in Eureka, did he Grandma?'

'Well he nearly did,' said Jane, grudgingly.

'You have never mentioned it before Mother,' said Hannah.

'Well, there's lots you don't know.'

'Come on then tell us.' Hannah and Flo brought some chairs to sit beside Jane, as Jean brought out a tray with glasses, lemonade and some small buns, warm from the oven.

Chapter 27

Creswick Creek November /December 1854

John believed once James Bentley was found guilty and sentenced to three years with hard labour, it might take the heat out of the situation. He thought it showed the government was beginning to sense that the diggers had a point to their grievances. But the opposite happened. Having let the diggers win once, the Governor came down even harder. Did the authorities not realise what they were unleashing by being so intransigent? The men were not just British but from all over Europe and America too, and the Americans had wrested power to themselves from Britain by bloody revolution. Did he think they would give in without a fight? Only one topic of discussion lay on the men's lips in early December.

The diggers at Creswick were not privy to everything that was going on at Ballarat. They heard of meetings being held with ten thousand miners present, of firebrand speakers, of resolutions and letters to the governor, but they also heard rumours of red coats arriving and sabres rattling. Jane received another letter from her mother via Isaac, this one even more desperate for her to return to Geelong than the last. The rumours there must be even worse than on the goldfields, Jane thought.

In the early days of her pregnancy, Jane felt well, too well according to Maggie. She did not suffer sickness or cravings, or anything that led her to change her daily routine. Only more tired than usual, she retired to bed early at night leaving John to chew the fat and drink a drop of grog with his mates. Once In bed, she cocooned herself against the outside world, and she tried to replicate this during the day. She closed her ears to the gossip and the whispers of the other wives queuing for bread and meat. Jane experienced an urgent need to secure a world of peace and calm for the scrap of life inside her to thrive. She could not explain it, and it would not last.

John wished to protect Jane from the worst news. He did not read her the latest newspaper reports. The diggers at Ballarat were on an inevitable collision course with the government. if rebellion came, which way would he jump? The newly formed Ballarat Reform League made demands the old Chartists had made ten years before in Britain. John knew that no Governor would accede to them and expect to keep his job. He could imagine the response in London to the granting of the vote to all men in Australia. If Australia why not the whole of the Empire? It was never going to happen without a fight, and was he willing to fight as the Americans fought eighty years before?

But how could things carry on the way they were? The hopeless management of the goldfields and abhorrent licensing system deserved to be kicked into the long grass, but at what price?

Back and forth his mind went over the arguments. Not least was his new responsibility to his family. Would he really leave Jane to go off to fight the troopers?

In his office in Melbourne Sir Charles Hotham studied the latest financial report with a mounting sense of despair. There appeared to be a two-million-pound shortfall again this year, and he had been charged in London with getting the State's finances under control. He needed money to pay the bills for the public works he had initiated. Melbourne was in great need of some fine buildings before it could claim to be a city.

His only money-making idea was to charge the Chinese gold seekers ten pounds to enter Victoria, but would it be enough? Only one thing would suffice, those damned diggers must be forced to pay their licences.

In the government camp at Ballarat, Gold Commissioner Rede was writing a letter to the Governor. How could he make him understand that collecting gold licences was a failure, and that a new way to make money must be found? Why not place a duty on the amount of gold exported instead? It would be fairer and more acceptable to everyone.

Policing of crime on the Goldfield also needed to be a higher priority, but there was no time. Instead, his troopers spent their days chasing diggers, who were mostly a decent, hard-working bunch. On the other hand, they were being stirred up by the seditious Henry Seekamp, writing in the Ballarat Times. Rede considered him to be a dangerous Chartist stirring up trouble for Her Majesty, here in Victoria. He cut out offending articles to enclose with his letter.

Rede knew the parlous state of the finances, but the Squatters paid next to nothing for their vast tracts of land. Why not impose a stamp duty on the sale of land and houses? He wrote down his long-considered ideas, praying that the Governor would see sense. But if not, he was prepared to do his duty and if that meant crushing the miners, so be it.

In the Star Hotel in Ballarat, members of the Reform League were meeting to discuss the results of their audience with the Governor, or rather lack of result. Sir Charles Hotham's hands were tied he told them. He was unable to overturn the guilty verdict handed down to those supposed to be the ringleaders of the destruction of the Eureka Hotel. A verdict agreed by jury was sacrosanct. Nor was he inclined to meddle with the new Constitution Bill. It did not grant universal suffrage to miners, nor representation, unless a digger be worth one or two thousand pounds by dint of ownership of freehold property. The only crumb he can throw at them was that a new commission had been appointed to look into the state of the goldfields, but the diggers will not be represented on the commission. Appointed members of the commission would only take evidence from the diggers. A crumb indeed!

The temperature towards the beginning of December started to heat the camp. There were days when the sun shone bright and showed the promise of the warmth to come. But there were also cool, wet days when thick red mud stuck to boots, and the washing hung limp and damp on the lines. Jane welcomed the ache and tingling of her swelling breasts and the darkening nipples, as a sure sign of pregnancy. But she could no longer ignore the gossip. It was too loud, resonating across the diggings like an echo reverberating around a valley. A shot-blast from an explosion sounding in one place then seconds later whizzing back at a different angle until it confused the senses. Her head rang with noise and worry.

She sat with Maggie, whose apron could not hide her growing belly or the voluptuousness of her bosoms. Her baby was due in the New Year, and she was slowing down, so Jane offered her help in many small ways, knowing it would be returned when her own time came. The air felt tense around them as they sipped at their tea, it crackled with rumour. The latest news was of whole regiments of soldiers arriving at Ballarat, of shots being exchanged in anger and confusion, of a digger's flag being raised and both men and women calling for action.

'How has it come to this?' Asked Maggie. 'I am frightened for our men. Jack doesn't say much, but I can tell he's troubled.'

'John too. I know nothing of wars or battles or soldiers. It's something that happens elsewhere, not in Australia and I'd rather it stayed that way. But we can't ignore how our men are treated. If it comes to a choice, will you be content if Jack takes up arms?' Maggie did not answer, her brow furrowed, and Jane noticed her teeth chewing on her lips in worry. Nor did Jane have an answer to that question.

Unbeknownst to either of them, a choice would be made sooner than they thought. The situation at Ballarat was becoming ever more grave. A meeting attended by thousands of miners to discuss the Governor's response to their demands, had started peacefully enough. But as the men listened to their delegates the mood changed to one of anger. No, they were not willing to wait for a commission to report, they had had enough of waiting. Be still the voices of peaceful reason; now is the time for action.

The miners were ready to be swayed by new voices, new leaders. Up stepped an Irishman, Peter Lalor, an Italian, Rafaello Carboni, a German, Friederich Vern. These men fed the fires of passion. Bonfires were lit. Diggers set fire to the hated licences and vowed that if the authorities tried to arrest a man without a licence, then two thousand miners

164

would free him. The journalists and the spies attending scribbled furiously.

A more judicious man than Rede may have let the situation cool before acting, but he thought things had gone too far. He was furious that the miners acted in open rebellion against the law and his authority. Strengthened by additional soldiers and seasoned officers, he sent the troopers out on a licence hunt, adding fuel to the flames lit the day before. Missiles were thrown at the troopers. Men refused to show their licences, rifle shots were fired on both sides, and the Riot Act read.

In mid-afternoon, Tom Kennedy arrived at Creswick from Ballarat, an hour or two before the miners packed up work for the day. They were already looking forward to a hot meal and a swig or more of grog, but instead, word went around that they needed to attend a meeting. Muddy faces emerged from the shafts after their partners called down to them below.

'Summat's up Mate. Best get thesen above.'

Jane watched the drift of men walking past her tent, John amongst them, all making for a spot of open ground on an incline well away from the original creek. She followed the diggers, as did some of the other wives, curious about what was to happen. Jane recognised Tom Kennedy as he stood on the hill waiting for the men to assemble and for voices to hush.

'Men,' he said. 'Your brother miners need your support. Ballarat fears attack from the redcoats at any moment. The men have had enough of harassment, of abuse and will nae put up with it any longer. We're burning our licences, refusing to pay another penny until they act to change the system. It's too late for talk.' On he went howling his anger at the authorities, whipping up the two thousand men and women who stood there. Jane felt the tension rising, but there was more to come.

A rider could be seen galloping towards them, his horse lathered in sweat. He jumped off and handed a letter to Tom and a man standing close by, who Jane did not know. This man opened the letter and came forward to read it.

'My name is George Black, and this letter has been sent to me and to all of you, good men of Creswick. The Ballarat diggers need you now, not tomorrow nor in a week. An attack on the diggers is certain and immediate. This letter I hold in the air is from Samuel Irwin of the Geelong Advertiser. He writes that the Joes were out in force this morning arresting miners who would not show their licences. The government means business, and the miners fear for their own safety. Shots have already been fired; men are hurt. Now is a time to stand together dear friends.'

Tom Kennedy stepped forward once more. 'Will we let them cut us down as they did at Peterloo Field?'

Jane wondered what he was talking about, as did some of the men nearby who glanced warily at each other. Others nodded and shouted out 'No!!

'The redcoats have a history of killing men, women and even children who stand up for their rights and act peaceably. They did it thirty-five years ago, and they will do it again. The time has come to stand up for your rights, and this time they will listen to our complaints and **our** weapons. But we need you **now**. Go back to your tents and collect your guns brave men, for we march tonight in support of our brothers. We will not let them down, will we? Remember the words of the great poet Shelley. They tried to silence the words. Let us now bring them forth and shout them aloud.

Rise like lions after slumber
In unvanquishable number
Shake your chains to earth like dew
Which in sleep had fallen on you
Ye are many – they are few.

Men **you** will not let them down, will **you**?'
'No' the men roared.

There was no longer a question to be considered. It had been answered. Jane recognised it, and though frightened for John, she was content that he would go. She hurried back to their tent to put together the things he would need for the journey, food, warm clothes, and a blanket. The nights were still cold. John came into the tent and gathered her into his arms.

'I saw you there in the crowd. Are you happy for me to go? Say if you want me to stay.'

'I think about what my father would have done, and he would go and so must you. I'm not saying I won't worry about you. But you have to stand up, don't you? I've seen how the Joes treat the miners. Just take care is all I ask. Come back in one piece.'

He kissed her and pushed a strand of hair away from her face, his fingers stroking her cheek as he did so. Then he turned and went to fetch his guns. Like all miners, he kept them in working order, cleaned and primed. Every evening before bed the air was shaken by gunshot as the diggers tested their weapons, firing into the sky. Jane shivered as she imagined a bullet piercing John's flesh. But she stood firm and calm as thirty minutes later the men gathered behind Tom Kennedy to march across country, through the Bush towards Ballarat.

Maggie and she held hands, their other hands waving madly at the column. A German band accompanied them as they began to march, and voices began to sing, men's voices.

'What's that they're singing?' Asked the women.

'It's the Marseillaise,' a Frenchwoman said.

'The working men of old Europe have gone to do battle with the redcoats.'

'Pray God it's not their Waterloo.'

The women stood until they could hear or see no sign of them. Night time was upon them. Jane and Maggie went back to Maggie's tent and got a fire going. It was going to be a long night. Neither could contemplate sleep.

Chapter 28

Melbourne March 1932

'What happened? Why was Grandpa not in Ballarat when the fighting started?'

'That night as we waited in the tent for news, the weather changed. What had been a perfectly calm evening turned into a storm, the likes of which we had never seen. Maggie and I ran out of the tent as we heard the thunderclaps and flashes. As did all the other women. True enough it sounded like a battle, and we imagined cannon being turned on our husbands and their bodies torn to pieces. Dogs were howling, the children screaming, and we were wailing in an agony of guilt and horror. We thought the end of our world was upon us. Then the rain started; huge, fat drops that quickly became torrents and we saw our mistake.

Our cries became laughter until we began to cry again. We imagined them out there in the storm with no shelter, either catching their death of cold, or drowning in a lonely gully. You know how fast flash floods can occur.'

'So, what did Grandpa do?'

'He tramped home, along with most of the others. They arrived well after midnight. There was no music to herald the men home, just the barking of those blasted dogs. Oh, those poor men they were sodden, covered in mud, freezing cold and plain miserable when they got back. They said they'd go on the next day, once they had slept and had some warm food.'

'But they didn't go back.'

'He did, they did. There was no band marching with them this time. The sun stood high in the sky as we women watched them march again, this time in silence. I supposed the storm was God's doing to keep your grandfather out of harm's way. But there he was again, marching towards a fight, possibly death, and I felt frightened.; a sense of dread creeping over me, making me cold despite the sun. I didn't know what to do to keep myself from going mad, so as I was telling Mary yesterday, I went to my little vegetable patch and dug as though John's life depended upon it.'

'But he wasn't at Eureka.'

'No that's true, thank God. Towards late afternoon most of them came back. You could see from their expressions they were annoyed, even downright angry. John told me they were nearing Ballarat when they met some diggers returning to Creswick in high dudgeon. There had been no welcome, no provision for them when they reached Ballarat that morning, despite battling through the storm. But worse, those in charge at the stockade, Peter Lalor for one, were high-handed, demanding that newcomers give up their weapons and horses for the cause. Then came the clincher, the password for their enterprise.'

'Vinegar Hill, the Irish call to arms!'

'Oh, so you learnt that in school did you Flo? Your grandfather could never support an Irish Rebellion. Most of the men turned back there and then, refusing to get mixed up with a bunch of Irish discontents.

'The few men who made it to Ballarat witnessed the attack on the stockade, telling us all about it when they got back. We were shocked, angry, horrified.' Jane's voice tailed off as she remembered the raw emotion of that day when the news came. If she closed her eyes, she could still picture the scene they described. Woken by a bugle in the predawn on a Sunday morning, they told of the confusion, the diggers shouting as they realised that the redcoats meant to attack. The first shot from the stockade, a soldier killed, more bugles, a volley of shots as the soldiers respond, the battle, the blood, the smoke, the screams, the slaughter, the rampage of revenging soldiers and then fire as they torched the digger's tents, not caring if women and children were inside.

'The men at Eureka went too far I suppose, but so did the soldiers. They tried to blame it on foreigners, but we knew the truth. There's only so far you can push men before something snaps, and the government held a great share of the blame. The people of Melbourne soon recognised that, and the diggers had the support of Fawkner.'

'Did you ever meet Fawkner?.'

'No, but your great grandpa drank in his pub in Launceston. He is part of the reason we moved to Melbourne.'

'The founder of Melbourne and my great grandpa actually drank with him. Why did you never tell us these stories before?'

Jane shrugged. It wasn't something you did, talking about the past. You were too busy struggling to make a living and bringing up a family. She never remembered her parents talking about their life in England or about their families for that matter. The campfire stories were about things that happened after their marriage, or sometimes her mother might tell legends of old Ireland. A sudden realisation that she did not even know the names of her grandparents, or where they lived. She sighed deeply.

Mary stepped in. She guessed Jane was tiring and told her daughter that she needed to rest.

'Before we go, Mary, do you think Mother is up to going for a drive tomorrow? I would like to visit my brother's grave in the Yarra Valley. It's not a long journey. Maybe you could both come.'

Jane's tired eyes lit up. Before Mary said a word, Jane answered for her. 'Yes. I don't care if I'm not up to it. I want to go, and I don't care if it kills me.' Her tone was imperious, and Mary knew better than to refuse the invitation, Jane would insist upon going.

The following morning dawned as bright as the day before. At around eleven o'clock, Hannah and Flo drew up outside the bungalow in a dusty, soft topped, black Ford A car. Flo stepped out of the driver's seat and helped Mary to get her grandmother out of the wheelchair and settled in the back. She was so light that Flo felt she could have picked her up herself. Mary placed a rug over Jane's legs. There was a heady smell of perfume in the car from the lilies and roses which Hannah held in her lap.

'It's a shame there's no room for the wheelchair. Grandma, do you mind sitting in the car while we lay flowers on Uncle Joseph's grave?'

'No, I'm just pleased to go for a drive.'

The car swung right out of Guest Street heading towards Lilydale. Flo was a competent driver, and Jane looked out of the window greedily taking in the sights that only a day or two ago she had never thought to see again. So many memories, more than many people's lifetime of memories, she thought with satisfaction. She pictured the route the first time she drove it, sat in the back of a wagon with her brothers and sisters. Not exactly the same route, the roads didn't exist, only a dusty track. The family must have been heading towards Plenty, northeast of here. It would have been springtime because she remembered the track lined by feathery wattles strung with golden jewel-like flowers. Slightly shocked, she realised that it was one of her earliest memories of the beauty and colour with which God had blessed the land.

She had loved Plenty. Her brothers taught her to fish in the river which was overhung by yellow gums. She explored every inch of the gorge on foot, and later on horseback. As children, they roamed free and barefoot, learning about the bush, the animals, the snakes and the insects. Jacob taught her to shoot. She remembered the first time she shot a wallaby and gave it to her mother, as proud as a rat with a gold tooth, as Charlie would say. She must have been around eleven. There were still aboriginals roaming the bush, dressed sometimes in the skins of opossums, and at other times naked as the day they were born. As a child, it didn't seem strange, she accepted them as she accepted the kangaroos and bandicoots living side by side with sheep and bullocks.

Flo broke into her reverie. 'So, Grandma, what did John Pascoe Fawkner do for the diggers?'

Jane wondered what on earth she was talking about before remembering where they had broken off the day before. 'Fawkner was a good man, a man of the ordinary people. His battle through early life was as tough as any. But, my father used to say, whatever life threw at Fawkner, he came back better and stronger each time. So, he used the opportunity the government had created to sort out the gold licensing once and for all. He was on the gold commission, and he brought it to

Ballarat and invited the diggers to take part. The Governor refused the diggers' representation; it was Fawkner who granted it.

He was against the squatters too, sixty million acres of land they held, paying next to nothing for the privilege. It was they who held power in the council. Ordinary folk could see it was unfair, but nothing had changed. Those men at Eureka they won the argument. One small battle and the government caved in. Everything changed for the better over the next few months and years.'

Jane sank back into the cushioned seats, while Flo chatted with her mother leaving Jane to her memories.

They turned north onto unsealed roads after reaching Lilydale. Mary had never travelled this far east from Melbourne before. She was struck by the beauty of the farmland they were passing through. It was a yellow-green landscape, lush, despite being March and framed by blue-tinged mountains beyond. Sleek black cows grazed the fields, and tall yellow grasses waved in the soft breeze as they drove along the dusty road.

'There were vineyards further up,' Jane said, noticing Mary's interest. 'My son had them taken up because he couldn't sell the wine, but his wine was so famous, it won awards in Paris.'

'I can imagine it. I don't think I have seen such fertile ground since leaving Europe. It reminds me of Normandy. But you don't get vines in Normandy; it's too cold.'

'He used to send his milk to Melbourne every day by train, for the children, so they wouldn't get sick. He was the first around here to refrigerate it, you know.'

Jane was proud of Joseph. Hannah overhearing the conversation said, 'We all know my twin was your favourite Mother. But yes, Joseph was a big man, in many ways. We adored him and depended on him, my other brothers in particular. They bound their lives to his rising star, and it was a great loss and a shock when his star crashed into the ground.'

The car came to a stop outside a graveyard to the west of a small settlement of neat houses and farmland. Mary helped Hannah get out of the car.

'Old age is catching up with me too Mother.' She stretched out her legs and stumbled slightly. Flo walked to the left of the car and took hold of her mother's arm. Mary took the flowers from Hannah and followed them up the path. She looked back at Jane watching them from the car, a wistful expression on her face and regretted the lack of her wheelchair.

Hannah and Flo stopped at a space towards the far-right corner of the graveyard. Hannah turned towards her daughter, and Mary saw that she looked stricken.

'There's no headstone. It's been almost three years since he died and there's no headstone.'

'He died bankrupt Mother. There was no money for one.'

'She could have paid, your Grandma Jane, she should have paid for it. I am sure she's got money.'

'Perhaps no one dared asked her for it.'

Hannah sniffed. Mary saw tears in her eyes. 'Where do I put these flowers? I can't just leave them on the bare grass.'

Flo pointed to a grave a few feet away. It was difficult to miss. A large plinth of Victorian bluestone supported a tall column, on which stood a graceful figure in marble; her eyes turned towards heaven. It was quite something Mary thought; ostentatious perhaps, certainly a statement of wealth and importance and hopefully of love.

They walked the few steps towards it, and Mary read the inscription.

'In loving memory of Isabella – dearly loved wife of Joseph Timmins who died 15th February 1906 aged 34 years.'

At the foot were two concrete slabs, the right one was inscribed 'Isabella Timmins' but the left one was blank. Obviously Joseph had intended that one for himself. A man who wanted to lie next to her for eternity must have loved her, and yet he was buried several feet away, in an unmarked grave. Mary felt saddened, and she thought back to the thousands of young men buried in an unknown field in France or Belgium. Her eyes began to fill. Would it ever cease to hit her, this raw emotion for lives cut down before they had scarcely begun?

Hannah sat on the blank concrete slab. There was room enough for three women, so Flo and Mary joined her.

'What were they like as parents, your mother and father?' asked Mary of Hannah.

Hannah looked at her, assessing her. She did not appear offended by the question.

'Hard as nails, both of them. They suited each other. I think it was difficult to be anything else on the goldfields because it was a tough life. There was no time for sentiment. I should have been tough myself, given the way we were brought up and being the oldest girl, but I did not want that life for my children. I married early into a more comfortable household.

People were afraid of my parents. I've seen grown Aussie men cower in front of mother, and you know how men treat women in this country. They never dared treat my mother with anything other than respect. Has she told you of her time in Broken Hill? No? Well, get her to talk about it. A widow, with several daughters coming up to marriageable age, running a hotel in Broken Hill. Who dares put herself in that position? Only someone as fearless as my mother.

Well, I came to place those flowers on Joseph's grave, but I'll leave them here, where he should have been buried, next to his second wife. Such a shame she died so young.'

Hannah was helped up by Flo. Taking the flowers from Mary she bowed slightly in front of the grave and said: 'Rest in peace Joseph my dear, we miss you.' Taking two roses out of the bouquet, she placed one on Isabella's grave and the rest on the blank slab. She shook her head in displeasure and walked back to the unmarked grave, letting the last rose drop to the ground, before turning back to the car.

Jane watched their progress. She did not need to get out of the car to remember the day they buried her son. It should have been a funeral worthy of him, but instead just close family came. Two of his children were in England; one was dead, so only two of his sons were present. Now Joseph and his son were buried there in unmarked graves, next to that ridiculous monument for Bella. It brought back sad memories of her father's pauper funeral. Jane paid for Joseph's coffin and offered to pay to have him buried next to Bella. His last wife stamped her foot and said no. Jane refused to buy a headstone which even mentioned that wife, and the 'grieving' widow refused to have one which did not.

Jane looked so frail and old and out of place in the large car. It enveloped her, making her appear insubstantial, something her mother had never been. Hannah lost the anger she felt over the lack of a headstone. It wasn't her mother's fault. She was too old to be blamed. Joseph's children were left without two pennies to rub together, and now with this depression, they most likely had less.

She imagined their shame, having been brought up in such luxury. No doubt their social connections abandoned them. People don't want to rub shoulders with the recently poor. It reminds them of their own vulnerability. I am pleased that I never was so well off that I ever feared losing my money, and comfortable enough not to worry about the lack of it.

Flo took the wheel when everyone was settled, turning right towards Healesville. A few miles down the road they had to stop the car before it collided with the local hunt riding along the road towards them. Huntsmen and women trotted by, giving the car scarcely a look, masters of their world.

'They're riding towards Yering,' Jane cried, in a strangled voice. 'I know these people. There's the Towts, the Gibsons and the .... oh, I forget the name. I sat at a dinner table with them, married my grandson off to one of their daughters, and now we are nothing.'

'Mother don't upset yourself. They won't recognise the car, and it's at least ten years since you met any of them socially.' How odd that her suspicions had borne such proof. Hannah had seen a jolt of recognition in one of the women's eyes and then a deliberate turn of the head. Hannah changed the subject.

'I thought we would go to the hotel in Healesville for lunch. I phoned ahead, and they have a wheelchair available.'

Jane was somewhat mollified as the owner of the Grand Hotel greeted her personally as a revered client from the past. He helped her from the car and pushed her in an aged bath chair into the lobby, saying how lovely it was to see her again. He told her he missed her son, Joseph and his family, without referring to how ill and drawn she looked. Mary took over from him, after asking for directions to the ladies' cloakroom. With Flo's help, they managed to make Jane more comfortable.

Later Jane pecked at her lunch of grilled trout. She felt exhausted, dispirited, her appetite deserting her. The pleasant memories she derived from the early part of the journey had been ruined by the sight of the hunt.

Twenty years ago, she loved to see the hunt leave Chateau Yering; her grandson and his wife were the most charming of hosts. She sometimes helped to organise luncheons awaiting the riders on their return. Jane revelled secretly in the delight of her family mixing with the great and good of Victorian Society. How proud her parents would have been to know that their sacrifices paid off. But then it turned to dust. A fortune is so easily lost in Australia; all it takes is drought or a bushfire killing an entire flock of sheep. Combining that with the Great War and the death of a generation of young men, depressing the economy further, ruin is no longer over the horizon, but staring you hard in the face.

Joseph was a risk taker. He built his fortune on hard work and taking on contracts that no one else wanted. It always paid off. For forty years his luck ran true but ten years ago, it finally ran out, and he lost everything. She wished she had not lived to see it; wished that she had not seen him broken and die a pauper, just like her father. Oh God, please take me soon, I can't bear this any longer.

Mary watched as Jane moved the food around her plate and wondered what she was thinking. Whatever it was it was making her unhappy. Hannah noticed it too.

'Mother, what's the matter?'

'I've lived too long and shouldn't be here. Please take me home.'

Hannah summoned the waitress to ask for the bill. A few minutes later saw them back in the car heading towards Melbourne. Jane fell at once into an exhausted sleep, her gentle snores no louder than those of a snuffling infant.

'Oh dear, this trip wasn't a good idea,' Hannah said, turning her face towards her mother in the back. 'She was always so indomitable, but now she looks a scared, lonely old woman. I'm glad she has got you to look after her Mary. She has taken a real shine to you. It's strange, her children always admired her, but she never let us come close somehow.'

'Jane is proud of you all; I know that. Your mother may not tell you, but her family means everything to her. I have never met anyone like her quite frankly. There's a steeliness about her which is difficult to penetrate, and I believe she talks to me because I am **not** family, but she doesn't tell me everything. The stories are a way of passing the time but they're intriguing. She has lived a remarkable life.'

'My children are afraid of her, which is very sad,' said Flo.

'How did your brother make his money?' asked Mary changing the subject.

'Joesph? He started out as a navvy on the railways and quickly learnt the business. His bosses, the Millar brothers, saw something in him and promoted him to manage the horse teams and then building stretches of line. He had a stroke of luck in the Northern Territories. A contract to supply rice for the Chinese labourers came up, and no one bid for it apart from Joseph. He won it, banked the profit and set out to make his fortune.

In the mid-nineties, he rode all the way over to Western Australia in a wagon. It was before they had the railway across the desert. He teamed up with another man, Henry Smith, and they bid for contracts, never looking back. Soon he was investing his profits in land and stock. At one time, he sold over 100,000 sheep, a record for anywhere in Australia at the time. Three thousand men worked for him, building bridges, roads, tram systems, you name it. Joseph was well respected as an employer too. The men knew he had been one of them and he never asked them to do anything he hadn't done himself.' The pride she had for her twin shone on her gentle face.

'He kept a string of racehorses too, but I doubt he made money from that. One he bought for 5000 guineas, only to see it break down soon after, much to my husband's disgust. He had rather a large bet on it.

I have never seen anyone with so much energy as Joseph, so much 'joie de vivre' as they say in France. He was generous to a fault and caring. Where he got that from I don't know, certainly not from my mother,' Hannah smiled wryly. 'He looked after the family, gave them jobs on his sheep stations, like Jack, Sophie's younger son, but when it all went wrong, they suffered too.'

'Don't mention Jack to Aunt Sophie, will you Mary. He shot himself accidentally on one of Joseph's stations,' Flo interrupted.

'Of course not, how sad. I often think she looks unhappy,' Mary replied.

'Yes, she's not been fortunate in life. Poor love.'

'Do continue with your story about Joseph, Hannah. What happened to the money?'

'The war happened. The country bankrupted itself and Joseph was one of its casualties. His luck ran out, like his energy. Suddenly he was an old man, an old, sad, diminished man. It was terrible to see him, and now my mother looks the same.' Hannah paused to look back at her mother. 'How much longer do you think she has?'

Mary looked at Jane, who was still fast asleep. 'It is difficult to predict. One day her heart will just stop, maybe in a week or two, but possibly a month, no more. She will get progressively weaker until then.'

Jane woke as they pulled up in front of her bungalow. Mary brought the wheelchair to the car and helped her to get in. She looked dazed; her face creased where she had lain against the seat.

'I'm going to get her straight to bed,' said Mary.

'I'll make us a quick brew,' said Flo. 'I am going to drive Mother back home before it starts to get dark.'

Twenty minutes later Hannah and Flo were taking their leave. Jane was sitting propped up against the pillows, her eyes, dark hollows against the unnatural white of her skin, peering up at them.

'Thank you, Flo, for driving me out to Yarra Glen,' she whispered.

178

'Oh Grandma, I am sorry if you didn't enjoy the trip.'

'I did enjoy it. It brought back many happy memories and some sad ones.' Jane paused to catch a breath. 'Seeing the hunt, I suddenly understood how life goes on once you're dead and forgotten, and that made me maudlin for a time. I will not see you again in this life, but thank you for bringing your mother to visit me. Look after her for me.'

Both Hannah and Flo leant down in turn to kiss Jane. They were almost overcome when she stroked their cheeks gently, telling each of them how proud she was of her family. Arm in arm they turned to make their way to the bedroom door, wiping their eyes with their other hand, then waved goodbye to Jane.

'I'll see them out,' said Mary.

As they stood by the car, Hannah turned to Mary and said: 'She seems softer, calmer less acerbic.'

'She is coming to turns with death. Jane has willed herself to be strong all her life, never giving in and overcoming every hardship, but she doesn't need to do that now. She can afford to show her love at last.'

'Thank God she has you with her Mary.' Hannah kissed her cheek, rather than shake her hand. The two women got in the car, waving as they drove away.

The outing had exhausted Jane, and by the time Mary came back into her room, she was fast asleep again. The following morning was damp and dreary, and Jane's spirits reflected the change in the weather.

'Why don't I tell you another of my stories,' said Mary. 'The diggers I knew were every bit as adventurous, hard-working, and ready for a fight as yours, but mine wore pea green khaki.

Chapter 29

Eastern Mediterranean 1915

How on earth had they got into this mess? They said it was Churchill's decision to fight the Turks at Gallipoli, but the scale of the catastrophe was evident to all on board this ship. Mary wished she could personally drag this Churchill, whoever he was, around the wards to see the state of the men.

The medics were overwhelmed by the number of casualties, not enough nurses for sure and not enough doctors. Mary volunteered to go overseas along with two thousand other nurses, but they were stretched to their limits and beyond. When the men arrived on board they were still filthy, a dressing over a wound if they were lucky, often dehydrated and raving in pain. These men, her countrymen, her brave and honest diggers let down by the foolhardiness of politicians and generals. Whoever said the Turks couldn't fight? The evidence to the contrary lay all around her.

She remembered the first voyage to collect casualties. How green she had been, not from the seasickness which they suffered, but from ignorance. How can you envisage a battlefield; the explosions; the chaos; the fear; the mutilated dead and the dying? Those same young men, itching for the fight back in Egypt; strapping tanned lads, taller and fitter than their European cousins. They broke just as easily; bullets, shrapnel, dysentery, typhoid, lice were each indiscriminating.

Oh, she wept when she managed to snatch a few minutes for a smoke. Silently her tears dropped into the inky sea; she had learnt to weep without noise, conscious of the need to appear strong and calm for the men. She may own a certificate to prove she was a nurse but these past few months taught her how unprepared she was. Her three years training in a Melbourne hospital did not prepare her for the carnage, but she and her fellow sisters learned all too quickly how to nurse in the army.

Had she known the conditions and the kind of wounds she would see, might she have changed her mind about volunteering? No, no and no again. Although she felt inexperienced, they needed dozens more like her; the men needed them.

As overworked as they were on the hospital ship, the conditions were even worse at Lemnos during the early summer months. Someone decided that it was in the men's interest to take them to a hospital nearer than Cairo. But there was a deal of difference between the decision and its implementation. She remembered the men stretchered down from the ship to the beach in scorching sun, left to lie there unsheltered; no beds prepared, scarcely anything to drink, hardly enough dressings. The only difference between their lying on the beach in Lemnos rather than Turkish beaches was that they were out of range of the guns, but they could hear them, see the smoke, imagine what their mates were going through.

How many have died from lack of planning, she wondered? It was as plain as the nose on her face that no one dreamt of the number of casualties. On and on the disaster rolled like a never-ending nightmare.

She always knew when they approached the battleground, even if she could not see it. The smell of decomposing bodies littering the rocky outcrops told its own story. On board, the soldiers spoke of the flies which feasted on the corpses and then plagued the living in a black and angry cloud. She thanked God that she did not have to see the sea red with blood after the failure of the landings at Suvla Bay in August. It was a small mercy that the evacuations were done at night time.

They were approaching Christmas, and the campaign began in April. A few weeks before, orders arrived that medical staff should adopt a hearty tone to raise the morale of the men; orders she received with both scorn and revulsion. Did that mean the men would be facing this battle next year as well? Mary prayed that someone would see sense soon. Everyone was exhausted. What had they achieved, other than sacrificing thousands upon thousands of soldiers, the cream of the empire?

In this last week of November, the weather was icy cold. Standing on the deck, she wrapped her thick grey woollen cloak around her against the bitter wind. She prayed the men had plenty of warm clothing and not just their summer uniforms. It rained non-stop the day before. She dreaded the state the men might be in when they picked them up from the beach, next to the one they called Anzac Cove. Whether it had a Turkish name or not, she did not care. She had seen it in the dusk of a summer's evening; hardly a cove, more a curve in the sand against a narrow shore of steep sandstone cliffs. She supposed it a mistake. No one could have planned to land there. Around the headland lay a wider strip of land, where the small field hospital tried to cope with the injured and sick, and it was there the ship was headed to evacuate the men.

It was worse than she imagined. The rain further south was a blizzard in the Dardanelles. Snow covering the pockmarked Turkish hills, glinted white in the clear starlit sky. Mary had never seen snow. Once upon a time she may have imagined the beauty and purity of it. No more.

This night's casualties were not wounded by bullets or shrapnel, but suffering frostbite and exposure. Their faces were white with cold, their bodies shivering uncontrollably, fingertips red and blistering if they were lucky, blue and frozen if not. Another thing Mary had not trained for. Instinctively she rushed around the men offering dry clothes, wrapping them in blankets, ordering cups and jugs of warm water from the orderlies to soak their damaged fingers and toes. She did not know what to do with frozen noses and ears but told the men to flannel them with warm water. An overworked doctor confirmed she was doing the right thing and told her what to look out for. Any signs of gangrene and she must call him. It proved a long night.

Mary was angry. She hid it from her patients, but she was furious, would have strung up Mr Churchill from the yardarm, whatever that was. She did not know he had resigned from the government two weeks before, nor would she have cared. Someone should pay for this wretched mess.

Her patients were as grateful as ever for her ministrations, their gratitude enough to make her weep again, but she smiled, kept smiling, offering words of encouragement even when she saw those signs of gangrene. Inwardly she cursed and swore and smoked some more whenever she grabbed that precious minute.

Mary was not alone. The other nurses and orderlies were a good bunch of people. Back in Cairo on a rare night off the nurses had a game of cards in one of their rooms. Occasionally a bottle of rum appeared, which a kind sailor purloined for them. The nurses were treated like royalty by the troops, but were guarded by a fierce matron who demanded unquestioning obedience to her rules.

'I might as well be a bloody nun,' the nurses would say.

'You are a bloody nun, didn't you know?' The laughing response coming from the others.

The best Christmas present that any of the medics could wish for came in the command to withdraw all the troops from Gallipoli. Kitchener had travelled there to see for himself what the generals in command had been writing about for weeks. Mary got down on her knees to give thanks when she heard the news after another dreadful trip to Anzac Cove. The hospital was preparing for major casualties from the evacuation, but for once God heard their prayers. Under cover of darkness, the diggers left the bones of their fallen comrades. The Turks woke to find the ridges, trenches and the beaches deserted. They had won this battle.

Matron told the nurses they would stay in Egypt until the last of the men had left the hospital. They would most likely be redeployed to the Western Front. With more time available, the sisters turned their hands to decorating the wards for as good a Christmas as they could give the men. They ransacked the bazaars for anything bright and glittery to turn into garlands or angels. They cut out coloured paper stars, cooked up sweets and biscuits for the men's stockings, anything to bring joy back into the lives of the men, who lay watching their attempts with no little pride.

There was one soldier who Mary became particularly fond of. He heralded from her state, Victoria. But he looked nothing like the muscular, fair-haired, bronzed Aussie men she was used to. His build was slighter and his hair blacker and wiry, his skin olive rather than tanned. His dark almond-shaped eyes were set in a face rounder than those of the other soldiers. He told her his name was Bert Farrell, an ordinary name for someone who looked so exotic. He was recovering from a bullet wound to his upper thigh, but it was a clean wound and would not trouble him too much in the future. She noticed that the other men did not invite him to join in. They did not isolate him for a reason known only to them; they just did not include him in their banter. Mary knew how the abbos were treated in Australia and their attitude verged on that, but without the blatant contempt.

'They're just not used to me,' he said, when she asked. 'My platoon was like them until I proved myself every bit as good as them at soldiering. I can shoot truer than most, and that's what counts'.

'And is that your real name?'

'Bert is real, short for Albert. Farrell's my mother's name. My father was Ah Wing, a Chinaman.' He looked for any reaction on her face and saw none. 'I've got three brothers, but I'm the one who takes after my father the most. I thought that by changing my name I might have more luck getting a job and a wife.' He smiled winningly at her, and she laughed. Over the next days, she always stopped for a chat with him until the other soldiers began to rib her.

'What do you want with a Chinaman Sister, aren't we good enough for you?'

'He's an Aussie born and bred, and underneath the skin, he's got blood and bones, same as you. I've dressed his wounds, and you're all alike. He talks like you and shits like you. And what's more, he's fighting the same war, and it's about time you bloody ....'

'Hey Sister, I'm sorry.' The soldier, whose name was Daniel, put his arms up in defeat. It broke the ice because the men began to include Bert. They admired Sister Mary Finnegan and did not want to be on the wrong side of her. Christ, she could swear like a trooper, good for her!

184

After that incident, Mary made sure she spent time with all the men in the ward over Christmas, which was as merry as any she could remember. A determined jollity descended on the day itself. The nurses focussing on placing a smile on their diggers' faces as they unpacked their stockings filled with sweets and fruit, bringing back memories of their beloved homes and families. A cobbled together choir sang carols and ended with a rousing Waltzing Matilda for good measure. Somehow enough chickens were found to provide a feast for dinner, and when a Christmas cake arrived filled with dates and almonds and candied fruit, the men declared it the best ever.

Later that evening Mary stood on the covered veranda lighting her cigarette. She was joined by Bert, who was hobbling on his injured leg. She offered him a smoke which he took with gratitude.

'Best not let Matron see us,' she said, drawing into the shadows, and cupping her hand around the lighted end. The night was cool, and Bert looked up towards the stars.

'What I wouldn't give to see the Southern Cross,' he said. 'This sky is not my sky.'

Mary asked him what he did for a living, and he told her he worked on a sheep station on the border of Victoria and New South Wales.

'Thanks for sticking up for me with the others. You didn't have to do that. I can take care of myself.' He took a drag on his cigarette, exhaling slowly, enjoying his first smoke in a long while.

'I'd do it for anyone. I can't abide anyone picking on others, must be the Irish in me.'

'You too! I had an Irish grandfather. He was a convict sent over for stealing a penny tart. Eleven years old he was.'

'My grandmother stole a sheep.' She turned towards him laughing. 'What a way to introduce ourselves. You don't get many Aussies admitting to convicts in the family, but it probably goes for half of us in that ward. Transported for a penny tart, that sounds real harsh.'

'And only twelve years old, but I don't know much more than that. Never met the bloke, never met my grandma either, she was Scottish.'

'I sometimes wonder why we got involved in the old country's war, when they treated our grandparents so badly. Half the people wouldn't have got transported if they weren't hungry and desperate.'

'Oh, I don't know about that. My mother had a shocker of a childhood. Some of those old lags were evil, born bad, died bad I reckon.'

Mary looked at her watch. 'I'd love to hear how your mother met your father. Right now, Matron will require my guts for garters if I don't get back. You shouldn't be standing for too long on that leg. Best get back to bed Bert.' He stubbed out his ciggy, saving the rest for later and returned to the ward.

Over the following few days, Bert and Mary struck up an easy friendship, but with little time to talk. Patients and nursing staff were to be evacuated to Europe by ship in the first week of January 1916. Mary was kept busy assisting in packing up the hospital and supplies. The more able-bodied men helped the nurses and orderlies fill cartons with bandages and dressings. Bedding was washed and packed for the voyage. By the time the order came to board ship everything was ready.

Despite the danger of submarines, life became more casual at sea. The majority of patients were on the mend or out of immediate danger. Matron kept to her bed, terribly seasick, and so Bert and Mary found lots of opportunities to talk, as she ambled slowly around the deck with him, helping to build up strength in his damaged leg.

'My mother was brought up in Ballarat,' he told her. 'Granny abandoned my grandfather to go off with another man, one Sammy Muldoon, another convict. He was a right bastard of a man, excuse my language, Sister Finnegan. Mother and her elder sister, Alice, more or less dragged themselves up, while Granny and Sammy drank themselves stupid. When Sammy drank, he became very handy with his fists. He was often in trouble with the police.

The two girls were neglected. Ma said they often went without food, although Alice stole food to share with her sister. But something happened to Alice when she reached eight. Ma didn't know what, but she said she changed, got moody, slovenly, unhappier if that were possible, given their way of life. When Alice got to twelve she began staying out at night, and the police picked her up for vagrancy, eventually sending her to reform school. But she didn't stay there. In and out of prison she was, up before the magistrate again and again. Ma said Alice stopped caring about herself, didn't care about washing, or what she wore, or even eating. Her eyes were hollow and empty, and it frightened Ma. She told me she saw herself in those eyes. By that time, it was all Ma could do to keep herself alive as her mother was a drunken tart, incapable of looking after anyone.' Mary saw how upset Bert was becoming and laid a hand on his shoulder.

'Don't tell me any more, shush Bert.'

'I don't think Ma told us everything that happened by any means, but it's my guess that Alice became a prostitute like her mother. Ma felt she had to escape or end up the same way. Isn't that a shocker knowing your granny and your auntie were on the game? You must wonder what kind of man I am.'

'No. I know you're a bonzer bloke, and I'm real glad that your mother made good. All credit to her, I say.'

'I've told no one else this. It's not the sort of thing you tell your mates. But I have this feeling I won't come through this war and would like someone to remember me. Will you remember this story and think about me from time to time?'

His dark eyes turned towards Mary, and she saw sadness, resignation. Nodding slowly, she said, 'I promise I will,' her voice grave and low. It was of no use telling him to stop thinking like that. It would demean the confidence he had entrusted her with. She felt privileged that he had shared his feelings with her. In another time, another place maybe they would want to carry on their friendship. It may have become the love a sister has for a brother, but it was unlikely they would meet each other after this week.

Before the ship reached Marseilles, where they were due to disembark, he told her the rest of the story.

'Few people know it, but there were ten thousand Chinese miners at Ballarat in the 1850s and 60s. Most of them, including my father, walked all the way from Adelaide and what they found there, upset them. The Chinese, a quarter of all the miners, but they were shunned by the Europeans. They were forced to live in camps set apart from the other men. Back in the hospital, I knew what my father must have experienced, that dislike of people with a different face, different culture. Given a choice, they would have lived amongst the Europeans.

Most of the Chinese wanted to return home once they had made enough money. Even those that died in Ballarat wanted their remains to be sent home to lie with their ancestors. It was an obligation. My mother obeyed Father's wishes to send his remains back to China to his honoured first wife when he died. I don't remember that. She told me much later of her pain. But she figured that she had the best of my father when he was alive. It was only fair his first wife had his body.'

'How old were you when he died?'

'Just a kiddie. I don't remember him at all. But I grew up with the Chinese; I felt Chinese, even spoke the lingo. I am more used to Chinese Opera than I am to Music Hall. Gosh, it was so more colourful than the rest of Ballarat. I can picture those singers now wearing costumes patterned with gold, red and yellow and my eyes stood out on stalks, seeing the beauty of it.

Best of all was the Chinese circus. You should go to a Chinese circus if you can. What those acrobats can do is something else. I couldn't believe how they could spin plates while balancing on the head of another man. They looked so sure about it, no nerves at all. Have you ever watched the lion and dragon dances? They held me spellbound. It's a different world. And I miss it.'

'It sounds wonderful. Perhaps I'll get the chance someday. But you haven't told me how your mother married your father.'

'There was no alternative but to go live with the Chinese. Her family's reputation was so bad that no decent European would marry her. Her mother died and then her stepfather a year or two later, and her only means of support disappeared. Mother told me that she walked to the Chinese Camp and offered herself in marriage to anyone who would have her, a seventeen-year-old girl; shoeless, mucky, as thin

as a rake who hadn't eaten in days. That took courage, don't you think?'
Mary nodded.

'My father was thirty-three when he took her, and it was a good marriage. He looked after her better than she was ever treated by Sammy Muldoon. And years later she married another Chinaman and lived out her days in Ballarat with him. Nowadays you would hardly know there were so many Chinese living there. They rubbed them out along with their buildings. Even the Chinese cemetery has been emptied and most of the bodies sent back to China.

I am proud of my father and proud of her too. They did the best they could do with the life they were dealt. I would like someone to remember my mother in their prayers once I'm gone. You're a Catholic aren't you Sister?'

'I am Bert, and my faith is important to me. I'll gladly remember her in my prayers. What was her name?'

'She was baptised in Geelong as Jeannie Farrell, in 1854, I think.'

'I will remember you both. How about I write to you, care of your Company? You can reply and tell me how you are doing.'

'Thanks heaps, Sister Finnegan. It will sure be good to have someone to write to. I've lost touch with my brothers. They may be mixed up in this war for all I know. But they're older so I hope they're not.'

Chapter 30

Melbourne April 1932

'What happened to him?' Jane lay in bed listening to Mary's story, her mind full of images of the Chinese communities on the goldfields.

'He died at the Somme in the early days of July that same year. They wrote to me, but I sort of knew. Like your sister did about Jacob, a shiver when it's blinding hot, that kind of thing. Not that I had much time to take notice. Hundreds of men arrived daily with injuries so severe my faith in God was put to the test, but it wasn't God's fault, I realised. Men make wars.'

'The Somme was where poor Bruce was shot, and Stanley got shrapnel in his head. What dreadful weeks they were.' Jane sighed remembering the anxious wait for news. She was visiting Joseph in Adelaide where he based himself while building their tram system. They waited for news, fearing the worst. Joseph paced the floor, newspaper held aloft and his hand slapping the article in the Advertiser. Jane only saw the headline word 'Carnage' and it chilled her bones. She had no interest in the heroism of the men on Pozieres Ridge. Why should she care about a war which took her grandsons and left Joseph bereft? All she cared about was that her grandsons returned home, preferably in one piece. She was present when he tore open the telegrams.

'Wounded, thank God! Not dead,' he had shouted. His eyes regained a spark of life; his moustache quivered with a perception of a half-smile as he fought back tears. 'They're both coming home.' Pursing his lips together he caught her up in his arms and squeezed her hard. She felt the relief course through his body. Why did it only seem like yesterday? She sighed and turned her attention back to Mary.

'I wonder if I met the Farrell family in Geelong? Maybe I did, but it's so long ago. They usually held baptisms after mass on Sundays; perhaps I was there.' Eighty years was too long to cast her mind back for a fleeting acquaintance or an insignificant moment in time. Instead, she returned to the subject of the Chinese.

'I have memories of the Chinese arriving at Creswick. We called them Celestials back then. Small, slight men wearing loose blue shirts, more like a tunic really, wide blue trousers and boots that didn't look strong enough for walking in, let alone for work. Then there were those hats, so wide with a point in the middle, just perched on their heads. I would have laughed, but for the loads they were carrying. Can you imagine a pole with a big sack of potatoes at each end? That was the weight they carried across their shoulders. One may have carried a cradle and a paddle, others tools or bedding, all in that way, most peculiar.' She looked at Mary who smiled and nodded, encouraging her reminiscences.

'They were good workers, helping each other out. They didn't appear to take notice of the heat or the cold. Creswick could be icy cold in the winter, but I never saw a Chinaman wear a woollen jumper or even gloves, just padded jackets. They had hardy constitutions.

A lot of diggers hated them, but that's because they were envious. John and I didn't because the Chinese worked in teams to dig gold, supporting each other, while the Europeans dug on their own or in twos and threes, and they liked their grog. It made them lazy, and you can't be a lazy digger and do well. You know, I don't ever remember a drunken Chinaman, but I must have seen a thousand or ten thousand drunken white diggers in my time. To be fair, that's how I made my money. No, the Chinese preferred to gamble their money away.

But your friend was right. There were plenty of blackguards amongst the ex-cons, thieves, drunkards, whores and madams. Ballarat was far worse for that than Creswick. It may have been bigger and richer, but debauchery was rife. We did our best to stay clear of it. When our claim got worked out, we moved north and then east, Whroo, Gobur, Alexandra, Toongabbie. We were like nomads, chasing the gold and after that the timber, like my father. In every place, I had more children. That's how I remember those places. Some of them only exist in my memory. They've returned to bush, gone back to the mosquitoes and the ants.' Her voice tailed off and her eyes closed.

Mary picked up her knitting as Jane drifted into a disturbed sleep. She watched as Jane's eyes flickered underneath their lids; a sheen of perspiration coating her brow, involuntary moans escaping her lips. She was dreaming, and it looked to be a disturbing one. Mary wiped her forehead with a cool damp cloth and stroked her hair, shushing her into a more peaceful slumber. Once sure that Jane was sleeping peacefully, she left her to arrange a light supper. Jane had eaten nothing for lunch or breakfast, saying she was too tired and had no appetite.

Jane felt much better when she woke and was hungry enough to do justice to Mary's efforts. Mary asked her about her dream.

'I'm not ready to talk about it yet, maybe tomorrow. It's too painful. There were awful times, but there were good times too,' said Jane, trying to cheer herself up. 'Dances and horse racing. I was never one for dancing, but it was fun to watch. There were too few women, so the men danced the mazurka to the sound of bagpipes. Thousands of men dancing together, can you imagine it? Their mucky boots clunking on the wooden floors sounded more like cows stampeding. Some even put on women's clothes, but their beards rather gave them away.' Jane chuckled.

'And after Christmas races were held halfway between Creswick and Ballarat, a time to meet friends and celebrate. Even the Christmas after Eureka they organised a race day. Everyone remained shocked by the events, but the men needed an occasion to lift their spirits because the treason trials were still to come, and no one knew if the diggers would hang.'

'They weren't hung though, were they?'

'No. Trying them for treason was a mistake. By the time of the trials, the people of Melbourne had lost the fear that the diggers would descend on Melbourne and shoot them in their beds. They came to understand that the miners had been treated badly and were shocked at the stories of burning tents and women and children being mishandled. There was no mood to find them guilty and condemn them to death. The innocent verdicts broke the governor, and he died soon after. We all looked forward to a new beginning.

Chapter 31

Creswick Creek 1855

Everyone knew everyone else's business on the goldfield. There was nothing to be done about it while living under canvas. Screams of women either in childbirth or being beaten by a drunken husband were nothing untoward. The constant noise of the day, and the nights punctuated by cries of pain, anger or joy took some getting used to. Barking dogs occurred throughout the day and nights. Pistol or rifle shots were common until everyone turned in around nine thirty. Then came the trampling of horses; the sounds of abundant wildlife and the not so occasional drunkard as he tried to find his way home. Even the scuffling of the ever-present mice kept Jane awake.

She was accustomed to snoring and the muted sounds of a man and woman lying together, having lived in a hut for most of her life. A slab hut with a tin roof was something she aspired to now. Jane thought fondly of the ones she had lived in with her family over the years of her childhood. But she realised it remained a pipe dream. Nothing was permanent on the goldfields. A claim might suddenly dry up and a new claim must be found on a different goldfield many miles distant. At least a tent could be taken down and re-erected in minutes.

As her time approached, Jane wondered if it would be her cries the diggers tried to ignore, her screams that woke children and frightened them. She was not afraid. Maggie was around to help, just as she helped Maggie a few months before, along with a kind-hearted mother of six called Esther, living a few tents away. Maggie patiently explained the process of childbirth and how to cut the cord. At first, she felt nervous, but Esther was so calm and confident that Jane soon began to enjoy the experience. It was an easy birth; second babes often are, Esther told her. When Maggie held her new-born daughter in her arms, and she started to suckle, Jane found herself longing for the day she held her own baby. The instant love that shone in Maggie's eyes as she studied her tiny puckered face nearly stopped Jane's heart with pleasure. She could not wait to experience the joy her own babe would bring.

Jane made John promise that he would not send for one of the quacks, who advertised themselves as doctors, but were clearly not. The signs outside their tents indicated the efficacy of their patent medicines, but their ruddy faces and swollen bulbous noses indicated drunkards. Jane wanted nothing to do with them. John had offered to take her to Geelong for her confinement, but she refused in words that brooked no argument. Other wives gave birth in tents and so would she!

Her mother did not know of her pregnancy unless Hannah let it slip. Mother still sounded distant and cross in her brief messages via Isaac. So be it, Jane thought, John is my family now, and my place is with him. Hannah sent up supplies of baby goods, and Jane began to sell these as well as the hardware. She was making a little income which John said she could save towards their own land. His claim still produced gold in sufficient quantities to keep three men, two women and two children from starving. The nugget that promised to change their lives never appeared, at least not yet. All diggers believed they would find it, otherwise, why do the filthy, bone-wearying work?

But Jane need not have worried about waking children with her cries. She woke at dawn with pain in her lower back. Saying nothing to John; she saw him off to work as normal. A vague memory of her mother's labour with Joseph came to mind. She had worked on until the very last minute, when she shooed the children out of their hut. Jane hung around the window opening and heard loud grunting noises. When Hannah arrived back at the hut with the woman she was sent to fetch, Jane was shooed further away and ran off to play with her brothers. What she did remember was how, with little fuss, she was introduced to her new brother only an hour or so later. She hoped her labour was going to be as easy, as her mother's appeared to be.

Jane's contractions started as she was washing up the breakfast dishes. Knowing that a first labour could last for hours, she put on a hat to guard against the early morning sun and went to tend her vegetables. As the sun rose higher, she left her bit of garden and laid out a clean old sheet on her mattress and put a pail of water onto the fire. The contractions were coming faster now. She gripped the edge of a wooden crate which served as a table, forcing herself to breathe through the waves of pain. It was only when her waters broke onto the compacted mud floor that she called for Maggie. The two women walked the few paces around the tent, again and again, Maggie supporting and encouraging Jane when the pains came. Jane did not utter a single cry, although she thought her body was tearing itself apart. Instead, she bit down on a piece of rolled up cloth to cut off the screams in her throat. It was only when Jane felt the urge to push that she crawled onto the mattress. At last allowed herself to bellow like a cow as she pushed and pushed again until Maggie said: 'I can see the head, one more should do it.'

With a mighty effort, she gave birth to a perfect boy, her firstborn. Maggie cut the cord and tied it up with twine, gave him a quick wash, before wrapping him in some clean cloth. Jane took the screaming mite into her arms, remembering how she reacted when Maggie held her son. What did she feel? First was a fierce sense of protection; the understanding that she would die before she let anything harm him. Then with terror, she remembered her sister Mary, and Hannah's daughter, Emma. Part of her wanted to die right then rather than live with the knowledge that her protection might not be enough. She cried out to Maggie to take the baby.

'Whatever's the matter Jane? He's beautiful, but you look sad. You are meant to be happy.'

'What if he dies? I can't do this. Maybe I won't be a good enough mother?' Tears ran down her face.

'Jane, you mustn't think like that, it will send you mad. You know what to do because I have seen you with mine. You'll be an excellent mother. Sad to say but we have all lost children close to us, maybe a brother or sister and mostly there was nothing we could do about it. We must trust in God to keep our bairns safe and if one dies, remember it is His will, and we must bear it.'

Jane calmed by her words asked, 'Does it matter do you think, if we pray to a Protestant or a Catholic God?'

Maggie smiled and said 'No. it doesn't matter. I was born to an Italian mother and a Scottish father and raised as a Catholic, but married a Presbyterian, just like you. God has not punished me for it has he? In my heart, I still use my rosary although you will not find one in my tent. Rest now, you're tired, and you will feel better for a sleep.'

By the time John arrived back from work, Jane presented her boy to his father in triumph. They had been married almost a year, and John was beside himself with pride as he picked up the boy and cradled him in his arms.

'Well now, my wee Johnny. What a sight for sore eyes you are! I hope ye didnae cause your mother too much pain?' He looked at Jane with love and concern.

'No John, I am made to have babies. There'll be enough for one of your football teams if we are lucky.'

'In that case, I'd best find that nugget pretty quickly.'

When little Johnny died in the dysentery outbreak six months later, which also took Maggie's baby daughter, Jane wondered how she would recover from the pain. In her head, she knew that there was nothing that could have been done to save the babies. They were always the first to go. There was no doctor for miles around. The heat and lack of clean water made for a virulent mixture. Strong single men lay prone and helpless in their tents as the disease took hold. They died a lonely death. Jane remembered Jacob and wept for him too. Her only solace was to pray that Jacob and her father might look out for her darling babe.

John dealt with his pain internally, refusing to speak of it, but Jane knew inside he grieved. For weeks, he worked harder and longer than ever, until Jane told him she was expecting a second baby. He relaxed, vowing to Jane that at the first sign of danger he would take them to

Geelong. Never again was he going to stand by and wait for disease to take his children.

Jane loved him for that. But from then on, Jane always held back an important part of herself from her large family. Yes, she would fight for her children, die for them, but she never dared to love them completely or let them pierce the shell which surrounded her heart. Over the years, the shell grew thicker, more solid, more impenetrable.

Chapter 32

Melbourne April 1932

'How many children did you have?' Asked Mary, holding her hand in sympathy.

'Ten that lived, four sons and six daughters, but you always mourn the ones that died. Let no one tell you any different. My children don't know about their eldest brother. I never mentioned him. But on his birthday, I say prayers for him.'

'Of course you do. No one forgets a baby they loved. How could you? It would be like cutting out your heart.' Mary turned away for a second and dabbed at her eyes. 'Look you've made me maudlin,' she said, with an attempt at a smile. 'Bringing up babies in a tent on the goldfields must have been fraught with danger; just the lack of clean water and sewers for a start.'

'Good water was difficult to be sure. If we had none in our rain barrel it might mean a long trek upstream to find it, but there were water carriers who sold it to us, and we had to trust them. It was the same in early Melbourne. They set up abattoirs along the Yarra River, with dead beasts and waste lying on the banks. Mother always questioned the carriers about how far up the river the water came from.

Sewerage wasn't a problem. One thing we weren't short of on the goldfields were deep abandoned pits. You just wouldn't want to fall into one.' Jane laughed in wry amusement at Mary's look of horror. 'You must have had the same problems in France.'

'Yes, but latrine pits were fenced off and managed with care, because of the chance of infection and disease. From what you said earlier, I guess the same care wasn't taken in Creswick?'

'Not in the early days. You might think that was something the gold commissioners insisted upon, but no. Everything was left to God's will or to the diggers to organise. By 1863 the miners and other residents of Creswick raised enough money to build a hospital. No doubt it saved lives, but not that of my dear friend, Maggie. The hospital refused to treat women in childbirth. Now my great grandchildren are born in maternity hospitals where their mothers get the best care. Back then you had to hope that nothing untoward happened. I was lucky, all my babies were straightforward, but my dear Maggie screamed for help for a day and a night.' Jane's face clouded with the memory.

'She called me when she went into labour. Everything appeared normal at first. Her waters broke, her contractions were normal. We sat having tea and talked about names. She wanted Robert for a boy, after her father, or Matilda for a girl. When she got the urge to push she lay down on the mattress and squeezed my hand, telling me how happy she was that I was there to help. It was a Sunday, and Jack had taken his son fishing way upstream.

But then nothing was happening when she tried to push. I knew something was wrong and ran to fetch Esther. Esther felt all around her bump and then tried to feel inside her. She turned to me, and I saw the panic in her eyes.

'It's a really big baby,' she told Maggie in a calm voice, but I had seen her expression, and my heart sank. 'You are going to have to push really hard.'

As the contractions got stronger, Maggie howled with pain and begged for help. I ran to find John and said he must find a doctor. This was well before the hospital was even built, even before good Doctor Lyndsay arrived in Creswick. John ran to ask the quacks for help, but they only suggested they cut her open to save the baby. We could not make that decision without Jack; it meant killing Maggie. How could we take that responsibility?

Willie offered to ride to Ballarat for a doctor, and John set off to fetch Jack. I remember Jack's face as he rushed into the tent.' Jane stopped talking, the glint of tears in her eyes. 'I have blocked that image for years. It's too painful,' she paused again. 'Jack and I, we held her hands all night as she screamed. Every scream tore into our souls. Torture would have been easier. If I had dared, I would have cut her open myself to stop her agony. How we prayed for that doctor to arrive. An hour before dawn, her screams turned to whimpers, and we felt her leaving us. I don't know how to describe it. It was as if her spirit was hovering above her body, choosing the moment to depart. Jack stared into that space, his expression puzzled and then clearing. Somehow, I believe she communed with him in that instant. It was private, and I wanted to look away, but I was drawn to it too. Mary, I was in the presence of God. He was in that tent, I swear.' Jane shook with emotion, and Mary put her arms around her until she recovered. She was the last person to deny an experience of that sort.

Recovering, Jane carried on, 'Her heart stopped an hour before the medic got to her. He still charged Jack thirty shillings for his trouble. Horrible man, I was livid. Willie was beside himself with guilt because he had taken so long to find the doctor. Do you think the doctor could have saved her if he arrived earlier?'

'Caesareans were carried out successfully in a tiny number of cases last century, but infection was always a problem. A dirty knife to cut her or a dirty cloth to wash the wound and she would not have stood a chance.' Mary took Jane's hand again, stroking the back of it.

'That's what I thought.' She sighed and paused. 'Jack left the diggings with his son soon after, to return to Scotland. Australia held too many painful memories, and I lost the best friend I ever had, maybe the only one.' Jane remained silent for a few moments and Mary, holding her hand, gave it a gentle squeeze. 'Too many of the people I knew died young. Why have I lived so long?'

'Yes, I can sympathise with that,' said Mary, her voice faltering as she remembered too many shadowy young men, the faces that haunted her dreams. She was taken aback when she looked at Jane's face to see tears pouring from her eyes.

The door to the bedroom opened, and Sophie walked in. Taking one look at her mother crying she said to Mary in an angry tone, 'This can't go on. I don't know what's been happening but whatever it is must stop. I can't see Mother upset like this. She's too ill and needs peace. I told Flo that the drive out would be too much for her and now this. Leave the room Mary while I settle Mother down and then I will speak with you.'

Mary left quietly, upset at how distressed Jane had become.

Sophie sat by her mother's bed and dabbed at her eyes. 'There, there Mother, please don't upset yourself.' Her mother never cried. Was she so frightened of death, or had Mary done something which made her upset? She felt no compunction about dismissing the nurse, even if that meant moving back in to look after her mother.

Jane laid a bony hand on Sophie's arm. 'Sorry,' she whispered, through her tears.

'No mother, there's nothing to be sorry for.'

'I failed you.'

'What on earth are you talking about? You did no such thing. You were always there for us.'

'But I didn't properly love you, didn't show you love, I mean. After Johnny died, I couldn't let myself love you too much.'

'Jonnie's not dead. He came to visit you last week.'

'My first baby, he was called Johnny too.'

'You mean you had a baby before our brother John was born. You never told us that. Not even after my baby died.' Sophie was shocked and angry. 'Don't you think it would have helped me to know you had gone through something similar?'

'No, it would not.'

'How do you know that?'

'Because only God understands what you go through then. A pain so intense that not even your husband can comfort you.'

'You see you do understand. Mother, it would have helped me to share that with you.' Sophie spoke with gentleness, her anger disappearing.

'Mothers are there to provide practical help. Look after the other children, cook dinners for you.'

'And you did all that, but what I wanted was your love and understanding.' Sophie spoke softly.

'See I told you that I failed you. It's only now I understand that. Of all my daughters you had the most to bear, and I stood back when I should have come forward. When your husband left, and then young Jack shot himself on Joseph's sheep station I didn't give you my love. I helped, but it wasn't enough, was it?'

'No, it wasn't.'

'I'm sorry Sophie. I felt Jack's loss immensely but did not share my sorrow. It was the way we were brought up, a different age.'

'I don't believe that. When a child you nurtured for seventeen years dies so suddenly and in such a way, are you saying we should keep a stiff upper lip?'

Jane remembered Jacob and how her parents displayed their grief, her mother screaming her grief, her father wracked with sobs. She quaked with guilt.

'No, you're right. For each of my loved ones who died, I added a pebble to my heart. That's a terrible confession to make. But Mary is helping me to shed each one, so don't think badly of her. I am peeling away the layers of guilt and sorrow, and I realise now I have erected a barrier around my heart. I thought it was the only way to survive. Sophie, I want to confess my sins before I go. Please let Mary fetch me a priest.'

'What? Do you mean Reverend Brown from the Unitarian Church?'

'No child, I mean a priest from the Church of the Immaculate Conception up on Burwood Road. I was born a Catholic, and I want to die a Catholic. I won't mind if you bury me as a Protestant, but I want the last rites when the time comes. Don't blame Mary. She has helped me to see what I have become, a hard, embittered old lady hiding her feelings for far too long. I buried my heart a long time ago before your father died. But I don't want to die with it still buried. I need to make peace with my children.'

'Oh Mother, we always admired your strength. You worked so hard to keep us together.'

'Don't excuse me, just forgive me. You are a good daughter, far better than I was a daughter to my mother. Will you kiss me to show you forgive me?'

Moments later Sophie walked back into the drawing room, no longer angry but bemused. Mary feared the worst.

'She says she's a Catholic. Is this your doing? She's always been a Protestant like my father.'

'Not before she married,' said Mary, in a quiet calming voice.

Sophie sank into the chair and put her head in her hands. 'I ought to be angry, but you have taken the burden off me now for many weeks. I appreciate that. But my mother just apologised for not loving me enough and asked me to kiss her. I don't understand how she can have changed so much, and I thought somehow....'

'What, that I have addled her brain, used magic or something else?'

'Yes, no, I don't know.'

'She wants to ask for absolution for her sins. She feels that one of those sins is not showing you enough love. Is that so bad?'

'No, of course not. It's just so unlike her. It's all any of us wanted, her love I mean. Now she's offering; it's hard to take in.'

'Let her make peace. It's what she wants.' Sophie sat awhile in the chair taking in Mary's words.

'You're right. I wish I knew what you talk about because it does appear to be working magic on her.

'I'm her nurse, and I promised I would not divulge what she says. All I can say is that she has lived through a lot. If that moulded her character to be as strong and hard as any man, then you should probably be grateful for that.'

Jane slept until the next morning. Mary checked on her several times, noting her breath becoming shallower. But when she went in with a cup of tea and a soft-boiled egg for breakfast, she thought Jane had benefitted from the good night's rest. After Jane had eaten as much as she could, Mary washed her, changed her nightgown, and brushed her thin grey hair.

'Do you feel up to sitting in your chair today?' She asked.

'No, I want to stay in bed. Will the priest come today?'

'Maybe, but it's not time for the last rites yet.'

'I know, but I want to confess.' Mary didn't say anything, looking quizzically at Jane. Something was on her mind.

'Sometimes you wonder if life can deal you any more blows. People who say there's a divine purpose to everything kid themselves. After too many knockbacks you can't help but begin to lose your trust in God, don't you think?'

'I am not sure. My faith was the only thing keeping me going forward during the war.' Mary replied. 'Losing people who are close is painful, but I find prayer helpful? Was that when you started to doubt; when you lost your friend?'

'No, my faith was stronger when she died. I remember my mother and the time she believed God had forsaken her. She was always so devout, but life dealt her blow after blow. Mother's mouth wore a permanent frown; she rarely showed emotion, 'though inside I knew when she was hurting. 'Grit your teeth and carry on', was her motto. I'm the same, but I had more luck than she ever did.'

'It's not a bad way to live. Most people who survive awful things become stoical. It does little good to dwell on things. What happened to make your mother doubt her faith?'

'It's a long time ago, just more bad luck. She had a lifetime of it, and I'm not sure I want to talk about it.'

'No, you have started a story, and I know you want to continue.'

'I don't think I want to tell this story. It's is the one giving me the most sleepless nights.'

'They say a problem shared is a problem halved.'

'Hmm, not this one, Mary; I only added to my mother's troubles.'

Chapter 33

Creswick Creek and Geelong 1859

Creswick Creek was thriving and without the constant licence hunts, a more peaceful township altogether. Two churches were built, a school started, and a gold office built from bluestone was due to open. Stores in Albert Street offered everything a digger and his family needed. Food was plentiful and cheaper than in the days of the last Governor. Jane ought to have been content, but life in a tent with three small children had lost its novelty. The twins were a long way from walking, but by the time they were, Jane wanted a hut. Daily she dreamt of it, longing for a table to sit at, a chair to sit in, a proper bed to lie in and most of all, a kitchen to cook in. After Maggie died, Jane took over cooking for her old customers. There were always single men who hankered after a home cooked meal, not just fried potatoes and meat, but a steak pie with vegetables, a chicken hot pot and the men's favourite, a shepherd's pie, just like mother used to make. John's claim was prospering, and he promised to find a plot of land to build a hut on before the summer heat arrived.

Regular letters arrived from Geelong with invitations to come and visit, the last one containing a plea they visit sooner rather than later, which concerned Jane, wondering if someone might be ill. She discussed it with John, and he thought it would do Jane good to visit her family. It was five years since she last saw her sister, mother and brothers. It was in a fit of anticipation that she packed for the journey. There was still no railway to the goldfields, but the roads had improved, and regular coach services plied the road between Geelong and Creswick. On what promised to be a bright sparkling day in September, the family mounted the coach at seven in the morning for the ride to Geelong. The coach made a stop in Ballarat, which in the five years since they passed through had grown into one of the richest cities in the country, if not the empire. Its wealth everywhere apparent in the amount and grandeur of building taking place.

As the journey progressed a quiet excitement gripped Jane. She longed to show off her family and husband. She was proud of them and could barely wait for her eldest son to greet his grandmother. Many hours were spent on coaching him to say, 'Good evening Grandma.' His childish lisp was adorable. Dressed in his first short trousers, shirt and his baby hair cut, he looked the proper little gentleman. The journey lasted the best part of a day, with several stops at pubs along the way, where Jane managed to find a quiet spot to feed the twins. The rocking motion of the coach kept them asleep for most of the journey, but Jane was relieved when the coach made its final stop in Geelong.

Joe, her youngest brother, was there to greet them and help them with their baggage. She hardly recognised him now at fourteen. He had left school and was taller than any of her siblings. Shyly he stooped to give her a quick kiss and then heartily shook John's hand, before picking up two of the biggest bags. Jane held baby Hannah while John held Joe's namesake, and his older son's hand as they walked at child's pace towards the house.

The first thing Jane noticed when they entered the house was her mother. It was a shock to see her head of white hair, the worry lines developing around her eyes and how thin she had become. In five years she had gone from the quiet strong force behind the family to an old woman. Her initial thought was that she might have some wasting disease. She pushed John junior forward to say the greeting he had practised for his grandmother, but when faced with the old lady, he burst into tears and could not be coaxed into saying anything. Shamefaced, Jane introduced her husband to her mother and then picked up her son to soothe him. Meanwhile, Hannah cooed over the babies.

'I want to get these children to bed, which room are we in?' asked Jane.

'The bedroom on the right, come I'll help you,' said Hannah.

Jane took the opportunity to question her about her mother's health, but thought Hannah's reassurance defensive. Something was wrong; she felt it in her gut.

In the dining room, Mother had set the table for supper. Everyone was present, apart from David. As tardy as ever, he had decided to try a bit of gold mining up in Bendigo. Jane felt relieved about that, as she could not see him getting on with John at all, Chalk and cheese sprang to mind. Isaac was telling John about a fire at his shop which had resulted in Hannah and her family moving in with Mother.

'Mr Finch, our oilman, was lighting the lamps with naphtha, something he does for me every evening in winter. But this time he spilled some near a lighted candle. Whoosh the oil exploded, the poor man was engulfed in flames, and he dropped the lamp as customers fled from the shop in panic. I tried covering him with my coat to stop him from burning further, while someone else kicked the lamp into the street. Too late because the fire spread quickly and before the water engine arrived it was up to the roof.'

'How's the poor oilman?' Jane asked.

'He's dreadfully burnt. They're treating him in hospital, but I'm not sure he'll survive.'

'Thank God you are all safe!' Jane grasped her sister's hand in support and Hannah smiled wanly at her.

'Yes, I was at Mother's with the children at the time. I dread to think what would have happened if we had been in the house.

'How about insurance; you do have it?' John asked.

'Yes, it was insured for five hundred pounds.'

'That should be enough to rebuild.' John smiled in approval.

'Does anyone want any more soup?' asked Mother, changing the subject, her face impenetrable, but Jane still felt there was more wrong than just a fire. They were all too common. All evening she could not shake off the bad feeling. She had been expecting recriminations over her marriage. Mother nursed her grievances, and even after five years, there should have been some fireworks before the inevitable making up. She never remained silent if aggrieved, but it looked as though the fight had gone out of her. She looked beaten.

John, who met Mother for the first time, noticed nothing wrong. She was an old lady, what was she supposed to look like? He was tired after the journey and wanted to sleep, not listen to worries about his wife's mother. It took Jane a while to get off to sleep. She lay in bed, relishing the comfort, but unsettled and mulling over the conversation that evening. She tried to pick out a sense of what was wrong, but eventually drifting off into the light sleep of a nursing mother.

The twins woke her abruptly around midnight for a feed. Wrapping them tightly in her shawl and binding them to her, she carried them out of the room trying not to wake her sister and family in the other bedroom. She headed for the dining room but saw the faint glimmer of a candle in the kitchen. Surely her mother was not still awake. She pushed the door, which was ajar only to see her mother sitting at the table, warming her hands on a cup of steaming tea.

'Whatever are you still doing up Mother?' Jane asked. Her mother looked so troubled that her heart went out to her as she saw her eyes glistening with tears. Jane gave her one baby to hold while she sat herself at the table and opened her nightgown to feed the other.

'I know something is troubling you. I don't think it can be my marriage. You have met John now, and he is a good provider. Please don't blame him.'

'It's nothing to do with you and John. I'm reminded so much of your father and me when I see you together with the twins. Your father would have been proud of you Jane.'

'What is it then?' Her mother took time to answer, her whole face working with emotion.

'Isaac's fire was the start of it. He has insurance for the house and the shop, but he lost more than that. When we moved to Melbourne, your father bought a parcel of land on Lonsdale Street with another man.' Jane's jaw dropped open at that; she was so surprised.

'We left Melbourne when land prices crashed, and it was worth next to nothing, but he held on to it. He gave Hannah the deed to the land for her children when she married Isaac.'

'But it must be worth a fortune now,' Jane said. 'That's good news surely.'

'Not if the deed burnt in the fire, along with Isaac's savings, which he kept in the house and not the bank. Hundreds of pounds in notes they tell me.' Jane's heart sank. 'He owes an awful lot of people money, Jane.'

'Oh no!' She understood now. Isaac had always been a dealer in goods besides his butchery business; he liked to pay cash and cut many a good deal that way. 'Is he insolvent?'

'Pretty much so, although he hasn't declared himself bankrupt. I think he is desperately trying to make money, but Hannah says he is just digging himself in deeper.'

'How much does he owe?'

'Hannah says it's over five hundred pounds and rising.'

'Oh, my Lord!' Jane was stunned, that was an enormous sum of money.

'If only we still had the deeds to that land, it would solve their problems.'

'Wouldn't there be a copy with someone, a lawyer, the bank or someone? You must know who Father bought the land with.'

'I do, and Isaac wrote a letter, but it turns out he is dead too. His son-in-law wrote back asking for proof of ownership, which we can't provide. Now we have heard that the land is for sale. He is selling it from under our feet, and we have no money for a lawyer. Isaac's a man possessed, trying every way he knows to make money. He hardly stays still for a minute, but he's making some daft purchases, then selling whatever it is at a loss. He's panicking, and It's hopeless. I worry he'll go to prison, and we'll be left with nothing all over again. How can we bear another catastrophe? I sit here night after night praying to God for help. But there is no answer. Haven't I been a good Catholic, repented my sins, attended Mass every Sunday? Why has He forsaken us Jane?'

Jane did not know what to say. Her mouth felt dry with dread. At that moment, she wished Mother had not told her, or they had not come to Geelong. In the back of her mind was Jane's nest egg, money she was saving for the land they wanted and for the business she intended to open. Mother looked hard at Jane and saw her floundering, hoping for an immediate offer to help. Not hearing it, she started to sob. She cried with little Hannah in her arms, rocking back and forth in her chair.

Do I save my children's future or my sister? Jane knew she would lie awake all night with this problem. Her family would not ask her outright for help but expected her to offer it if she could. It's why they were so keen for us to come she thought bitterly. Her eyes concentrated on little Joseph's head as he nuzzled her breast, hardly daring to glance at her mother who still wept, though quietly. What should she say? Was there anything that would comfort her other than a gift of five hundred pounds? Jane did not have that kind of money, and if she gave what she had to Isaac, she would never see it again. It wasn't enough to get him out of trouble but might pay for a lawyer to argue that the land belonged to Hannah. Would that be of any use, or just waste more money? After all, whatever was Hannah's belonged to Isaac, in British law.

'I'll talk to John about getting a lawyer,' Hannah said at last. She sat baby Joseph on her knee winding him and then swapped babies with her mother. This should have been a happy moment with Mother, a chance to forgive and forget their differences, talk of happy times and look forward to future visits. Instead, Jane felt sick to her stomach with guilt.

All night she lay awake and in turmoil. When John woke, he turned towards her in bed and said, 'Did you have a bad night? You look worn out.' His finger traced the shadows under her eyes. The gesture made tears well in her eyes.

'We need to talk John. I'm afraid there is a problem which Mother told me about last night. I have a horrid feeling it's going to break the family. Please, can we take the children down to the sea this morning so that we can talk in private?'

At breakfast, each of the women appeared pale and washed out, while Isaac looked determinedly cheerful. He offered to take his oldest son to school and then suggested taking John for a drink before dinner.

'No, make it before supper. It's a nice day, and we want to go for a walk this morning,' said Jane quickly. Isaac frowned, sensing he was being diverted but gave in with good grace. Hannah's younger son was only a few weeks older than the twins, and Hannah offered to go for a walk too.

'I could do with your help here,' Mother said. Hannah looked at her and understood from her expression that John and Jane needed to be alone.

Flushing with embarrassment, she replied, 'Of course Mother.'

In later years Jane remembered that walk and conversation as one of the most difficult of her life, not because there was disagreement, far from it. It was the time she irrevocably discarded her birth family for her new family, and the guilt ate into her, however much she tried to suppress it.

John had no allegiance to her family, reminding Jane of the message sent by her mother following their marriage. As for Isaac and Hannah, he liked them, but it was their problem, not his. When Jane suggested hiring a lawyer, he poured scorn on the idea. All that would do was tie the family up for years in legal arguments or bankrupt them faster. Jane felt she had to defend her family from John's onslaught, but at the same time, she agreed with him.

'One thing is certain Jane, we are not giving Isaac and Hannah any money. I will go out with him for a drink and try to get to the bottom of his problems. See if there is any advice I can give, but that is all I am prepared to do.'

That afternoon, as the children slept, an awkward silence filled the house. Once they woke, Jane busied herself with them and at last got her oldest to say the words she had taught him to say to his grandmother, although it was not yet evening. Her mother's face softened a little, and as a reward, she gave him some bread and apple jelly. Patting him on the head, she turned towards Jane and said, 'You and I are alike in so many ways, but not in the one way that matters. Whatever happens, I want you to know that.' Jane felt her insides curdle. What did she mean? She knew one thing for certain, it had been a mistake to come to Geelong, and despite the hardships, Jane longed for her tent.

In bed that night, John told her of his conversation with Isaac. 'He wanted me to invest in one of his schemes. He has lost his mind, and I told him so. Get the shop up and running again I said to him. He replied that it would never pay enough for his expenses. I suggested he write to John Brooke to ask for help on the matter of the land in Lonsdale Street. He is the member for West Geelong, perhaps he can advise on what he should do. But that is it Jane. We will return home tomorrow, do you agree?' Jane nodded in relief. She could not stand to stay in Geelong another day.

That night when the babies woke, she fed them in their room. Not for anything would she face her mother again.

On the journey home, there was no anticipation or excitement. She sat still with her hands clasped stiffly in her lap, trying to forget the awful scene of departure. Hannah cried in despair, never having said a word but knowing she was to be left to fend for herself. Her mother looked haggard and lost. Her brother, Joseph, was puzzled by the shortness of the visit. They haven't told him realised Jane. She kissed him and begged him to take care of himself. Isaac was nowhere to be seen; no doubt he was angry with them. She kissed her mother and sister too, getting nothing in response; no expression of regret they were going; no wishing them luck, not even a wave goodbye. I have cast them adrift, and they know it. Will I ever see or hear from them again, she thought in sudden panic?

Chapter 34

Melbourne April 1932

'What did your mother mean by her comment?'

'Family is everything. Protect and fight for them at all costs. She brought us up to believe that, and I let her down by choosing my family with John, not my sister. That was unforgivable in her eyes.'

'Choices are hard, and sometimes we make mistakes.'

'I did not make a mistake. I would do the same again, and I also brought my family up the same way. They looked after each other, but it's easier when money is not a problem. Poverty is a hard taskmaster.'

'What happened to Isaac?'

'We only found out from newspaper reports. A few months later John read to me an account of Isaac's and Hannah's interrogation in court. I remember the turmoil in my mind, and my promise to my father to look after my mother. John told me not to blame myself; it was Isaac's own doing. Never before, had I blamed Isaac for my father's death, but coupled with my sister's ruin, he had to be at fault I thought. All these years later I don't blame him, John was right, Isaac became ill with worry and acted irrationally.

The way the reporters wrote it, my sister spun on a web of lies and deceit as she tried to protect Isaac. Money had been squirrelled away in a bank account in her name, maybe two or three hundred pounds. She swore it belonged to my youngest brother Joseph, and she was only looking after it. Where would a fifteen-year-old butcher's assistant get that kind of money? They didn't believe her, and Isaac was tried for fraudulent insolvency, then sent to prison with hard labour for two years. Of course, they never saw any money from the sale of the land in Melbourne. Why didn't he keep the deeds in the Bank? Such a stupid mistake to make.'

'Did you ever see any of your family again?' Mary hoped for a positive answer. While her sympathy for Jane had grown these last weeks, she could not bear to think Jane had abandoned her birth family forever. How could she live with herself? Mary pictured them living in Geelong, longing for a visit or a word from Jane.

'Don't judge me Mary. I have spent so many hours regretting the decision I made to cast them off, and only God will be my judge. I wanted to protect my own family; please understand. You've guessed from my stories that my parents were convicts, and I vowed my children would never be tainted by that. I convinced myself it was the right thing to do. Isaac went to prison and then young Joseph too for some petty larceny or other, and I realised my family would hold us back, always be a drain on us. John agreed with me.'

Mary forced the words of disbelief back in her throat.

'Years later I did go back.' Jane whispered, 'But I am not sure I want to go there yet.'

Chapter 35

Melbourne and Geelong 1879

At breakfast, Jane made a mental list of the Christmas gifts she planned for her family. The eldest girls always craved the latest dress patterns and materials. That was easy and would afford her the most pleasure. Gone were the days of two dresses, one for Sunday and the other everyday dress of grey or brown. Having daughters had taught her to love fashion, and she looked forward to her new dress once a year, as much as any other woman.

The eldest boys wanted tools or saddles, and John promised he would take care of those which left the younger children, always the most difficult. She hoped the shops of Melbourne were going to inspire her.

As she sipped her coffee, a sudden frisson of uncertainty gripped her, nothing to do with presents. Something or someone was calling to her. The waitress passed by and offered to fill her cup.

'Are you alright, Ma'am, you look pale, as though you've seen a ghost?' Jane shivered despite the December heat. The hairs stood up on her neck. It was at that moment that her plans for the day changed irrevocably.

On the train heading west, she decided that her sister, Hannah, was calling her and must be in trouble. She had no argument with Hannah. Why had she not thought to make amends before? She cursed her stubbornness. On alighting in Geelong, she stood at the station trying to get her bearings, picturing the town she knew of old. Once decided she made for a hotel she knew well. Someone at the Lord Nelson would recognise the Evans name and tell her where to start her search.

'Are you sure?' No one seemed to know of the Evans or the Dugmores. The staff had changed, and the landlord was new to the town. After all, twenty-five years have gone by, but it still surprised her. She wondered where to go next.

She found herself outside the ironmongers. Looking up, she saw the name Richardson in large letters above the door. Entering, she expected to see a son standing behind the counter, but it was him, dear Mr Richardson, seventy years old at least and looking greyer. The bell above the door tinkled her arrival and her boss of old looked up from the newspaper he was reading. Customers were fewer on the ground since the gold rush ended. There was nothing wrong with his eyesight, however,

'Jane is it you?' He walked from around the counter and took her hands, Looking her up and down. 'Why have you never called in before?'

'We live way over to the East of Melbourne, in a town called Traralgon, and it only recently acquired the railway.' She smiled at him. 'It's so good to see you again. If it hadn't been for this shop, I might never have met my husband.'

'Is John well? Do you have children?'

'Yes, he's very well, and we have nine children. Life has been kind to us.'

'Good, I'm pleased. I often wondered. You must be here to visit your mother.' Jane tried to expel the startled shocked expression from her face.

'Y..yes,' she stammered.

'I haven't seen her for a year or so. I hope she's well?' What was she to answer when she did not know, had thought her dead for ten or more years.

'Is she still at her old address? She never writes to me.'

'No Jane, I'm sorry. She lives in Ashby.' He gave her an address which was familiar for its poverty, frequented as it was by drunkards, thieves and harlots. She did not try to hide the shock this time.

'I would not want my mother there Jane. I hope you can do something for her.' She nodded close to tears with shame.

What was she going to find? How did her mother end up there? This day was not going to be a happy reconciliation with her sister. She understood that now. The something which called to her this morning was a voice of desperation.

She had never ventured down the street where her mother now lived, because it was an unspoken rule that this was no place for the Dugmore children. The odour hit her first as she approached the corner of the street, a stink of outside privies percolating in the heat of summer, of decaying rubbish, of vomit and manure. Holding a handkerchief to her face, she made her way to one of the hovels, watched by grimy, underfed children playing barefoot amongst the filth. She knocked on the door, made of simple nailed together planks it neither fitted the space surrounding it nor kept the weather out. No one came to the door, but she heard a faint cry from inside. Emboldened, she lifted a latch and let herself into the one-room shack.

If she ever imagined her mother still alive there would be a picture of a neat, trim old lady, hair bound up tight in a bun, either sitting in a rocking chair on a veranda, or working in her vegetable garden. Not the dirty, ragged woman sitting before her on a crate with long straggly hair flopping around a filthy grey face.

Jane dropped her bag and ran to the woman, unable to believe she was the woman who gave birth to her. Falling on her knees, caring nothing about the dirt floor which had not been swept in months, she swept her mother up into her arms.

'Jane, is it you?' croaked the toothless crone. Unable to speak Jane hugged her tighter.

In the gloom, she had not noticed anyone else until she detected a snore coming from a pile of assorted rags in the corner. She looked questioningly at her mother who said, 'It's David.'

Jane jumped up in a fit of rage so potent she would have swung for him. Instead, she walked over slowly, deliberately and aimed a hard kick at his ribs with her boot, guessing he was too drunk to do her much damage. He swore. She kicked him again and again until he grabbed hold of her ankle and she stumbled. Angling her body, she fell with the full force of her knees onto his stomach, winding him.

'What the hell!' He roared.

Jane scrambled to her feet and returned to her mother.

'Get me out of this place, Jane. Take me with you.'

Jane didn't know what to say. She stood up and faced David. 'Why is Mother living like this?' She screamed at him.

'I'm the only one who stayed to look after her, you bitch,' he snarled.

'You've sold everything to pay for drink, haven't you?'

'And what have you ever done for her?' He whined. 'If you want to help, give us some money.'

'So you can drink it? Never!'

'Jane, please take me with you,' her mother whispered, clutching at Jane's dress.

'I'll get you out of here, I promise. First I will clean you up.'

She went over to David who had finished coughing and spluttering and was now feeling sorry for himself. Jane fished a few shillings out of her pocket and threw them on the floor.

'Go get yourself drunk while I wash mother.' He grabbed at the coins, climbed to his feet, and left, swearing at Jane but with no attempt at any physical retribution. Had she not known it was him, she would have passed him unrecognised in the street. He was a wreck of a man, soft, cowardly, and bloated.

She searched the shack but found no food, no cleaning materials no wood for a fire, just a bucket, acting as her mother's toilet, two stained, stinking mattresses, and various empty bottles.

'Mother I need to shop before I clean you up. Stay here, and I will return soon.'

'Take me with you Jane.' Her mother was stuck on that phrase. Did it mean her mind had gone?

Jane walked to the closest shop, her mind racing. How was she going to keep her mother safe from David? How was she going to make sure she was looked after? The problem was urgent. She could not leave Geelong without solving it. Jane fell back into practical matters, discarding the emotion and anger, which raged in her moments before.

218

The shopkeeper was delighted to have a lady with a full purse walk through his door. The list of her requirements made his eyes sparkle until he discovered the delivery address.

'I don't deliver there,' he said. Jane was in no mood for an argument.

'Find me a boy to carry the box of shopping, and I will take it with me. If not, I will go onto the street and find one myself and give him a pound for his trouble.'

The shopkeeper did not want any disease-ridden ragamuffin entering his shop, and for a pound tip, he would sacrifice his son to the lady.

Jane noticed a shop selling second-hand clothes opposite. Instructing the boy to wait for her, she wandered over to buy a complete set of clothes for her mother instead of the rags she wore. She had no time to wash them, so she hoped they were clean, lifting each purchase to her nose as well as subjecting them to minute observation. When satisfied, she paid for her purchases and marched back to the shack, the boy trotting along in her wake.

The look of relief on her mother's face as she walked through the door followed by a curious boy laden with assorted food, clothes and cleaning materials, gladdened Jane's heart. She gave the boy another shilling to draw some fresh water from the nearest well, then set to light a fire in an ancient, soot-stained range. Thank goodness for small mercies she thought. It was entirely possible, no probable that a hovel like this, would not possess a range and yet it did. Once a pan of water was set to heat, she stripped her mother of her rags and began to clean her up.

'How did it get to this, Mother?' She asked, washing her skin with care, noting the insect bites and sores. She would burn the ragged clothes in the range later. She hoped her mother could tell her and not simply repeat the phrase of earlier. When she began to talk, it was in a whisper, but her mind was as agile as ever.

'David returned to Geelong after trying to dig. He went bankrupt like Isaac, owing hundreds of pounds from a bad mining speculation. Jane, I don't blame you for not giving Hannah the money. I sat watching Isaac's trial and realised that it was hopeless. He owed too much. We should never have asked you, and I have regretted the words I said every day since then.' Jane kissed her mother on her brow.

'I am sorry too. I should not have abandoned you. We read of Isaac's and Joseph's trials, but I thought Hannah would live with you and take care of you with Isaac in prison.'

'When Isaac and Joe came out of prison, David encouraged them to leave Geelong to make a new start. Half of me believed he did it for the right reason. I pray it was for the right reason, but I never understood why we did not get any letters. Neither of us can read, but the priest would have read them to me.

Little by little things started disappearing from the house. I was still taking in lodgers and thought it was one of them. David offered to pay the rent to the agent as he passed the office on his way to work. I had no idea he wasn't working, but spending all day playing cards.' Jane's anger rose again. What a despicable thing to do to his mother, stealing from a mother who always loved him and always protected him.

'We lost the house and ended up here. David was full of apologies. He stopped gambling and promised me he would mend his ways. I thought we would only be here for a month or two, that was ten years ago. I hired myself out as a domestic servant, but the money was never enough once David went back to his old habits. Work gave up on me once I got arthritis in my hands and then my knees. I have prayed for release Jane, from the pain and the shame of living here. Please take me with you.' Her beseeching look almost undid Jane, a sob catching in her throat. She had to get her out of this midden.

'Can you walk?' Helen pointed to a stick beside her. Jane picked it up. It was no more than a stick of splintery wood, a castoff without so much as a handle for comfort. Handing it to her mother, Jane thought regretfully of the beautiful walking sticks her father made. She helped her mother stand. Watched as Helen took no more than two painful steps before her legs gave way. Jane had to catch her and stumble with her back to the crate so she could sit.

'I'll make us some food while I think what to do.' Jane thanked her foresight in buying a pan, because the sum total of implements in the shack were two cracked bowls, a mug, a knife and two spoons. She poured some oatmeal into a pan with water to make gruel, adding a banana to sweeten it.

'What do you eat, Mother?'

'David brings a pie back from the pub most days. If he's earned money at the docks, he'll bring me some battered fish. I rarely go hungry.'

'Still making excuses for him,' Jane mumbled, under her breath. She's skin and bone. The clothes she had bought for her drowned her tiny frame.

'Here's what I propose,' Jane said, as her mother sipped at a mug of black tea, following a tiny helping of oatmeal and some tinned sardines. 'I will have someone collect you later on today. They will take you to a hotel where you can stay, until I find a bungalow and a housekeeper to look after you. In two weeks, I'll return to settle you in.'

'You won't take me with you?'

'Mother, you're unable to walk.'

'I mean to live with you.'

Jane's heart sank. 'I can't take you with me, no.'

'Is it your husband? Won't he allow it? Ask him Jane, beg him. Please. I don't want to die alone. David can't look after me the way a daughter should.' Those words would haunt Jane for all the years to come.

Chapter 36

Melbourne April 1932

Jane turned her tear-stained face to Mary, all her defences defeated. Mary shushed her and stroked her hair, understanding that this was the biggest regret of Jane's life. Eventually, Jane calmed down enough to carry on with her story.

'Before I returned to the station to catch the train back to Melbourne, I called in to see Mr Richardson. He agreed to act as agent for buying me a bungalow and finding a housekeeper, bless him. I found a small, clean hotel and gave them my mother's address. I paid for a room and meals for a fortnight and asked them to send a carriage around for her that same day. I did try my best, didn't I?'

Mary held onto Jane's hand, reassuring her.

'But before I left Geelong, I bumped into David. If only I had ignored him, that would have been the sensible thing to do. I was so angry with him. I blurted out what I had done. Of course David did not want me to buy a house for her. He knew I would not let him live in it. He swore at me, calling me names, saying they wanted no help from a filthy Proddy. But Mother had begged me to get her out of that stinking cottage, so I told him he was a disgrace. If it weren't for the fact that we were in the street on public display, I would have given him the hiding he deserved. Me, a woman of no more than five foot, but he was all blubber and bluster.' Jane allowed herself a half smile.

'I returned two weeks later with the deeds to a two-bedroom house. First, I went to the hotel to find Mother to tell her the good news, but they told me she wasn't there. They had sent someone to the address I gave them, but no one answered the door. The following day they tried again but the place was locked up, and a boy in the street told the coachman that the people had left.'

Jane gasped in distress, recalling the panic she felt, almost running towards the hovel and then bursting through the door, only to be accosted by a man demanding to know why she was breaking into his house.

'Mother and David had gone. No one knew where. I wandered around Geelong asking in every pub and every shop, but no one knew. By chance, I asked a porter at the station if he knew David and he did. He told me that he had last seen him two weeks before, helping an old lady onto a train. Which train he couldn't say, maybe the Melbourne one but then again maybe up to Ballarat.

'The funny thing is,' he said, 'I found a wheelbarrow on the platform that day, no one ever claimed it.' Years and years later I found out where they went. David died of drink when he was living in a tent with my mother in Saint Kilda Road, south of Melbourne. She was eighty years old. Rather than let her live out her days in a clean house with someone to look after her, he put her in a tent. Can you believe it?' She turned to Mary, a mixture of anger and puzzlement in her eyes.

'Who knows what is in the minds of men such as him? He sounds weak and troubled. But what I don't understand Jane, is why didn't you want to take her to live with you?' There was a long pause before Jane looked up at Mary, her face crumpled in misery and guilt.

'Because I told my children she was dead, and they did not have a granny.' Jane cried, in despair. 'Just like Peter denied Jesus, I denied my mother; I did not want my children to know her because I was ashamed of my family. It was wrong of me. She was a good woman, hard but fair and she did not deserve the way we children treated her.'

Jane attempted to gulp back her tears as Mary took her trembling hand in hers, the parchment skin barely troubling to cover the knobbly bones beneath. No wonder Jane held this huge burden of regret and guilt, bottled up for decades, eating away at her.

'Your mother forgave you and you were trying to do right by her. Don't blame yourself, blame David.' Jane shook her head, refusing to be comforted.

'I should have made sure that she got to the hotel, but I was in a hurry to get back to Melbourne before the shops shut. I told my family I was staying an extra day to do Christmas shopping. I could hardly go home empty-handed.' Jane lay silent, her lips drawn inwards, in mental combat with her conscience. Finally, she gave a big sigh and turned towards Mary.

'Please bring me that priest, Mary. I want to confess now, while my mind is made up. I cannot die with this guilt eating into me.' The pain in Jane's eyes made them appear overlarge in her wizened face. The flesh had all but melted away over the last few weeks.

Mary attended Mass most Sundays at the Catholic Church around the corner, since she moved in to nurse Jane. There were two priests she knew of; one, Father Riley, an elderly man, hard of hearing and with an air of impatience, the other, Father Donaldson, young and engaging who turned to God after fighting in the war. As she picked up the telephone to call the presbytery, she hoped it would be the young one who answered. Mary was in luck.

An hour or two later he arrived, and Mary took him in to meet Jane, who insisted on being out of bed and in her chair for the visit. Mary looked out her best dressing gown and combed her thin silver hair, pinning it back away from her face.

'If I'm going to say my confession after all this time, I want to look my best. Mother always insisted on us looking our best for church.' Mary smiled. It seemed that Jane had recovered some of her verve.

After making the introduction, Mary was on her way out of the door when she heard Jane say, 'Bless me Father for I have sinned. It has been,' a pause as Jane calculated the years, 'seventy-eight years since my last confession.'

An hour later Mary heard the bedroom door open. Father Donaldson came out. Mary went to hand him his hat and coat. He smiled, his gentle brown eyes crinkling his pink cheeks.

'Remarkable, quite remarkable,' he said. 'I am so glad you asked me. I'll come again soon.' Mary ushered him out as the sky was growing dark and went to the kitchen to make tea for Jane.

'You made an impression on the good Father,' she said handing Jane a cup.

'What a pleasant young man. Thank you Mary, for finding him. I feel so much better for having confessed. Maybe I should have done it years ago. The weight has lifted from my shoulders.' She dabbed at her eyes with a sodden handkerchief. Mary went to the drawer and found a clean one to give her. Jane took it and unfolded it to blow her nose and stopped.

'Find me a different one, not this please.' Mary obliged. Taking it back, she noticed the embroidered initials CB in the corner, in red chain stitch. The cloth was old but good quality cotton with a fine lace edging.

'Who did this belong to?'

'I forgot I had it. I always meant to return it to its owner, but I only met her once, and our paths never crossed again.' Jane sighed, she looked exhausted. 'Tomorrow, I'll tell you tomorrow, if I live that long. Just let me sleep I am so weary.' Her eyes closed, and Mary watched as Jane's face slackened and her breath became shallow.

'Not much longer Jane,' she murmured, before leaving the room.

Jane dreamt again that night. She was sitting with her mother studying her coarse hands as she showed Jane how to sew. Her mother's needle appeared to fly through the thick cotton, and Jane wondered how she would ever become as skilled. She looked up at her face; those battered glasses wedged on her nose, her chestnut hair glowing in the candlelight and her lips pursed in concentration.

'Here Jane, you try.' The apron was handed to her and Jane attempted her first stitch. The needle slipped in her fingers, and she was surprised at the resistance in the cloth as she poked the needle through. Her stitch was ungainly, large and clumsy, and tears pricked her eyes.

'It's too difficult Mam,' she cried.

'No, that's the first try. Trust me it will get easier with practice. Let me show you again.' She pushed the needle through the cloth and back out again, almost in the same hole, it seemed to Jane. But when she looked there was a tiny neat stitch, difficult to see with the blue thread against the indigo cotton of the garment.

'It doesn't matter what the underside looks like Jane, but the outside must be perfect. Think of it in this way. God only sees the outside of things, and they are a reflection of his glory. In church, the tapestry kneelers look beautiful, don't they?' Jane nodded. 'If you cut one open you would find a jumble of cut threads, a mess of colours inside, but outside the kneelers are flawless. The same goes for life. Inside you may have mean thoughts, but God judges you on your actions. That is why we go to confession to confess those bad thoughts and receive a penance for them. In that way, both our thoughts and our actions are judged and forgiven.'

It sounded too complicated for Jane, but she nodded again.

'What God has forgiven, I can forgive Jane. So, if you do anything wrong, you must confess it, and I will love you for it.' She planted a kiss on Jane's forehead.

In her sleep, Jane felt the pressure of that lingering kiss on her brow and relaxed into a deeper, dreamless sleep. She awoke the following morning at peace, without the burden of guilt she had borne on her shoulders for more than fifty years. She knew that she could never undo what she had done all those years before, but in her heart, there was a sense of forgiveness she had longed for, and never thought to receive.

She was more than ready to die, but on that bright April day she was still alive and smiled as Mary brought her tea and toast.

Propped up in bed, having had a refreshing bed bath and the luxury of a freshly laundered nightgown, she was ready for another story or two. She still had a few up her sleeve, and although her voice was less strong than it was a few weeks ago, and her breathing more laboured, she looked forward to sharing them. God had been good to bring her Mary.

Mary noticing a bluish tinge to Jane's lips, was less sure about tiring her.

'Perhaps you ought to rest,' she said. But Jane would have none of it. She wanted to complete this story of her life. It was important to finish it and let Mary be the only living witness to her tales.

Chapter 37

Whroo, Victoria 1865-1867

Little by little money trickled in, and their savings grew. After eleven years of gruelling work, there was enough. Enough money to build the small hotel that Jane dreamed of, ever since her ride up to the diggings. There was guaranteed income from running a licensed hotel on the goldfield. She had never forgotten the piles of bottles outside each grog tent they passed, on that first journey to Ballarat. Eleven-years of experience proved that miners had a thirst, an almighty thirst, needing to be assuaged each and every night. Publicans grew rich off the money that miners worked hard for, and Jane wanted never to worry about money again.

At twenty-eight and with four children under nine, she longed for the security which evaded her parents and siblings. There had been no word of them for years. John never mentioned them, perhaps for fear of upsetting Jane, but maybe because he too was still angry after that short visit they made to Geelong. The money they worked for and saved was going to reap dividends. She felt sure about that.

John was still a miner working on the Coy diggings at Whroo; several days walk to the northeast of Creswick. Had there been a choice, they would have preferred to stay at Creswick, but the easy gold had disappeared. The big mining companies moved in as John predicted. A company compensated him for his claim, asking him if he wanted to stay and work for them, but John preferred to work for himself. The money made as a wage slave would keep them at poverty levels, never part of John's plan. He chose Whroo because the big companies were unlikely to want to mine in what was one of the most difficult Goldfields. Better still, the Coy Diggings were a new find and yielding good results.

John built Jane a hotel, the Sydney Hotel, made of wood with a tin roof, like all the buildings in Whroo. They were not built to stand the test of time. When the gold and quartz were worked out, Whroo would disappear back to bush. Who wanted to live in a town with no access to water during the summer months? The Sydney Hotel may sound grand from the name, but it had just three extra bedrooms and two sitting rooms for guests. Simply furnished, each bedroom had a single bed, a washstand, containing a jug and bowl for water, a chamber pot and a cupboard with a drawer for clothes. Their own accommodation fared little better, but for Jane, it was a palace after the years spent living in a tent. There were two bedrooms, one for the children and the other for Jane and John, a sitting room cum dining room and a separate kitchen outside. Fire remained a constant threat with forest all around.

Whroo had been carved out of the bush and stood seven miles south of Rushworth. It boasted a church, a one-roomed school and a mechanics institute and library. John said a Scot would have set that up, and if he ever had the time he would use it, but Jane was grateful for the school. She wanted her children to have an education and was happy to spend the shilling a week to send each child.

Around a third of the population were Chinese some of them ran stores and market gardens, the others worked as miners. Of the European population, few were women and children. The single men would be in need of a good meal and clean lodgings and, it went without saying, drink. That winter, four hundred miners worked on the Coy diggings alone, plenty to give them enough custom.

Gold had been discovered at Whroo early on in the gold rush, but conditions were not ideal. The Goulburn River was twelve miles away, too far away to provide a useful water source. In a dry year, the miners upped sticks and left, not returning until the rains fell, the creeks and dams filled, and it was feasible to puddle again. Jane hoped they wouldn't have too dry a season in the coming summer. They needed business, after the expense of building the hotel.

The geology was also against the Whroo diggings. Everything was upside down. John said it was as if a giant hand had twisted the earth and the best alluvial gold lay under rather than above the water level. One reason the big companies displayed no interested, because of the expensive equipment required to pump out the water to get at the gold.

John applied for a publican's licence in July, just two weeks before their neighbour, one James Bentley, applied for his own beer licence in Whroo. But while Bentley built a house with three rooms Jane's was double or more in size. She could not believe the irony. Jane had once marvelled at the grandeur of the Eureka Hotel, and now she owned a hotel, while he ran a small pub with scarce enough room to swing a cat. She forgot that six years before, a three-roomed house was her dream. Bentley's was not the only pub, there were several others. Jane meant to have the cleanest, the best run hotel, where drinkers would know that their grog had not been tampered with or watered down. As well as drink, she planned to serve her home cooked pies and mashed potato, with whatever greens she grew in her patch of garden.

Not for the first time, was she grateful for the 'miner's right' won after Eureka. For the sum of two shillings and sixpence a year, John could now mine, fell trees, build a house and a fence on a half-acre of land and vote. In her prayers, she rarely forgot to thank God for Fawkner and those that died at Eureka to gain that right. John never talked now about moving to America. Australia was his home and would be for all their children, including the little one she felt fluttering within her. Her hand stroked the slight bump rising underneath her skirts, a New Year baby she reckoned.

Her eldest daughter, Hannah, was ready for her first responsibility. Jane considered that helping out with the little one would be the training she needed for her own babies when they came. Each of her children had tasks, otherwise, how would she manage when the hotel opened. As it was, she rose at six in the morning and scarcely sat down until eight in the evening. John promised her help if the hotel took off, maybe someone to do the laundry. Jane smiled at that thought. Laundry work was the bane of her life.

Looking out of the window, she watched the boys working in the garden, weeding as she had done for her mother. She heard Jonnie moaning at Joseph.

'It's not fair, even Alfred does more weeding than you, and he's only three.'

It made her smile. Joseph was happy spending hours moving soil from one place to another, weighing it, then measuring it. Jane did not understand what went through his mind. The boy was fascinated by structures and machines of any sort, wanting to know how they were made or how they worked. At six he was more of a help to his father than his older brother, measuring wood for the house, bringing him water in the heat of the day, holding the nails. 'He's an engineer in the making, that one,' said John proudly.

Jonnie preferred the land, growing things for the table and hunting. Show him a gun and nine times out of ten he brought something back for the table, like Jacob. She sighed at those memories of childhood, recognising traits of her brothers and sisters in her own children.

John employed three miners to work his claim. They did most of the digging, while he worked the horse-drawn puddling machine and sifted the gold. He wanted a steam quartz crushing machine, because that was where the money was. Every week he scoured the papers for bankruptcy sales. He could not afford the hundred and fifty pounds for a new one. Maybe with the hotel, they could make the money within the year. A lot rode on the success of the hotel.

It opened for business in October as the weather warmed up. Men flocked to the bar for Jane's home-cooked meals and stayed to drink. After the children went to bed, Jane joined John in the bar, and both were kept busy, filling up glasses and tankards until they closed at ten or eleven o'clock, depending on business. Sometimes they had to shoo men out. Other places opened longer, some of the diggers weaving their way towards them, after the Sydney hotel shut its doors.

Jane soon learnt how to deal with men who became unpleasant drunks. On one occasion, not long after they opened, John left her on her own in the bar while he fetched another keg of beer. A customer, who Jane had not seen before, grabbed her behind as she collected glasses. If John had seen it, he would have thrown him out after a few punches to his face, because the man was too drunk to put up much of a defence. Jane simply used what she had to hand. She brought an empty wooden tankard down on his head with sufficient force to lay him out on the floor. He complained of seeing stars, before his friends picked him up and carted him away. The men around laughed and clapped her on the back.

'Fair do's Missus,' they said, and then carried on drinking. When John returned, they told him he had a right little demon for a wife. 'Best not get on the wrong side of her, I reckon,' said one.

One night in the bar, a digger told Jane that he had been drinking in Bentley's pub, but got fed up with the landlord.

'He's a madman, that one,' he said. 'He keeps going on about a man who was not murdered but spirited away somehow. He swears he spent time at Her Majesty's pleasure for a murder he didn't commit. Then he says all his money was stolen by the government.' The digger was a recent immigrant and knew nothing about Eureka. Jane did not enlighten him, storing the information away to tell John later.

She caught sight of Mrs Bentley several times when she was visiting the store on the main street. At first Jane felt a little sorry for her. It was plain she was on her way down in the world. One look at the remains of her well-darned skirt, a blouse straining to hold in her slackening chest, her bedraggled bonnet, which had once sported pink silk rosebuds, but now faded to a nondescript grey, was enough to convey poverty. Although only a year or two older than Jane, her face was lined with worry. But when she caught Jane looking at her she stared back, a haughty, angry expression in her eyes.

Bentley himself looked years older than the eight and forty years Jane understood him to be. He walked with a limp, his right foot turning inward with deformity. His grey hair showed little of the dark brown hair of his younger days, and his hazel eyes held a wild air of desperation. It was difficult to reconcile these two sad people with the couple who flaunted their wealth and connections in Ballarat. Time had dealt them a heavy hand indeed.

It was clear from the gossip in the shop that neither of the Bentleys felt guilt or responsibility for poor James Scobie. Exactly the opposite, they were incredibly aggrieved by events, which they swore were not of their making. The troops should have stopped the destruction of their hotel. Of the murder they knew nothing.

One day, between Christmas and New Year, when the heat of the day threatened to overwhelm Jane, she was gathering in her washing from the line. From the corner of her eye, she saw Mrs Bentley walking or rather stumbling with a shopping basket down the track towards Cherry Tree Diggings, where her own property lay. Jane watched as the woman stopped for a second and then sank to the ground, immobile. There was nothing for it but to help her. Jane walked as fast as her heavily pregnant body would allow. As she approached heard the woman sobbing quietly.

'Mrs Bentley,' Jane said in a quiet voice, so as not to alarm her. 'Please let me help.'

She looked up at Jane, her face white and tear-stained. 'Thank you,' she whispered, with no sign of haughtiness this time, just despair in her blue-grey eyes. Jane saw that her basket was empty. She offered her hand to pull the woman up, placing an arm around her waist before Jane led her back towards her house.

'A sit down out of the sun, and a cup of strong tea will see you better. It's too hot to be walking out now.' Although Mrs Bentley did not answer, Jane sensed her relief in the idea. On entering the kitchen, Jane sat her down in a chair and then turned to put a pan of water on to the range, making small talk as she did so. The tea was quickly made. Jane set out two cups on the table, a teapot and a plate of biscuits, made earlier that day. Jane saw, with surprise, how the woman's eyes were drawn to the biscuits with longing, noticing the gauntness in her face. She's hungry, Jane thought with sudden pity for the woman and her situation.

'I'm sorry to put you to so much trouble Mrs...'

'Timmins,' Jane offered. 'And it's no trouble at all.'

'It was the heat; you're right. It's too hot to be out. I'll never get used to the heat here.' She dabbed at her face with a handkerchief.

'Please take a biscuit,' said Jane, holding the plate towards her. She watched as the women took it, restraining herself to take a polite nibble rather than wolfing it down, before thanking Jane and commenting on the fine quality of her baking.

'That's a good range you have,' she said.

'It is the latest model and makes life so much easier than cooking on a fire, don't you find?' Jane asked.

'I suppose, although I have never yet cooked on a fire.' An unspoken inference led Jane to believe the woman feared sinking low enough to experience the unwanted delight of a campfire. Further stilted conversation followed, until the woman had drunk her tea, eaten the biscuit and politely refused a second.

'I must not take up and more of your time, Mrs Timmins. Thank you, I feel so much better and must be getting home.' She stood to take her leave.

'Would you like to take some peas with you, I seem to have an overabundance this year,' said Jane, pointing to a pile she had intended Hannah to shell.

'No, I could not possibly,' she replied, uncertainty and longing in her eyes.

'Of course, you could,' said Jane, bundling them into her basket. She threw in an onion and a couple of potatoes for good measure, as the woman tried to mask her gratitude. It was not until after she left that Jane noticed the handkerchief on the floor. She picked it up meaning to return it, after it had been laundered, but never got the chance.

It was no surprise to learn later that Mrs Bentley had been refused further credit at the store. Nor that she and her family had scurried off back to Melbourne, their pub failing to make sufficient profit to see them through the dry season.

'Good riddance,' was all John would say after Jane had told him about her encounter with Mrs Bentley. He told her she was too kind.

'I can't see a family go hungry. A few peas will make a thin enough soup. I felt sorry for her. But she's proud; I'll give her that.'

Only Hannah was upset by the Bentley's leaving, because she looked up to Matilda Bentley, two years her senior at the small village school. The nearest child she had as a friend. Few of the miners bothered to send their daughters to school. As it was, the teacher made the girls sit at the back, while she controlled the boys at the front, with frequent use of her cane. Hannah depended on Matilda to help her with her letters. When Matilda left the village, Hannah became dumb with panic at the thought of returning to school after the long summer break, until Jonnie promised to help her with her reading. After supper, Jane sat with them, at first to rest her swelling ankles. She wanted to encourage Hannah, who was a sweet child, although no match for her ebullient twin. They were as different from each other as they could possibly be. Joseph had all the energy, enthusiasm and charm, while his sister was placid, cautious and shy.

As the three sat around the kitchen table, Jane began to take an interest in what they were doing. She asked Jonnie if he would mind teaching his mother how to sign her name. He picked up his slate and taking a nub of chalk; he wrote her name out in large letters telling her the name of each one as he wrote. When he finished, he handed the slate to her. She stared, trying to embed each shape into her brain. It was the first time she had seen her name written. Yes, she had her birth name written on her marriage lines, which John kept in a safe box in their bedroom. From memory, she knew that there were so many squiggly words on it, she could not have found her name without help. But these two words she could learn, and one day she would write them herself. She knew that as sure as the sun rose every day and the stars shone in the night sky. Never again would she have to shame herself by marking her name with a cross. With a patient teacher like Jonnie to help her, she would learn in God's good time.

Joseph found most of the lessons boring at school, other than arithmetic, which he found easy. Learning about English Kings and Queens had him itching in his seat. He frequently felt the cane on his knuckles, his hand idling beside his slate. As soon as the bell rang for the end of lessons, he escaped to help his father feed, water and bed the horses. His own special pony was Billy, a gentle piebald three-year-old, who neighed with pleasure when he smelt Joseph. Before he even saw him, he whinnied in pleasure. Then nuzzled his hands to get at the carrot or apple, which Joseph never failed to save from his lunch pail. Joseph did not know what he loved most, engines or horses. They both filled him with so much pleasure, he could not wait to discard school forever and spend his days with them.

Towards the end of January Grace entered the world. 'We could do with a bit of God's grace, Jane,' John said, cradling his latest child in his arms. He had laid off his workers through lack of water, and the miners who wanted a room for the night dwindled to nothing. 'We need rain sweet Grace. Can you intercede for us?'

'Hush John, that's no way to talk to the child, taking God's name in vain.'

'I mean it, Jane. We always knew it would be a risk moving here, but I hate being idle and losing money. We have tons of quartz lying on the claim and no means to crush it. No one can afford the cost of carting it miles to the crushing mill.' John was thankful that he did not buy the quartz crusher, because several were standing idle on the diggings. He was beginning to feel that this move to Whroo was a mistake, but there were so few independent goldmines now. If he did not mine gold, what else was he to do?

For Jane, despite the worry of drought, the slack time allowed her to regain her strength. Thank goodness, they had not taken on a laundry maid. By the middle of March, Jane was as perturbed as John to see their savings and water dwindle in equal measure. But then the rains arrived in abundance, and with them, the miners returned. They breathed again, as the hotel and the bar sprang back into life. Jane took on a sturdy twelve-year-old girl as both laundry maid and nursemaid. Freda was an apple-cheeked, flaxen-haired girl of Germanic stock. Her solid arms and work hardened hands were a good sign of her usefulness and Jane was not disappointed. The girl worked ferociously at the laundry but was as gentle and loving with Grace as Jane herself, allowing Jane to prepare food for the ravenous miners who flocked to their hotel after work.

It was one of the good years; the water lasted through the following summer until March. Gold in the alluvial seams was plentiful and easily extracted. Their savings grew again. But months later it all turned sour. Because there had been rain in the summer of 1867, by the time winter arrived, the alluvial seams became flooded and unworkable.

In August, with money in the bank, but no likelihood of it remaining there for long, as work dried up, John decided to explore the Red Gate Diggings, where gold had been found the year before. He took a horse and rode seventy miles south-east to prospect the land. Two weeks later, he rode back brimming with optimism. Jane could see the excitement on his face, but he did not get a chance to talk for a while as the children ran to greet him. Even little Grace toddled to him, demanding to be picked up.

Later as they talked before bed, he said, 'You'll like it, Jane. It's a real bonnie place, not far from the Goulburn River. There are wide valleys and snow-topped mountains to the east and south. If the grass weren't all so yellow, it would remind me of Scotland. They already have a post office, and a school will open soon when a teacher's been found. Best of all, I bumped into a young man, by the name of James Shore who is looking to invest in a mine. He has the money and I the experience; it's a good combination. Think Jane, for the first time we'll have the capital to become a gold mining company, one of the bigger boys. No more being just a digger. We can lay the foundations for our family.

We've marked out a likely fifteen-acre plot beside the creek, and James and I bought the land last week. He's putting in the licence application, but I need to return to buy the machinery we need. In a few weeks, we can move if you start to pack. Let's hope we've turned a corner in our fortunes.'

Chapter 38

Melbourne April 1932

Mary thought of Jane's stories as a potted history of Victoria. She should be rolled out into schools and children would lap up the lessons.

'Did you hear any more of the Bentley's afterwards?' Mary asked.

'He was a wreck, and you could see it in his eyes. He took a laudanum overdose a few years later. I remember John reading out the story in the paper.' She paused, looking blank for several seconds, and then smiled. 'They said he was a pickle maker in Bourke Street. That street again; the one where I lived as a child, and he committed suicide. Don't you think that there are patterns in life Mary? You just have to look for them.'

Mary shrugged. Sometimes the dying began to have moments of confusion or strange visions as the oxygen becomes depleted from their blood. Could that momentary lapse in her conversation be a sign?

Something else that Jane understood at last; Mary was her guardian angel, leading her towards a peaceful end. Every day she sensed the growing presence of her mother waiting to greet her on the other side. She could almost feel her, touch her. It would not be long before her mother's arms would embrace her and lead her to eternal rest. Why should that matter more than being reunited with John? It was John she missed most.

Mary had been guiding her. She said when she first came how she only worked with the dying. What could be more obvious that she was sent to do this work by God? The dreams were a part of it; the messages clear. Her mother waited for her and had forgiven her. Jane felt blessed and loved. In turn, she knew she would wait for her children to join her. John, her husband, and Joseph her son, were already there. She must give this message to her children. It was important for them to know. Dying was not something to fear; she welcomed it with open arms.

'Will you ring the family Mary? I want to see as many of them as can make it. I only have another couple of stories, and then I can go.'

Chapter 39

Victoria 1870s

Jane thought of the eighteen years after they left Whroo as her golden years, not because of the gold itself, but because of the golden beauty of the lands they inhabited. First, she fell in love with the land surrounding the township of Alexandra, renamed by the time she arrived from the original Red Gate Diggings. It reminded her of the estate at Plenty and the good farmland she always coveted. Before the diggings, it had been a sheep run. Despite the evidence of new mining, there was sufficient beauty remaining in the creeks, the gum trees, the wildlife and the mountains to the south. East of the town were lakes and on rare summer Sundays the family took picnics there, the only holidays that Jane ever had time for until she was in her eighties, by which time she was too old.

It was also a time of greater prosperity. Hard work yielded the rewards necessary for their growing family. Five more daughters arrived in quick succession, four of whom survived. John arranged for their hotel in Whroo to be taken down in sections and moved to Alexandra, where it reopened under a different name, the Mooltan Hotel. Jane considered it a strange name, but John explained that it was the name of the Indian Regiment which his father was attached to in his youth. Years later Jane thought it a good omen when her grandson sailed for the war in Europe on a troopship called the Mooltan, a liner which had been plying the route between England and India until called into war service.

They did not stop moving in the years they based themselves around Alexandra. It was only as the gold returns diminished that they moved south over the mountains towards Walhalla. The boys left school at twelve, working with their father, first in mining and later, sawing wood. Timber was now in great demand for the steam engines at the Walhalla mines and the new railway line to Sale.

At last, there were trains.

'About time too,' said John, often enough. He won a contract for supplying the railway with red gums from their saw-mill at Boola. He took Joseph with him to make the first delivery to the line. Joseph saw the canvas tents strung along the route the railway was to take and was captivated by the excitement of the enterprise. Is it true, he asked his father, that people will soon be able to travel to Melbourne within one day? Indeed so, he replied. His father talked to him about the railways of the old country and the changes they brought.

'Mark my words,' he said, 'railways will be the making of this country. There's money to be made for those lucky and enterprising enough build them.'

Joseph watched as the men laid the iron tracks interspersed with the wooden sleepers. It was tough work in the boiling heat of the day, but he saw their sweat and labour as something noble, as they described the engine that would ply the tracks within the year. He imagined it eating up the miles and spewing them out in the gritty steam, clouding the onlookers in dirt and grime.

Joseph was beside himself with excitement on the journey home, talking non-stop to his father about what he had heard and seen. He begged his father for permission to revisit the navvies, whenever he had a spare moment. His father agreed, as long as he finished the work he had been set for the day. John knew it was the right path for his son. A career as a railway engineer would be the making of him.

Whenever he had the chance, Joseph went armed with cool drinking water, enticing the navvies to take a break and talk more about the track and the engines. It was not long before he came to the attention of the overseer, and by the age of sixteen, Joseph was taken on by the contractors to cut sleepers from the gums he helped to log.

Jane remembered the anticipation and excitement of the day in December 1875 when the newly shipped engine got up steam and ran down the track between Sale and the first bridge over the river. The whole family was there to see it. She and girls stood beside the track, completely overawed by the sight. Little Sophie, only two at the time, put her hands over her ears and screamed as the engine passed.

'Not like, Mama,' she cried. Jane shushed her, picking her up and placing her face against her bosom as the engine whistle blew long and hard. Joseph stood proud as punch, watching the engine passing, staring intently at it, wanting to know how each part worked.

A different invention caused Jane to be waiting at the station three years later. The day before she had received a telegraph while weeding her vegetable patch. She ran into the house where Grace confirmed it was addressed to her and offered to read it.

'Joseph's been ill, but he's out of danger,' she read. Jane snatched the telegraph back, attempting to read it for herself, her heart racing with concern.

'What's this name?' she asked, pointing to the end of the telegraph.

'Mrs Carlotti, she says Joseph is in her guest house in Euroa.'

Jane hailed the telegraph boy who was waiting patiently at the door. 'Reply that I am coming,' she told him, searching out some coins in her bag.

John offered to go, but Jane would not hear of it. Ever since the telegraph arrived she sensed that she was meant to make this journey. Perhaps, she thought, Joseph was worse than this Mrs Carlotti claimed, although John reread the message several times to her assuring her that Joseph was on the mend.

As she stood waiting for the train, she tried to dismiss her nerves, supposing them to be her motherly instincts. It was the first time she had made any journey without John, let alone a journey which involved travelling by train. The railway line was built only as far as Oakleigh, where a Cobbs coach service took passengers from there into Melbourne. She would stay overnight in a hotel before catching the train north to Euroa from Spencer Street Station. It was all booked, including the hotel on Bourke Street, so she only had to walk west a few blocks to get to the station.

There should be nothing to worry about, only, of course, there was. The whole journey, at this point, seemed a series of what ifs, despite her brain telling her that nothing could go wrong. The worry was a little worm burrowing into her mind. 'Strange', she thought, 'I'm not the worrying kind'. She considered herself strong and independent in any circumstances.

Once she got underway, she forgot her fears, becoming interested in the unfamiliar country passing by amidst the strange sensation of speed. There were odd sounds too, a clickety-clack and then a jerky rattle as the train went over points. She relaxed into her seat enjoying the comfort of the journey, comparing it to wagon rides on the backwater cart tracks of rural Victoria. Ruts, mud and boulders were a common hazard, and the consequent journey, a series of bone-shaking jolts, or worse if you lost a wheel or an axle broke. This train journey was as smooth as a boat travelling downriver, she supposed. Not that she had ever been on a riverboat.

The train appeared to fly over rivers and gullies, the new bridges so sturdy and strong, not the broken-down ones she was used to. They were often a disgrace with so little money in the small townships to pay for repairs. The arrival of the train was changing everything, bringing prosperity and new blood in its wake. John was talking about bidding for contracts to repair roads and bridges, with Jonnie and Alfred joining him in a new contracting business. Things were looking up for the family, as long as she found good husbands for her six daughters.

Her nerves melted away and she began to enjoy the journey. She felt disappointed when they had to step down from the train and mount a coach for the remaining miles.

She arrived in Melbourne in time for a late dinner. As they passed through the city streets, she saw no evidence of the Melbourne she once knew. Wooden huts and muddy streets had been replaced by stone pavements and impressive buildings of brick and stone, all lit by gaslight. It was her first sight of a modern city, and she was impressed.

The hotel was large with sixty bedrooms and gas light in the lobby. A lackey picked up her valise, the leather still so new that it had no scuffs and the pleasant rich smell of a new saddle. he carried it her room on the third floor. The boy lit the lamp, and she gave him sixpence for his trouble. She washed and changed and went down to dinner.

After her main course of poached fish, she was presented with a concoction in a tall glass. It looked colourful with cherry syrup on top and a dark brown sauce underneath and sandwiched between, something creamy-white. She dipped her spoon into the mixture and took her first bite of an ice cream sundae. Her eyes opened with shock and pleasure. She had never tasted anything so delicious, and she imagined the response if she were ever able to put this on the menu in her own hotel.

The owner said he would be delighted to show her his new soda fountain, sent directly from America. Jane started to make mental notes. In the few hours since she left home, she had entered a new world, modern, intriguing and exciting. She had much to tell her children, and her mind spun into overdrive, planning for a hotel of her own with gas lamps and soda fountains and who knew what else.

The following morning, she walked to the station to catch the train north. She knew that she was walking along the same road where their family lived many years before, but it had changed out of all recognition. She stopped for a moment where she thought their cabin might have stood and turned slowly around, but it was no good. Nothing looked familiar.

Arriving at the station, she found a porter and asked him for directions to the Euroa train. He took the valise from her and found her an empty carriage. She had plenty of time to wait for the train to set off and she watched the bustle of the station as travellers arrived and departed. It made her dizzy to see the commotion, but it also made her mind buzz with excitement. The nerves of yesterday disappeared, and her confidence returned.

Perhaps carrying another child had perturbed her the day before. At forty-one she hoped that her childbearing days were over, but the signs were unmistakable. She prayed for a son.

After changing trains in Seymour, Jane arrived at Euroa in mid-afternoon. The sun beat down on her, causing beads of sweat to run down her back as she walked along the street looking for the Myrtle Guest House. The little town was busy for a Monday afternoon, surprisingly so. She had been given directions by the man in the ticket office, but it was no more than a minute or two's walk and took her hardly any time before she saw the sign. She still tried to memorise the shapes of words, especially if they were unfamiliar, but in this case, the owner had a sprig of myrtle painted next to the name on the board. Jane was convinced she was at the right place.

The door opened before she knocked three times. A cheerful, motherly figure opened the door. Jane guessed the woman was in her fifties, with round, dimpled cheeks and dark brown eyes containing the kind of warmth that drew people in.

'You must be Mrs Timmins; Joseph will be so pleased you're here. Do come in, dear lady.' The woman spoke with an accent, which Jane could not pin down.

'Your Joseph is a delightful boy, and we were so worried about him. The doctor came every day for a week. Come you must be thirsty; I will make you a nice cup of tea. Are you hungry?'

Jane could scarce get a word in. The woman was everything Jane was not, garrulous, plump, unconstrained and Jane liked her at once. Taking Jane's valise, she ushered her into Joseph's upstairs room saying, 'I know you won't be happy until you see the invalid for yourself and make sure he is being well looked after.'

He was sitting in a chair beside a window facing the street. Jane thought he looked wan and pasty. She crossed the room to kiss his face and stroke his hair. Turning towards the landlady, who stood in the doorway smiling, Jane said, 'I can't thank you enough, Mrs Carlotti, have I said it right?' She looked for reassurance from Joseph.

'Yes, my dear, Angela Carlotti, a good Italian name. I'll leave you with Joseph while I get you some refreshment.' She turned from the door, beaming at the reunion between mother and son and padded off across the hallway.

'She's been my nurse and a saint, Mother. I think I would have died but for her.' Joseph's voice sounded thin and reedy. 'I still feel as though

I have been hit by a sledgehammer. The doctor says I will need a few weeks to get over it, but I must get back to work on the railway. Mrs Carlotti sent my boss a telegram to say where I was, but I'm not sure how long they will keep my job open.'

'Don't worry about that for now. You need to regain your strength. Otherwise, you will be ill again. What were you doing in Euroa anyway?' Joseph blushed, and the pink in his cheeks stood out like a furnace in his ashen face.

'There's a girl I thought I was sweet on here. As I had a night off, I came to visit her, but I found out she was courting another beau, so I drowned my sorrows instead. I'd paid for a room here, as I have in the past, but I don't remember much after going to bed. I suppose I had a skinful. Mrs Carlotti came to my room after I did not turn up for breakfast and found me thrashing about with a fever.'

'It was a fever you could boil water on, Mrs Timmins' Mrs Carlotti walked in with a tray of tea and sandwiches, covered with a cloth. 'I wanted to send a telegram sooner, but I searched his bags and could not find any letters or anything, so I did not know who to contact. It wasn't until he had been ill for nearly a week that he was able to tell me your name and address.'

A sudden chill swept over Jane. Joseph was not far off the same age as Jacob was when he disappeared. Had Joseph died, would she have found out what happened to him? It did not bear thinking about.

She clutched at Mrs Carlotti's hands. 'Thank you, a million times, thank you.'

'You would do the same, my dear. Come and eat a sandwich. You must be hungry after your journey.'

'There must be expenses, Mrs Carlotti; the doctor's bill and the room here.'

'Yes, but don't concern yourself with that now. All in good time as they say.'

Looking out of the window Jane saw a bank, the side entrance facing the street. 'Please I can't be in your debt, I'll not be happy until it's paid. It's just the way my parents brought me up. After I have drunk this tea and freshened up, I'll visit the bank, over the road. Please give me the doctor's bill.'

'If you insist my dear.' Mrs Carlotti went to fetch it.

'Mother let me pay it.'

'No Joseph, you are in no condition to leave this house. I doubt you have enough ready cash for this doctor's bill and in any case, I want to pay it. Let that be an end to it.'

Joseph knew enough about his mother to recognise when to give in. Once she decided to do something, there was no changing her mind. He was delighted to see her. As wonderful as Mrs Carlotti had been, he thought he had been calling for his mother when he was full of fever. He remembered a dark tunnel, a voice far off in the distance and the word mother, echoing around his head. He wondered if she had any sense of his illness before receiving the telegram.

'No, I didn't. If I had, I would have been terrified because of what your Aunt Hannah experienced when Jacob died. I remember her face to this day; it was ashen. I thank God, I did not inherit the second sight as my mother called it. Neither has your twin, and that is a blessing.'

'You never talk about your family.'

'Haven't I got enough of my own family to keep me occupied? I lost touch with my brothers and sisters. My parents died before you were born, so what's to tell you?' She stood up and smoothed her dress as Mrs Carlotti returned with the bill. Jane took it and pursed her lips when she saw the amount. Doctor's always knew how to charge, and by the sound of it, without the nursing of Mrs Carlotti, Joseph would not have pulled through. She would be added to Jane's daily prayers.

It was almost four o'clock when Jane entered the bank. There were few customers and enough tellers, so Jane was served straight away. She was grateful that John insisted she have her own bank account, knowing some husbands refused to allow their wives this independence.

A few minutes later she was exiting the front door of the bank, stuffing the money she had withdrawn into her purse. When she looked up, she noticed a wagon and spring cart draw up just around the corner.

Four men got down and came towards her, making for the front door, leaving a youth on the cart. The men were young, heavily bearded, but well dressed in grey check suits and dark coats. Three were wearing white hats with elastic chin bands and the other a drab felt hat. They only looked odd because they were dressed almost identically. One brushed against her as he passed and gave her a brief apologetic smile. She would have forgotten about it, but as the heavy door closed behind them, she thought she heard it lock. Faint shouts came from inside. She paused, vaguely uneasy, and looked across the road to the guest house. Joseph was sitting in the window beckoning urgently to her, so she crossed the street to return to him.

As she entered the house, she heard someone banging on the bank door. She turned to watch a frustrated customer walking away. The door was definitely locked, but why?

'Mother, thank God you are back,' Joseph said, as she walked into his room. 'I think the bank's being held up. I am sure I saw rifles underneath those men's coats as they got down from the wagons.'

'Guns! We must call for the police,' said Jane, shouting to Mrs Carlotti who came running.

'Whatever is it, Mrs Timmins, is it Joseph? Has he taken a turn for the worse?'

'The bank's being held up. There are four men with guns in there, and they've locked the main door. Go fetch the police, quickly.'

'But there aren't any police in town. They are away tracking the Kelly Gang after the murders at Stringy Bark Creek a few weeks ago.' The three of them looked at each other and realisation struck.

'Oh, mio Dio! I'm going to lock our doors,' said Mrs Carlotti. 'Keep away from the windows, in case bullets start flying around.' Jane sank onto the bed; she felt faint. All that nervousness from yesterday rose screaming to the surface, but never in her wildest imagination did she think of getting mixed up with the Kelly Gang.

'Mother lie on the bed. You look awful; your face is as white as a sheet.' Joseph turned back towards the window. It was minutes now since the gang entered the bank. They must surely come out soon, maybe with guns blazing. People were walking along the street, some were mothers with children, all oblivious to what was going on in the bank.

'We should warn them somehow. I think I should go and warn them.' He stood but then sank back down, his head buzzing and his body refusing to move.

Mrs Carlotti crept back into the room as though the Kelly gang were going to hear her and shoot at her.

'I've bolted the doors. Is anything happening? Oh, Mrs Timmins are you alright?' She noted Jane lying prone on the bed.

'I am a bit nauseous.'

'Let me fetch you some water.' She crept out again.

'Something's happening now.' Joseph said, a minute later, as the side door to the bank opened. People were streaming out, men, women and children. They began to climb up into the wagons.

'Why that's Mr Scott, the manager, and his family,' cried Mrs Carlotti, who had arrived back with the water. 'Where are they going?'

Jane rose unsteadily from the bed to peek out of the window. She recognised the teller who had served her, but it was the women and children who most struck her. They looked terrified, even though, what she took to be the manager's wife, tried to calm her children. They must have been warned not to make a sound, as the gang directed them towards the waiting wagons.

'A minute earlier and it would have been me.' Jane held on to Joseph's hand. She could see two of the members of the gang pointing rifles at the hostages, the tips of the barrels visible from underneath their long coats. When everyone had climbed into the wagons, the drivers flicked the reins, and they set off at a trot. One of the gang members sat amongst the hostages in each wagon with a gun across his lap. The hostages' heads remained down, and the younger children sat on the women's laps with hands lightly placed across their mouths to stop them from crying.

Their journey through town was as inconspicuous as possible. No one appeared to realise what had happened, although the bank was in full view of the railway station and the town's largest hotel. As audacious as their plan was, it was succeeding without a hitch.

Joseph and the two ladies remained where they were, not daring to believe what they had witnessed. It seemed like minutes but was, more likely only seconds. The silence was broken by yet another customer banging on locked bank door across the road.

Mrs Carlotti came to her senses and rushed off. Joseph and Jane watched as she flew out of the house screaming, 'Carabinieri, we need carabinieri, robbery, Kelly Gang.' Her anguished words were jumbled and incoherent, but 'Kelly Gang' came out loud, and strong.

In an instant, men and women gathered around her like a flock of birds alighting on a cast-off scrap of bread, so much so that she disappeared from view. Screams were heard as women found out about the kidnapping of the Scott family. A minute later, a pathway cleared. Jane saw the landlady pointing towards her house and the room upstairs, where Joseph and his mother sat watching. People began streaming across the road towards the house. Jane watched Joseph grow even paler as they realised that soon enough they would be inundated with questioners. She stood up saying, 'I will deal with them, Joseph. You stay here.'

'But Mother you are not well yourself.'

'I am much better now,' and it was true, the shock was fading. She left the room closing the door firmly behind her.

Later she did not remember how many times she told her story. First, the crowd gathered around her in the lobby of the guesthouse. She remembered the questions shouted at her until her head ached. She also remembered the welcome interruption when a man arrived saying the telegraph wires running alongside the railway track had been cut. That caused great consternation as realisation struck that they could not summon help from Benalla Police Station. Someone would have to be sent there by train, and the crowd began to speculate on the time of the next train. At last, they drifted off, but the following day a reporter asked to interview her. She agreed but asked for her name not to be printed as her family did not know what had happened. Then a policeman wanted her to make a statement, and every time she set foot out of the guesthouse during the next two days, someone felt bound to approach her to ask her to repeat her story.

Why not ask the Scott family or the bank staff, she wondered? Their tale sounded far more dramatic than hers. The hostages had been taken to a sheep station a few miles from Euroa, where more of the gang were holed up. The hostages, numbering around thirty in total, said they were treated well enough, but Daniel Kelly acted like a brute. They were grateful that his brother, Ned, was there to restrain him. Jane thought back to her fleeting encounter with the gang. Did one have a more threatening air than the other? She could not say that in truth.

Eventually, the gang left the sheep station with their haul of money and silver. They told the hostages to wait three hours before raising the alarm. Out of fear for the consequences, they complied. The Kelly Gang were a law unto themselves and capable of anything. So now the bushrangers were back on the loose, and the rumours about their probable direction abounded.

After she got home, Jane's family and neighbours wanted to hear the story too. She became sick of the tale and never repeated it after the gang was killed, and Ned executed. When she saw his photograph, she studied it to see if she recognised the one who brushed by her. It may have been Ned, but she could not swear to it.

John had been wild with worry when he heard about the holdup, knowing she and Joseph were in Euroa. She sent him a telegram, as soon as the wires were repaired to put his mind at rest. Joseph was recovering well from his illness and received word that his employers agreed to grant him three weeks of unpaid leave. So, after a few days, Jane felt able to leave him in the care of Mrs Carlotti and returned to Melbourne.

She always intended to stay an extra day in Melbourne to do some Christmas shopping, but something told her to visit Geelong instead. She had never listened to any inner voice before, but after what happened in Euroa, she knew she must. Perhaps she too was affected by the curse of second-sight, however faint the signs until then.

Chapter 40

Melbourne May 1932

Jane was fading. The last story exhausted what remained of her energy. She had arrived at the point when her life became both more difficult and her soul most troubled. The guilt of not removing her mother from David's clutches tormented her, along with the decline in John's health. He depended more on her and the eldest boys while, at the same time, she had her last child, Charlie, to care for. She needed to file away the guilt she felt for leaving her mother. There was nothing to be done about it. Her husband and her baby consumed her time and her energy. John's was a long decline. He was not yet sixty, but years of toil in the mines and the timber business broke his health. Little by little she watched him fade. When Charlie was not yet four-years-old, John had a stroke, which rendered him bedridden and helpless. Jane and her daughters nursed him to the best of their ability until he died aged fifty-eight.

In her remaining moments of lucidity, she only had thoughts for John and their life together. It had been a strong marriage between equal partners, and she longed to be reunited with him. Nothing else mattered now.

Every day saw her sleep more. Although that sleep was fitful, her breathing becoming shallow and wheezing. Rattles accompanying her outward breaths as her lungs became congested. Most of her family had visited in the last two weeks. Mary was at last able to put faces to the names she had come to know so well since she started nursing Jane.

Little Jonnie was a stooped, balding man in his late seventies, Mary had met him before, and Alfred not much younger. Charlie, the youngest was lean, fit, energetic and in his fifties. Stanley, the grandson who married an English woman and bought an opera company was short, amiable but sad looking. Sophie whispered to her that his wife had refused to bring their children back to Australia, after an extended trip to England. Emily made a fleeting visit from her home in New South Wales, Grace was shorter than the other daughters and walked with a pronounced limp, but nevertheless, the likeness to her sisters was unmistakable. Sophie and Eleanor came every day to sit beside Jane, chatting softly as their mother slept and appearing alarmed when she struggled for breath.

Mary brought in tea for Eleanor and Sophie one afternoon in the second week of May. The women had been there since mid-morning and looked tired themselves. This vigil was wearing for Jane's children, especially Sophie, to whom most of the lot had fallen.

'Your mother never got to tell me about Broken Hill,' Mary said as they sipped the tea. Their expressions told a story in itself; eyebrows raised and a simultaneous look of wry amusement.

'After Father died she spent the next twenty years confounding us with her energy. Look at her there. She looks so frail now, but there was no mother like her anywhere. Most widows of her age settle for a comfortable if impoverished old age. But my father dying, freed her to be this whirlwind businesswoman, who never took no for an answer. She fought other people's expectations, businessmen, the law and for the most part she won. She and Joseph what a pair they were,' said Eleanor, a year older than her sister. They may have been twins, in the way that they dressed, talked and finished each other's sentences.

'I'm sure it was Joseph who put Broken Hill in her head,' said Sophie. 'I remember him arriving in Traralgon with his son after his first wife died. He wanted Mother to care for little Joseph. He'd been working on the railway from Adelaide to Cockburn but was then off to work on a line in the Northern Territories. Mother took out a wine licence on the house in Traralgon. It brought little money in, but she couldn't get a beer licence. The strict, Scottish Presbyterian Council thought there were too many pubs in town already. Unbeknownst to us, she began to plan a move.'

'Those old fogies should have seen Broken Hill. How many pubs were there when we arrived Sophie? Sixty pubs for nine thousand men, and everyone of them full of men drinking their wages away.' Eleanor answered her own question. 'Now that's the profit my mother was looking for. Do you remember the journey, Sophie?'

'I do. I'd never been anywhere else but that little corner of Victoria. It was exciting but frightening at the same time. We left at New Year 1891, having spent a final Christmas together, surrounded by packing cases. Jonnie and Alfred, who were staying to carry on with the saw-mill at Boola, took us to the station. Jonnie kept on trying to get my mother to change her mind. He was beside himself with worry, thinking that Dad would be up there blaming him for this crazy idea she had. I loved the train ride to Melbourne, but I would have been happy to take the train right back, because I missed our home already. You did too, didn't you Eleanor?' Her sister nodded.

'I mostly remember the crowds of people milling around the station. More people than I knew existed and it unnerved us. Mother, as usual, was in complete control. She hailed two cabs to take us to down to the port for the steamer to Adelaide, so we did not see much of Melbourne. We were looking forward to our first sight of the sea. Unfortunately, it was dusk by the time we arrived to board the ship, so we had to delay that pleasure until the next morning. Charlie ran around getting in everyone's way until Mother slapped him. I took tight hold of little Joseph's hand, because I was terrified of him falling overboard. We all watched as the lights of Melbourne faded into the distance. It was hard saying goodbye to Victoria, not knowing when we would be back. I know I shed tears.

Adelaide was pleasant; I remember thinking it a good size for a city, not too big but well laid out. Not that we stayed there long, just a day for Mother to collect the keys to the hotel she had bought. Then off by train to Cockburn and tramway from there into Broken Hill arriving in the middle of the night.'

'The night was clear,' butted in Eleanor. 'I remember the stars shining and they appeared nearer somehow than they did in Victoria. It must have been the desert air. We all felt the chill as we climbed down off the tram, didn't we? I remember shivering, not thinking we would long for the cold over the days ahead. There was a different kind of smell too, not the sharp, tangy Eucalyptus scent we were used to. The air reeked of chemicals, engines and grease. Later we learned that it was the smelter pumping out fumes. You could never get away from the stink until they moved it down to Port Pirie.

We didn't know what to expect. Mother told us she had bought a hotel and there it was, across the road from the station, the Terminus Hotel, larger than we expected, twenty bedrooms, built of wood with a tin roof. I think we were all so weary that we crossed the track and fell into it the moment Mother unlocked the door. I don't remember how we got to bed. I do remember waking up the next morning. Mother said we should sleep in and meet for a late breakfast at nine o'clock. We shared a bedroom, didn't we Sophie?'

'Yes. We woke much later than normal, washed, dressed, and I opened the curtains, excited to see our new home. Oh my, what a let-down. There was the scarred Broken Hill rising high into the air not far away, the colour of rust. The unpaved streets were full of dust, and you could see the horses kicking sand up as they trotted by. The sun was already shining white-hot in the blue cloudless sky. It looked unrelenting, fierce, and I swear the sandy ground shimmered with heat, even at nine in the morning. You joined me at the window Nellie, and we wondered where the trees and bushes shading the streets were? We did not know we were coming to a desert. She must have known, but she didn't warn us. We stood at the window, open-mouthed until Emily burst into the room in tears, saying she wanted to go home.'

'Of course it was no use complaining to Mother. We must have sat around the breakfast table with long faces, because she told us, in no uncertain terms, that this was our future. We should be grateful for a mother who was going to work hard to put clothes on our backs and food in our mouths, and make sure we made good marriages,' said Nellie.

'Here is where the money is,' she said. You have to give her credit, she was right.' Sophie sighed and putting her cup down, she picked up her mother's hand again, stroking it. 'None of us but Joseph inherited her drive and ambition, well maybe Charlie too.'

'Do you recall our first visit to church there, Sophie?'

'Oh yes. How can I forget the stares as we trooped in? Mother in front, followed by Grace and Emily, then me and you with Florence, Charlie. Little Joseph brought up the rear. All of us dressed in our Sunday- best. We doubled the number of marriageable girls in the town, in one stroke.' The sisters began to giggle.

'Did you all find husbands there?' Asked Mary

'No, only Emily. She married a brewer, dear Frederick. What a lovely man he was. He drowned at Manly, trying to save a woman from the sea. Poor Emily and her children watched the whole thing. I don't think she ever got over it, although she married again. But you don't want to hear about that, Mary.' Sophie smiled. 'Let's tell you about the strike of 1892. What an eye-opener that was.'

Chapter 41

Broken Hill NSW 1891-2

Jane herself wondered many times, in those first weeks in Broken Hill, if she had made a mistake in moving there. It was not a lack of drinkers in her public bar. They were too numerous to count. More so when they realised how many daughters accompanied her. Rather the daily battle to live in the town took some getting used to. The heat in Victoria reached a hundred degrees frequently, but never lasted for weeks on end as it did here. Yet the nights were cold, it was a rare cloud that scudded across the inky, open sky. Then there were the dust storms. When the hot winds blew, there was no vegetation to anchor the rusty red soil, and it became a maelstrom of gritty dust. When the first one blew, she felt a moment of panic, recollecting the fire that followed back in 1851. She was convinced the wooden town would burn, until an old timer at the bar told her not to fuss so.

'They are a fact of life here Missus. We all get used to them in time.' His face told of resignation, his eyes bloodshot with grit.

Then there was the water or lack of it. Jane watched in amazement the first time she saw a tram full of large metal containers arrive at the station outside her hotel. Water was hosed from the tanks into a man-made ditch, where it flowed into town to be sold to rich and poor alike. Having to buy water made a bigger hole in her profit than she had bargained for.

Firewood was another added cost. She had lived most of her life surrounded by trees, majestic gums in all their guises and shrubby ones too, but trees for all that. Here there was scarcely a leaf. Any tree that existed in this barren, dusty town had already been cut down to burn and make way for a town where none should exist.

Her children complained about the lack of shade, and the lack of a wooden walkway through the town to the shops. Their clothes were constantly dusty and dirty, and while she agreed with them silently, outwardly she glared at them and told them to put up with it. She was never going to admit that it had been a mistake to come here. In her heart, she did not believe that it was. It was a matter of adjustment. Life had been too soft these last few years.

'In any case,' she said, 'the town is still young, hardly six years old but look at how rich this place is. Verandas, pavements, and parks will come later. We have to be patient.' They continued to grumble. But who could dispute that the town was becoming as rich as Ballarat had been in its heyday? Some might think it odd for a town to name its streets after chemicals and metals, but not Jane. Argent Street, Bromide Street, Sulphide Street showed a brashness and confidence that appealed to her, just as long as the silver, which the town produced in such awe-inspiring quantities, also found its way to her bank account.

Jane watched approvingly as her children began to adapt to the town. It did not take long before they found amusement. Her daughters threw themselves into whatever society had to offer, and there was no doubting that Broken Hill offered more than Traralgon. For a start, there was a roller-skating rink where they could hire skates and parade around the ring, at first holding hands and tottering unsteadily, but within weeks be gliding around as graceful as swans. There were theatres and various musical clubs which both Eleanor and Sophie loved, being more frivolous than their older sisters. They inclined towards the charitable societies. For Charlie, a bicycle became his replacement steed. Despite the heat, young men who had no access to horses took up cycle racing, and for Charlie, it became a passion and his name featured high in the winners of races around Broken Hill.

They still had tasks which they could not escape from. But Jane paid for help with the hotel, a cook, a barman and laundry maids assisted with the heavy jobs. She wanted her daughters to be ladies, not drudges. Although she was not averse to training Grace to deal with the accounts, nor the other girls acting as waitresses and barmaids when the hotel grew busy. Grace walked with a limp after falling from a tree back in Gobur days. At twenty-six she had not yet found a husband. What a burden all these daughters were, thought Jane for the umpteenth time, but they were the driving force behind her decision to come to Broken Hill. Running a hotel and pub was one of the few respectable occupations for a woman, other than teaching or nursing. Jane she was not equipped for either of those professions, nor would they pay the money she needed, while she knew the hotel business backwards.

In its first year, the hotel made good profits, but as the months passed, she realised that troubled times lay ahead. How could she not help but hear it in the miners' conversation after they piled into the bar at the end of the shift? While in the dining room, managers brought their colleagues or wives to dine and discuss the falling price of silver. Fortunes had been made, and the Adelaide Stock Exchange created to benefit from the rich lodes discovered by a few lucky men. Jane was between two worlds, and her loyalties were divided.

Jane's heart bled for the men who worked in appalling conditions, broiling heat and dust that brought disease, and poor safety practices. Accidents, which happened all too frequently, were treated in a charitable tented hospital, unsupported by the mining companies, no matter that accidents were caused by their lack of care. All the men paid into the union, and it was the union who supported the men unable to work because of their injuries. Broken Hill was a union town through and through.

On the other hand, Jane's head was all about profit, and without the mines, there would be no profit. How was she going to navigate the perils ahead if the miners struck over the loss of the pay agreement? That agreement had brought peace and prosperity to the town for the last three years. She listened to the men bemoaning the directors' attempt to break the agreement and bring in contract work.

'It will result in us fighting each other for work, undercutting each other out of desperation, and not earning enough to feed our wives and children.'

She listened to the directors saying that now was a good time to break the agreement and the closed shop. Hadn't the Queensland shearers been brought to their knees by the firm action of the pastoralists. Could they not do the same to the miners? Why pay more than they needed? She knew where her loyalties should lie, with the men of course, but she could not afford to alienate the managers, and she remembered the time over thirty years ago, when John faced a similar conundrum, whether to stand up and fight or not.

All Jane's savings were sunk into this hotel. The staff relied on her, and she had her own children to feed. If the coming strike proved long, would she be able to keep going? She found it difficult to sleep at night as doubts gripped her mind, making her toss and turn, sleep only arriving as the clock struck four or five. She dreaded its chime as it counted away her sleepless hours, but the thought of going bankrupt terrified her and would not let her rest.

Again, and again she wondered if she did right by leaving the safety of Traralgon, but she did not trouble her children with her worries. Jane needed all her wiles and cunning to survive; there was no one else to rely on.

Whereas shopping at the stores in town might have been a chore to avoid, now she listened patiently to conversations anywhere in town as well as at her bar. She instructed her daughters to pass back any gossip they thought useful. What kind of gossip they asked? Her reply was, anything. She had to prepare for the worst, and who knew what titbit might prove useful.

The men struck on July 5th, and the effect was immediate. Several men checked out of her hotel on the same day, to leave town. Their faces apologetic as they paid their bills. But what good would it do to stay, when there was no work for the foreseeable future? Jane smiled and wished them well, expressing her desire that they might return when the strike ended. As each walked out of the door, a mental pound sign disappeared with them. The bar was unusually full during that first day. Miners met to bemoan the necessity of the strike, but little drink was consumed. It felt like a tee-total wake to Jane, in spite of her attempt to be cheerful and press the men to buy another drink. But most were watching their pennies, especially if they had wives and children at home. Elsewhere she found shops began to accept cash only rather than credit, even for her! Her worries trebled. Had she not paid her bills on time at every month end?

There was plenty of gossip in her bar as men made a pint last an hour or two. They told of pickets being posted at the mines who refused to let anyone pass unless they had permission from the union. A rival hotel owner had his whisky destroyed on the first day of the strike by an angry mob. He unwisely attempted to take a couple of cases into a mine office. The striking miners laughed uproariously about that. Jane made a mental note not to get caught out if she should receive such a request.

But the town was orderly, and support was behind the miners rather than the directors, who refused all attempts to negotiate while breaking their own clause on binding arbitration. Even the mayor called their actions dishonourable, while in her dining room Jane heard whispered conversation of contempt for the town council. How dare they admonish the directors who brought prosperity to the town and the companies' shareholders.

It was Jane's daughters who brought back the news that the miners' wives were organising. They were women whose lives were as tough as Jane remembered. She felt an affinity with the families who lived in tents made from stitched together flour sacks or in corrugated tin shacks with dirt floors. This was one story her daughters knew. It had been told many times. Their family lived in tents for years, but they escaped only because of the hard work and determination of their parents. Life for the miners' wives of Broken Hill was far more difficult, because their husbands worked for a company and not themselves. Without wages, they had nothing left but their united strength and willingness to fight for their men, and Jane wanted to help them.

Jane decided on a plan she hoped would keep her in with both sides. Her daughters must help the wives in practical ways, without getting involved with the strike, and she would continue to court the managers and the authorities. A foot in both camps she remembered John calling it.

Fifty extra policemen were ordered to Broken Hill to maintain order. Not that there was much disorder; the strike leaders kept their men well in check. As the police were due to arrive at the station, Jane planned for her girls to greet them with an offer of one free drink that evening. In the meantime, she offered to billet some of them in her hotel, and with the profit she intended to offer soup to miners' children, making sure she charged the police for the additional vegetables required.

Other tradesmen like Marshall's butchery offered free meat to needy families. It was a business decision, he told Jane, because the wives tended to remember who helped them long after strikes were over. Something that made perfect sense to Jane.

She went shopping on the third day of the strike. Men passed her walking in the opposite direction to catch a train to anywhere where they could pick up work. Miners stood in knots on street corners discussing the strike in low voices. She paused in Argent Street to listen to bands entertaining the strikers with jolly, cheerful music. It was a working day, and strange to see men lingering, chatting or passing the time of day. Unless needed for picket duty, the men were at a loss and had little to do. On such a day as this, miners normally gravitated to the pub, and that they did not, meant there was no money for such pastimes. Jane knew it. It did not raise her spirits, however much she might enjoy listening to the music from the band.

The noonday mass meeting of strikers in the Central Reserve ended. Men drifted away, but without money in their pockets, they added to the crowds on the street. There was no trouble, no anger, just a sense of belief in a righteous cause. Nor was there anger from the tradesmen, or the wives of businessmen, whose shops or hotels suffered a loss of trade. Small acts of kindness were the order of the day. Jane watched a shopkeeper hand a bun to a small child and saw the grateful look on his mother's face. In the greengrocer's, she looked on as slices of apple were cut up and offered to other children, while mothers bought the cheapest potatoes to fill their children's hungry bellies.

Yes, in these early days there was sympathy for the men and their families; so much so that a deputation of concerned citizens set off on their way to Sydney via Adelaide and Melbourne in support of the men. The government was in disarray and unable to offer leadership, another reason the directors had chosen this moment to break their agreement. A weak government suited them fine.

Grace read the newspaper reports to Jane. In the Adelaide papers, she read of support for the directors who claimed that the men rarely did a full day's work, many being idle, while the union insisting that two men were required for one man's job. Jane wondered how many of these shareholders, who wrote letters to the newspapers, knew what a miner's life was like. As for the suggestion of bringing in British miners to break the strike, how many would work in the conditions that faced the Broken Hill men. Few she guessed, although knowing something of the appalling conditions in British coal mines. But were they accustomed to the temperatures of the ones in Broken Hill? Working temperatures of one hundred and twenty degrees were not uncommon.

The delegation was received badly in Adelaide. The shareholders did not want to hear of support for the men. 'What about our investments', they cried. They shouted down any delegate attempting to tell them how the directors had broken the agreement; how many of the men were affected by lead poisoning and how their wages had to extend to buying water as well as food, with so little rain at Broken Hill.

How quickly the country's population divided, and sides were taken, thought Jane, watching from the side-lines. Her daughters reported how strike funds were being collected, with wealthier miners supporting poor families, and workers in other cities collecting funds to buy food.

'Even the barmaids are promising a pound a month from their wages,' reported Emily, her bookish daughter.

Neither Jane, nor her daughters, attended any of the mass meetings of unionists, but reports were given by the wives at their own meetings, which Emily and Grace attended. At the end of the first fortnight of the strike, they learnt that a new magistrate was being sent from Sydney. The previous one, Mr Lane, had been giving false reports of the bad behaviour of the men, a fact that the Mayor, Mr Topperwein, contradicted in his own telegram to the government. Jane did not think this information would help her, but it might mean the miners would be looked on more favourably by a fair magistrate, encouraging the strike to last longer. The unions managed to amass six thousand pounds to feed the families of miners, and they were preparing for a long strike. Union stores were to be set up around the town and food distributed using coupons.

Neither of these pieces of news was good for Jane, and her heart sank further. Her hotel was suffering an enormous loss of trade, and if no money was to be given out in strike pay, she could not see any improvement for several months. If the merchants provided food for the stores at near wholesale prices, then they might hang on, but all Jane could do was to try and negotiate similar discounts from the merchants and brewers to cut her own costs. She worked out that she had enough money saved to carry on until November. Surely the directors or the miners would give in by then.

She snorted with derision when she heard that barmaids were going on strike, because a landlady told one off for giving cold potatoes to an old man. There's one less rival she thought, fancy alienating the miners when memories of such behaviour would remain and fester a long time. Slowly men returned to drink in the hotel, although a mug of ale lasted longer than before. The union stores brought prices down around town, and the men had a few more pennies to spend on beer. A bakery funded by the oldest Kidman brother, Sackville, was supplying free bread to the miners' wives, much to the disgust of his younger brother, Sidney. And in a roundabout way the bakery helped Jane, just those few extra pennies she thought, let them keep on coming.

To her thirteen-year-old son, Charlie, she supplied a gun. 'Go shoot some dinner,' she told him after hearing reports of hares and wild turkeys being shot by miners outside the town. She did not fear for his safety; his brothers taught him to shoot before he was eight years old.

Perhaps I'll dig out those old recipes of kangaroo steamer and parrot pie Jane thought. She was happy to feed such meat to her family while keeping roast beef for the few managers who still ate in her hotel. As for Charlie, he was delighted to help out, and with two other boys from the school, set out to find any unfortunate animals to grace their plates. He was proud to be the man of the family.

In mid-August, the directors threw down the gauntlet by advertising the reopening of the mines and asking for miners to apply for work on August 25th. Only the advert wasn't in the Broken Hill newspapers, but in those of Sydney, Melbourne and Adelaide. They were seeking blackleg labour and the miners, and their wives were outraged.

Emily and Grace were well in with the miners' wives. Jane needed them there, helping out in whatever way they could, whenever they were not behind the bar in her hotel. They reported back all the gossip and told her about a meeting of women to be held at the Masonic Hall on August 24th, the day before work was planned to resume. Her daughters pleaded with her to let them go. While she would not be persuaded by tears or sulks, at last she gave in as long as their mother accompanied them. Leaving Grace to look after the hotel they set off for the hall, the streets crowded with women walking in the same direction. What an evening it was. Hundreds of women filed into the place. The wives of miners heralded from Ireland, Cornwall, Italy, Austria, Greece and any other country, where times were hard. The accents reminded her of that meeting in the tented theatre in Ballarat, shortly after her marriage.

The atmosphere was orderly but gay with chatter from a hundred voices. At the stroke of seven o'clock, one of the ladies on the platform at the front brought down her gavel on the table, and hush descended. Speaker after speaker stood up and spoke in impassioned voices about why they supported the strike. They described the petition they had made to the governor supporting the men. Jane was reminded of Tom Kennedy, any of these women were as stirring as he. She had never imagined or thought for a moment that women could stand up and be heard as equals with men. It was a revelation to her, and she was not sure she completely approved, but her daughters did. They had worked with the women's committee and imbibed their philosophy.

'You're a businesswoman Mother, but are you welcome in the Trades Council?' Jane had to agree she was not. 'These women are saying we should have as much right to vote as any man. Once the strike is over, they will work to change the law on female suffrage.'

How life revolves in circles, thought Jane, remembering Eureka. A new generation is fighting for the same rights our men won all those years ago, and here I am on the sidelines of it again, watching, not participating.

The speaker was talking about the next day. 'Women are needed for the picket lines,' she said. 'Blacklegs must be stopped from entering the mine. Bring broom handles, bring sticks, we will be on the front line.' She rallied the women with stirring words and instructions. 'In the afternoon, we will process through the streets of Broken Hill to the Central Reserve. Join us; show us your support, women of Broken Hill, women of Australia. Let us win here and then let our voices be heard.'

The hall broke into cheers of support and applause, but Jane shuddered as she felt a tingling up her spine, which she recognised as fear. Please let there be no deaths. Not this time. Do these women understand the danger? As for her daughters, she was prepared to lock them in rather than let them go tomorrow morning. She need not have feared as none of the girls made any mention of the morning, asking only to attend the procession in the afternoon.

'We'll see how the morning goes,' said Jane firmly, but secretly longing to be there to wave the women on.

That night she could not sleep at all, mulling over the evening's meeting and worrying about the day ahead. She rose at six as normal and from her window, in the half-light of dawn, she saw men and women already marching towards the mines, their faces grim and determined. The women carried sticks while the men carried nothing.

'Are the women really going to fight?' She asked herself, amazed at their foolhardiness. She dressed, scarcely stopping to pin up her hair, before grabbing a shawl to wrap around her in the cool morning air. Silently she padded downstairs and entered the kitchen, telling Cook to lock the door behind her and allow none of her children to leave. She left the hotel and followed the crowd westwards as they marched towards the Proprietary Company's office. It was a strange atmosphere. Usually, with crowds of people, there would be conversation, laughter and a general levity. Jane only heard muted voices, and the seriousness of their endeavour was written on their faces.

When she arrived, onlookers stood everywhere taking vantage points to view the proceedings, and the air of excitement was palpable. The miners and their wives moved into the crowd below, welcomed by handshakes and hugs for the women. They did not have long to wait for action.

Some of the onlookers had managed to get themselves up on a platform thirty-feet or more up in the air, and one of them shouted 'Blacklegs.' Jane worked her way to the front of one of the many mullocks of debris in front of Block 10. In the distance, she watched two men approaching the mine. A crowd of howling women rushed forward surrounding the men, carrying them away back off the road away from the mine. Undeterred one of the men tried again, but the same thing happened. Jane watched as the crowd below pushed forward again. Push, shove, backwards, forwards, it was difficult to tell who was winning, but the women were in no mood for failure, and they propelled him back once more.

Two policemen accompanied him on his third attempt, and once again the women surrounded them refusing to give passage. The crowd roared 'Blackleg and Scab,' the noise deafening Jane. The man was jostled, but this time he managed to reach the mine, exhausted but successful, amidst groans from the watching miners. Another two men tried, but the women were determined this time to get their way. Jane calculated there must be two thousand women and men pushing against the two men. She thought it impossible for them to succeed, until at last the younger man appeared to faint in the crush. Room was made for him and the police escorted him to the mine amidst more groaning from the miners. These miners were fair Jane decided. That young man could so easily have died if they did not give way for him. Despite her fear, her heart swelled with pride for these principled men and women.

Jane was caught up in the excitement of the crowd willing the miners and their wives on. She found herself shouting with the rest. The excitement and emotion gripped her. Minutes later a buggy left the mine carrying three men, and rumours flew around like wildfire, but they were not left to wonder for long. At precisely the time the mine was due to reopen, and as the whistle blew for the commencement of work, the buggy returned, followed by the whole of the available police force. Some mounted, some on foot but all armed, with the bright sunlight glistening on the metal of their bayonets. Jane's heart rose to her mouth in anguish, believing the bloodshed of Eureka was about to be re-enacted. She hid her eyes, could not bear to look, but her worries proved needless. The strikers and their wives knew they were no match for guns and metal.

The miners and their wives met the police with shouts and dismay but thankfully no resistance. The policemen were not molested as they marched through the jeering crowd. Arriving at the mine, they lined up two abreast outside, their bayonets pointing towards the massed thousands. Silence fell. Jane shivered with tension. Horses pawed the ground and snorted in fear.

Had they wanted to, the men and women might have overcome the hundred-strong police force, but at what cost? It was not something the miner's leader, Richard Sleath, was prepared to contemplate. He made his way to the front of the crowd. Standing on a crate, he thanked the men and praised them for their forbearance and their good behaviour in not rising to the challenge to riot.

'They wanted a showdown where they could say 'look at the miners see they're no more than ruffians.' But you, good people of Broken Hill, have proved them wrong.' The applause for him was genuine, but after it faded there was nothing left to do.

The crowd drifted away as quickly as it arrived and Jane with them, the atmosphere still muted and now despondent. With her ears ringing from the noise earlier, she walked back towards her hotel grateful that no one was hurt in the scrummage she had witnessed. She was full of admiration for the women who took the fight to the police and the scabs. Their view that they were less likely to be beaten than the men had proved correct. In Jane's mind, the miners had won the moral victory, even though the final show of force defeated them.

When she arrived at the hotel, her daughters surrounded her, full of questions.

'Let me sit down first,' she said, and as she sat, her legs suddenly turned to jelly. Her hands shook when she lifted the cup of tea Grace pushed in front of her, the tea slopping back into the saucer.

'Was it dreadful Ma?' Asked Sophie. 'Did anyone get hurt?'

'No, it wasn't dreadful girls. It made me proud to be a woman and a digger's wife. But it could so easily have become violent. All credit to Mr Sleath for calming the crowds, otherwise there may have been a bloodbath. There were mounted police with bayonets.' Her voice shook with emotion. 'Have you heard of Peter Lalor girls?' She asked.

'The hero of Eureka?' Emily queried.

'Some may call him that,' her mother replied, frowning. 'I think Mr Sleath was more of a hero than Lalor, because he stopped any violence before it began. He brought the crowds back to their senses, but his name won't go down in history like the fiery Irishman who brought death to the miners of Ballarat.'

'Did you know Peter Lalor, Ma?' asked Grace.

'No, we saw him once. He owned mining interests in Creswick, but your father held him in contempt.'

'What!' the girls were shocked. 'Why?'

'He started out fighting tyranny, so he said. But in the end, he became one of the establishment bosses. He stood for the legislative council to fight for miner's rights. But as a politician, he voted against all men having the vote. No, John could not abide Peter Lalor, not so much for his Irishness, but for his hypocrisy.

As a boss, he tried to use cheap Chinese labour from Creswick as scabs at his mine in Clunes back in 1873. Like the directors of Broken Hill Mines are attempting to do here by advertising for men to break the strike, he did the same. The men were fighting for better conditions, not for more money but for a reduction in hours to spend more time with their families. Lalor was a fallen hero in the end, though people tend to forget it. He did not win at Clunes, thank God. Beware of men who talk big and encourage violence. It is the poor working man who suffers, believe me.'

Casting her mind back, Jane suddenly remembered that the Clunes wives supported their men on the picket lines as they had here. But would these strikers win? It did not seem likely after what she witnessed today. Oh, for another Fawkner, a powerful friend to the working man, she thought. No present-day politician could hold a candle to him.

Jane took her older daughters to cheer on the women in the procession that afternoon. She told them how the women stood up to the police and blacklegs a few hours earlier. Their enthusiasm and determination were exhilarating. Jane vowed to herself that she would not fail as a businesswoman, no matter what difficulties she had to overcome. The morning's events had renewed her determination to succeed.

They watched as five hundred women marshalled outside the Masonic Hall, led by Mr Sleath and Mrs Poole, both on horseback., The women began their march towards Argent Street, followed by a brass band and several thousand men, cheered on by the crowds lining the footpath, three abreast. As they marched on to the Central Reserve the crowd followed, parasols shading them from the bright winter sunshine. On reaching the Reserve, Mr Sleath stood on a trolley and asked the women to close their parasols, so everyone could see. A reporter described the scene in a newspaper as a sea of gingham, ostrich feathers and flowers as this flock of women stood quietly to listen to the speeches of women; a scene unheard of in the history of Australia. Women joined together to fight for the right to speak out as equals, to speak out in support of their families and to speak out in condemnation of the behaviour of the bosses.

Heads nodded, and Jane cheered along with her daughters and the rest of the crowd. Her daughters looked at her with puzzlement on their faces. They had never seen her show so much emotion, and it was true, she kept her feelings in check all the time. She had to; it was her armour against the male world that she lived in. How could she be successful as a hotel owner if she showed any weakness? This crowd of women were not displaying weakness, however, but strength and hurrah for that. She was all for strong women, women of business, women as providers for their families.

History keeps on repeating itself, she thought, barely two weeks later as she heard about the arrest of Richard Sleath and six other strike leaders; but for what? Did she not witness them refuse to let the strikers retaliate in the face of police aggression? Despite the overwhelming numbers of strikers, there had been little trouble. Yet police now poured into the town, and seven men were arrested for conspiracy and sedition.

Grace read in the newspaper that the member for the Barrier in the New South Wales Parliament asked if the directors would be arrested for conspiracy too. He was told he was being frivolous. 'Always one rule for the poor and another for the rich,' Jane murmured to herself. The new magistrate was clearly on the side of the companies. Where was the evidence for sedition, she wondered? Who would testify against them?

'I'll bet it's those spies, just like Eureka,' she said out-loud. Her girls needed a history lesson, and she gathered them round to tell them about life on the goldfields in the weeks leading up to Eureka. She wanted them to understand, that although the strike leaders may be convicted, it did not mean they were guilty but that people in charge always looked for scapegoats.

'It's a way of keeping the working man down,' she said. 'If you want to succeed you have to play them at their own game. Become a property owner, a landowner or business owner and people listen to you. But never forget where you have come from. Help others less fortunate than you.'

No one in the town thought the arrests were fair, certainly not Jane who was convinced of the men's innocence. But with the government now on the side of the directors, hope for the success of the strike diminished.

Over the next month, Jane contributed to the strike funds even as scabs arrived in the town, and as miners drifted back to work. Drinkers returned and paying guests too, but she heard different conversations in her bar and dining room. Some of the new labourers in town expressed apologies for helping to break the strike, but they needed the money when they had families to support. Jane understood their dilemma.

The managers in her dining room crowed with delight as the strike collapsed and the leaders were sent for trial. That sickened her, and she made sure any tips went to the strike fund. Walking around town in November, it was plain to see the misery of unemployed men and the hardship of widows and children. What had it all been for? Desperation and hunger were rife. Those who could, set off with a swag on their back to do harvesting work in South Australia. Jane had seen the town in good times and now the worst of times, but she was never tempted to leave. The poor needed her soup more than ever. She intended to stay and help rebuild the town in any way she could.

Chapter 42

'How long did your mother stay in Broken Hill?' Asked Mary.

'Oh, until the turn of the century,' replied Sophie. 'But, that wasn't the end of her troubles. The Terminus Hotel burned to the ground in 1894 while Mother was in town shopping. We suspected that one of the guests left a cigar burning in the parlour. The whole thing went up so fast; we were lucky to escape with our lives. The fire left us with nothing but the clothes on our backs.'

'Goodness! What did she do?'

'She obtained permission to erect a beer tent on the ashes and started over, having sent me to stay with Joseph as Bella needed help after the birth of her first child. Grace and Eleanor, she sent back to Boola to stay with Alfred and Jonnie. Emily was already married, so Florence and Charlie stayed at her house in Broken Hill. Mother received the insurance money, and with her savings in the bank, she bought another hotel and then another, always bigger and better, each one closer to the main town.

In 1900 she built a brand-new hotel, The Federal Palace she called it, brick built with thirty-three luxurious rooms, was how she liked to describe it. She was cock-a-hoop. Do you remember Nellie, that palaver about finding a lamp to put over the main door? I don't remember if it was gas or electric, but she said she could picture it in her mind. Eventually, she had it made for her.'

'I attended the grand opening, and I have to say it was a beautiful hotel. It had a soda fountain, electric light in each room, bathrooms with running water, but as soon as it opened, she sold it at a great profit and moved back to Victoria. She said she had achieved what she always set out to do, and it didn't matter anymore,' Eleanor continued.

'I think that Joseph buying Chateau Yering was too much of an enticement. She wanted to share in his glory and could only do that by moving to Melbourne.' Mary thought Sophie sounded a touch jealous.

'And all her girls, but me were married with children by then. I suppose she wanted to be nearer her grandchildren,' said Eleanor. 'At least that's what she told me.'

'But she was not exactly a warm and loving grandma?' Sophie with a wry smile, looked at Jane, who slept on. 'She worked as hard as ever taking in paying guests, not retiring until twelve years ago. I don't know how she did it. I'm nearly forty years younger than her, but she always had more energy than me.'

'Sophie, I think she still owns a hotel in Broken Hill,' said Eleanor. 'The rent will come in handy, she always told me. Her will may surprise us. She always kept her investments close to her chest.'

'And yet she didn't offer to bail out Joseph.'

'He owed far too much. It almost broke her heart when he went bankrupt. For some reason, she had a lifelong fear of bankruptcy and the debtors' prison. I don't believe they send them to prison these days, but the thought of it terrified her.'

Mary kept quiet; there was much these daughters did not know about their mother and never would. How sad that the words that had never been said, the confidences never shared, the secrets kept. How were sons and daughters to learn from their parents' mistakes?

'She always called me a fool for marrying my first husband, and I suppose I was. He was handsome and charming, and I was desperate to get away from being an unpaid nursemaid to Joseph's children as much as I loved them. But it was a mistake; he was a bankrupt and Mother told me he wouldn't amount to anything. She was right of course. Being handsome is no virtue, she told us. Do you remember, Nellie?'

They opened their mouths and spoke in unison, 'Being handsome or pretty doesn't pay the bills, but hard work does.' Their heads almost touched as they bent over with laughter.

'You'll think us uncaring Mary,' said Eleanor, looking up again.

'No, not all,' Mary assured her.

273

'It's all down to Mother that we girls had the lives we have lived. None of us had a lot of education, but we did have some. I know women of Hannah's and Grace's age who were never taught to read. That's shameful, isn't it? Emily's daughters went to college and how proud that made mother! She may be harsh in her manners and her ways, but that's all she knows. She served her family well. Can you believe she was born the year Queen Victoria gained the throne and you know how buttoned up those Victorians were?'

Mary hastened to correct any misapprehension that Eleanor had about her.

'I admire your mother; please don't think I don't.'

'We know you do,' said Sophie 'and you have been wonderful with her. We're very grateful that you agreed to nurse her. Look she's beginning to stir.'

Jane's eyes opened a fraction but did not focus. Where was she? There were shapes around her bed but whose? Her mind was groggy; it hurt to breathe. She felt a cool cloth touch her brow and something moistened her sticky lips. She heard a voice, but the sound did not register. Why was her head so fuzzy? A hand stroked her face, the fingers soothing. She closed her eyes again and drifted back to sleep.

'She's going, isn't she?' Sophie whispered.

'Soon, maybe tomorrow. Why not get some rest? I will stay with her,' Mary reassured them.

Once the daughters left, Mary picked up the telephone and dialed, and a female voice answered.

'Can I speak to Father Donaldson, please? I have a lady here who needs the last rites.'

Jane was still asleep when the priest arrived. Mary shook her gently, and she opened her eyes.

'It's Father Donaldson, Jane.' Jane tried to speak, but nothing came out. Mary went to the drawer and pulled out the crucifix, kissed it and returning to the bed she placed it in Jane's hands. Jane held the crucifix as tight as she was able; her anchor to this world. She smelt the aroma

274

of the wood, and it took her straight back to her childhood and her faith. She mouthed 'Thank you' to Mary.

'I am going to give you the last rites, Mrs Timmins,' said the priest. Jane tried to nod.

Once the priest left Jane pushed the crucifix towards Mary, using all her remaining strength.

'Keep it Mary, it's yours. Remember me.' Her voice a mere whisper.

'I will treasure this always.' She bent down to kiss Jane's face. 'Thank you for sharing your life with me, and now it's time for me to tell you my final story Jane. I have only ever told this to one other person. It is my penance.' Mary took hold of Jane's hand. 'If I tire you too much, just give my hand a squeeze.'

Chapter 43

France 1917-18

You talked about mud Jane, in those early days of Melbourne and the goldfields. Let me say, no one has really seen mud unless fighting at Passchendaele. I nursed at the Somme in 1916 and thought hell could be no worse; that was until the autumn of 1917. The French had taken a beating at Verdun in 1916. They fought and died in their thousands until they became mutinous and no general wanted to risk them in a fight, so the British forces were sent up the line instead. The front there was only about ten miles wide, but they told me there were almost half a million casualties in the three months they fought.

Along with Churchill, I learnt another name to curse, Field Marshall Haig. If you should come across him up there, will you spit on him for me? But I truly hope he's in hell.

We were much nearer the front than we had been at the Somme. The manure in the fields of France got mixed up in the wounds and caused gas gangrene. We learnt that the hard way. Men needed to be treated much closer to the line. I lost count of the men who died because they were not treated until too late.

We nurses did not remember ever working as hard as we did that autumn, and still the casualties kept coming. Many more drowned in the acres of mud. I have never seen rain like it, but Haig kept ordering the men forward, all for an insignificant, ruined village which served no purpose. When it was finally captured almost forty thousand Australians had died in battle. Men who would never marry, leaving women behind who missed out on having children, and it's left us the poorer for that.

After it was over, I was sent on leave, exhausted, broken by the futility of it all. I longed for sun, so I caught a train to the south of France and ended up in Marseilles. We had landed there from Egypt eighteen months before and stayed there for a few weeks, monitoring the men for diseases such as typhoid and cholera before sending them up to the front, where they might otherwise infect other men. Marseilles was the only place I knew of, but I had an image of the sun shining on the water, which is all I wanted.

Every day I walked down to the sea or caught a bus to a little town called Cassis. I remember a beautiful bay and beaches lined by white houses, where red geraniums still flowered in abundance. It was as though the rest of the world had disappeared. There was such peace there, and I wanted to stay for the duration if possible.

Then one day, I was sitting in a cafe by the port in Marseilles, drinking the best coffee I had tasted in Europe. I heard a familiar accent. It was an Australian digger ordering a beer. I looked up at him. He was tall, thin and in his face, I recognised the exhaustion and pain I had been feeling myself, but he was beautiful. We both smiled when he caught me looking at him. I gestured to him to join me, and he brought his beer over to the table. At that point, he may have taken me for a loose woman, but I did not care.

When he took off his slouch hat and laid it on the table, I saw deep blue eyes, thick brown hair and a face lined by the sun of Australia. He shook my hand, introducing himself as Patrick O' Hara. His fingers were long, and his nails scrubbed clean, showing not a trace of the Western Front, but I knew he had been there. I was not in uniform, and so until then, he had no idea I was Australian too, and from his hometown of Melbourne. When he found out, his face shone in amazement.

'Why have we not met before?' He asked, his face crinkling in a wide grin.

'Because we were meant to meet here,' I replied. 'In the time of our greatest sorrow. It is God's will.' I really believed that Jane. There he was, an Irish Catholic Australian, sent to me by God to comfort and love me, and I the same for him.

We spent the rest of our leave together. He left my side, neither day nor night. In Cassis, we persuaded a priest to marry us, and it was as if I had never known happiness before. I suppose our marriage wasn't legal in the eyes of French law, because we didn't get the Mayor to do his bit. But I'm sure it was in the eyes of God. Of course, we didn't get permission from our commanding officers either, so it had to be a secret. I would have been sent home if the authorities found out. It was forbidden for us nursing sisters to consort with anyone of lower rank than a Lieutenant.

We forgot the guns, the mud, and the fear, taking only joy in our surroundings. All the little things which mean so much; a child's smile; a couple of dogs chasing each other on the beach; the divine aroma of a bouillabaisse; the forgotten taste of ice cream. We often stood in silence, his arm tight around me to stare at the blue-green sea which turned to slivers of silver in the winter sun. Sometimes we watched the red-orange sunset from the mighty cathedral on the hill above Marseilles. It was magical. If it were raining, or the mistral blew, we stayed in bed, fortified by crusty bread, goat's cheese, and rich red wine.

We had ten wonderful days and nights together. Then we travelled back north towards the Front, even though he was owed two more days' leave. Patrick said he wanted to spend every possible second with me. But we stopped in Paris for a night, and then I left by the morning train to the Front, so that we would not be seen by anyone we knew.

As we approached the station, I took his ring from my finger and placed it on a ribbon around my neck. At that moment, I knew I was losing the best part of myself. We could not even kiss goodbye for fear of being seen. He stood on the platform as I climbed into the carriage. The tears in his eyes mirrored my own. I put a handkerchief to my eyes, complaining of grit from the steam engine to another nurse sitting opposite. I dare not wave goodbye, but as the train slowly gathered pace, he lifted his hand and placed it over his heart. I lifted my hand to mine, regretting the invisible air between us, wondering if we would meet again in this life.

Those ten days sustained me over the next few months. But we managed one weekend together on a wangled pass in February. Patrick booked a perfect hotel in a tiny village on the Normandy coast, one that was not so popular with the British forces. I remember the hotel, it was typically Norman. There were four stories with a window in the steep gabled attic roof, but narrow, with just two windows on each level facing the road. It looked like a little doll's house, despite the peeling blue paint of the door and its air of neglect. I entered, and there he was waiting for me. How can I describe the joy of seeing him again?

Ah, you squeezed my hand, Jane. Are you too tired? No? You want me to continue? Well, I will.

Madame brought us breakfast in our room. Patrick had explained our predicament and shown her proof of our marriage, and she could not have been more helpful. All our meals she brought to us, and we only left the room to walk by the sea as the sun was setting. Arm in arm we walked until it was dark. Had we met anyone we knew, we would have told them we were cousins. Once again, I did not wear my uniform; that would have been too dangerous.

We said goodbye in our room, and I left the hotel after kissing Madame on each cheek as is the French custom. She begged us to visit again. How I wished that we had been able to keep that promise.

Three weeks later the Battle of Amiens began. I was there when he was brought into the hospital, but I did not recognise him. He had no legs from the thighs down, and his face was a mass of purple flesh. One of his eyes was gone completely, the other sightless, but he recognised my voice, grabbing my hand as I tended to his wounds, whispering 'Mary is it you?'

What went through my mind? It's difficult to remember all the emotions. Pity, rage, sorrow, love, anguish. Everything seemed to come at me at once. I remember my whole body shaking, and then my training kicked in. Taking a deep breath, I forced myself to be professional and carry on treating his wounds, talking to him as I would to any other patient. While all I wanted to do was kiss his lips, lay my head on his chest, as I had done so a few weeks before.

He kept saying, 'Mary, I'm sorry.' I shushed him while my heart was breaking for him. There were other patients who needed me, but I kept returning to him and whispering 'I love you' in his ear. At the end of my shift, I longed to stay with him, but I knew Sister would not allow it even if I told her he was my cousin. She may have moved him to a different ward, and I could not have borne that. How did I get through the night? It was torture.

More men had been brought into the ward when I arrived on duty after breakfast, and I was kept busy, while always aware of Patrick listening for my voice. I glanced over at him as I was tending to some of the other men, and saw him trying to lift his bandaged head when he heard me speak. At last, I got to him and spent an age changing his dressings, talking calmly as he winced in pain. After I had changed the dressing over his missing beautiful eye, he caught hold of my hand.

'Mary, you have to let me go. I'm no good for you. I'll never be a husband to you,' he whispered.

Through gritted teeth, I said, 'Your injuries don't matter. I don't care about them, and I'll devote my life to looking after you.'

'But I don't want that. It would kill me slowly, to think you were doing that. Eventually you would begin to hate me. What use am I? I can never earn a living. All I am is a labourer on the docks at Port Melbourne, and I will never be able to work again.'

'I don't care,' I told him and turned away before I started to sob.

Two days this went on. He continuously pleaded with me to let him go. I thought he just meant for me to forget our marriage, but towards the end of my third shift, he told me he meant something altogether different.

'They're moving me on tomorrow, probably to England. Please, will you let me die? I want to die in your arms Mary. I can't live, not this way.' Jane, I backed away from his bed, my hand over my mouth. How dare he ask that of me?

The soldier in the next bed caught hold of my hand. 'Do it love. It's what he wants.'

'No!' I wanted to scream. God would never forgive me, or him. I did not want him to die. I wanted above everything else for him to live. Was I selfish Jane?

All that night I prayed to God for guidance, and I thought about my Nana Kathleen's tale. What would she do? Was it a case where I should break the rules, but I rejected that, and by the morning I was determined to make him change his mind. He needed to understand that he did have something to live for. With prosthetic legs, he might walk again, and we could still have children.

When I got to the ward, there was a screen around his bed. The night duty Sister saw me looking and said, 'Corporal O'Hara has passed during the night. The orderly found him dead when he was delivering breakfasts. I haven't had time to lay him out, so can I leave that to you.'

'How did he die?' I stammered stupidly, feeling sick enough to throw up my breakfast.

'To be honest Mary, I don't have any idea. He was fine when I turned out the lights, and I checked him at midnight, and he was still alright. There's no sign of infection in his wounds. I called the doctor, but he wasn't concerned, and he said that it was perhaps the best thing, poor blighter.'

How did I get through that day and the ones that followed? I realised what had happened as soon as I saw the faint bruising around his nose and lips. The soldier in the next bed looked me straight in the eye and whispered.

'All Pat wanted was to die in your arms. I would do it for my best mate, but I can't get out of bed with these broken legs. We know you were his sweetheart. He couldn't help himself talking about this wonderful Aussie nurse who loved him. But you didn't love him enough to do the one thing he asked. None of us wants to live with the injuries he had. We all knew what had to be done, so it was done.'

I looked around the ward, and none of the other men would look me in the eye. They were all complicit and so was I because, I did not tell on them. Jane, I still feel the guilt of not having done the one thing he asked of me. I live with it every day. But I also live with the anger that he would not live for me, when I so desperately want his arms around me, still comforting me. You're squeezing my hand again, have I tired you? There's more to this story, do you want to hear it? Is that a nod?

A few weeks later I realised I was with child. How did that make me feel? Both overjoyed and terrified. The baby was due in late October, and I knew that my belly would show around July. Who would help me?

That was my main concern. My mother and grandmother were dead; my only friends were the nurses working with me. What was I going to do? Then a letter arrived for me from Melbourne, and I held it in my hands puzzling about who could be writing to me. At last, I tore it open and read the misspelt words. It was from Patrick's mother. He wrote to her telling of our marriage and gave her my maiden name and bless her. She wrote to thank me for making her son happy and looked forward to meeting me after the war. The letter must have been posted before the priest arrived, informing her of his death. Now at least I had someone who might help. I wrote back telling her that I helped nurse Patrick. That he died peacefully, and I told her about her grandchild.

It happened as I expected; I was sent home in disgrace. I had no proof that I was married, as Patrick's clothes were cut off him and burned. I thought the priest's letter confirming our marriage burnt too. In fact, it was sent home with his effects, but I doubt it would have made any difference to my disgrace. I disobeyed orders any way you want to look at it.

I arrived on her doorstep in September having sailed from Southampton. She took me in and looked after me until the birth of my son. We named him Patrick of course. We saw the likeness in him straight away, and I was overcome by the way he regarded me through those deep blue eyes. Something in him recognised my love for his father; I am convinced of that.

His grandma adored him naturally. She was a widow on a small pension, and I had no money. Our few savings bought the things we needed for Patrick, but I did not really worry because I knew I could get a job nursing.

My husband had an older sister, Bridget, a pleasant woman, gentle but filled with sadness that she was childless. She and her husband, Jim, came to visit me when little Patrick was a few weeks old. He had just started to smile. I remember the first time I saw him smile as if it were yesterday. I took him with me in the backyard to hang out laundry when he caught the sight of sheets blowing in the wind. I swear he chuckled. I picked him up and danced around the sheets with him and he just smiled and smiled. Anyway, Bridget asked me how I would manage, and I told her that I would have no trouble getting a job.

'But who will care for Patrick while you work?'

'Your mother has offered.' I was surprised she needed to ask.

'Mother's getting on and not in the best of health. I worry it will be too much for her. Why don't Jim and I take him?'

'You mean every day until I come home from work?'

'No. I mean why don't we adopt him? We will give him a loving home. He'll not lack for anything.'

It was out of the question I told her but thanks for the offer. I can feel your hand again Jane. You know what's coming, don't you?

Irish families are like glue they stick together, and after that visit, I no longer felt part of the family. A shift in the atmosphere occurred around me. I became an outsider. They worked on his mother until she told me she could not look after my son while I was at work. I was at my wits end not knowing how to manage. I never thought about my husband's war pension until it was too late. His mother had proof of my marriage and his death, but claimed the pension for herself as his dependent; she never told me that.

Eventually, it was suggested I visit the parish priest for advice. I can't remember who suggested it, but it made sense to me. Perhaps there was some practical solution I had not thought of. I forgot he had been their priest for more years than you could throw a stick at. He had christened my husband and buried his father and been a support to his childless sister. Who was I? An interloper, half married by a foreign priest. A woman who nursed at the front, handling men's bodies, when I should have stayed at home, keeping myself pure. I only worked that out later.

He heard my confession. I never dared confess how Patrick died until then, because I was afraid an army chaplain might make enquiries to find out who suffocated him. I could tell this priest was shocked, by his sharp intake of breath. That gave him all the ammunition he needed.

'A life for a life' he said. But I did not, nor would have killed Patrick. I never wanted Patrick dead.

'You stood by,' he said. 'You said nothing. If you told your superior officer, Patrick could have been moved to a different ward away from his comrades, so you are just as guilty. What right do you think you have to his child?'

'The right of any mother.' I said, incensed at his words.

'No, you must give up the child. You will never be a fit mother in God's eyes.'

I protested, oh how I protested.

He was implacable. 'You committed a mortal sin.' How I shrank at those words. Me, commit a mortal sin? His words cut me to the bone.

'If you do not give up the child, you will not be welcome again in the church. How can you nurse when you stood by and let someone, your husband no less, be murdered?' He paused and then said with all the moral rectitude of a man who knew nothing about war or love, 'Your penance is to give up the child to his father's family and nurse the dying until the end of their natural lives. If you do that only then may you seek God's salvation.'

Jane, you are thinking I should have run, gone anywhere away from Melbourne, taking my child with me. That is what my Nana meant when she told me to break the rules if I must, and I did not. Why did I not? I ask myself that over and over again. All I could see in front of me was penury. No money, no job, a starving child and no redemption for my sins, I wasn't thinking straight. Why did I not go to my own parish priest and ask him for forgiveness? He was a kind man, and I am sure he would have helped.

It was years later, when I visited Patrick's mother on her deathbed, that I found out Bridget's husband had given a large donation to the church when they adopted my baby. She begged my forgiveness. I don't think I ever felt such anger as I did then, mostly with my husband, Patrick, because had he lived, even with a body as broken as his, they would never have dared to take our son. I was also angry with myself for allowing it.

I still visit my beautiful boy on Christmas Day. He's growing up to be the image of his father, and he loves his parents. He is happy, well-educated and wants to be a doctor, although Jim wants him to join the family drapery business. When I asked him why he wanted to be a doctor, he said, 'so I can save people as you did in the war, Aunt Mary, people like my Uncle Patrick.' I wanted to hug him and kiss him, but I told him his uncle would be proud of his dear nephew.

When I look at my boy, I try to convince myself that maybe I did the right thing. But it is not what Nana Kathleen would have done and nor you Jane. I see that in your eyes. I also see the wariness in Bridget's eyes when she looks at me, trying to assess my mood. I see only threat in her husband's eyes, knowing I will never be invited again if I say anything. But he's my son, not theirs. The days after Christmas are the worst, knowing I must wait another twelve months to visit him. Sometimes I weep so much I can't get out of bed with the pain of my loss. It never gets easier. Do you think me weak Jane?

Well no more! Listening to your stories and learning about the trials you overcame has restored something in me. I thought I'd lost all courage and strength of purpose. You took risks, ignored convention, broke away from your family when you thought it right. We both carried a burden of guilt and regret around for too long. Isn't it time for us to let go? For years, I have hidden in this bitter cloak of penance, but I want to cast it off and start living again.

This is what I have decided; I am going to apply for a hospital job, although I may need to retrain. I look forward to the challenge. I want to be a midwife sharing in the joy of new life, breathing in the scent of a newborn innocent child. How I miss that, even after all these years.

Next week, I will start to write my son a letter to give him when he is eighteen, explaining the circumstances of his birth and begging his forgiveness. It may take the three years in between for me to get the words right, but I refuse to be cowed anymore. I spoke to Father Donaldson, and he has given me absolution for my sins. He was kind enough to tell me that I have suffered enough. So Jane, my dear friend, thank you for telling me your stories, they changed my life. It feels like being reborn.

You are squeezing my hand again. Do you approve? You don't know how much that means to me. But you are exhausted, and I have kept you awake for far too long. Close your eyes now, and I will sing you a song, the one I used to sing to my son, Patrick.

I will be here holding your hand. I won't let go.

Mary continued holding Jane's hand as she slipped into a final fitful sleep, her breaths laboured and shallow. Just before dawn, her breathing paused, and then a slow rattling breath as her hand grew slack, falling back against the sheet. Mary checked her vital signs but knew Jane's suffering was over. She made a note of the time, thankful for a peaceful death, something that Mary wished for all her patients. She took a moment to pray for her soul, wishing that Jane was now at peace in the arms of her loved ones, before phoning the doctor. He assured Mary he would come later in the morning to sign the certificate. But her work was not finished. Before the daughters arrived, she needed to lay Jane out. As she gathered the things, Mary began to hum the lullaby she sang to Jane to stave off the melancholia she always felt at these moments.

The relatives often told Mary she had the patience of a saint to work with the dying. If only they knew. She was a sinner through and through. How many times had she told that story, spoken those words of hope for the future? Her patients appeared to take a little comfort from it, thinking they had made a difference to poor Mary's life. She took some perverse enjoyment in making them feel good in their final moments.

So much of the story was true, and she loved to tell it because it was the one part of her life that had truth and meaning. She missed Patrick every day, every night and every year that passed. She missed his arms around her, his gentle kiss upon her lips, his humour and his optimism. She shivered with sadness.

Mary sometimes wondered if she told the story enough times, it might become true and her life change for the better. But in her heart, she knew it would never improve. Next week or the week after she would pick up the telephone in the shabby boarding house she returned to between jobs, and it would begin again. Another old man or woman sucking up her energy, taking away the best years of her life. But there would be no one for Mary when her turn came.

No Australian hospital would employ her. They told her in France her card was marked. She never confessed her guilt, but they thought they saw it in her eyes, and then there was the evidence, a missing lethal dose of morphine. Did she not know that he had begged each doctor and nurse to let him die?

Mary had succumbed to Patrick's begging and the entreaties of his fellow soldiers. She had broken the rules and see what her life had become; a dried-out husk of a life, without hope, without love, without peace. Her only consolation was the absolution for her mortal sin. The priest gave it in return for her son and told her to be grateful. But she still rued the day when she copied down Patrick's address from the hospital records before taking the transport back to England.

Whenever she had a day off, she stood across the road from her son's school, watching him leave with his friends, rejoicing in his beauty and his laughter. He did not know her. She was told never to contact the family again, and she had stuck to that promise, but would not cease her lonely vigil.

There would be no letter on his eighteenth birthday. What was she to write? I am your mother, and I murdered your father. She refused to lie to her son.

The End

Thank You

Thank you for taking the time to read this second book in The Currency Girls saga. The first book in the saga, Search for the Light, tells the story of three girls transported on the ship, Henry, in 1825, one of whom was Jane's mother, Helen Fitzgerald.

If you have enjoyed reading this book, please consider writing a short review on Amazon or Good Reads and tell your friends. Word of mouth is an author's best friend and much appreciated.

There will be a third and final book in the Currency Girls Series, Sadie's Wars, planned for publication in December 2018.

Spanning continents, Sadie's life is a rollercoaster of love and heartache. As her youngest son joins his brothers in the RAF in June 1940, a letter arrives from her brother, Eddie, in Australia, reawakening memories of the glorious years of her early childhood. The Great War changed everything, wrecking fortune and family. Can old wounds be healed, and new love found or will this second war destroy everyone she saved?

The author's latest novel, Ranter's Wharf, is set in England in the early part of the nineteenth century. For more information on this, see the author's notes.

Find me at rosemarynoble.wordpress.com

Twitter @chirosie

Facebook – RosemaryJaneNoble

Author's Note

This book is a work of **fiction** but based on fact, with apologies to any of the wider family, who take issue with my imaginings. Thanks to the Australian Trove newspapers online, I have been able to track the family all the way from the 1830s to 1932 where this story ends. Actual court cases and license applications provide the framework for the story. The story is that of Jane Timms and her husband Thomas; my husband's great, great, grandparents. I changed his name to John to avoid confusion with her father. Her first two sons were also called Thomas.

Jane's obituary as it appeared in a Tasmanian newspaper
The death occurred on Friday of Mrs. Jane Timms, of Guest Street, Hawthorn, who was aged 94 years. Mrs. Timms was born in Perth, Tasmania. She was married at Geelong to the late Thomas Timms, who was one of the pioneers of the Ballarat goldfields. Later the family went to Traralgon, and then to Broken Hill, where Mrs. Timms conducted a business. The late Joseph Timms, one of the leading railway contractors in Australia, was a son. Mrs. Timms had 10 children, of whom six are living. She leaves 30 grand-children. 72 great-grand-children, and two great-great-grand-children.

Advocate (Burnie, Tasmania.) 25th May 1932

What happened to the missing members of Jane's family?
Sarah Dugmore There is a sighting of her being imprisoned for a month for fighting another woman in Melbourne in 1866.
Joseph Dugmore was in and out of trouble in the early 1860s. A man of the same age and name died in 1885 after being run over by a wagon leaving a wife and six children in South Australia. Could it have been him? There is no proof.
Hannah Dugmore Evans disappears from view after her husband was

imprisoned for fraudulent insolvency. Their son, Isaac, died in Collingwood, Victoria in 1900.

Jacob Dugmore – there is no further sighting of him at all.

James Dugmore left a document describing his life in Victoria from the 1830s through to the goldfields; some of his story is written here and attributed to Jacob or James. The document was transcribed by Lance Pritchard, at Werribee Historical Society, with many thanks to the society for sharing this document with me. James lived until at least 1903, when he told his story to a live audience, and it was written down by someone unknown.

Their mother **Helen /Ellen Dugmore** died in 1889 in the benevolent institution in Melbourne leaving £53. This was annexed by the state as no children were found.

Further Reading

This book could not have been written without giving credit to the books, and articles listed below. To anyone wanting to read more about Eureka I recommend Peter Fitzsimmons' book. It is extremely readable and very helpful. I hope the author will forgive me for using it extensively.

Annear, Roby. Bearbrass: Imagining Early Melbourne. Black.Inc. Australia. 2014

Bloodworth, Sandra. The Rebel Women of Broken Hill 1889-1817. La Trobe University. 1996.

Brown, Henry. Victoria as I found it. T. Cautley Newby. London 1862.

Dugmore, James. Memoirs. 1903 Original document held at the State Library of Victoria.

Fitzsimmons, Peter. Eureka the Unfinished Revolution. Random House. Australia 2013.

Howitt, William. Land, Labour and Gold. Volumes 1 and 2. Longmans, London 1855

Powell, Ann. Women in the War Zone: Hospital Service in the First World War. The History Press. 2013

Read, C Rudston. What I Heard, Saw and Did at the Australian Gold Fields. T & W Boone. London 1853

Trove Newspaper Archive

Unbroken Spirit: Women in Broken Hill. Australian Women's Archive Project. 2009.

Wright, Claire. The Forgotton Rebels of Eureka. Text Publishing. Melbourne 2013.

Ranter's Wharf

One moment, William is running around barefoot, ragged and more often hungry than not. Then Aunt Betsy appears from nowhere. She needs an heir to drive away suitors and William fits the bill. He leaves a family torn apart by Betsy's decision. One day in the future, that action will come back to bite her, with devastating consequences.

Set in Lincolnshire, in the early years of the 19th century, this moving family saga sees William grapple with the loss and betrayal set in motion on that fateful day. It doesn't end with him, as his son, John, also discovers. Will love conquer the Victorian demands for respectability and duty?

A story of three generations working out, not only their place in the world but also how to navigate the pitfalls of living in a country fearful of invasion and rebellious ideas.

Praise for Ranter's Wharf

'Woe betide anyone that doesn't have tissues ready when they read this book - This is an intelligent study of the harsh conditions of the times. One is shocked, educated and made to feel compassion like the central characters. I tasted 'the grit and grime' of the novel from the safety of my armchair and felt the warmth of 'the straightforward good folk with no pretentions or guile'. Yet, I did want to get on my soap box and rant on behalf of my ancestors who would have struggled as 'wealth and poverty oozed through the smoke from the chimneys.' I wanted to call on Sir Titus Salt for help!' Books in My Handbag blog.